THE TIPTON'S OF TYBBINGTON

Before and Beyond, Part Two

The Tipton Crest "Causam Decidit"
"The Sword in This Hand Caused the Decision That Ended the War"

REBA RHYNE

The Tipton's of Tybbington
Before and Beyond, Part Two

ISBN: 978-1-952369-19-3

When the author started this epic tale, she knew the story could be lengthy, but certainly not as extensive as it turned out to be. If placed in only one book, the font or print would have been very small, and the book would have been weighty and cumbersome — maybe over three pound — too heavy to hold for any length of time.

She had no choice but to think of two books for her story. This narrative is not complete or finished unless you read Book Two. And, starting the second book without reading the first, means less understanding of the setting, characters, and actions described therein. **So, she highly advises YOU, the reader to buy these two books as a set**.

All Scripture quotations are taken from the KING JAMES VERSION (KJV): KING JAMES VERSION, public domain.

and

THE ENGLISH HEXPLA: 1841,Samuel Bagster and Sons, London, Reprinted by THE BIBLE MUSEUM, Copyright 2008. greatsite.com

Published by EA Books Publishing a division of Living Parables of Central Florida, Inc. a 501c3 EABooksPublishing.com

Acknowledgements

Thanks To:

Ken Raney for the excellent cover work. This Crest is the official one of the Tipton Family Association of America. All members are descendants of Jonathan Tipton of Anne Arundel Co., Maryland.

Ben Belandres for ALL the beautiful maps in the book.

Maria Kercher for her editing skills.

Dawn Staymates, my formatter, for putting up with me, and EA publishing for another great job.

Foreword

Just a brief note to my reader. If you haven't read the first book of The Tiptons of Tybbington – Part One, I highly advise you to do just that. Some of this book will not make sense if you haven't read the first book.

Have you ever been to a show or seen one on television where they said, "This will require audience participation?" Well, **The Tiptons of Tybbington requires reader participation**, beyond that of reading. So, if you aren't willing to put the effort into doing the research, which is provided within its pages, then this book may be the most boring book you will ever read.

This is a book of history. The first book, or Book One, starts in 500 A.D. or thereabouts, and ends around 1350 A.D. This book, or Book 2, starts in 1350 and ends at 1700 A.D.

First, let me explain about the word *"thereabouts."* Since a lot of the book is written before names, dates, and actions were adequately recorded, this writer used her imagination and made up *rational facts* to go along with the time period and story.

Mark Twain once told the English poet, Rudyard Kipling, "Get your facts first, and then you can distort them as much as you please." Mr. Twain would not be happy with me, because I tried not to distort the facts. But as I gleaned information from one chronicler to another, I did find *the facts may differ.*

These two books cover around 1200 years of history, in places where most of my readers haven't been, and within situations they haven't participated. In the first book, you'll start at Germania in the 500 A.D.'s or *thereabouts,* and follow Tybba and the growing Tybbington family as they participate in the evolving English history of the different time periods being followed.

So where does the reader participate?

In both books, **I have added maps** so you can maintain a reasonable idea of where the characters are in the world — at least, the point where they are in the present time period being covered. In most cases, I've been there and can describe the area. You can go to the internet and find other information between chapters for further facts if your interest is piqued and if you desire.

I've also **added a chart** of the important rulers and Kings of England and coupled them to my characters, those in the same time period. So, instead of being confused, you can put your finger on each, as they are in chronological order. How many Kings were named Edward or Henry in 1200 years? Several, I can tell you.

At the start of each chapter, I've **given a brief summary of the events between time periods**. This shows up in a different font. I know this will be boring to some, but read it. The commentary leading up to the next section, in most cases, is very interesting.

The settings in this book are true, and the Tiptons lived through these times, but in order to people the story, it was necessary to put fictional persons through the history, alongside some real ones.

Some of the Tipton people are real, but their interaction in the historical activities are fiction — but possible? Since most of the Tipton descendants that I know have been honorable, God-fearing, support-your-government kind of people, this is the way they are portrayed in the book. My Tipton family is full of fact and fiction, legend and lore, each addressed in these pages.

This is a fun story of several generations, reminding me of where I came from, how I got here, and the sacrifices my ancestors may have made to dream of a different life.

Dedication

At times, I've found the dedication for a book a bit tough. But not this time. This very intelligent man is a keeper of his word.

Starting a project of this magnitude (which I hadn't planned to do) is a daunting task. I needed someone in England to keep me on track—read the manuscript, point me to websites, and make suggestions…someone who would stay with me from start to finish. He promised to do just that, and he did.

We have e-mailed back and forth for many months as we worked on the manuscript for *The Tipton's of Tybbington*. Slowly, we have gotten to know each other much better.

Jeff Worsey has lived in Tipton all of his life, and is proud of his country and his town. As an avid reader, he became Chair of the Friends Group of the Library in Tipton, England. That's how I met him.

The Tipton Family Association of America planned a trip to England to visit the town where **_it is believed_** our family originally settled. Several signed up to go. When time came to finalize our arrangements, I couldn't find anyone planning on making the trip. I e-mailed this stranger. He hadn't heard from anyone … but me. I told him if no one else came, he and I would have all the fun. He had planned several activities, but couldn't complete the arrangements until he knew the final number. In the end, he had seven coming, all at staggered times, making his job even harder.

Without his help and traveling alone, I would have struggled with logistics, especially getting back and forth to my lodging and the library. At home, I drive a car and have little experience in riding the train, bus, or calling a taxi, especially in an unfamiliar location. He gave excellent instructions.

It turned out that most places were in walking distance. My Travelodge was next to the Dudley Zoo, in the shadow of the ancient castle on Castle Hill, next to the Dudley Archives, and in a short walking distance of the Black Country Living Museum.

At the library, Jeff had arranged for our group to be honored with an English Tea, hosted by Edwina and other ladies of the Friends of the Library. The ladies 'did us proud.' Keith, from the Tipton Civic Society, and David, whose family once operated businesses in Tipton talked to us about the history of Tipton. There was also commentary and slides on the canals and narrow boats from a lady who lived it with her parents. Graham, who teaches an art group at the library, presented signed prints to the Tipton Family Association of America. Robert Hazel, the library manager, made sure our stay while there was comfortable — meeting any other need.

The following day, we attended the Canal Festival and went on a narrow boat trip along the canals. Sadly, Jeff did not arrange the weather. It drizzled almost non-stop. He did make sure we met some of the locals, and their cheery welcome soon drove the dark clouds away. This included two women who were patrolling the area as Bobbies. We stopped to take pictures.

In particular on day three, I enjoyed the Black Country Living Museum with his daughter, Caroline, as my tour guide. The BCLM took me back to the glory days of coal, blast furnaces, and steel. Within its boundaries, I visited period homes, observed a school session, and talked with people who told and showed me some of the history of the area. It's a must for anyone staying in Tipton or Dudley. Finally, to cap off a wonderful day, we had an early dinner in one of the museum's restaurants.

Jeff Worsey, you were there to help with great directions and support. So, as you folks in Tippin say, "I ull tek me cap off to yow."

In *The Tipton's of Tybbington*, I wrote the story, but you gave it more English places, language, and flair than I could have. Your fingerprints and suggestions are everywhere in these two books. It is fitting that this book is dedicated to you.

So, I say a simple, "Thank you, so much."

Introduction

Have you ever wondered how far back you could go in your family history? Since my mom was the genealogist of the family and researched many sides of my ancestors, I was interested in just this. I'm not a genealogist, but I am a lover and an avid reader of this world's history—from the ancient Israelites in the Holy Bible, Egyptians, Romans, and English, right up to how the United States of America came to be.

This two-part book is written as a history and should be read as such. It is the fictionalized story of the Tipton Family, who left Germania in 500 to 550 A.D, or *thereabouts*. This was the time period when many of the tribal peoples left the coastal regions of northern Europe for more favorable areas in Brittania. After many years and a sojourn in the West Indies, my Tipton ancestors arrived in the Chesapeake Bay of the New World in the late 1600's, *or thereabouts*.

This manuscript, along with Book One, encompasses around 1,200 years of European and New World History, and includes some of the historical happenings during this time. I concentrate on the areas the Tiptons inhabited—Germania (now northern Germany), Brittania (England), Barbados, Jamaica, and the New World (North America). I've traveled through most of the areas in the book.

Many of the characters are real, such as the first recorded Tipton who went by the name Tybba. In 500

A.D., people generally went by only one name. The community he founded on the River Tame in Brittania was called Tybbington, meaning Tybba's farm or village. This name changed several times over the centuries before it became Tipton, England.

The interactions of the characters in the book are totally fiction, but based and set against actual movements and activities in the different areas. You will discover what is happening around the Tiptons and their possible response to the situation.

Almost two years were dedicated to this manuscript. Lots of hours to write down descriptions of areas, events, and people who lived during these centuries.

In 2018, on my third trip to England, I visited Tipton, and walked in the area where *it is believed* my ancestors had walked before. I looked up at Dudda Hill (Dudley), saw the ruins of the castle, stood outside and felt the drizzling rain, and watched the sun come up and go down. Many of these activities would feel the same to Tybba, should he come today.

But, I'm sure Tybba would be totally bewildered if he could return and walk down shop-lined, busy Owen Street, through modern Tipton Green and past the statue of the Tipton Slasher. He would see the canals which have replaced the River Tame, cross multiple paved roads, and look confused at a traffic-controlling roundabout, filled with horseless carriages and flashing red or green lights.

What would he see, if he climbed Dudda Hill (Castle Hill) and looked over his old home? What had transpired during the years to make Tipton the town it is today? These two questions will be answered at the end of Part Two. Instead, we start in 1350 A.D.

So, let the adventure continue …

Contents

Rulers of England

Tybba's Family

Edward III, Fifty Year Reign Victory at Crecy and Start of Order of the Garter, Pestilence	1327-77	Adventures of Roger of Tipton, Sir Ralph de Stafford. Ralph's Death of Roger and Ralph
Richard II, Son of Black Prince Grandson of Queen Joan, Peasants Revolt	1377-1399	Mary Tipton, Maid-in-Waiting Niece of Roger of Tipton
Henry IV, Son of John of Gault	1399-1413	
Henry V, Skillful Soldier Battle of Agincourt, John Duke of Bedford, Thomas Montacute, John de Dunois William Glasdale, Siege of Orléans, Jeanne d'Arc	1413-1422	Edmund Tipton, William Tipton from Bristol, George Beaufert
Henry VI, Lost All of France but Calais, Had Mental Lapses. Richard, Duke of York Made Protector, The Printing Press, Start of War of Roses	1422-1461	William Tipton, George Beaufert Hugh Tipton, Martha Tipton, Laurence Tipton. Bristol, England
Edward IV, Not Popular War of Roses Continues	1461-1483	
Edward V, Reigned Two Months. He and Brother Disappeared in the Tower of London.	1483-1483	
Richard III, Disposed of Nephews in Tower. End of War of Roses, Battle of Bosworth Field Where He was Killed, Henry Tudor	1483-1485	William Tipton, Young George Tipton, of Bristol, Durwin Tipton of Pontesburg

Henry VII, First Tudor King, Won Battle of Bosworth, John Cabot Adventures, Columbus Discovers the New World, William Tyndale is Born, The Reformation and Renaissance Start	1485-1509	Laurence, Son Young George, Grandson Isaac, of Bristol. Harold Tipton and Sons, Paul and Andrew, of Portishead
Henry VIII, Greek and Hebrew Writings Come from Europe. Colet and Linacre Read Scriptures in Greek. Martin Luther tacks 95 Theses on Church Door. William Tyndale, Edward Stafford, Cardinal Wolsey, Mary and Anne Boleyn, Church of England. Start Of Plantations Policy in Ireland	1509-1547	Isaac Tipton, Eleanor, Young George, Hugh Tipton becomes Consul for Andalusia Company in Seville, Spain
Edward VI, Son of Henry VIII and Jane Seymour	1527-1553	
Mary I, or Bloody Mary, Tried to Reestablish Catholic Church in England.	1553-1558	
Elizabeth I, Mature, Level Headed, Spanish Armada, Francis Drake, Loved Greenwich Castle and Shakespeare's Plays Continuing the Plantations Policy In Ireland. First Virginia Colony	1558-1603	Hugh Tipton, Consul in Spain, Wife Joan, Sons John and Harold. Harold's Grandson, Dudley, Jeffery the Pie Maker, Shakespeare
James I, Authorized Version of The Bible. 1620 Pilgrims to America, United Scotland and England, *Mayflower* Sails	1603-1625	

Charles I, Personal Rule, Civil War in 1642, Royalist Forces Defeated by New Model Army led by Oliver Cromwell Beheaded. Republic Called Commonwealth of England	1625-1649	
The Commonwealth	1649-1653	
Oliver Cromwell Lord Protector Puritan Figure, Crushed the Irish Clans, Sent Irish as Slaves to the West Indies. Waterford, Ireland	1649-1658	Harold Tipton, Hugh Tipton, Paul Tipton, Paul's Grandson Samuel, Keera, Aron, Roisin, Ciara, The West Indies
Charles II, Takes Throne After Oliver and Richard Cromwell	1660-1685	Jonathan, The Hurricane and Earthquake, New World, Sarah Giovanni, The Wedding

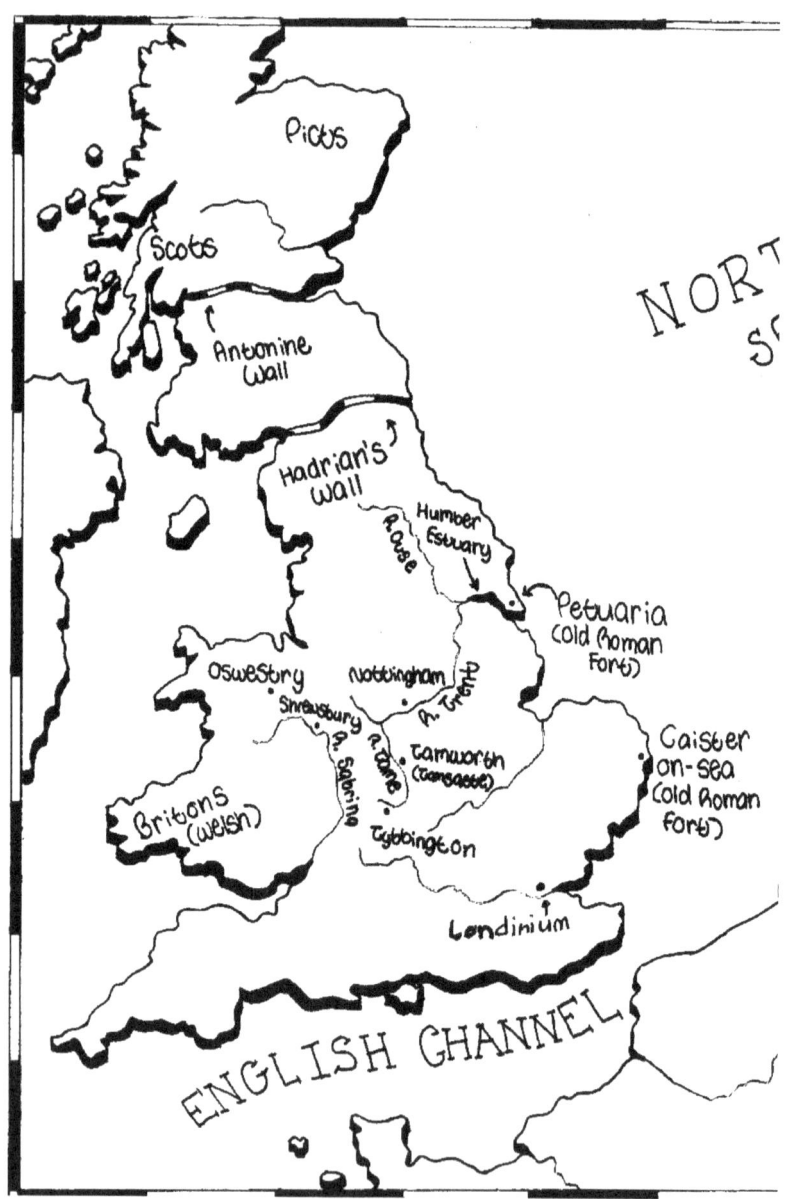

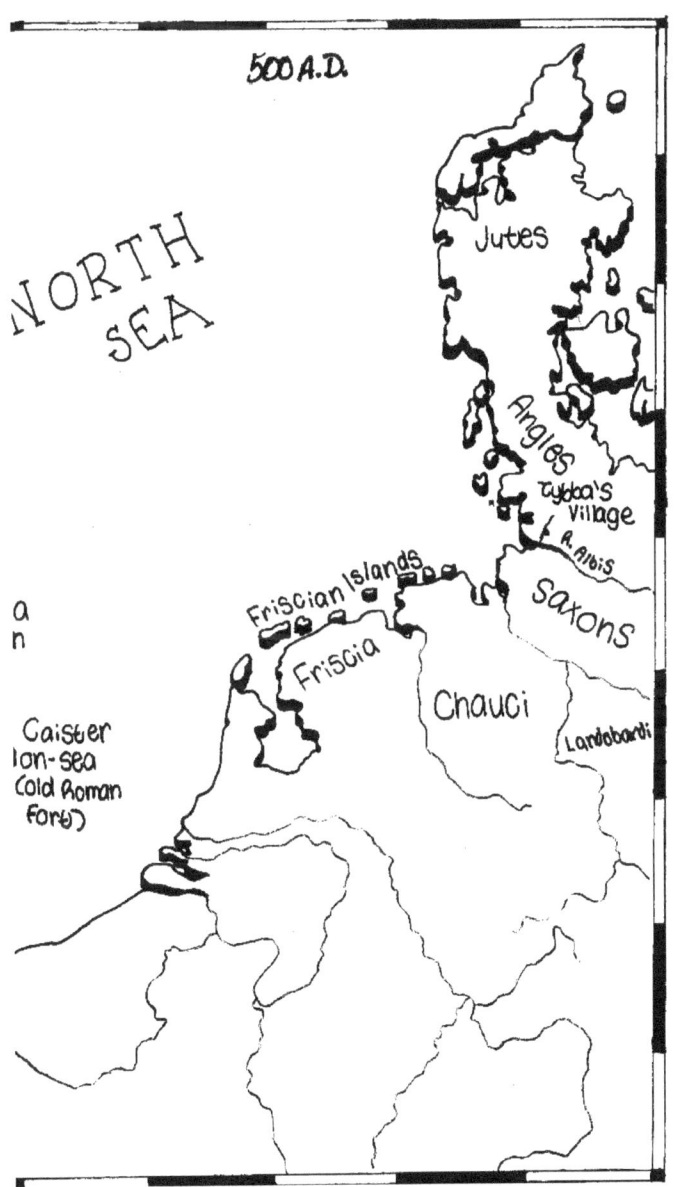

500 A.D.

NORTH SEA

Jutes

Angles

Tydba's Village

R. Albis

Friscian Islands

Saxons

a
n

Friscia

Chauci

Landobardi

Caister
lon-sea
(old Roman
fort)

Setting the Stage

1348 was a year of change for the civilized or feudal world. Besides the escalating French and English War, a dark shadow was sweeping across Asia toward the west. Possibly starting as far away as China, this sickness was so terrible that it killed millions, almost fifty percent of the known world.

For eight hundred years the literate world had been relatively clear of the plague, after it struck with vengeance the Byzantine or Holy Roman Empire and its capital, Constantinople, wiping out millions of people. This was during the reign of Justinian I, who was the emperor during the initial start, and who contracted the disease himself. He survived, so it was possible to conquer this dreaded killer disease. The emperor was not one of the ones stacked in the streets waiting to be buried.

That was hundreds of years ago, and now, this scourge was on the march again and had arrived in Genoa.

THE TIPTON'S OF TYBBINGTON

Before and Beyond, Part Two

The Tipton Crest "Causam Decidit"
"The Sword in This Hand Caused the Decision That Ended the War"

REBA RHYNE

❧ Chapter One ❧

Late 14th Century A.D

The Start of the Pestilence (Black Death) 1348

In late September, 1348, Francisco da Grata stood on the aftcastle of his ship, the *Sancta Vittoria* in the Genoa harbor, watching the loading of his cargo bound for the English city of London. Because of an unusual period of rain, or maybe a leftover year from the Little Ice Age, there was great demand for grain from Egypt or any other country with a good harvest. Much like during the former cold spell in England, the crops were rotting in the fields, and people were starving.

Prices had rose dramatically, and Francisco intended to make all the money he could off the disaster which was likely to occur. The last sheaves of Egyptian wheat and bales of straw disappeared below the deck. Other supplies, such as olive oil, dates in crates, and wine in barrels had been loaded aboard. Finally, the open holds were covered. His ship was ready to set sail. This would be the last voyage of the season.

Crossing the aftcastle to the port side, he watched as the rest of his crew walked down the wharf. Singing some silly sailor song, they were just barely going to make the ship's shove-off time.

This was nothing unusual for them, and so he did as they expected. Cupping his hand, he yelled at them, "Hurry, make haste!"

The men threw up their hands, acknowledged his admonition, swaggered a bit more, but didn't quicken their pace.

Francisco grinned and shrugged his shoulders. With his sailors, it was always this way. They were never in a hurry, except to leave the ship when it went into port.

Below, on the wooden boards of the gangplank, where it touched the wharf, something caught his eye — a slight movement.

Nudged on by the noisiness of the boisterous group, a large, black wharf rat hesitated, head jerking from side to side, and then it ran up the boat's ramp.

Francisco yelled at one of his crew members who was sweeping the deck beneath where he stood, "Bernotti, kill the rat!" The captain motioned toward the gangplank as the rat jumped to the deck.

Bernotti ran for the rat, drew back and swatted hard at the running rodent, breaking the broom's handle. The rat fell over on its side — either knocked out or dead. Bernotti picked it up by its long tail and tossed it overboard. Leaning over the gunnel, he stood looking at the water until the rat sank out of view in the harbour. He'd certainly killed the rat, but he'd also killed his broom.

Francisco threw back his head and laughed heartily at his crewman, who had looked up at the captain, expecting to be chastised for his cumbersome charge. "At least the rat is dead," the captain said. "We'll have no more trouble from him."

Bernotti, who hadn't moved from the spot, reached down to swat at something biting him on his exposed leg. "No, Captain, I watched it sink in the sea. There'll be no more trouble at all," he predicted, now scratching at his ankle.

The rest of the *Sancta Vittoria's* crew climbed up the wooden board and jumped from the gangplank to the deck.

"Bernotti," asked a man with a large belly and a kerchief wrapped around his head. He stood with his hands on his hips, "Why did you break the broom?"

"I was killing a rat," said the sailor, spreading his hands palms up with a sheepish look on his face.

"Sure! You were trying to kill the ship, and the ship won," his mate responded, coming near. "I see no rat," he waved toward the ship's rail and took the piece Bernotti still held in his hand—the handle part—and examined it. Then he picked up the brush and fitted it to the other piece of wood. Looking up at the captain, he said, grinning, "I think I can salvage it."

"Good, Fante," the captain responded. To the rest of the crew, he said, "Take your places. The holds are full, and we're ready to sail."

With a booming laugh which caused sailors standing on the wharf to look in the ship's direction, Fante headed for the door to the crew's quarters. He stopped at the door and flicked something off his hand to the deck. Then he promptly began scratching at a red welt which appeared.

One of his companions paused beside him. "Did something bite you? Was it a mosquito? Or a gnat? I've been swatting them all day. Seem worse this year for some reason. Maybe the rain."

"No, it must have been a flea, but I can't be for sure. It jumped or fell just as I hit it."

"Probably one of the ones they loaded with the sheaves from Egypt. Did you hear any scuttlebutt while you were in Genoa?"

Fante wrinkled his brow. "There's some kind of illness going around. Didn't take time to learn much about it, because with sailors they're always complaining about something — the weather, the food, the rough seas. I was more interested in drinking as much ale as possible, since the Captain won't let us imbibe while on the ship. What did you hear?"

"Same as you. There's whispers of the pestilence."

"Pestilence, you say! Like I said, 'sailors' tales.'"

"Several people have died, Fante," his mate shook his head. "I can't just dismiss it."

"You too." Fante turned and headed on to his work area.

The mate following, continued gushing news. "There's talk of a war between Constantinople and Genoa — something about custom duties through the straights of Bosporus. Captain says this is the reason we've loaded grain from Egypt. None is coming from the Pontic states around the Black Sea. Plus, all the talk we heard about the rain being back in England and how badly they need food. Makes me glad I live here in Genoa. We may have hills, but food can be found on the nearest tree or vine. At least, we don't starve."

Fante stopped his walk and lowered his voice to say, "I'll wager the captain will make a bundle when we arrive in London. Think he'll split some of it with us?"

His friend laughed and didn't bother to answer. The boat made a sudden movement. They were under sail.

~

Leaving the Genoa harbour was always a treat to Francisco. He could look at the empty sea ahead with the small white caps, indicating a steady wind for sailing, or he could look up at the green hills, towering over the city. Both positioned against the harbour below.

The one place he directed his gaze was to his hillside house and the large piece of green cloth floating on the wind from an upstairs window.

Goodbye, his woman said, and please return safely. She was expecting their fourth child.

This was the life of seamen sailing the seas. They came home and stayed around long enough for the wife to be with child and then they left again—some men gone so long, they hardly knew their children.

Francisco waved. He couldn't see her, but he knew she'd be there watching.

His ship was known as a cog vessel, not very picturesque or pleasing to the eye as the newer tall-masted sailing ships, but serviceable for shiping men or cargo. It had one large mast and a smaller sail.

This trip would take around two to three weeks, if the wind held. Sailing west along the coast of France and Spain, he would pass through the Strait of Gibraltar, cross the Biscayan Sea, head northeast in the English Channel, and enter the River Thames east of London.

Away from the wharf, the crew set the sail and the ship picked up speed as it left the harbour for open water. The azure blue waves of the Mediterranean Sea slapped its side and then the boat caught the first swell.

Without knowing it, the *Sancta Vittoria* was carrying The Pestilence to England. The rats already onboard the ship would all become infected, along with the fleas traveling on the sheaves out of the granaries of Egypt.

When the ship arrived at the London port, only four men survived. The captain was one of them.

King Edward's new chapel at Windsor Castle was ready for the ceremony to establish the Order of the Garter, which was planned to take place after the morning meal. His choice of October 13th, a well-known feast day in England to celebrate his ancestor and namesake, Edward the Confessor, was the perfect day.

Sir Ralph and Roger had been up for several hours preparing clothes for the day and for the trip into the Great Hall for the morning meal. This repast was likely to happen right on time, because the King insisted on punctuality.

For some reason, the Garter habits had almost arrived late. Roger observed, "I'm glad I wasn't in charge of getting the habits here."

"Yes, poor soul. Shaking in his boots, I heard some say, when he saw the King's anger."

"Why do you think he was late?" Roger asked, handing Sir Ralph his tunic—the last piece of clothing he would need before the morning meal.

"Probably the weather—maybe flooding is the culprit." Sir Ralph added.

"That would certainly explain it." Roger had hung Sir Ralph's cloak up with a carved wooden hanger, so any wrinkles would fall out. He couldn't help but finger the carved wood. It reminded him of his father, Henry, and his talent of carving wood. Most of it he gave away, but Baron Dudley often bought articles he carved to use and display in his castle—animals, he especially liked.

"Will we come back for the cloak after the meal?" asked Roger. Sir Ralph would not need it going to eat at the breaking of the night's fast, because the walk was indoors, but the short hike to the chapel was not, and it was cold and rainy outside.

"I'm sure that's what everyone will do. So, leave it hanging. The procession to the chapel won't line up until after the meal."

"Are you ready to go?"

"Yes. Remember, you have one of the assigned seats at the ceremony, which from what I've heard will be a long one. Did you go and find it, as I suggested?" Sir Ralph could choose those of his own people to watch the ceremony. He'd chosen Roger and, of course, his brother, Sir Richard de Stafford.

"Yes, I found mine and Sir Richard's also. I'll be able to lead him to his seat. Have you heard anything from him?"

"No. Nothing."

"I hope Sir Richard makes it back in time from France." Like Ralph, he was always on the King's business somewhere in the Kingdom.

Sir Ralph started out the door with Roger following.

"Yes. I'm still hoping he'll be able to make the ceremony, but time is close. Don't say a word, but the King intimated to me he may be nominated in the future when a seat becomes vacant."

"What an honor. To have two from the same family and shire to be Knights in the highest order in the land."

~

The morning meal was over. Roger looked around the room. A signal from one of the arched doorways caught his attention. Looking closer, he was shocked to see William of Tipton's son, Henry, from Bristol, motioning to him from inside the doorway to the Great Hall. Since others were rising, he went quickly to embrace and stand beside him.

"Why are you here? Is something wrong?" was his first thought and words.

"Yes, something is very wrong. This morning, I arrived from France with the *MaryRose* at my usual wharf in London, and while visiting our merchant's offices there heard the news of another boat, the *Sancta Vittoria* from Genoa, which arrived earlier in the day with most of the crew dead of the pestilence. Have you heard this?"

"No. Not a word. I'll have to tell Sir Ralph, so he can tell the King." Roger turned, but Henry caught his arm.

"Wait, there's more. The office had just got word from father by messenger. The pestilence is now in Bristol. Two of our wharf hands have died from it— only three days for them to be gone from this world."

"Dear God. What will become of England? Where are you headed, Henry?"

"Back home. I am fearful for my family—my wife and children."

"Thank you for coming with this information. I'll see that Sir Ralph knows." Roger embraced his cousin again, looking him squarely in the eye. "God be with you until we meet again."

"And you too, Roger."

Henry turned and went out the arched doorway.

Roger went immediately to Sir Ralph who'd risen from his seat and was engaged in pleasant conversation with another inductee.

Making eye contact, Sir Ralph realized it must be important. He said his goodbyes and came to Roger.

"Something has to be wrong," stated Sir Ralph, looking serious. "You never interrupt me in conversation."

"Yes." And then Roger filled Sir Ralph's ear full of the conversation he'd just had with Henry. Sir Ralph was fairly dark-skinned from being out in the sun for long periods of time, but Roger could see he blanched underneath the facial tan.

"The King will have to know," he said, looking over the crowd. He spotted the monarch and headed in his direction.

Waiting until he could talk to the King, he said in a low voice. "Your Grace, I have some rather shocking news. May we step to the side and converse?"

The King took his arm and led Sir Ralph a few steps away where some privacy could be had. Then he said, "Is it about the ship in the harbour this morning?"

"Yes. How did you know?"

"I had news an hour after it happened, and not wanting to damper this glorious occasion, did not communicate it to anyone. I will after the ceremony in the Great Hall is over, and we are finished with the noonday meal."

"I won't say a word," promised Sir Ralph.

"There's more to the story. After being told not to open them, vandals wishing to make some pennies ripped open the holds and started taking the supplies off the boat. Afterwards, I ordered them arrested and their greed covered up, until I decide what to do about them Things are really desperate in the country with all this never-ending rain. I even thought of cancelling our ceremony."

"Do you suppose they've introduced the pestilence on London?"

"I wish we knew more about the disease. I hope not. This isn't the first time a boat has come into a port with dead men and the distinct appearance of this disease, but it's the first for England."

Sir Ralph noticed the King did not want to use the word — pestilence.

King Edward continued, "A few days will tell us the answer, but let us pray we are wrong. For now, let's get through the coming hours."

"Your Grace, there's something else you should be aware of also." If Sir Ralph could've withheld the next words coming from his mouth he would have done so, but the King needed to know. "Two men died of the pestilence in Bristol in the last few days."

"Oh, dear God! Then this dreaded disease is in our country already. Now it's on both our coasts. How will this change England?" The King's question ended the conversation. He thanked Ralph and, composing himself, he returned to his guests.

Those who were honoured in the ceremony finished their robing, and the long procession to St. George's Chapel was completed. The ceremony was long and drawn out. Sir Ralph's mind was so occupied with the fate of England he could hardly concentrate.

Finally, he was conducted to his stall and, with a short ritual, given the blessed Garter, which they buckled on top of his hose on his left leg. Next a red riband was placed over the left shoulder and under the right arm and secured under his belt. The brooch of St George was pinned to this riband on his chest.

Two more items were necessary. A robe or surcoat went over what the Knight was wearing to the ceremony, then buckled over the surcoat was Sir Ralph's crimson velvet girdle — all this done with a ceremony for each. Finally, a sword and its hanger were belted on by those performing the service. Then they administered the actual oath taken by the Knight, which stated:

"You being chosen to be one of the

honourable company of the Most

Noble Order of the Garter, shall promise

and swear by the Holy Evangelists, by you

here touched, that wittingly and willingly

you shall not break any statute of the said

Order, or any article in them contained, the

same being agreeable and not repugnant to

the will of God, and the laws of the Realm,

as far forth as to you belongeth and

appertaineth, so help you God and

his Holy Word."

The ceremony continued with pieces of the robe presented, including a hood and collar.

"Wear this collar about thy neck, adorned

with the image of the Blessed Martyr and

Soldier in Christ, St. George, by whose

imitation provoked, thou may'st so

o'erpass both prosperous and adverse

encounters; that having stoutly vanquished

thine enemies, both of body and soul, thou

may'st not only receive of this transient

combat, but be crowned with palms

of eternal victory."

Finally, he signed the Statute Book of the Order and then the placing of his ceremonial cap with feathers on his head ended the ceremony for him. Sir Ralph was an official Knight of the Order of the Garter. He was the fifth one to go through the ceremony. There were nineteen more to go.

Next, after the secular ceremony for all the chosen was concluded, was the divine service, spoken in Latin, but when translated into English ended with this verse of Matthew 5:16…*Let youre light so shyne before men, that they maye se youre good works, and glorify youre Father which is in heven.*

It was very late afternoon when the procession from St. George's Chapel took them back to the castle to rest.

Before the sun went down, the participants headed to the Great Hall. When all was ready for the sumptuous feast to follow, there was a flourish of trumpets announcing the King. He arrived with his Captain-of-the-Guard who seated him at the table, whereupon the whole retinue sat down to a splendid banquet. The King was served first, along with those selected to sit at the head table.

Next, the Knights of the new Sovereign Order of the Garter, sitting at tables in the center of the room, received the meal and its condiments.

The soothing music of a band of roving minstrels put all the attendees at ease. They played until all were sated with good food and drink.

When King Edward stood to address the attendees, the noise in the room abated, as everyone looked expectantly at their Liege Lord.

"Knights of the Order of the Garter," he proclaimed loudly, his words echoing in the vast reaches of the room. "We hold the future destiny of

England in our hands. You have sworn a great oath to God and our country. With His help, we will vanquish our enemies in combat and adhere to the laws of the English Realm. We will overcome every difficulty, fight and labor with honor. We will accomplish great deeds—eternal deeds. You have valiant hearts and the most virtuous of souls, for I have chosen you well."

King Edward looked around the room, surveying his men with affection. He continued in a lower tone, causing his audience to lean forward to catch his words.

He reflected, "How much of the past can we understand? How far into the future can we see? What is my hope and dream for our country?"

He did not elaborate on these questions, instead the King cleared his throat, looked pointedly at Sir Ralph, and plunged into the part of the speech he'd been dreading. "Today, I received some terrible news." He watched as the Knights looked wonderingly at each other—bad news? They weren't at war, so no battle was lost. What could be worse than that?

"Today, a ship from Genoa, carrying grain, came into London's harbour. Most of the men on board were dead. Knights, I fear we may have the Pestilence in our country."

There was a noise of the men sucking in their breaths and rustling as they turned to look at each other with a question in their eyes and on their lips.

King Edward held up his hands to quiet them. "There is also a report of the Pestilence in Bristol."

Shocked silence now reigned in the room.

The King's voice was full of emotion as he continued. "Rain, snow, and cold we can contend with, but this death ... no one knows the final and complete end for our country. I would say more, but I fear this cloud will hang over England as it has elsewhere for many years. We will not dance tonight as planned. Here is my admonition to you. Go to your homes and take care of your families until England needs you again."

He turned and, with his Captain of the Guard, immediately left the banqueting hall.

Several of the Knights stood around talking, but Sir Ralph and Roger did not tarry.

Back in their quarters, Ralph told Roger as he prepared for bed, "If I was an older man, I don't think I could have survived the ceremony—and the other news. Now, I fear, our country must endure a worse fate."

To which Roger replied, "Sir Ralph, you've survived worse than a ceremony, and you're only forty-seven."

"Tonight, I feel twenty-years older," said a sleepy and tired Ralph.

When Roger left the room, he looked back and murmured, "And you've lived and experienced enough in those years to be that age." He went to the wooden hanger and put Sir Ralph's new habit in safe order. They would be returned to the King for secure keeping tomorrow.

～

It turned out the vandals had off-loaded the plague onto England. By All Saint's day, November 1st,

England was in shock. By Christmas, as The Pestilence spread, it turned to mourning.

Sir Ralph continued to serve King Edward, and, in March 1351, the King rewarded him by making his longtime warrior, the Earl de Stafford.

Many times, with either the Duke of Lancaster or his own brother, Sir Richard de Stafford, he traveled to France to complete treaties, fight battles, or to protect the King. He also helped the King's son, the Prince of Wales, later known as the Black Prince, in the Realm's struggles with the Welsh peoples at Chester and other sites across Offa's Dyke.

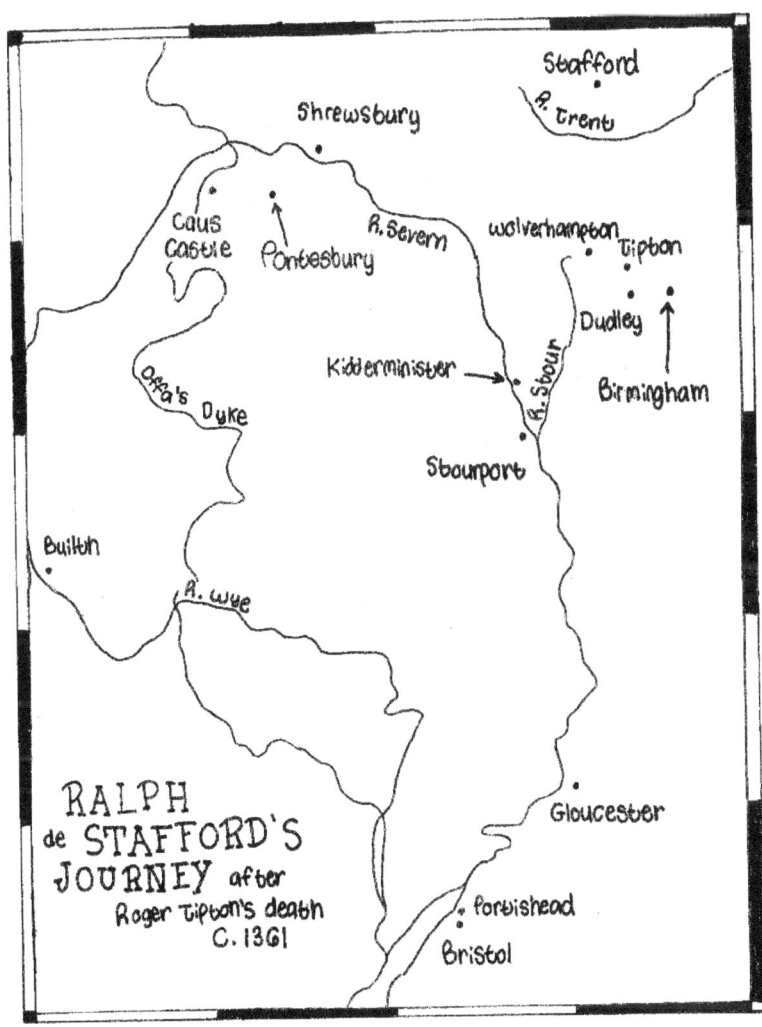

✣ Chapter 2 ✣

Late 14th Century A.D

The Death of Roger of Tipton and Sir Ralph de Stafford Changes in England Brought About by the Pestilence

When Sir Ralph was sixty years old, during one of the few times they were at Stafford Castle, his Constable Roger fell ill. The Knight sat at his bedside when it became obvious that his long-time friend, who was going in and out of consciousness, was sick until death. On one of the trips, when Roger came back into the world, they had their last conversation.

"Will you take me back to Tipton and bury me on Summerhill at St. Martin's, beside my father?"

The Earl de Stafford had to bend his ear close to Roger to hear what he said. "Yes, I will do that, my friend."

"Bury me in my Constable clothing, but not with Anthony's sword. Please take it to William in Bristol and give it to him or the son who has the Ancestry Book. My Lord, ask them to see that I'm in its pages."

"I will do that. What else?"

"I'm a simple man. There is no 'what else.'" Roger said this with a slight smile on his face. Then he turned his head away a little and shut his eyes.

Sir Ralph did not hesitate but said, "You are not a simple man, but one with great feeling and honor. Your name should have had Sir in front of it, for you went through the same battles and complications as I. Not only that, but you've been my great friend and companion these many years." Sir Ralph hesitated until his emotions settled down and then continued, "Going on without you will not be the same. The glory will be diminished, because you've always been part of that glory. Goodnight, my dear friend and companion."

Sir Ralph wasn't sure Roger heard him. So, he reached for his hand and felt a slight squeeze. He was sure that was a "Yes." At least, he convinced himself it was.

~

In 1361, Sir Ralph supervised the burial at Tipton and gave the final prayer over the grave. Standing outside the church, with the leaves turned in the golds and reds of autumn, and the English morning sun shining brilliantly over the Glebe fields opposite the burial ground, he read from a parchment prepared especially for the service.

"O God, who didst call thy servant, Roger of Tipton, to an earthly existence that he might help advance your heavenly kingdom here in the King's service, and didst give him zeal for thy Church and love for thy people: Mercifully grant that we who commemorate him this day may be fruitful of good works, and attain with him to the glorious crown of thy saints; through Jesus Christ our Lord, who liveth and reigneth with thee and the Holy Spirit, one God, forever and ever. Amen"

Sir Ralph picked up a handful of dirt and tossed it into the burial place. He stood back while the grave diggers filled the grave.

After the service, he headed for the old home where he'd first met Roger. Roger's sister, Anne, who was now a widow, still lived there with a nephew, Martin, and his wife, and children.

"My other nephews and nieces live near," she said to his question as several of Martin's children ran into the house.

"Children, we have a visitor," exclaimed Martin's wife. "Please be quiet."

The children went up the same ladder that he, Roger, and Anne had used as children. Soon, snickering was heard overhead. Nostalgia hit Sir Ralph with a heaviness hard to bear as he remembered another time and place—happy memories, never to be forgotten.

Anne looked at his sorrowful face and smiled. Then she explained, "My other brothers and sisters did not survive the Pestilence." She had raised six of them, nephews and nieces—those young ones who had survived. Some lived in Tipton. Some lived in Dudley—with one in Wednesbury among other distant kin. Martin was the oldest boy.

On the fireplace front, hanging in the old place of honor, was the second sword, the one which King Edward I had given to Sir Anthony de Tipton. The sword was now Martin's—given to him by Roger when his father, Henry, had died.

Sir Ralph did not stay long. He left with a sufficiency of food for the trip to Portishead and Bristol and a pillow Anne had sewn herself and stuffed with wool. "To remind you that you have friends here in Tipton, and that you are welcome at any time, my Lord." The pillow had the silhouette of a rabbit embroidered on the cloth. Sir Ralph quickly turned his head to hide his tears at the memory of the time spent on the Coneygree field.

After visiting with Anne, Sir Ralph immediately went on to Bristol and Portishead to leave the sword of Aethelflaed with William of Tipton. On arriving, he found that the plague had taken both William and MaryRose in their attempt to save Henry and his family, but Samuel continued to run the shipping business. He had possession of the Ancestry Book, which he gave to Sir Ralph, inviting him to write Roger's history within its pages.

Writing and visiting, Sir Ralph stayed three days with Samuel's family, riding to Bristol with the exporter/importer each afternoon to stay the night. He and Samuel trudged the hills and Downs above the port, talking of days gone by and Roger's involvement in the many English wars.

"He saved my life more than once," Sir Ralph concluded.

Their walk had ended before William's stone house above the harbour at Portishead. "Do you intend to move here to your father's old house with your family?"

"Yes. Much of our household goods have already been moved. I need to be closer to the expanding business, and my wife loves this house," replied Samuel. Turning, the men headed down toward the floating wharf. "She hopes our children will fill it with grandchildren, and I do too. My exporting business has increased since the pestilence continues to wipe out most of the competition. I could use more little ones to learn the operation."

"What is your major export, Samuel?"

"The exports, from up and down the River Severn and the River Avon, change all the time. We still ship raw wool and woven wool cloth from the sheepherders of Shropshire and even Wales, especially when we aren't at war with the Welsh. The wool cloth, which is of high quality, is sent to be finished in Flanders and Gascony."

"Some of the French goods are shipped back after being dyed with the surface smoothed, but my suppliers tell me that several men are proposing and actually setting up facilities along the rivers to produce wool goods comparable to the French ones we import. Everything in the shipping area is subject to change."

"What happens to the finished goods after coming back to England?"

"They are taken to drapers who sell cloth for making clothes or household goods, and we have several sellers of cloth goods in each town on the River Severn. They've set up guilds to ensure quality of their supplies and to protect their markets."

"Cloth can't fill up all the holds on a ship, can it?"

"No, you are right, Sir Ralph. Most of a ship is loaded with wine when we return from France, some of it coming to us as far as the Italian markets through Genoa. There we might also find olive oil, olives, dates, spices or other goods to be loaded and imported, these resting in the warehouses on those distant wharves."

"Do you take goods to English ports?"

"Yes, and we're looking at Ireland, especially if we have an overload here and it isn't profitable to transport them over the English Channel to France or the Italian markets. Those supplies might include salt, tanned hides, and iron-working products. We've also sent apples, pears, and bottled honey. During an excellent harvest, we've even moved dried corn for milling to the London markets."

"You don't see any downside to the import/export business?"

"No. There's always something to ship by sea. We've expanded our airtight barrel and box making warehouse at Gloucester, and started making buckets and chests in Bristol—something my family has wanted to do for years. This is a buffer against any slowdown in the shipping business. I'm sure we'll find other items to make."

"What about owning your own ships?"

"In the back of my mind, but probably not in my lifetime," Samuel grinned as he said this.

The two men were back at the warehouse at Portishead. Samuel went to curl a dock rope into a circle on the wharf. Sir Ralph continued on into the building and returned, holding the Ancestral Book toward Samuel.

"Have you written the story of your family here?" asked Sir Ralph of Samuel.

"Not yet, but I will. It's complete to my father. He wrote his in there."

"This book will be important to your family someday. Cherish it and protect it. I've signed my part, so your family will know who wrote it." He handed the book back to Samuel. "I have something else to go with the book." Sir Ralph went to his horse and unstrapped a long object wrapped in leather from his saddle.

"That looks like a sword," observed Samuel.

"It is. A very important sword."

Sir Ralph handed it to Samuel, who took it out of the leather casing and from its scabbard. He hefted the piece of metal. "It's very curious, heavy—not like the ones of today."

"Swords have changed," Sir Ralph agreed. "Look at the hilt. It's engraved with the Staffordshire knot, which means it came from a Stafford native, in this case Aethelflaed, when she was the Lady of Mercia, ruler of part of our country."

"How did we get it?"

"Her scribe, Meta, saved her life at the Battle of Tettenhall, and she honored him with her own sword. He was from Scrobbesbyrig or Shrewsbury now, of the Tybbington people who moved there. The story's in the book. You must go back and read it."

"It is a small world, isn't it? There's something written on the blade." Samuel moved the blade so it would catch the light, because as was often the case in England, there were clouds coming in from the south, threatening rain later in the day. "Do you read Latin, Sir Ralph?" he asked.

"Yes." With the sword back in his hand, he read, "*Strike hard*, on this side."

"Very appropriate, for a sword," said Samuel, nodding. "And on the other—"

"On the other there's *We are bound as one*."

Both men stood in silence, thinking their own thoughts—one of family, the other of friendship.

~

Sir Ralph de Stafford left Bristol very early the next morning. He rode without his armour except for his sword and knife — a little dangerous considering there might be highwaymen on the road, although the path was frequented by daily travelers. So many Englishmen were destitute since the ravages of the Pestilence had broken up families. Food, clothing, and shelter were still scarce for the very poor. Even children had become scavengers, dirty and unkept.

Samuel promised to send his extra supplies back to Staffordshire by several gentlemen headed to Leicester.

During the night, he had decided on his way back home, to call on a castle which the King had given him in Shropshire. When he and Roger had traveled this way to sail to France, he'd decided to not take time to make the detour toward the Welsh territory. His property was called Caus Castle and was located west of Shrewsbury.

Oswestry, where Eggen had helped build Offa's Dyke, was only a few miles northwest.

Not in any hurry, he walked his horse and enjoyed the countryside as he went north. His life had always been one of haste, and out here the King could not fi[n]d him. This was his pilgrimage into the world ar a him — alone to mend his heart from the de'ging lifelong friend. He paused to hear the bi·w and and to watch the sunset turn the clo·er, getting orange to match the colors of autum· large castle The third night, he stayed ·le mint which there early enough to ride an·· built by the River Severn had made royal coins for three hundred years. He could have identified himself at the castle or at Charles of Tipton's home and spent the night in opulence or at least comfort. Instead, he preferred to spend the night over the local tavern, where his roommates made a joyful noise during the night. The next morning, after a breakfast of eggs, fried pork, and rye bread, he headed out for Worcester with his water bottle full, walking his horse through the market-place and riding past Gloucester Abbey as he left the town—one of many churches in the area.

He and Roger had missed Worcester on their way down to Portishead and Bristol. Its rapid growth since the Norman invasion had necessitated sandstone walls being built to encompass the town and the construction of a thirty-foot wide ditch filled with water as a deterrent to any attacker. Ralph entered through the southern Sidbury Gate, immediately passing the castle within, and more than one set of walls as he headed for the center of town. This time he managed to get a single room and spend the night in relative quiet, except for the noise from the tavern downstairs.

His next encounter with the public was at Kidereministre (Kidderminster), a small village mpared to Gloucester and Worcester. He must have ʰd like a stranger because …

oldʳ, do you need a place to stay the night?" an from man wielding a broom, sweeping minute dirt pass ʰ nt door walkway, asked as he prepared to "Ye

stay, and ʰo you have a room for strangers to ʰhe afternoon and morning meal?"

Sir Ralph replied, looking over the establishment. She had to have a few pennies, because the place was stone with a thatched roof and real windows with glass panes. The glass panes did not have a speck of dust on them. Who was this woman? He was more than a little curious.

"And fodder for your horse," the lady nodded in the direction of the back of her home. She came to the street and held his horse's reins as he dismounted, obviously determined he'd be her guest.

"Please come around to the paddock at the back of the house. You can unsaddle and leave your horse there. Then I'll show you to your room. We can enter from the enclosure," she stated, leading the animal down a narrow path between another house.

Making sure the horse was comfortable and fed, she led Sir Ralph into the house. The downstairs was separated into two rooms—a large bed chamber, with the other room used as a combination cooking area and sitting room. The fireplace on the outside wall separated the areas so it could be used for heat and cooking. A pot heating on the hearth emitted a stomach-growling smell.

"Something smells good," commented Sir Ralph.

The elderly woman grinned, showing a missing front tooth. "Rabbit stew, and a very good rabbit stew, if I do say so. My name's Mary. What's yours?" she asked.

Sir Ralph started to give his full title. He caught himself and said, "Ralph, just Ralph."

The woman looked at him with a question on her face. She'd noticed his hesitation. "Well, just Ralph, where are you from?"

"From Staffordshire—one shire over." Now Ralph grinned at her boldness. "Where do I sleep?" he asked.

"Oh, up the stairs." Mary went to a door they'd passed on the way into the sitting area and opened it. The stairs, as she'd called them, was almost a ladder leading to an upstairs loft.

Ralph went halfway up the stone steps and hefted his traveling bag to the floor above before climbing the rest of the way into the area which was large and contained a cot and chair. Openings at either end of the gabled roof let in air and a dim light. The place was adequate.

From downstairs, Mary called, "I'll bring you a coverlet and pillow for your head."

The meal was delicious. Mary hovered over him, making sure he had a knife and spoon, a napkin which she'd sewn herself, and enough food to fill his trencher and stomach up. Finally, Sir Ralph ordered her to sit down and eat, which without objection, she did.

"What does your husband do?" he asked, after she'd made herself comfortable with a trencher of food.

"My husband has been dead these five years. He was the Coroner of this County, appointed by the King—a gruesome job many times. He stood by as a man was executed and collected any fines the dead man owed his Majesty, and many times he was called in the dead, excuse the term, of night to investigate a death. Was it murder, suicide, accidental or natural causes?" Mary shook her head, remembering her husband's position in the village and surrounding area.

So, Mary's husband was a court official, thought Sir Ralph. That explained the upgrade of the house. Every position on the court was subject to being bribed by those in conflict with the laws of the land, which with each passing year increased in number. They all worked in concert—the Sheriff, Bailiff, Coroner and the newly created position of Justice-of-the-Peace. That didn't mean all courts were corrupt, but more were joining those ranks, since the areas were far-flung and difficult to monitor.

Sir Ralph responded, "I'm sure he had a difficult job," he agreed, thinking he was getting his eyes opened to the ways of the common people on his ride north.

Mary interrupted his thoughts. "Will you be staying long in the area, Ralph?" She was sopping her bread in the soup from the rabbit stew and almost done with her meal.

"No. I'll head on to Shrewsbury tomorrow morning. I'll be visiting my (he almost said castle) friends there, and then I'll head on to Staffordshire and home."

Mary nodded, agreeing with him.

"Where did you come from?" She got up to light candles around the room, pausing by the table as she returned to set one beside him.

"From Bristol and Portishead. I have friends there also."

"You have a lot of friends, Ralph," she said, wondering why they lived in so many places. She let the obvious question go and pulled a large pottery bowl from a shelf above a wooden counter. Dipping hot water with a large cup from an iron pot hanging over the fire, she poured it into the bowl. Turning to Ralph, she said, "My husband insisted on the dishes being washed."

Ralph watch her clean the table and place the dishes into the water. "Ouch! That's hot," she exclaimed, shaking her hand.

Sir Ralph stood and went to the door to look out. It was pitch dark outside with only a few candles lighting the open doorways in the area. He heard the murmur of voices. Some people were taking advantage of the last warmth of summer to sit outside and talk, discussing the events of the day with their neighbors. "Mary, I'm going to bed," he said, taking the candle and heading for the loft room.

Mary turned and watched him approach the stairs. "I'll be up early, Ralph, with your morning meal ready for you to eat. It's been a pleasure to have a man sittin' at my table. Sleep well."

Sir Ralph left Kidderminster with a sack of bread and meat for the day's ride toward Shrewsbury. Mary had called after him, "I don't know where your next meal will be coming from. Not many people live along the road."

Sir Ralph had turned and waved. "Thank you, Mary. God go with you."

"And to you, too, Ralph."

He wondered if she'd known she had just entertained Sir Ralph, Earl of Stafford and proprietor of Caus Castle, if she'd have been any different. He guessed not. Mary was Mary. In the large pot where she'd washed the dishes, he'd left several extra pennies for her kindness.

Shrewsbury was a hard two day's ride away. He started out at a fast pace, covering over one-half the way before starting to look for an area to stay the night. Mary was right. There wasn't one place along the road to stay or eat. Thankfully, she'd given him enough food for the night, and if he was careful, it would last until the morning. Bedding down was another problem.

At dusky dark, just as he was about to give up on a place to lay his head and stretch out under a tree against a tree trunk, he saw a glow coming through a stand of trees along the road. Curious, he led his horse toward the light.

As he got closer, he realized a crackling fire was burning, and a man in a gray robe sat by the fire. "Hail, there."

The man got clumsily to his feet. "Hail to you, Sir."

Sir Ralph recognized a Franciscan Friar in his gray monk's robe with its huge hood, tied with a rope belt from which hung a cross. Over this attire was the long mantle reaching down to the tops of his shoes which were sturdy with thick leather soles. He had no horse, so he walked everywhere he went. His head was shaved on top with a circle of hair sprouting from where the shaving stopped.

"May I join you, Friar?"

"Sure. The more the merrier," said the religious man. He laughed. "I'm Friar James. Who might you be?"

"Ralph from Staffordshire."

"Have you eaten? I don't have much, but such as I have, I'm most willing to share."

"Thank you, Friar James, but I have eaten. Do you know of any place to stay the night in the area?"

"If I did, do you think I'd be sitting in the forest, eating over an open fire? No, there's no place." The Friar led the way to his fire. "Pull up a chair and sit down," he laughed again. This time at his witticism.

Instead, Ralph took off his horse's saddle and made a chair of it. "Do you plan to sleep here tonight?"

"Yes. But I'm used to sleeping in the open. You don't appear to me to hanker such a plan," the Friar looked Ralph over. Something about this man wasn't stacking up. "Where are you going?"

"To Shrewsbury."

"You might make it by in the morning, if you keep on riding."

"No, I think I'll spend the night here with you. At least, I have a pillow, and my cloak will be my bedding. A few branches from one of the evergreen trees, and I should be comfortable enough for one night." Ralph took out his knife, grabbed his horse's reins so he could tie him in a grassy spot, and looked for a tree with small leaves and limbs. Nearby alder trees supplied both, and some willow trees growing in a wet-land only a few yards away made a rather bumpy bed, but at least they kept him off the ground. He put his saddle on the limbs and his rabbit pillow on the saddle. Spreading his spare cloak on top of all, he lay down to test his bed.

"Where did you spend last night?" asked Friar James.

"At Kidderminster," he said from his reclining position.

"With Mistress Mary?" asked the Friar.

"Yes, do you know her?"

"I often stay with her. She must spend all day sweeping the doorway to her house so she can snatch visitors to the area."

Now it was Sir Ralph's time to laugh. "She caught me," he said, closing his eyes.

⁓

The next morning, the two continued on toward Shrewsbury with Sir Ralph walking beside the Friar, while leading his horse.

"Where do you live Friar James?"

"I live outside the walls of Shrewsbury—land is available there where the poor live, and their numbers are growing rapidly."

"Do you think the Church has lost sight of its earlier ideals and is mainly interested in gaining wealth?" Ralph knew this was a loaded question, but he was interested in this man's opinion.

"The Church *is* wealthy. And to an extent, I believe that's a true statement," he said, being delicate when addressing the situation. "Of course, when the pestilence swept through the country, the ministers were the ones with the highest losses, since they did not refuse to go to the dying and sick."

"That's true," said Ralph, thinking over what Friar James had stated.

"We have schools at Shrewsbury, where we teach the children and even adults to read and write English."

As they continued down the road, the conversation turned to the different friaries in the area.

"Do you know Friar Joseph?" he asked.

"Oh, he's long gone. Lost his mind along the last. He wasn't at my Church, but I knew him—everyone knew him. How did you meet him?"

"Fifteen years ago, I visited this area with my Constable. He gave us directions to my servant's people. We had planned to stop and visit." Ralph had let the cat out of the bag, but the Friar didn't or pretended not to notice.

Friar James laughed. "Along the last, Friar Joseph would ramble on about whatever came to mind, changing from one thought to another."

"He sure did," Ralph agreed.

When the two arrived in Shrewsbury, Friar James gave him a tour of the building and the area where he lived. Ralph left a donation with the good Friar to help continue his work.

"Goodbye, Lord Ralph," called Friar Joseph as Ralph rode away. Ralph waved and smiled and kept going. Finding the inn in Shrewsbury where he and Roger had stayed wasn't hard.

~

Caus Castle sat on a long hill with a view of the surrounding valley around it—open lands, separated by stone fences with sheep grazing and drinking out of irrigation ditches, which funneled water into the fields, after being backed up by small earthen dams.

Offa's Dyke was only a little over two miles beyond the stone building, making the castle valuable to protecting the border with Wales. Kings had garrisoned the castle with troops, and the bailey below the town had grown enough to have a weekly market. Sir Ralph rode through the Wallop Gate into his castle with no one expecting him. In the years it had been his property, he'd never been there. To cause less confusion, he'd donned his surcoat with the Stafford coat of arms emblazoned on the front.

The Constable approached him after he'd entered the gate and greeted him, recognizing him as someone from the next shire over. "Who are you here to see?" he asked, looking at the surcoat.

"You, for one, and the Steward of the castle. I'm Sir Ralph de Stafford."

The Constable looked at Ralph with a puzzled look on his face. Then he bowed and said, "Will you wait here, my Lord. I'll get the Steward."

When the Steward walked quickly from the Great Room to greet Sir Ralph, he just kept apologizing. "Sir Ralph, I'm so sorry. We had no idea you were coming."

Sir Ralph looked at him and smiled. "Neither did I. My coming was a spur-of-the-moment decision. I couldn't let you know. Will you take me to my rooms?"

"Yes, sir. My name's David, Sir Ralph. I'll be your Chamberlain and Steward."

"Are we short of staff, David?"

"Yes, sir. The Pestilence took care of much of the bailey and village. There are still houses in the village, but they are mostly empty. The peasants who are left charge high wages, and I don't have enough money to pay them, even with the 'Ordinance of Labors' which was King Edward's attempt to reduce the wages back to before the plague's ravages hit our country." David wasn't complaining, he was stating a fact.

"This is much the same way all over England. There is much grumbling among the peasants. I wouldn't be surprised if they revolted," returned Sir Ralph.

"Do you think feudalism is on its way out?" asked David.

Sir Ralph grinned, knowing he was giving an opinion that was controversial to say the least. "The Pestilence has brought great changes to England. One of them is the increased value of peasant labor because of its shortage. One way to keep the wages of the peasant's low is to tax them greatly. I fear they will soon test the system, and change is in the offing." This was all Sir Ralph was prepared to say. He'd felt the undercurrent of change all over his country.

He stayed three more days. He and David had long talks in the Great Hall—about England, the King, and the plight of the peasant—about feudalism.

Sir Ralph returned to Windsor and continued to serve King Edward in any capacity that became necessary. He was joined by his second son, Hugh (by Margaret de Audley), who in the future became the 2nd Earl of Stafford. As Sir Ralph grew older, he became a patron of several priories in the area, and even founded a house of Austin Friars in Stafford. In 1372, a worn-out old man in the King's service, Ralph died at his castle at Tunbridge, Kent. He was buried at the Tunbridge Priory next to his second wife, Margaret, and her parents.

Because of internal struggles in England and in France, the war over the French kingship was mostly put on hold for the remainder of the 14th century.

꙰ Chapter 3 ꙰

Late 14th and Early 15th Century A.D

Continuing the Hundred Year's War Changes in
England Brought About by the Pestilence (Black
Death)

The nobles and elite—who had the best living
conditions in their castles and manor houses—managed
to survive in greater numbers during the Plague. But the
Black Death ravaged the lower classes in the English
countryside. Coming in waves for several years, it wiped
out between thirty to fifty percent of the English
population. Within England, established around a
manorial system controlled by Lords and Barons, the
trading, commercial, and financial systems collapsed.

The Black Death first changed the agricultural
system of England. Two reasons were responsible for
this. Since grain was grown in great quantities, the
population, which decreased dramatically, caused its
consumption to decline proportionally. This resulted in
the flooding of the market and a huge reduction in
prices. The peasants, already slammed with so many
deaths, started to rethink their way of maintaining their
livelihood. The Lords and Barons were shorthanded, and
they were doing the same thing.

Because there was a labor shortage caused by the plague, and sheep and cattle were easier to raise, with less people needed to maintain a flock or herd, why not switch to raising them exclusively?

The battle didn't rage long between the cultivators and the herdsmen. The herders won and, because fewer men were required to maintain large herds of sheep and cattle, whole villages were abandoned by the produce farmers. They moved elsewhere within a shire or out of the shire to gain wages.

In the struggle to survive, some of the larger herders encroached on the smaller herders. Quarrels erupted with the invaders, but in the end, this doomed the smaller herders to failure. There was no one to stand up for them when the ambitious and more wealthy herdsmen took over their land. Fights broke out, and people moved or were pushed out of areas where they had survived for centuries. Land, which could be inherited from one generation to another, was abandoned for other more promising prospects.

Now the Lords jumped into the fray. Realizing the peasants who were left under their rule, were making an increased amount of money from the cattle and sheep they herded, the Lord's forced the peasants to sell them their land. Fewer tenants meant more for the Lord's coffers and more to pay the King's taxes. The process was a never-ending, confusing circle.

During this time and always before, the land was subject to famine or flooding. When the crops and grass were poor, whether by excessive rain or lack of rain, this increased the misery of the peasant and the poor and also reduced the Lord's revenue.

It was obvious that the shortage of labor, due to The Pestilence, would do nothing to increase the plight of the lower classes. When they tried to ask for more money, the Ordinance of Laborers and secondly, two years later, the Statute of Laborers were established to return wages to the lower pre-plague levels.

～

The Black Prince, heir to the throne, died of dysentery, a byproduct of the war in France in 1376. His father, King Edward, died in 1377 (five years after Sir Ralph de Stafford), leaving the Prince's young son, Richard II, as the King of England. King Richard was only ten years old.

During the first years of his reign, his relatives (uncles) and the Parliament, consisting of the Lords, titled aristocracy, and the senior clergy, were part of the courtiers advising the young King during his minority.

King Edward left Richard with an unfinished war in France, including a huge military to support. This put the Kingdom under great financial strain. The lessening of the internal revenues which were due the Crown because of the confusing climate of agriculture and trade, and the collapse of international trade, all due to the Black Death, meant England was close to default on its national debt. Most of it pertained to the long war.

This resulted in the establishment of the first Poll Tax—four pence for every person over fourteen on movable goods and stock, which did not generate the amount of money the kingdom needed but hit the lower classes a hard blow.

Because of the failure of the first Poll Tax, a second one was enacted. When this tax also failed, the third Poll Tax followed in 1381. This one levied a tax of fourteen pence on everyone over fifteen years old. For the peasants, it was the final straw.

The taxes would have generated the money needed for England's bills, but rampant corruption by the higher nobles and those charged with enforcing the new tax laws, plus the continuing migration of the lower classes to find work, made collecting them impossible.

The whole of England was unsettled. On the cusp of the 14th century, the peasants, artisans, and some village officials revolted, mostly in London, southern and southeast England, plus a few other out-of-the-way places such as York, East Anglia, and Shrewsbury.

The southeast of England was hurt the worst and complained the most—the populations of London and the counties of Essex, Kent, and Suffolk. In June, the peasants, poor, and others of Essex were the first to revolt. From there, portions of the dissenters advanced into the other areas and, along the way, a man named Wat Tyler from Kent became the rebel leader.

"My Lady," the lady-in-waiting, Lady Joanna, addressed the Queen Mother, the Dowager Princess of Wales and the widow of the Black Prince.

The Queen Mother came from Canterbury Cathedral after visiting the shrine and praying at the tomb of Thomas Becket. Becket was the former Archbishop of Canterbury, who had been murdered, it was said, at the orders of an earlier King.

The Queen's entourage had come from her castle at Wickhambreaux that morning on the way to London.

"What is it, Joanna?" asked Queen Joan, proceeding at a brisk walk to her carriage with Lady Joanna catching up behind.

"There's news from London."

"What news?" the Queen Mother slowed her walk enough to turn and look at her favorite servant. "What is the news, Joanna? Speak up!"

"There's a riot in the countryside at Essex, and some men left Canterbury a few days ago to join them. They're heading toward London."

The Queen Mother stopped at mid pace and turned. "Who's rioting?" she demanded.

"I'm sorry, my Lady. Here's the Knight who brought the warning from King Richard. He can tell you better than I." Lady Joanna stepped back, letting the Knight advance.

"Come forward, Sir Knight. Let us hear the news." Queen Joan narrowed her eyes and looked at him. She recognized the man as being one of those who was often in her son's inner circle, but she couldn't remember his name. She stood for several minutes, plying him with questions, until she asked, "Where is my grandson, the King?"

"Your Highness, he's at the Tower of London with many of his courtiers." The young man answered.

"And what exactly are they advising?"

"I'm not privy to that conversation, my Lady."

Of course, he wasn't, thought Queen Joan, who paced two times before the carriage. She turned to her servant, "Joanna, we mustn't tarry a minute longer. Tell the coachman to head for London and not to waste anytime about getting there," she said, heading for the carriage. With the aid of the Knight's proffered hand to steady her, she entered and sat inside. "You will follow with the rest of my group," she ordered the Knight as she settled on the softly, padded bench.

"My Lady, we can't reach London before nightfall," said Lady Joanna, always the practical one, poking her head through the carriage door. "We must stay somewhere for the night."

"Yes, we must. Sir Knight, ride ahead to Hever Castle. Tell the Boleyns to expect the Queen Mother to stay the night. It's a little out of the way, but they'll welcome us there for tonight."

Lady Joanna gave the orders to the driver and followed the Queen into the carriage along with a chambermaid. These young women always accompanied the Queen on trips. They were the two of her servants she trusted completely.

When they were off the grounds of Canterbury Cathedral and riding through the Kent countryside, Lady Joanna asked, "Your Grace, are we in danger?"

"We'll find out when we get to London," was the Queen's short answer.

The white carriage was enclosed as they rushed through the countryside, with windows covered by canvas flaps. Glimpses of houses, water, and trees flashed in the openings made by the rush of air through the flaps, which cooled the three women riding inside.

A shower of rain caused Lady Joanna and the chambermaid to scramble and thoroughly close the flaps. After the short downpour, and with the steamy, afternoon heat, it seemed like they were riding in moisture. Hand fans appeared from concealed compartments in the carriage, moving the stuffy air.

∾

Hever Castle was a beautiful moated castle belonging to the Boleyn family. The stone walls had lots of glass windows and the gardens were extensive. Lady Joanna always enjoyed the Queen's visits to the grounds.

As they approached the castle, the sun went down and the heat of the day abated, leaving a chill in the air. They clattered across the drawbridge into the courtyard. Obviously, there was no riot here—yet.

Recognizing the royal carriage by the coat-of-arms on the door, footmen came running to help. The Knight and the Constable welcomed the ladies in the courtyard and led them to the Great Hall, where all was prepared for the evening repast.

The Master of the house rose immediately and, coming to the Queen, bowed deeply. "My Lady Queen, will you join us at our evening meal?"

The Lord of the house escorted the Queen Mother to the head table and seated her to his right, where a place had been laid out for her arrival. The Queen joined the family, as men and women scurried to serve the meal.

Lady Joanna and the chambermaid walked to the kitchen to find something to eat and be escorted to the bed chambers the Queen would use. The rooms were familiar, because she'd used them before on other visits.

Once in the Queen's rooms, Mary Tipton asked Lady Joanna, "Are we in danger?"

Mary Tipton of Staffordshire was Martin Tipton's daughter. This made her Roger of Tipton's niece.

Katherine de Stafford, Sir Ralph's granddaughter, hearing from her friend Lady Joanna, of her burden of work, had recommended Mary Tipton to the Queen Mother. Mary had been with her Majesty for three years, becoming a great friend of Lady Joanna, who was the Queen's favorite among the ladies-in-waiting.

"Doesn't seem to be any trouble here at the castle. I wonder what they're saying in the Great Hall."

"Are you scared?"

"I'm not happy about going into harm's way, but we may not get even close to the rioters." Lady Joanna shrugged her shoulders. "At this moment, we must prepare for the Queen to go to bed."

"I still think the Queen will ride through the midst of the whole disturbance. She's never been one to dodge trouble."

Joanna replied as she opened the Queen's traveling chest and arranged the Queen's bedclothes, "Except when she got married secretly to a much older man, Thomas Holland, without royal permission and while married to him, was betrothed and married another. When Thomas Holland came back from serving in the French War and wanted to claim his wife, she then acknowledged it to King Edward."

"What a predicament," said Mary.

"Predicament?" laughed Lady Joanna. "It was a trying time, but my Lady was the most beautiful woman in the land, known as the Fair Maid of Kent. It was only natural that men would think of her."

"Even the Black Prince?" Mary loved to hear this story.

"Especially the Black Prince. He harboured a love for her for years. Even though they were close in kin and had to get special permission from the Pope to get married after her husband, Thomas Holland, died."

Mary turned around to the open door. "Hush, I think I hear her coming."

"Yes, you do. Turn down the bed and please lay her slippers out on the carpet."

~

In the late afternoon on the following day, the Queen's carriage started through Blackheath on its way to cross the Tower Bridge. Once over the bridge, they'd be within a few yards of the gate to the Tower of London, where King Richard was waiting to handle the outcome of the riot. As they continued through this section of London, the noise outside the conveyance increased in volume, and the carriage came abruptly to a halt.

~

Obviously, the rioters could see this was a royal carriage. The question in their minds was who rode inside?

Outside, there was pandemonium as men grasped the harness of the carriage horses. A man yanked open the door and looked into the interior.

"Wat," he called, "the King's mother is in here."

The first head vanished and another stuck inside.

"Your Grace," said the second man, raising his hand in a salute. The head disappeared and a discussion took place outside in the street. The Queen Mother was held in a higher regard by the lower classes—like the older ones in any family. What course would they take against her?

The din had died down. This wasn't the King or any of his high-minded nobles.

Joanna scooted across to sit by the Queen, who remained in the carriage saying nothing. Was she resigned to whatever fate the men outside decided for her?

"Stay quiet until these men decide on a course of action. Then, as a last resort, we will protest loudly and make a run for it. We aren't far from the bridge," she commanded.

The discussion outside involved many voices, but the main gist of the conversation seemed positive. "My Lady … good, always … can't hurt … send escort … safety … where … Tower."

Joanna and Mary looked at each other. Were they actually going to let the carriage roll onto the Tower Bridge and cross to safety with an escort?

The second head returned. "Your Grace, I have men who will escort you in safety to the Tower Bridge." That was the end of the conversation. When the head disappeared, the carriage started to move — slowly at first and then faster as they neared the bridge.

"Clear the way," demanding voices cried, as they moved forward. "Stand back!"

As the carriage clattered onto the bridge, Joanna lifted the flap to see if they were alone. The men were standing behind the carriage at the bridge entrance, blowing kisses to the Queen as they went across. They were free from the mob.

For a brief moment, Joanna looked west toward Westminster. From upriver, a huge cloud of smoke billowed into the sky.

"Look, my Lady, is that from the Savoy Palace of John of Gaunt?"

The Queen leaned forward from her seat. The home, on the lavish Strand which had paved streets and fronted the River Thames, was the most opulent in the English kingdom.

"The brigands! Outlaws!" she exclaimed, slamming her fist into her palm. She was appalled at the scene she saw in the distance. She did not know the rebels were killing anyone associated with the King's government. They had spared her life.

John of Gaunt, the brother-in-law of Queen Joan, and son of the late King, was hated by the rioters because they thought he was responsible for the Poll Taxes, and there was widespread suspicion that he wanted to be King. His house was one of the first to be raided, torn to shreds, and torched. Prince John was not there. He was on the border of Scotland, preparing to invade the highlands.

The coach proceeded on across the bridge at breakneck speed. The Constable inside the Tower saw it coming and gave the order to open the gate. The resident ravens flew squawking from the gate into the air, and then settled back down on the top iron bars. The Queen's coach was safely inside.

∽

As the coach rolled onto the cobblestones, King Richard approached on his horse. He did not get down to welcome his mother as usual, but rode up to the carriage with several men behind him. "Mother, go into the castle where you'll be safe," he suggested. He never commanded her, for it was well-known that she had a mind of her own.

The Constable and his men helped the Queen Mother out of the carriage. "Where are you going, Richard?" she asked. Richard was just fourteen years old.

"We ride out to meet the rioters and listen to their list of complaints," said the young King.

The Queen opened her mouth to protest as any mother would but closed it saying nothing. She did as her son suggested, and as she strode forward, she heard the clatter of horse's hooves as her son and his guards passed through the gate to his meeting.

In the comfort of her suite of rooms, she sat down in a gilded chair and breathed a sigh of relief.

"My Lady, would you like some refreshment?" asked Joanna, concerned that her Lady might faint as she sometimes did under pressure.

"No. I'll stretch out on the bed and rest," said the Queen, feeling slightly ill. She got up to sit on the side of her feather bed, while Joanna took off her shoes, and helped her into position, reclining on her side. She closed her eyes, meaning she did not wish more conversation.

Seeing the King and his guard ride from the Tower to meet the rebels at Mile End, which was in the opposite direction, was an open invitation to the four hundred men who waited on the other side of the Tower Bridge, especially since the Tower guards, left the drawbridge down, in case the King needed to make a quick return. This tempted the men to do something desperate. They stood around, mulling the possibility of rushing the guards.

The impressive Tower of London, with King William the Conqueror's White Tower protruding into the sky, looked impossible to occupy. Built to sustain any assault, the edifice was sure to contain one of the two men they blamed for their plight.

The first man was the despised Lord High Treasurer, Sir Robert de Hales. The second was the hated Archbishop of Canterbury, Simon Sudbury, also known as the Lord High Chancellor. Sudbury's attempt to escape downriver on a boat had failed, and he'd retreated to the Tower. Getting at Sudbury was too tempting to resist. They knew he was inside.

Being whipped up into a frenzy, they dashed across the Tower Bridge, over the open drawbridge—scattering the ravens once more by their loud cries—and confronted the garrison of soldiers, protecting those within. The guards put up no fight whatsoever. In fact, the rioters shook hands with them. Then the interlopers dispersed and headed into the interior of the castle, looking for traitors. They found Sir Robert de Hales and quickly dispatched him. With loud shouts of triumph, they went in search of the Archbishop.

∼

Queen Joan, hearing the hue and cry from without the walls of the castle, as the invading men separated into groups, and the cries of victory as Hales died, rushed out of her bed chamber followed by Lady Joanna and Mary. She headed for the chapel and entered a side door, where she found the Archbishop praying at the altar.

Before she could join him, a group of men burst noisily through the main door, slamming it back on its hinges, and rushed toward the kneeling man, dragging him from the room.

Seeing the Queen and her attendants standing in the chapel, some of the men approached. These weren't as kind as those she'd left at the entrance of the Tower Bridge. They demanded kisses from the 'Fair Maid of Kent,' whereupon the Queen fainted.

Lady Joanna and Mary, both frightened at what might next transpire, rushed to the Queen's side, kneeling alongside her.

At that moment, the men were distracted by one of their companions, rushing through the entrance door to the chapel, as he beckoned, his face red with excitement, "Come quick! Hurry! They're going to behead the Archbishop," he announced.

The group hurried from the room. The beheading of this hated man was something they wanted to see.

As soon as the rioters left the chapel, Joanna gave instructions to Mary.

"Make haste. Go find someone to help us carry the Queen to her chambers," said a disturbed Joanna, tears running down her face in relief. "And bring some water to wipe her face. Run quickly."

Mary headed toward King Richard's bed chamber where she stopped in shock, as some of the rioters frolicked on the King's bed.

One of His Majesty's attendants came down the hall. "What's going on Mary?" he whispered to her, wandering what all the boisterous behavior was all about.

"Look. They're in the bed chamber," she pointed.

The attendant looked and quickly drew Mary out of the line of the rebel's sight. "Where is the Queen Mother?" he asked.

"Oh, she needs your assistance. Come." As they hurried to the chapel, Mary explained the scene at the altar. "Our Lady fainted. We need to take her back to her chambers."

The attendant grabbed another servant as they passed through the Great Room, and between them and the two ladies, they returned Queen Joan to her bed.

~

The beheading of the Archbishop of Canterbury on Tower Hill was a gruesome sight. When it was done, the rebel's rage was assuaged somewhat. Fearing the King might return at any minute with his guards, they left the Tower and crossed the Tower Bridge back to their mates-in-arms.

At Mile End, King Richard was busy promising the rebels most of their demands, including the abolition of serfdom. He agreed to meet them again at Smithfield on the morrow. After returning to the Tower and seeing the results of the rioter's rampage, he may have determined something different on the next day's meeting.

After arriving at Smithfield, some pushing and shoving broke out amongst the two factions, and in the end, Wat Tyler was killed. The King rode forward shouting, *"You shall have no captain but me!"* He did not honor the promises made to the rebels.

Raising an army, King Richard put down the rebellions around the country, especially those where many royal officials had been killed and meted out punishment to the perpetrators.

Queen Joan died four years after the rebellion in 1385.

In his later years, King Richard wished to marry a French woman. He enlisted the services of Geoffrey Chaucer, a diplomat for King Edward III, who was experienced in the art of negotiations. Chaucer is best known as the 'Father of English Poetry.'

Anne of Bohemia became the bride of King Richard in 1382. She would be called 'Good Queen Anne,' by the English people. Truly loved by the King, she died in one of the waves of the Plague in 1394. After her death, Richard went a little berserk, wiping out those he considered to be conspiring against the crown and generally causing discontent among the powerful in the realm. Who would stir the King's ire next?

Prince John of Gaunt—son of King Edward III, brother by marriage to Queen Joan, and King Richard's uncle and advisor—died in February 1399. This was the same year that King Richard banished John's son, Henry of Bolingbroke, from the country. Henry fled to France and Richard confiscated his inheritance, distributing the vast holdings to his friends.

Banishing Henry and taking his property was the beginning of the end for King Richard. This happened quickly, all within the same year.

∼

Mary Tipton had remained with Lady Joanna when she established her own household as her chambermaid. "My Lady, is it true that John of Gaunt's son, Henry, is back in England?"

"Yes. I understand he returned many days ago, landing at Ravenspur on the Humber Estuary with a small army. He went straight to his Pontefract Castle to secure it and add to his numbers those who would fight. He may be in London by now."

"What do you think will happen," asked Mary, always concerned for her Lady, the Tipton family, and their friends.

"Nothing good will come for King Richard, since he's out of the country in Ireland with much of his army. Everyone says that's the reason for Henry of Bolingbroke being here. He knows the King is away, so he's come to take the throne from him. He has royal blood like Richard."

"What do you think?"

"Henry has a lot of backing from the English barons and he's mobilizing an army. I wouldn't be surprised if he didn't declare himself to be King. He has just as much right as King Richard, except not in as direct of a line."

"The King has no heirs." Mary made the statement.

"No. It's always awkward when that happens. I suppose that's something Henry is thinking about. Mary, will you get my cloak from the wardrobe? I don't want to go outside in the cold without it."

Mary left the room. She came running back without the cloak. "My Lady, there is a rumour that King Richard was arrested several days ago at Flint Castle upon his return from Ireland. He is being returned to London where he will appear before Henry."

"My cloak?"

Mary laughed. "I'm on my way."

∾

Lady Joanna came back from visiting her neighbor with more news.

"It's no secret now," she said as Mary helped her off with her cloak. "Henry did arrive at Ravenspur and go to Pontefract Castle. From there he marched south through Leicester and confronted King Richard's Regent and uncle—Prince Edmund, the Duke of York—who decided he didn't want to fight. Henry went on to Bristol Castle, to await the King's arrival from Ireland.

"Richard did come south from Ireland, but he was suspicious of a plot, so he turned and headed north to Flint Castle, with a small contingent of his army. Last August, King Richard was arrested at the castle, and Henry brought him to London.

"Henry says that Richard abdicated his crown and the next day September 30, Henry of Bolingbroke was crowned King of England. Richard's been confined to the Tower of London until the new King decides what to do with him."

"So, the servant's talk was true."

"Somewhat true," said Lady Joanna nodding.

"I feel sorry for King Richard—such a tragic figure. What do you think will happen to him?"

"I'm sure we'll find out in a few days. Will you check on Harry for me? Tell him I'll be in shortly."

"Yes, Lady Joanna. Right away." Mary left the room to check on Joanna's youngest son.

∼

Not long afterward, the former King was taken to Pontefract Castle in York where he could not oppose Henry's reign, and it was there, he died. Some said he starved himself to death, while others said he was murdered. Tales circulated for years about his death, with many swearing he was still alive, and these stories haunted Henry's reign.

Rumours flew in all directions, along with small rebellions in the land. Henry IV busied himself with putting them down—all except one stubborn man who declared himself the Prince of Wales—Owen Glendower. Owen aligned himself with Henry Percy, the Earl of Northumberland and his son, Henry called Hotspur. The rebellion ended when Hotspur was killed by Henry's forces around Shrewsbury in 1403.

Henry's success was mainly due to the military prowess of his oldest son, who soon presided over much of the King's business. Henry IV was very sick. He died in 1413, and his son was crowned Henry V.

Henry V was a brilliant military general. He, like others before him, declared himself King of France and didn't delay in sailing to the continent to claim his throne. His most spectacular success was at the Battle of Agincourt.

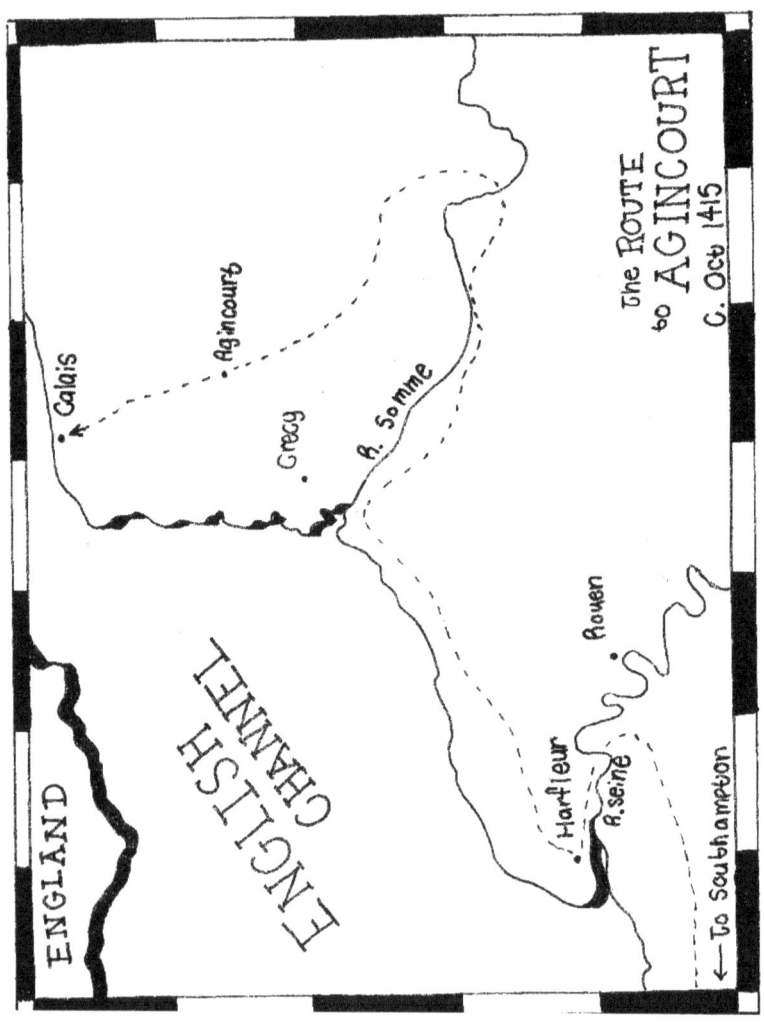

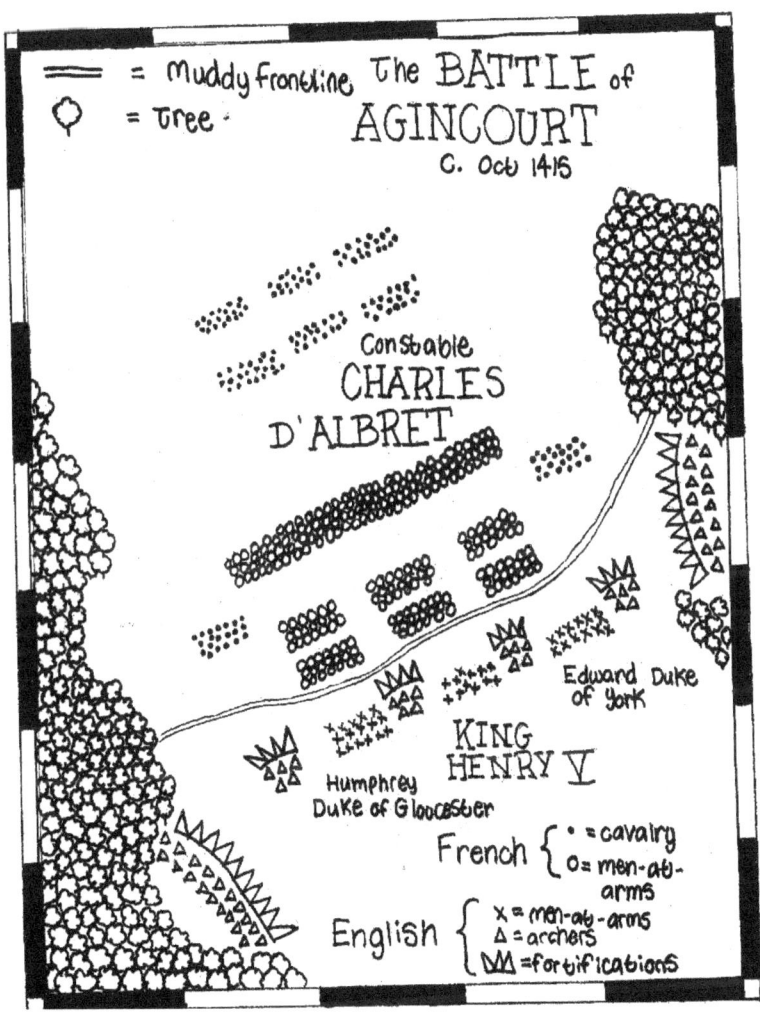

❦ **Chapter 4** ❦

15th Century A.D

Continuing the Hundred Year's War King Henry V, Battle of Agincourt, The Tiptons

The year was 1428, and a middle-aged Edmund Tipton sat in his home on Tipton Green, talking to his cousin, William Tipton, who had come from Portishead and Bristol on the Severn Estuary.

After greetings and a catchup on the family which lived in this area, the conversation had turned to the main focal point weighing on young William's mind and heart—his impending trip to France to fight for the King. Who better to ask, than someone who had served with the King's army in the battle at Agincourt?

"You were there at Agincourt, so I was told, and headed to France with Prince Humphrey, the Duke of Gloucester?" William, a young eighteen, asked of Edmund. This famous battle was won by the present King Henry V.

"Yes. Thirteen years have passed since we camped at Southampton, while gathering an army, until we set sail for France," returned Edmund.

"I'd like to hear the whole story, if you don't mind. Maybe it will give me an idea of what fighting in France will be like." It was early spring, and

William had taken a detour to Tipton to see Edmund on orders of his father, Harold Tipton of Bristol.

There was nothing more Edmund liked to do than tell the story of the Battle of Agincourt, unless it was bouncing his two-year-old grandson, Hugh, on his knee. Edmund was the last elder Tipton left in Tybba's town — the grandson of Martin. His own son had died of the pestilence on its last ravage through England, leaving his wife, and four children for the grandfather to raise.

Watching his son die, in a few short days of the pestilence's black buboes, which rose on his body and knowing he wouldn't survive, had been the worst time of this father's whole life. The wound was recent and hadn't healed as yet.

"You understand I had a wife and two young children when I went to France. Leaving them was hard, heart-wrenching, especially since my wife wasn't well. But you don't refuse to go as you are finding out. At least, you don't have a family to deal with," said Edmund, smiling at William.

"Maybe not, but there may be a young lady at home who's crying that I'm gone."

"I hope she's there when you get back. The way the war's going now, you may be gone some time, and the King won't care if you have a woman friend or not. He's just there to be crowned King of France no matter the cost in men or money — such an obsession." Edmund paused and shook his head at the words he'd just uttered.

William looked at him and asked, "Why does the King need land in France? We haven't recovered from the pestilence. We both know people who died, leaving many farms abandoned.

"Yes," responded Edmund. "There's not enough people left to till and plant."

"Don't you think we need to use our strength on growing food for our fellow citizens to eat?"

"I agree, or if we're to use men and spend money, shouldn't it be available to shore up England, build or improve roads, bridges, and develop other projects which are sorely needed."

"This is exactly the same long discussion my Father and I were having before I left Portishead."

"So true. The money is being used on perpetual wars or taken by the nobles for their own pleasures—so much corruption and greed. The King can't run this country, if he isn't there." Edmund shook his head. "This Realm has taxes on everything."

"Father pays tax to come into a port and one to leave. And then, the export and import duties on goods are high." William chuckled and continued, "Father says they'll have taxes for crawling out of bed in the morning—*a good morning tax*, if you will."

William and Edmund shared a hearty laugh.

"I agree with you. Good morning tax, indeed. How will the King's men collect that one?" Edmund laughed again at the preposterous idea. "King Henry did attempt to become the ruler of France without going into battle, but after negotiations with the French broke down, he went to Parliament to get their approval on going to war."

"Why does the King think he has claim to Aquitaine and Normandy?" William asked.

"Shall we say, it's all in the royal family and much too complicated to explain. Our King felt he had a direct claim to the throne through Isabella, King Richard II's mother, and he wanted to pursue that possibly. Besides this assertion, the wine and other trade which flows freely between our claimed French provinces and England is worth fighting for—at least the King thinks so. Money, money. The world revolves around money. The exchange of goods is making many rich men even richer, which is always the case," observed Edmund.

Edmund's comments smarted somewhat. "My father is part of the wine-for-wool trade. The land in Shropshire and Wales is known for fine wool, and he often sends a cargo of wool, cloth, and other supplies to France—the wool to be processed and returned as finished goods. The rest to be sold at French marketplaces. He's outfitted our ships to carry passengers from up the River Severn to English coastal cities and others back—some even go to France, and if he feels like chancing a run-in with pirates as far as the Mediterranean."

"When I last visited, years ago, he was continuing the Tipton business in shipping boxes."

"Yes. That's become a serious market for him. His watertight boxes for packing goods, and barrels for shipping liquids, olive oil, wine, and other things by sea, are sold and sent as fast as he can make them, to every trading market of the English and French. Before I left, he said he's thinking of buying a ship."

"Business is very good." Edmund agreed and asked, "Where is Harold making boxes?"

"Father's maintaining the operation in Bristol and Gloucester. He's kept the Tipton idea of spreading out the manufacturing process, so that more people can be involved. He's still a member of the trading guilds in both towns."

"Your father isn't like most of the English merchants. At least, he's into sharing his wealth."

William nodded. "What about the war in France?" he asked. They'd strayed from the subject he'd previously asked about.

"Ah, yes. The continuing war." Edmund sat for a minute in silence. "Where shall I start? Let's see, I mentioned we waited at the port of Southampton for the army to gather. Once we were all grouped there, over a thousand ships and other vessels came to transport the fighting men and their officers to the coast of Normandy. That was a sight to see."

Edmund paused, remembering His Majesty's vessels coming into the estuary in waves. "The docks were full of men, rushing to quickly load the ships with boxes of supplies, armour, horses, and men. With sails unfurled, we headed for open sea. Most of the fighting forces had never been on a large boat."

"I've heard of seasickness," mentioned William, making a grimace with his mouth.

"Some got sick and spent the whole voyage with their heads hung over the rails. Not me. I made the trip just fine. In August 1415, we left the ships, put on our armour, and started our tramp inland. King Henry had his brothers, Prince Thomas and Prince Humphrey, to help him lead 11,000 men with 20,000 horses into battle.

"When I looked back, the hands on the wharf were off-loading our supplies onto pack horses, carts, and waggons. Coming up the rear of the army, these would haul food and extra fighting equipment. Did you know that we had a supply, so I was told, of 150,000 extra arrows to shoot at the enemy?"

William shook his head. "I can imagine every fletcher in the London area supplied arrows."

Edmund continued, nodding, "At least that. I think the whole of the south must have been involved. We continued marching, but only a few miles inland, where we laid siege to the village of Harfleur. This was just above the River Seine. In September, with the chilly air of autumn pointing to winter, the siege finally ended. The conflict wasn't going as planned. The siege had taken too long."

"Did Henry intend on coming back to England for the winter?"

"No, he didn't. I heard he *thought* about coming home, but decided to march north to English-held lands — Calais, where King Edward III, had gone after the Battle of Crecy. He took about 9,000 of his army and left a contingent to guard his new village. Since the French didn't respond to Henry's challenge for combat at Harfleur, the war dragged on and on."

Edmund continued. "What Henry didn't know is this. The French had raised a small army while Harfleur was being besieged. But there weren't enough men, and those they had weren't trained or ready to fight the English during the siege."

"So, most of you marched north?"

"Yes, and the enemy followed us, gaining in numbers and hurrying to block the English march.

They needed to keep us from Calais, where we could replenish our supplies and rest the army."

"Why didn't the French go ahead and attack?"

"That's a good question. King Henry's thinking followed this line. Since the French didn't have enough men, the officers wanted to see if the Lords of the territory they were walking through, and their Knights, would join the rest of the marching army."

"Seems to me, the different bands of men would have made an army of different factions and not a smooth fighting whole."

"You *are* exactly right, and this may have been one reason that the French lost the battle. Of course, everyone said the French King was mad."

"Was he crazy?"

"I think he did have some mental illness, but who knows to what extent."

"I heard he wasn't on site and didn't command his army like Henry?"

"No, he wasn't. The French Lords are more disloyal to their King than our nobles seem to be. But maybe that depends on the ruler. We've had a few Lords who rebelled against their English Sovereigns.

"In October, at Agincourt, we faced them on open ground, but they still didn't want to fight. Instead, the next day, they sent negotiators to stall a confrontation. Our King knew he needed to attack. He couldn't wait any longer, because we were running out of food and we had trudged 260 miles in a little over two weeks. We were exhausted and suffering with dysentery in large numbers. Delaying the battle was not a choice."

"Who helped the King besides his brothers?"

"Edward, Duke of York, was one. I don't remember the others."

"When you got to Agincourt, what did you see?" asked William.

"We waited, huddled together in the rain the night before the fight. The ploughed field between the two armies had become a muddy, water-logged morass. I was a longbowman as you are. We were given the flanks of the battle line as usual with dense forest on each side of us. In the middle were the heavily clad men-at-arms on horses. We spent some time driving stakes in the ground to prevent the French cavalry from approaching us. Our side had 6,000 archers, 2,000 heavy infantry, and 1,000 heavy cavalry. The French, as far as our spies had informed us, had 9,000 heavy infantry, 3,000 heavy cavalry, 1,500 archers, and 500 crossbowmen—a total of 14,000 men."

"The French had you outnumbered."

"Very much so."

"What happened when the battle started?" asked William.

"It was slow to start, so King Henry advanced our forces to within an arrow's range and we dug in again, placing more stakes in the ground to hinder the French horses. The French didn't realize or understand the force of our longbowmen. When our army was ready, you could cut the tension with a sword."

"Were you nervous and worried before the battle?"

"No way to get around it. We did maintain a quiet night on the King's orders and said prayers for our souls and safety, while the French reveled and hurled insults across the field."

"Did you sleep at all?"

"Not much. Most of us dozed until morning. Some of the men had nightmares and were calling out in their troubled sleep.

"After the sun had risen and started to warm the earth, the King gave the order to shoot our arrows. 6,000 arrows flew through the air at the French cavalry and infantry. From our stance, the arrows could wound at 250 yards. The battle was on. The first wave of the French cavalry charged across the muddy field, slinging mud into the faces of horse and man riding behind the line. Horses slipped and slid through the waterlogged meadow. During the first minute of their charge, 50,000 arrows flew through the air—the sun was darkened as if a cloud went over the battlefield."

"Could you shoot that many arrows?"

"Some of us could shoot twelve arrows a minute."

"What happened next?" William was getting into the narrative.

Edmund took a deep breath and continued, remembering scenes he'd probably put from his mind. "The closer the French came on the horses, the more deadly our arrows were, until they penetrated through the armour and mortally wounded the riders. Some found their horses shot from under them. The French cavalry turned and beat as hasty a retreat as possible, running over another wave of French infantry which was on foot, slogging through the mire, and coming toward them and us.

"We slowed the shooting of our arrows and started taking careful aim at the French infantry. With armour not as strong as the Knights, it was pierced easily by our arrows. Soon the battlefield was full of men and horses, dead and dying. This clogged up the field. We stood our ground, not rushing into the muddy area, because our arrows were winning the war—a rain of death," Edmund said, the cries of the wounded and dying still ringing in his ears. His tone was more reserved as he finished his story.

"I wonder if I can kill a man?"

"You won't have any choice, because you'll have to. It's kill or be killed. The French kept charging our lines and our heavy infantry on horseback went to meet them. Riding to the outside of the battle, they surrounded and killed those on the ground. Then they penetrated into the midst of the melee. The Frenchmen in the saddle were so close together, they couldn't heave their swords for wounding each other. I saw King Henry fighting hand-to-hand, raising his sword and slashing at those who managed to come toward him. At one point, he took a blow to the head which would have killed him, except for the helmet he wore. Later, I learned he was protecting his brother— Humphrey, Duke of Gloucester, who'd been wounded—until the Duke could be removed from the area.

"When we ran out of arrows, we picked up swords, battle axes, anything we found on the field that we could use to fight the enemy, and jumped into the fray. Because they had on heavy armour and we were lightly clad with thick leather pads, we could move easier and faster in the muddy field. Although the fight seemed like an eternity, we were only engaged for three hours. There was no third French wave.

"Standing back and surveying the muddy field, there were piles of dead. The French left the battlefield in disarray. The battle was over with only mop-up operations to finish. We carried the Duke and the other wounded to Calais."

"Then you came home?"

"Yes, we sailed for England. When I got home, I knelt down and kissed the ground." Edmund stopped—his eyes filled with tears and his voice was full of emotion. "I wasn't the only one," he finished, putting a finger up to his cheek to remove a tear.

There was silence in the room for several minutes, as both men contemplated those uttered words—the ones of the battle and then coming home.

Finally, William said into the quiet, "You never went back for the siege of Rouen?"

"No, I didn't. When Henry returned to France, he conquered Normandy first, and then the King conducted a successful siege of Rouen in 1419. The following year, after signing the Treaty of Troyes, he attempted to be crowned King of France. The treaty gave him this right, and it added the possession of all the northlands of France.

"If I remember correctly, part of the language in the accord revolved around his future marriage to Catherine of Valois, daughter of the French King Charles VI. They lived together long enough for him to father a son.

"Although Henry was winning on the battlefield, he wasn't politically. Some of the French people loved him, but most did not. This, because of their deep hatred of the English. His Kingship didn't last long, because he died of dysentery two years later in August 1422. His infant son, Henry VI, became our King."

"How can an infant run a country?"

"It's happened more than once in the history of England—a young lad is crowned King. Most of the time, there are relatives who take over, but in this case, a group of men known as the Regency Government started running the country." Edmund, tired of talking about war and battles, paused to see if William had another question. Then he asked, "When will you be leaving, William?"

"Do you mind if I stay until the end of the week, then I'll head on to the Southampton port? Our forces will ship out in a couple of weeks. We're to reinforce those already in France, something about a big operation being planned. It's a big secret until we get there."

"There's something I'd like to give you." Edmund got up and walked to the fireplace. "One of your ancestors was a Knight. Did you know that?"

"I think I read about him in the Ancestry Book."

"Yes, you did—Sir Anthony de Tipton. When King Edward I knighted him, he gave him a brand-new sword to replace a relic Anthony cherished." Edmund pulled the sword from the front of the fireplace. "This is the second sword. I want you to have it. At least, you won't have to pick one off the battlefield like I did." Edmund pointed to another one which had been positioned above the one he had removed—a souvenir of the Battle of Agincourt.

"Thank you, I'll bring it back safely to you."

"No need. I want you to have it. I'll give the other one to Hugh, when he's old enough to handle it—and you are welcome to stay as long as you like. I'm enjoying having another man to talk to. May I suggest a walk to the market in Dudley. We should do something different. Get our minds off of battles and war," suggested Edmund, ready to forget again. As he stood, he looked over at William, knowing when he saw him again, he'd be a changed man. He refused to put an if in the thought.

Outside the house, William looked up at Castle Hill. "Do you ever feel overshadowed by the presence of the castle and its occupants?"

This was a loaded question. So, part of the walk included Edmund's comments on the inhabitants of the castle and the goings-on at Tipton Green.

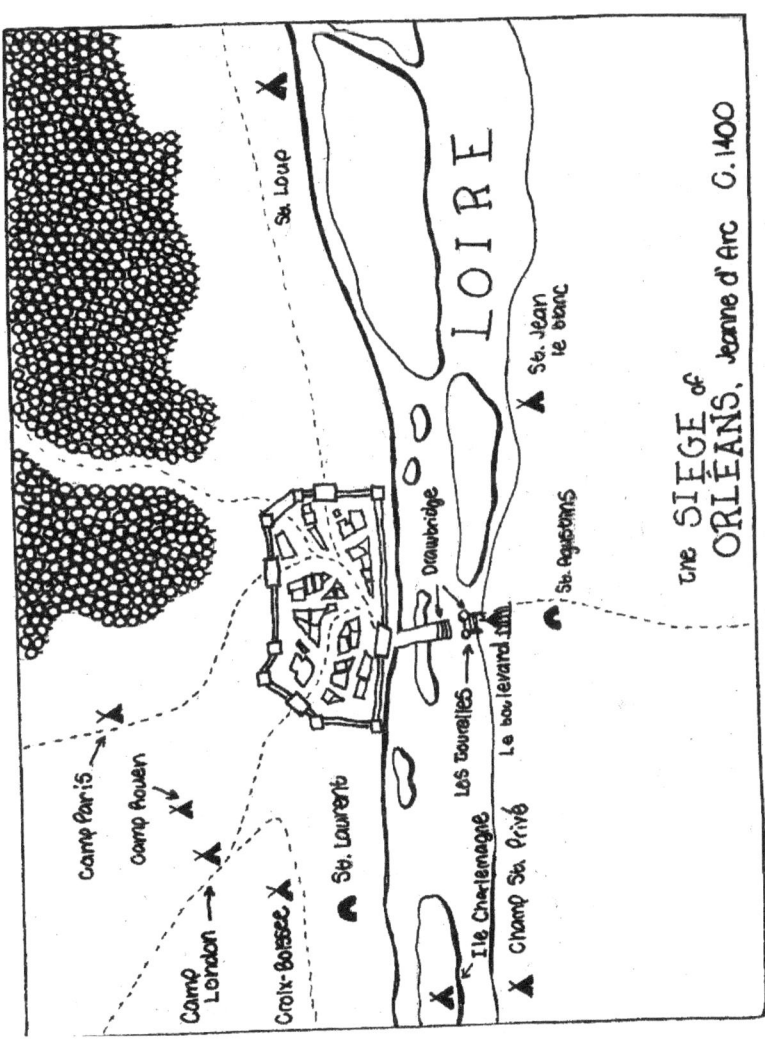

❦ Chapter 5 ❦

15th Century A.D

Continuing the Hundred Year's War Siege of Orléans, Jeanne d'Arc, The Tiptons

In the spring of 1428, John, Duke of Bedford, was made the English Regent, head of the Regency Government which was controlling the monarchy and the war in France. As the leader, Bedford made a failed attempt to place the newly crowned infant, Henry VI, on the throne of France.

The Duke was a large man, plump with short brown hair. His nose protruded oddly, and his forehead slanted backward, while his chin seemed to disappear beneath his mouth, which accented his prominent hawk-like nose.

Since the English had made inroads into the territory of France under the late King, the Duke called a war council to establish the plan for prosecuting the war in France.

One of the French Lords, Phillip, the Duke of Burgundy, supported the English in the execution of the war in France.

On the French side was Scotland, fighting against the English domination of their territory to the north of

England, and helping the French in return for their assistance against a common enemy.

The French City of Orléans was not on the original agenda, because the Duke of Orléans was in an English prison after being taken at Agincourt. Normally, one did not seize the property of someone in captivity.

But plans changed.

Bedford said the siege was *"taken in hand, God knoweth by what advice."*

Maybe the choice was by the Earl of Salisbury, Thomas Montacute, who had spent several successful months sieging cities and battling armies—generally mopping up the area as he swept through the area southwest of Paris. Then he turned northeast into and prepping the area around Orléans.

Or possibly, Phillip of Burgundy persuaded the Earl to take the city, which was located next to his territory in France. What kind of ideas could he have had about this area?

Orléans was the largest, northernmost city not under English control. Salisbury made the final decision to approach the city from the south. Orléans would be a prize catch, because it was still loyal to the *Dauphin of France*, Charles, who was the uncrowned King of France.

Reims was the official city to crown French Kings, and it was held by the English.

Salisbury's antagonist in the siege was the Frenchman John de Dunois, illegitimate son of Louis I, Duke de Orléans. Dunois watched as the English prepared to commence the siege of Orléans.

Realizing the English would be close to the southern entrance—a bridge into the city over the River Loire—

he gave an order to one of his commanders, "Since the English are coming from the south, build an earthwork at the southern end of the bridge at the Boulevard, and pack it with troops."

Then he turned to another, "Evacuate the southern part of the city and level all buildings and do the same across the river, along the southern bank. I don't want these locations to be a place for the English to utilized as protection to shoot into the city."

From along the Silk Road in China, hundreds of years ago, came a chemical compound called potassium nitrate or gunpowder. It had advanced through Asia, the European continent into England, and was known by King Edward III. First, used sparingly at the Battle of Crecy and the Battle of Agincourt, the developing cannons were pulled into position by the English to bombard the City of Orléans with the biggest one at St. Jean le Blanc.

The cannons of the French were positioned within the city of Orléans to return fire across the River Loire to the south.

William Tipton reported to William Glasdale, who was under Thomas Montacute, 4th Earl of Salisbury's command. A brilliant military strategist, Salisbury was the General commanding the siege. Glasdale was intrenched in eastern fortifications at St. Jean le Blanc, on the south side of the River Loire, where the biggest cannon rested. There were two more fortifications on the south side—one to the west and a large one in the center at the convent of St. Augustins in front of the French encampment at Le Boulevard.

A Junior Officer under Glasdale sent William to George Beaufert. Beaufert was a soldier sergeant over a group of archers under Glasdale's command. George, dressed in archer's armour, turned out to be an aimable and talkative man who needed a friend.

"William Tipton, where are you from.?"

"From Somersetshire, the city of Bristol. Have you been there?"

"No, can't say that I have. I'm from the other direction—to the east. Isn't Bristol in the southwest, close to the River Severn?" he asked.

"Yes. Just a short walk downward along the Avon Gorge to Portishead, and you are at the Severn. My family lives all along the River Severn as far as Shrewsbury. Where are you from?"

"I guess you could say I'm a transplant to East Anglia—on the opposite side of England." Sir George pointed to a rough cot where William could deposit his traveling case and armour. The roof over William's new quarters consisted of rough thatch, and there were no sides to the lodging.

"You aren't descended from the Beauforts of Somerset? They control property on the Severn Estuary where it opens to the sea."

"No. I'm not sure of my ancestry. The plague spread us everywhere to keep from starving. All I know is the name I was given. I resided at St. Benet's Abbey in East Anglia until I was apprenticed to a small bolt maker at Cambridge. He taught me to shoot both the crossbow and the longbow." George paused, watching as William spread his cloak on the rough cot and deposited his case.

William's armour of thick leather for torso, arms, and legs, he placed at the head of his cot, along with a padded gambeson which fit his body. This was worn beneath his leather protection so his body could breathe.

George picked up William's helmet. "What, no visor?" he asked.

"No. I prefer to see where I'm aiming."

"You *can* see much better," he nodded. "My helmet doesn't have one either. Of course, you and I are taking a chance of getting an arrow in the face." Looking at William's sword, he observed, "That's a fancy sword."

"It was given to one of my ancestors by King Edward I," responded William.

"Now that's a story I'd like to hear, but some other time. Come on, I'll show you the rest of the area and where food can be had. That is, if we get to eat. You need to put your armour on." George waited until William was armour-clad. He picked up his own helmet as the two went outside and headed toward the fortifications at St. Augustins. "From now on, your sword, longbow, and arrows are stuck to you like resin from a pine tree."

"George, I've never been in a battle before."

"I guessed as much. What do you want to know?"

"What is the object for us?"

"To stand firm, fight, and suffer for the King's cause, which is at present the taking of Orléans. The reason, so it can be added to the land the sovereign possesses. There will be sleepless nights and days of nothing but hunger, dirt, and lots of bloodshed. Just make sure none of it is yours." George gave a wry smile. "Does that help?"

"Yes," but William's response didn't seem like he was fine with George's answer.

George decided to elaborate. "You and I are entangled in this war not of our own choosing, but to please the King. Keep that in mind. Be strong. Don't waver. Don't pause before you shoot your arrow, once you have selected your target. Keep the goal in sight. You'll be all right. Experience comes quickly when the battle starts. I can guarantee it."

"You haven't been fired upon here at Orléans?"

"Cannonball fire, but nothing much else. We're waiting at present, digging in." He motioned to the dirt ramparts as they walked along the riverbank.

"And, if we lose?"

"Not likely, but if you do your best, there's nothing to be ashamed of, is there? You're in my section of archers, so stay close to me. You'll be — "

George didn't finish his comment. A cannon ball landed in the river, splashing water almost onto the path where they walked. "Run!" George shouted. The two men ran toward the cooking tent out of cannon range and went inside.

∽

The siege, which started on October 12th, escalated quickly after William arrived. Nine days later, the French assaulted the English position at the convent of St. Augustins, which was beyond the end of the bridge, and before the Boulevard, which the French occupied. They were repulsed.

Two days after that, the English took the French occupied Le Boulevard and, on October 24, the Earl of

Salisbury and his foot soldiers stormed the towers at Tourelles, which was the stoned entrance to the bridge. The French position was now pushed to an island in the middle of the River Loire.

"William, Salisbury has ordered Glasdale to fortify and occupy the towers—that means us," George said gathering his gear. "It's one of those pick-up-your-bed and walk kind of things. You don't know how many times I've done that in France."

"We'll be staying in the towers?"

"Yes, until the siege is over and we find a soft bed in the city," George winked at William. "Don't count on that, my friend."

~

Three days later, the Earl of Salisbury returned from inspecting the reinforcements around Orléans and climbed the steps to the top floor of the Tourelles. He stood looking out the upstairs window, talking to Glasdale. "We've encompassed the whole of Orléans, except the northeast. Our defenses are nonexistent there, but a thick forest exists, which will slow down anyone coming from that direction—hopefully until we get there. I've instructed those in charge on the perimeter to see that there are patrols morning, noon, and night."

A distant report from the direction of Orléans meant a cannonball was incoming from the city. It hit below the window on the lower stonework of the tower. "They're getting better at aiming their cannon," laughed Glasdale as the tower shook with the thud.

Salisbury turned from the window. "Have you put the extra reinforcements in place?"

"Yes, Sir." Glasdale gave a report of his buttressing. "And my men's quarters are at Le Boulevard as a last bulwark for the French to conquer before Les Tourelles. I don't see any way the French can overpower us."

Salisbury nodded in response and turned again to the window, looking toward the east. This was a mistake. Another report from the city, and this time the cannonball hit the windowsill where he stood, sending shards of stone flying in all directions. Salisbury threw his hands to his face and turned from the window. Then he fell to the floor, his face—what was left of it—covered in blood.

Glasdale rushed to his side, yelling loudly, "Beaufert, come here."

George and William rushed up the stairs to the horrible sight. One eye was gone, and the commander of the English force's face was cut to the point he wasn't recognizable. Gushing blood pooled around his head.

"Go get the barber surgeon," ordered Beaufert to William, who had blanched white at the sight.

Glad to be on the move, William ran down the stairs to summon the barber surgeon. They arrived back within minutes.

The barber knelt beside Salisbury, who was now mercifully unconscious. From a bag, he took out compresses to place on the wounded man's face. Motioning to George and William, they came forward to hold them in place.

The barber backed off to talk to Glasdale. "I can't do anything for him here."

Salisbury was lashed onto a stretcher. George and William helped others take him carefully down the stone stairs to the barber's tent, where he was placed on a more comfortable bed.

William and George waited outside. Neither had been given further orders.

"What can they do for him?" asked William.

"I'm not sure in a case like that," returned George.

The two were standing there discussing the situation when Glasdale showed up and asked, "Is he still alive?"

"We think so," answered George.

Glasdale went inside the tent and came out minutes later. "We'll transfer him from here to better facilities in Meung Sur Loire and let the monks tend him there. Go back to your posts," he ordered.

On November 3, the men at Tourelles received word. Lord Salisbury had died at Meung.

The successor to his command, William de la Pole, Earl of Suffolk, did nothing to force an end to the siege, until John Talbot and Thomas Scales arrived to urge him to build more siege works, and establish other forts in strategic places outside of Orléans.

Weeks went by. The English war supplies dwindled. Having sent word of this problem to Paris which too was held by the English, a supply train of three hundred or more carts left the city for Orléans. The load it carried, consisted of armament and dried salted fish for the meatless days of Lent, which was coming soon.

For once, the French with their Scots allies made a valiant attempt to stop the constant flow of supplies to their enemies. As the train of waggons made its way toward Orléans, going to the north of the city, they provided a perfect invitation for the army under Dunois to attack, since the English had no forts in the area.

∾

"George, have you heard?" an excited William asked. "The waggons, loaded with supplies coming from Paris, have been attacked."

"Yes, I heard. Glasdale said the person in charge is John Fastolf. I knew him at St. Benet's. Let's go see what happened."

John Fastolf stood in a circle of men, explaining the results of the battle. Turning, to answer a question, he noticed an acquaintance. "George, it's good to see you."

"And you too, sir. I hear you had a *minor* skirmish on your way here."

John laughed. "I wouldn't call it minor, unless you consider a French force of three or four thousand men against a few hundred a small one. Our group came through the fight very well."

"What happened?" George asked.

"The battle occurred near the town of Rouvray, on a flat plain where you could see for a mile. We saw them coming, circled the waggons and carts, and prepared for battle. Our longbowmen and crossbowmen laid waste to the Scottish forces, who evidently went against the French battle plan and attacked prematurely. This caused the French to hesitate, obey their orders, and not join in the fighting. When we saw them hesitate, we rushed the Scots, and they ran. We killed the Scottish leader, and we think we wounded Dunois. He was almost captured. As you can see, the herring got through, so our men will have fish to eat during Lent."

On February 12, 1429, when the French lost this battle and the fish went through to the English, Orléans was desperately feeling the pinch of the siege. Discouraged because he was wounded, John de Dunois seriously considered surrendering the city. This was not to be.

Miles away a young woman of sixteen had predicted the loss of the Battle of the Herrings, as it was sarcastically called. Jeanne d'Arc's prophecy, convinced those objecting to her previous comments, to believe her statements that God had sent her to save the French people. She was given a horse and was soon riding toward Orléans with reinforcements. Her arrival would change everything.

Chapter 6

15th Century A.D

Continuing the Hundred Year's War Siege of Orléans, Jeanne d'Arc

Jeanne d'Arc's life in France was one of being a farmer's daughter, at least until she started hearing voices in 1424. The voices told her she would save her beloved country by banishing its enemies, thus fulfilling an old prophecy of a virgin who was destined to save France. Jeanne, taking the voice literally, chose a vow of chastity and headed for Vaucouleurs, where it took nine months for her to convince the local magistrate, Robert de Baudricourt, to send her to Charles VII, heir-apparent as King of France.

When she predicted the defeat of the French at the Battle of the Herrings at Rouvray, before the messengers arrived with the news, Baudricourt relented, agreeing to send her for an audience at the future King's residence.

Jeanne shortened her hair and donned men's clothing, consisting of long boots, trousers, and ropes which could be tied to the tunic, giving her a measure of safety and modesty while traveling with an army of men. With an escort of several French Knights, she made the eleven-day journey to Chinon, where the French *Dauphin* resided.

Charles VII hid among the crowd when Jeanne arrived, but to his surprise she picked him out and addressed him thus, *"Most illustrious Lord Dauphin, I have come and am sent in the name of God to bring aid to yourself and to the kingdom."*

Hearing her earnest and persuading words, he soon became convinced of her sincerity, but ordered her examined by the ladies-of-the-court to verify that she was a young woman. Then he sent her to church leaders at Poitiers to prove to them that her visions were divine.

Both reports were positive. Against the advice of his counselors, Charles sent Jeanne to Tours to be outfitted with armour—all white—mail, banner, and horse. She left there in men's clothing, with her sword attached to her belt, to meet up with her army at Blois.

With her entrance and her position at the head of her army, the fight turned from a political to a religious war.

Finding the men at Blois without discipline, she immediately expelled the prostitutes and camp followers, sent the men to church for prayers, banned swearing, and demanded they not harass the local populace.

With her arrival, hearing and seeing her devotion to the Church, and to clearing France of the hated English, men from all over the region began arriving and volunteering to fight the war. This was an about-face, since the French people didn't want to fight because of the decline of morale in the forces, due to the multiple losses they'd suffered.

≈

Jeanne loved to send letters. She could not read or write so she dictated her words to someone who could.

One, she sent to the King of England, saying among other things ... *Return the keys of all the good cities which you have received to the Maid (Virgin). She is sent by God to reclaim the royal blood, and is fully prepared to make peace, if you will give her satisfaction, render justice and pay back all that you have taken.* She went on telling him, *she would make them flee the country, and the Maid will have them all killed.* Continuing ... *And believe that the King of Heaven has sent her so much power that you will not be able to harm her or her brave army.*

Another one was sent to ... *William de la Pole, Count of Suffolk, Sir John Talbot, and Thomas, Lord Scales, Lieutenants of the Duke of Bedford, who calls himself Regent of the King of France for the King of England, make a response, if you wish to make peace over the city of Orléans! If you do not do so, you will always recall the damages which will attend you.*

And also, to ... *Duke of Bedford, who call yourself Regent of France for the King of England and the Maiden asks and requests that you will not cause your own downfall. If you do not do right, you will be able to see before your very eyes that in her company the French will do the finest deed ever done in Christendom.*

She had covered all the bases with her words.

These letters were sent by couriers. The English response was to detain the messenger.

Afraid she would alert the English to her incoming army and the supplies for the people of the city, Jeanne decided to approach Orléans in stages with smaller contingents of soldiers. She rode toward Orléans and went into the city under cover of darkness by the Burgundy gate.

Lord de Dunois was not happy with Jeanne's presence, and at first thwarted or went against her advice, because she demanded he immediately attack the English. John de Dunois was not prepared nor was he willing to listen to her. After he headed to Blois, to collect the rest of her army, he arrived back in Orléans on May 4th and, without telling Jeanne, he went straightway to attack the northeast English fortifications at St. Loup.

The French were in the process of retreating when Jeanne, aroused from her sleep and hearing of the battle, went to check on the fight. Her appearance at the head of the French assault on her white horse with her banner held high, turned the men from their retreat, and they ended up winning the battle—finally a victory for the French.

The next day, resting to honor the Feast of Ascension, Jeanne composed her final letter. On May 5th, fresh off the victory at St. Loup, Jeanne sent her finest bowman with instructions to put it through the top window of Les Tourelles, one of the turreted gates across the bridge to Orléans, where William Glasdale, George, and his bowmen were guarding.

"William, what was that?" George asked as something went flying by him, thudding against the wall on the other side of the room. They were acting as lookouts on the top level of one of the Les Tourelles turrets. The same one where the Earl of Salisbury had received his fatal blow. Shards of concrete and a dirty, dark spot where he had fallen still marred the upstairs floor.

"It's an arrow with a note attached." William bent over picked up the arrow and walked to George, handing him the missile.

"I'd better take this to Glasdale. It's probably to the commanders."

George went down the steps and out of the building to Glasdale's quarters. He handed the letter to his commander.

"Another one from the French harlot," Glasdale exclaimed. He unrolled the parchment and read …

You men of England, who have no right to this kingdom of France, the King of Heaven orders and notifies you through me, Jeanne the Maiden, to leave our country, or I will produce a clash of arms to be eternally remembered. And this is the third and last time I have written to you. I shall not write anything further.

On May 6th, after convincing Dunois of her plan, Jeanne crossed the River Loire. She went over on a floating pontoon bridge with her army to take the southeastern stronghold of St. Jean le Blanc. It was empty, because Glasdale had received orders to repair forthwith to the convent of St. Augustins. Under cover of darkness, the large cannon and the men had left.

Jeanne and her men continued to advance, bypassing Augustins and routing the other smaller English forts on the southwest side of the river. At this point, they started to advance toward the last stronghold, the hardest one to take, the convent of St. Augustins. If they could control it, Le Boulevard and Les Tourelles would be next. The English would be put to rout and the siege of Orléans was over.

~

"George, come and look at this?" William asked, standing on the makeshift, wooden scaffolding and staring over the palisade toward St. Augustins.

It was twilight with just enough light to see, but not to see clearly. Behind the convent, the glow of a hundred camp fires lit the sky. Only two hours ago, the sound of battle was heard, but now there was silence — deathly silence.

The two men and those with them were the last defense before the French rushed to Les Tourelles. If the twin turrets were stormed and fell, the English siege would end in disaster.

The older man came to stand beside William. "Who is that?" George demanded.

Before the convent of St. Augustins was Le Boulevard, where the two men stood. And, in the distance, a ghostly figure on a white horse with a white banner had appeared.

The thump of boots on the wooden steps and rattle of heavy, metal armour signaled the arrival of William Glasdale. Noting the intense stares of the men, he asked, "What is so interesting, gentlemen?"

"Sir, come and look."

Glasdale ambled over and looked out the window at Jeanne d'Arc, dressed in her coat of mail with her banner held high over her head. "What has happened? Did St. Augustins fall to the French? That harlot has got a lot of nerve coming this close to the fort," he exclaimed angrily. Glasdale wasn't in a habit of standing and watching any opponent parade their horse in front of him, much less a woman. He backed away from the disturbing scene framed by the window.

William and George resumed their stares, each thinking, if Augustins had fallen, this dirt and wood fortification was next on the list, but not tonight— tomorrow perhaps or the next day.

"Men, is there a better way to prepare our fort for a battle?" Glasdale asked, realizing if there were any chinks in the fort's armour, the soldiers would have discussed them.

William and George both turned to look at him. George answered, "William and I've discussed your question. If they've got their cannon set to fire on us, the balls will go straight through these flimsy walls. Where we stand now will collapse and the archers, those who survive the fall, won't have an advantage of height or sight to shoot at the enemy. It's too late now to make adjustments for that, but in the turrets of Les Tourelles, we still have enough distance for our arrows to make a difference."

Glasdale looked over the scaffolding and realized his sargent was right. He would lose his greatest defense—his archers. "Then take half of the archers and go to the turrets. If a battle starts tomorrow," in his mind he thought it would, "fire any arrow you can get your hands on. And, I want you two and two others you designate, to specifically focus on the woman-in-white. She's your special target. With her gone, the English forces will win. This is our only hope to save Les Tourelles." Glasdale said these words with conviction.

"Sir, how is the siege going?" George asked. What he was hearing wasn't very positive.

Glasdale didn't answer the question. Why should he discourage these two men? He added, "If losing the turrets seems imminent, then de la Poole says we are to fall back and regroup to the west.

"Will you stay with the men here at Le Boulevard?" asked George.

"Yes. We will join you, should the French overrun the fort. Now hurry. Gather your men. There's still enough daylight to find your way."

After predicting the night before, that an arrow would enter her shoulder above her breast, Jeanne d'Arc arose at the first light of dawn for prayers. Soon the sound of her army, cooking the morning meal, and donning the rest of their armour for the day's battle rang loudly in her ears. It was time—the moment she'd been preparing for these many months.

There was a verse the men at her Church had made her memorize, knowing what she might face. She repeated it from the Book of Isaiah... *Voici, Dieu est ma délivrance, Je serai plein de confiance, et je ne craindrai rien; Car l`Éternel, l`Éternel est ma force et le sujet de mes louanges; C`est lui qui m`a sauvé.* (Behold, God is my salvation; I will trust, and will not be afraid; for the Lord God is my strength and my song, and he has become my salvation.)

Jeanne bowed her head, made the sign of the cross, and arose with head held high. She trusted those words. They were a promise kept many times in the last few days.

On May 7th, the French stormed Le Boulevard, routing Glasdale and his fighters. Jeanne, sitting on her horse at the front of the battle, and seeing Glasdale and his men, clad in their heavy armour, heading slowly for Les Tourelles, yelled at him, "Glasdale! Glasdale! You called me a harlot, but I have great pity on your soul and the souls of your men!"

George and William watched as Glasdale and his men retreated under the force of the French attack. Turning again to the turret's windows, they renewed shooting arrows at Jeanne.

"We hit her," yelled William. They were shooting so many longbow arrows at the woman-in-white, this was almost to be expected.

Thinking they had killed their nemesis, the men in the tower gave a loud cheer. Glasdale pumped his fist in the air.

～

The arrow hit Jeanne in the shoulder just above her breast. Taking both hands, she pulled it out and rode to the back lines, and into the newly captured Le Boulevard to clean her wound and dress it.

When Jeanne left the field, the French hesitated. Seeing their leader with an arrow in her shoulder caused the French army to waver. Could they win without her?

Noticing the hesitation, Glasdale turned his men.

William and George watched as Glasdale and his men dug in and stopped retreating. The English regrouped and fought again, pushing the French back along the route they'd just come.

Jeanne rested a few minutes, got back on her horse, and returned to view the battle. Observing the results of her leaving the forefront of the fight, she held her banner high and returned to the front, urging the men to fight on and win.

~

"Look, George."

George could not believe his eyes. Jeanne was not dead.

Jeanne never fought physically, but her presence gave her troops added inspiration to fight harder and not to give up. This they did, and the battle turned once more.

Glasdale headed for the stone turrets again.

"They're headed for the drawbridge," George exclaimed.

The scene unfolding in front of their eyes was a race for life. If they could cross the drawbridge, and pull it up behind them, they would be safe. Progress was slow, because their armour was heavy.

"Look! George. Upriver!" William pointed at something in the water.

In horror, George noted a barge was lit ablaze. It floated between the river's islands toward the wooden drawbridge, which it hit and lodged underneath. Soon the bridge's old, dry underpinnings were aflame. Glasdale and his men, backs to the bridge, and fighting for their lives, did not realize this.

The shock of what was happening continued, when the English turned to cross the flaming structure. The drawbridge collapsed under them. Glasdale and many of his men fell into the water. Because of the heavy armour, they drowned.

The men in the turrets continued to shoot arrows into the melee below, trying to give the English who were trapped on land some relief. When they were out of arrows, all they could do was watch.

Since the drawbridge was gone, the French headed for boats upriver. This was the only way they could get at the archers who wounded their leader. Walking to the boats would take some time in their heavy armour and dusk was drawing near.

In the approaching darkness, George gathered the archers together. "Our orders are to meet up with de la Pole to the west. The only way we can get off this island is to swim. Take off your helmet and any metal armour. Your leather protection will not be heavy enough to send you to the bottom of the river. So, I'm ordering those who can swim to do so. If you can't swim, grab something which floats and ease into the water. This is your only hope."

With those words, George turned to William, "I hope you can swim, my friend."

"Yes, sir. I learned in the River Avon."

"Then, let us be first. Remember men," he called. "No splashing, no noise."

As the sun set, the smell of smoldering wood wafted through the air, and the men of England silently abandoned the two turrets of Les Tourelles. Slipping into the dark waters of the river, William Tipton wondered what was in store for England.

When both Edmund and George had told him he would learn quickly when thrown into the thick of battle, they were right.

The English had lost the fight, but their efforts for the King were valiant and brave. There was nothing they could have done better and nothing to be ashamed about. He swam down-river, satisfied there would soon be another day in the not too distant future to prove he could fight again.

～

The south bank of the River Loire was gone. The siege, for the English, was over. When the English lost the blockade of Orléans, this became the turning point of the Hundred Year's War. The French had won a major victory, and the story of the rout was relayed over the land.

Jeanne d'Arc went on with her army to clear the intruders out of most of the territory claimed by the English. Perhaps her greatest military victory was at Patay, in June 1429, where the French army slaughtered the force under the English commander Lord Talbot. The English lost several thousand men. The French less than a hundred.

In July, with a path cleared to Reims, deep in English territory, the Dauphin was finally crowned King Charles VII with Jeanne in attendance. She had accomplished her main goal and kept her promise to him.

In September, she was again wounded by a crossbow bolt while trying to free Paris. This time to the thigh. Carried from the field of battle with the intention of returning, the French King ordered the assault ended. The English-Burgundian position in this great city was well fortified. The King suggested there would be another day and there were other easier targets.

In May 1430, Jeanne was captured by the Burgundians at the fight for Compiegne. The French Burgundians were allies of the English, fighting for money or other favors. Several months later, she was ransomed by the English for ten thousand francs.

Chapter 7

15th Century A.D

Continuing the Hundred Year's War Jeanne d'Arc and The Stake Back in England

George was visiting his young friend in the surgeon-barber's quarters at Rouen, in Normandy, France. This was where many of the seriously wounded were recovering from the last battle at Melun.

After taking his helmet off to help a fallen soldier, William had taken an arrow in the head. The arrow had struck an almost glancing blow, hitting the skull bone and slicing a pathway through the thin skin on top of his head. The gash looked terrible, and at times, still oozed a trace of blood.

The surgeon-barber had carefully bathed and stitched up the gaping wound and ordered him to bed. "You may get an infection. That would be bad with an open wound into the brain, even if it is very tiny," he admonished, rubbing ointment on the injury. "Try not to move. And lay quietly," were his final instructions.

George sat at William's bedside. He leaned forward with hands clasped and elbows on his knees, and said quietly, "William, I have news. Jeanne d'Arc is in Rouen to be tried for heresy."

"Now that's news," William exclaimed, getting up on his elbow, disobeying the doctor's orders. "What happened?"

"Lie back down, William, and I'll tell you."

William did as told, and the older man leaned toward William to speak confidentially.

"The Duke of Burgundy captured her at Compiegne. As was her habit, she was at the vanguard of her army. They approached the drawbridge into the city, which I hear was intentionally left down to entice her. Jeanne looked over the situation. No one appeared to be guarding the wooden structure. So, she took advantage of what she thought was an opportunity to enter the town without a battle. She rode over the bridge with several of her men. As soon as she was safely on the other side, men appeared from the shadows and the drawbridge was raised, trapping her and those men with her. The fight, with the Duke's men, did not last long."

"What wonderful news. What will happen next?"

"There'll be a trial."

"What will they try her for?"

"I've heard for a witch and a heretic."

"Serious charges."

"Yes, but the ones expected so I hear."

"Are you going to the trial? If you do, I want to go," stated William.

"No, William. You obey the surgeon-barber's orders, and I'll report back to you." George leaned closer to examine the top of William's shaved head. "It looks like the swelling is going down somewhat."

"I hope so." William returned to the news of the day. "How long do you think the trial will last?"

"There's no way of knowing. The English will want her gone from the face of the earth. I'm sure the only verdict is guilty. It's only a matter of how to make it happen."

"How much longer will we be in Rouen?"

"When fresh troops arrive, I've been told my group of archers will leave, but there's no date on the arrival or my departure. Of course, I hope you'll be well enough to go with me. We don't want to lose contact."

"No. I think you would fit in perfectly at our business in Bristol. You could establish a bolt and arrow making operation for us. That is, if you are interested. Think about it."

"I'll definitely give your suggestion some thought. I don't have any plans and really no one to go home too."

~

Months passed as the trial got underway. Jeanne, chained to her prison bed, was being accused of being a heretic and witch. Sadly, the French King did nothing to help his court's favorite, preferring not to associate with someone called a witch/heretic, nor did he offer to negotiate her release.

Finally, after a year in captivity, Jeanne relented and signed a confession saying that she had never received divine guidance, nor would she don men's clothes again.

Then, in some way, deceived by the men holding her in prison, she put on men's clothes, breaking her signed confession. That, in itself, was a reason to send her to the stake. She had relapsed, they said.

George came to tell a recovered William of the plans. "Do you want to go and witness this sight?"

"Not really, but I'll go with you," he said, after having time to think about the horrifying act.

∼

On May 30, 1431, Jeanne d'Arc was led from her cell to the market place at Rouen. George and William Tipton stood on a slightly raised stand to the side of the crowd. They watched as she stopped before mounting to the hurriedly constructed wooden platform. Kneeling, she said a prayer to God.

On the ground, below the two men, the observer's lips were moving with whispers...*she said she heard God's voice. She wore men's clothing. Was she a witch? What is heresy? The French King abandoned her, poor thing. Have you ever seen someone burned at the stake?*

Making the sign of the cross, she arose and with heavy steps slowly walked up the stairs to the platform where the stake protruded. Her eyes followed its rough, brown surface, rising to the sky, where birds flew, taking advantage of the upper air drafts. White clouds floated, one by one, across the blue heavens.

Nearby, the priest she had requested prayed in French and quoted Psalms from a parchment he held in his hand … *Quand je marche dans la vallée de l`ombre de la mort, Je ne crains aucun mal, car tu es avec moi.* (Yea, though I walk through the valley of the shadow of death, I will fear no evil: for thou art with me.)

With her head bowed, Jeanne did not resist when two men roughly tied her hands behind the wooden stake and her ankles to the front. All was ready.

The crowd was hushed as the fire was lit and started to burn. She looked over the crowd. Her eyes lighted on William. Their eyes locked and hers rested there for a second or two while the flames licked upward toward the stand. Then she looked toward the priest, listening as he quoted more from the scriptures. And finally, lifting her head, she watched the birds in the heavens as the flames licked through the boards on the platform and smoke filled the air around her.

Someone in the crowd murmured and pointed, "See. She's looking for God in the clouds." The crowd started praying, pleading to God for relief, theirs and hers. Still … she said not a word.

The flames and heat increased and the smoke, boiling up from below, suffocating her, making her cough. She moved her head to keep from breathing the smoke—but to no avail—and saw the cross on top of the nearby church.

William looked at George. "I can't take any more of this. Let us go." Slowly, they threaded their way out of the crowd. Behind them they heard a loud cry …

"Jesus! Jesus! Jesus!" The last words she spoke. Jeanne d'Arc slumped forward. She was unconscious. The fire burned the rope holding her hands onto the stake, and she fell to the platform. The Maid of Orléans was dead.

William and George turned to look one last time. The platform was engulfed in smoke and fire. Only a dark lump appeared infrequently through the flames.

∽

Three months later William and George appeared on Edmund Tipton's doorstep. He welcomed them into his house. Three years had passed since William had left for France. Edmund looked the young man over. He'd grown up.

"Edmund, let me introduce you to George Beaufert from East Anglia. He makes bolts and arrows, and he's going on with me to Bristol to set up a shop to make them for the Tiptons."

"George, welcome to my home." Edmund extended his hand and indicated a chair which sat close to the hearth. Since it was August, no fire burned in the fireplace.

All three men sat down, two breathing a sigh of relief. "You don't know how wonderful it is to sit and not worry about which direction an arrow or cannon ball is coming from," William exclaimed.

"What is the status of the war in France?" a curious Edmund asked.

"I don't know what you're hearing here in Tipton, but the war is not going well for us."

"The French continue to gain land. The English army's morale is at an all-time low," added George.

"I've heard we are in deep debt to many in England and even in France and other places," said Edmund.

"We don't know about that, but we did get compensated somehow." William jingled pennies in his pocket and grinned.

"Were you there when they burned Jeanne d'Arc at the stake?"

The grin disappeared. William looked at George and then back at Edmund. "Yes. I prefer to forget the sight," he said. He continued with an abbreviated version of what happened.

After hearing the short narration, Edmund nodded. "I understand the difficulty in sharing the horror of the scene. I've always avoided such happenings since returning from France."

"You would have to be there to appreciate just what happened," said George.

"Are you going to stay awhile," Edmund asked, as four-year-old Hugh Tipton and his mother came into the room. Hugh headed straight for his grandfather's lap.

"No, we are headed toward Stourbridge to stay the night, and then on toward Bristol. I wanted to talk to you about coming with us. There's nothing here in Tipton that you can't find in my hometown. "Why don't you load up the family and come. There's plenty of work to go around or you might end up a ship's captain and sail the seas.

"Ah, I'm too old for sailing the seas, but I'll keep your offer in mind. Our roots have been in Tipton for almost one thousand years. If I decide to come, I'll send you a letter."

The two sat and conversed until the noon meal, which they ate with Edmund and his family. Then they went outside, mounted their horses, and rode south.

∽

After the Maid of Orléans died, Philip of Burgundy left his English allies and came to terms with King Charles VII.

Twenty-two years after Jeanne died in 1431, the English had lost all of France but the port of Calais. The war to capture all of France was over. After hundreds of years, lots of treasure, and many men's lives, the English were basically out of the country.

Because of the failure in France, Henry VI's government had diminished respect. He had lost generals in the war, friends at home, and some of his trusted counsellors had left his court.

At this vital time in 1453, when strength was needed to rule instead of weakness, something caused the King to withdraw and become unresponsive to the world around him. He did not even acknowledge his wife, who was carrying their first and only child. Secrecy was the order of the day. His courtiers were adamant that no one know, but his insufficiency did get outside the court. Richard the Duke of York took over every-day duties in the position of Protector of the Realm.

❦ Chapter 8 ❦

The 15th Century

Back in England William Tipton, George Beaufert, Hugh Tipton

In February 1455, William Tipton received a letter from his cousin Edmund, talking about the state of things at Windsor. He sat in the house he occupied on the Bristol bridge, talking with George, his permanent resident since they had returned from the war in France.

"Here's the latest letter from Edmund, George," he said, slipping his finger under the wax seal.

The older man reclined on a couch, stocking-feet up, because his whirlbone (hip bone) was hurting. He moved and grimaced. "Ouch! Arthetica, the doctor said," he explained to William.

"Hip still hurting?" William asked. "Did you take the potion containing the rue and vinegar which the doctor said may take care of the ache?"

"William, that stuff is so bitter, it makes my tongue curl. I don't recommend it. Yuck!"

The younger man laughed and shook his head. "It's your decision."

"Yes, I know. What does Edmund say?"

William had been looking over its pages as they talked. "He says the word from Windsor is that the King regained his senses last Christmas after being totally indisposed for one-and-a-half years. He recognizes his wife and baby boy, asking the child's name, and being delighted with the name Edward. He says that Richard the Duke of York has resigned his position of Protector since Henry's health is better."

"Wonder what happened to Henry?"

"Everyone has an opinion, but no one really knows."

"Where was he when he quit responding to the world?"

"Remember, he was at the Royal Lodge of Clarendon in Wiltshire when it happened and there was lots of unpleasant news coming to the King each day. Edmund continues that there is much intrigue in the castle at Windsor with rumours that his cousin, the Duke of York, is after his life and crown."

"Are we going to have another war?"

William did not get to answer the question. His wife, Martha, and three of their children came noisily into the room—all boys. The youngest child, John, headed straight for George, jumping onto his lap. The older man grabbed the child in a hug and forgot totally about his whirlbone.

Martha came to William, kissing him on the cheek. "We were busy this morning," she told her husband. "I left Laurence downstairs to tend to the customers while I fix something for the children to eat. Do you and George need me to make something for you?" Her shop, on the main passageway which crossed the bridge and directly under the house they lived in, contained many products either imported from the continent or beyond. Some were made locally by the members of the Bristol guild, and others supplied by the many Tipton projects in the local area.

William stuck the letter in his pocket and responded, "No, we ate as we came home. George needed his spectacles, since he's working on paperwork this afternoon. I hope they didn't get crushed in his pocket," he observed as the wrestling continued.

George ran the bolt and arrow making division, and William oversaw the box making part of the Tipton enterprises in Bristol.

The delightful din from the couch continued with laughter and squeals, as the other children piled on, all of them totally spoiled by the older man. William shook his head and whispered to his wife. "And only minutes ago, he had aches and pains."

Martha grinned and waving her hand, cautioned her sons, "Boys, be careful. George is very old."

"Ah, Mother, you spoil all the fun," said John, quitting his roughhousing with *the old man*. The other boys did the same.

"Do what your Mother says," said his father. "George, do you still have your spectacles? Are they unbroken?" William watched as the old man patted his shirt pocket and nodded his head. Then he added, "We need to get back to the warehouse and finish what we started today. I have a large order of boxes to send on the boat heading to Portishead, and you have orders to send also."

William went to his wife and with another quick kiss, the two men were out the door and going down the steps to the busy market area on the Bristol Bridge. A noble's carriage clattered noisily on the stones toward the city of Bristol, followed by a man on a horse, and across the street several men were loudly discussing the affairs of the day.

"William, George, come here," exclaimed one, throwing up his hand in greeting.

William acknowledged the greeting but did not join them.

Instead of waving at Laurence, the two men went into the open front of the store. The smell of ginger, cinnamon, and nutmeg from the spice isles of the East Indies beyond Araby, and saffron from the Eastern Mediterranean greeted them. George sneezed as they passed by fresh ground black pepper from India.

Laurence laughed. "George, you know the black pepper is always in the same place, and that this is the day I grind the dried pods. If you'd walk a little to your left, you would avoid it."

"Yes, you are right. But if I did that, we wouldn't have anything to talk about." George smiled and shook hands with his favorite salesman.

"Son, how are sales today?" William stopped to finger the beautiful bolt of blue silk cloth which lay on a counter.

"Father, I sold some of it a few minutes ago. A lady in a carriage bought enough for a dress to be worn at a future wedding. She said a local tailor will make the dress."

"Did you recommend Edward Onslow's wife to tailor it, since he's a member of our guild?"

"Yes, I did, and also there was another man by here early this morning trying to sell both men's and ladies' stockings. I sent him to the guildhall, telling him we couldn't buy anything from him unless he was a member."

"That's the protocol," said William, nodding. "George and I are headed back to the warehouse. Your mother will be down with your food shortly."

The crowd of men had dispersed by the time the two went outside the building. William and George followed several people who were on foot, crossing the bridge with its banks of houses sticking out over the River Avon.

The first time George had crossed the bridge, he'd been amazed. Upon looking closer, he saw great beams protruding from the edge of each side of the wide stone bridge. These oak beams were supporting side-by-side houses all along the pathway. These dwellings hovered over the water which served as their waste disposal. Frequent rains and flooding washed the Avon clean of deposited, murky matter, sending it downstream to Portishead and into the vast Severn Estuary.

William and George's destination was on the northern riverbank, where the carriage had disappeared. Feeling the pages of the letter in his pocket, William continued, "I didn't get to tell you, but Edmund said he's encouraging Hugh to come and work with us. He says not to count on it, because Hugh's best friend is in London, and he's asked the grandson to join him."

～

Hugh Tipton's return home from his cousin's home in Wolverhampton to Tipton was always uneventful. He had started early just after the morning meal, walking briskly and usually whistling as he followed the road. Often, he stopped to wave at a passerby on horse or in a cart. Today, traffic was light and he concentrated on the mud puddles dotting the path from the downpour of rain which soaked the ground yesterday.

"English weather," he groaned. "Rain, rain, and more rain. No wonder there's no one on the slick and muddy road."

The sun shone brightly as it always did when the torrential downpour washed the atmosphere clean of dust, coal, and wood smoke. Halfway to Tipton, he came to a narrow place in the road. Two low hills on the north and south funneled the traffic into a narrow isthmus, where the puddles became deeper in the road's ruts, and a curve made them worse — muddy water splashing, coating the bushes whose limbs stuck out on the side of the narrow road.

He stopped to check out the situation. He was going east. On the left side of the road, the forest was dense. There was no easy way to avoid the messy route in that direction. But looking into the woods to the right of the lane, he saw a trail, probably made by wildlife in the area. Using it, he decided to detour around the slick roadway and upon entering the woods, he heard the sound of approaching horses and cart. There was another sound he did not recognize. He could have sworn it was a sneeze — a double sneeze. Where was it coming from? Deciding he was hearing the wind in the trees or the crack of a broken limb, he did not investigate.

The conveyance was approaching at a higher rate of speed than normal. He heard hooves pounding the ground and harness squeaking abnormally loud —

unusual because here a waggon or coach slowed down. He heard it slow somewhat as it entered the long curve and men's voices yelling, telling the conveyance to, "Stop. Stop."

He jerked his head around. On the other side of the trees, which shielded his position, other horses emerged on the roadway, and the unexpected, loud report which came from one of the horsemen caused him to jump, and the animals pulling the cart to halt and rear up.

What more perfect place for bandits to rob an unsuspecting person, Hugh thought, sucking in a quick breath as he understood the scene unfolding before him.

Peering through the trees toward the direction of the loud blast, Hugh saw a handheld weapon with smoke coming from the barrel. What was that thing, and more importantly had they seen him before he entered the woods?

He directed his gaze back toward the bandits. The cart had traveled most dangerously on two wheels, with the driver struggling to control its progress. It settled back down on four wheels as masked robbers with swords rode alongside, grabbed the horse's harness, brought it to a halt, and prevented it from moving.

The drama kept unfolding before him. "Your money or your life," was loudly shouted to whoever was inside with a sword, for punctuation pushed through an open window.

A gray-headed man poked his head out of the window and with his gloved hand pushed the sword aside. "Sir, you shall have my money. Please spare my life and those of my companions." He handed out a small bag which he jingled, meaning there were coins inside.

Hugh watched as some of the robbers rode to the opposite side, demanding coins from the others.

Suddenly, the hair on the back of his neck stood straight up, as rough hands grabbed him by his collar. "Stand still," ordered a harsh voice with authority.

By now, the cart and its occupants were leaving, and soon it was out of sight. The masked men were laughing and removing their face coverings.

"That was easy," a bushy headed man on a brown horse stated.

Hugh recognized one of the men. He was a ne'er-do-well, Richard, nicknamed Three Fingers, who frequented the local alehouses in Dudley, Sedgley, and surrounding areas.

Richard had lost two fingers in a drunken knife fight. He was unemployed, and rumours circulated around Dudley and Tipton that he lived on ill-gotten gains.

"Stay away from him," the inhabitants whispered.

The other man he did not know.

Shoved onto the road, he waited with his captor for the two men and the rest of the robbers to ride over.

"Well, looks like we got us a witness, Sir Haywood," Richard exclaimed, waving his gloved hand, the one which covered the two missing fingers, toward Hugh.

Ah, so that's who he is, Hugh thought. Sir Welden Haywood, he was. He'd never seen this man before, but his petty acts of banditry over the Midlands were well-known.

Haywood wasn't a local Knight, and there was some question about him even being a Knight. He supposedly hailed from somewhere north of Staffordshire. Some even said he was from London — a notorious place for bandits and robbers.

Maybe London's where he learned his craft, ran through Hugh's mind as he stood there, looking the two men over, realizing his fate was in these men's hands.

"Who are you?" asked Sir Haywood, who was dressed in a nondescript brown peasant tunic, which didn't represent a higher rank in the hierarchy of England's nobility.

"Hugh Tipton," he responded, thinking there was no reason to give this man more detailed information.

"I thought so," said Three Fingers. He turned to his companion. "He's of Edmund Tipton's family. The Tipton family has served the Lords of Dudley for many years."

"Tie him up and blindfold him," instructed Sir Haywood to Hugh's captor. "He can ride with you, and we'll decide on his fate later. Right now, we need to get back to our hideaway and divide our loot."

The ride to the hideaway was uncomfortable, with Hugh holding onto his captor as best he could. Pulled from the horse, he was tossed to the ground. This is where he lay — out of earshot of the conversation around the campfire.

At nightfall, he shivered in the English Midlands cold, but finally, his blindfold was removed, and he was permitted to eat some roasted meat which had been cooked over the open fire, where he was allowed to sit and warm. When he took a moment to look around, he realized he was outside a cave, one he'd discovered as a child, playing in the forest between Sedgely and Bilston. Here a trail cut through the woods. He wasn't far from home.

Evidently, his fate had been considered and decided while he rested on the cold, wet ground. Sir Haywood spoke to him. "Not taking any chances, we've determined not to upset the Lord in the castle at Dudley, but you and your family will leave the area immediately, and we will see to it that you do. On Thursday week, after dark, we will bring a large, covered cart to your door. Have your affairs in order and your family ready to go. Your goods will be loaded as quickly as possible. Should you not agree to this, we will see that your house is burned to the ground, your cattle and garden destroyed, and your mother and sisters, well …"

Haywood did not finish the threat, but Hugh got the message. He nodded his head in agreement, feeling these men would do as they said.

"I want you out of Staffordshire, as far as possible. Where can you go?" Haywood asked, looking at him.

Before he could answer, Three Fingers butted in. "I hear they've got relatives on the River Severn. Is that far enough away, Sir Haywood?"

"Perfect," responded Haywood. "Three Fingers, take him home. Use the extra horse and bring it back after his delivery to Tipton. We'll harness it with another horse to the glorified cart we have secreted in the woods. The one we inherited when the last Liege

Lord we robbed bolted from it to avoid us." Haywood's laugh was more like a sneer.

"Thought he could out run us, so don't get any ideas, Hugh Tipton," laughed Three Fingers with his leader. "Better not to stir up more trouble in the shire, Weldon. Don't want people nosing around with questions we don't want to answer."

"Exactly. Thus, we will get rid of a potential problem and the odd cart so it can't be found." He turned to Hugh, "And, you'd better hope no one sees you with it. You do realize they hang bandits for stealing carts and horses, and this one is distinctive and may be known around this area. For that reason, we will deliver it to you in the dark, and escort you to the edge of Tipton. My advice to you is to keep to the road, traveling with all speed at night, my friend, as far from Tipton as possible, and stopping to rest during the day."

My friend, thought Hugh. *No chance of that. And, what had happened to the Liege Lord? The one Sir Haywood had sneered about. I don't know of anyone missing in the area I live within, and what did a glorified cart look like?*

~

"I still don't think you should go," Edmund Tipton had said as they waited for Haywood's men to appear.

To which Hugh had replied, "You weren't there when they were talking. They meant what they said," he had tried to explain.

Stubborn Edmund had stated, "I'm not going." He would stay with friends until it was safe to return to the only home he'd ever known. He'd sternly told Hugh, he would be buried at Summerhill with his other ancestors, next to the Church of St. Martin, rather than go to another place and start anew.

Although he'd considered moving when he was younger, now he had no desire to leave. When it was obvious Hugh wouldn't change his mind, he had suggested to his grandson, making Bristol his mother's and sister's new home. He gave some instructions on where to stop for the day and night, since he'd been visiting in the area before.

When the sounds in the night meant the band of robbers were coming, Edmund had given quick kisses to his family and disappeared into the shadows to watch until his family was gone.

Quickly, the men on horseback dismounted and helped load the enclosed cart with wooden boxes and leather bags. The carts underneath suspension Hugh did not recognize in the darkness—different from others he'd driven.

Hugh helped his family into the interior, where they sat on plush velvet seats with backs. He mounted to the driver's seat, which was padded and covered in leather. He flicked the reins, and they were off.

The girls leaned from the cart for a last glimpse of the only home they'd known.

The highwaymen rode alongside for a few minutes, and then, as quickly as they had come, disappeared into the night.

Right on time and as if planned, the rain came come down in torrents. Now on the road, they risked floods in the lowlands, but Hugh knew this area. He would avoid the muddy roads and streams, if possible.

What was his problem? Why did he feel as if the world was ending?

Because of the rain, Thursday night was dark with heavy clouds in the sky.

Occasionally, the rain let up and a glimpse of the moon as a round, silver orb darted between the storms.

Hugh Tipton and his family rode southwest in the plush cart with covered sides in brown leather toward their new home in Bristol.

Large oaks made the drive even gloomier, and the low bushes, heavy with raindrops and leaning into the dirt path, sometimes scraped the side. This added to the feeling of being closed in on the muddy road.

Hugh sat on the driver's seat, carefully urging the horses when he could see, but mostly letting them feel the way, because the road was rough and rutted with many potholes. The cart's suspension left little doubt as to the results of dropping into the holes in the road. With each bounce, the riders left their seats, or slid sideways, almost falling to the floor.

∽

After driving south for two hours, his mother called out, "Hugh, we need to take a short stop." He pulled the covered box next to a stone fence where sheep stood in a close group. He eyed them, and they eyed him. Alighting from the driver's seat, he pulled the sidestep down and helped his mother and sisters to the ground.

He wondered what his mother and his two sisters thought about the whole situation. They hadn't questioned him about leaving when he'd firmly said they would go. She caught his eye and smiled. "How much longer before we sleep?"

"We'll find a secluded spot before daybreak and try to stay hidden until nightfall. We must sleep in the coach this first day. Can't take a chance on someone recognizing our transportation. Tonight's and tomorrow's travel will be the worst, but maybe we can put the girls in a real bed soon."

"How long is it before we arrive in Bristol?"

"In three days, we'll be there. I promise."

The girls came back. Hugh helped them inside, and then he mounted up to the driver's box.

"Is everyone ready?" he called.

"Yes," came the faint reply.

Although his team of horses weren't of the muscled bay breed known for pulling carts, they made good time, and after some inquiries, he drove to the front entrance of William's shop on the Bristol Bridge just as he had promised—in the afternoon of the third day.

After a short greeting with Martha, while Laurence ran to get his father, the three men, Hugh, William, Laurence, and the women left for Portishead and the large stone house above the estuary. This is where the family stayed the night with Harold and his family, upstairs in the same rooms which were previously occupied by Sir Ralph Stafford and Roger.

"We'll decide on a plan for you tomorrow," nodded Harold, grinning. "I wish Edmund had come. He'll be lonely in Tipton by himself. We would have had lots to talk about, but I understand his need to stay in his home. Please sleep well."

Hugh stopped him as he headed for the stairs. "We need to get rid of the cart. My captors said it was stolen."

"I understand Hugh. We can use it, so I'll make sure my men change its appearance so no one will recognize it. Consider it gone."

Hugh slept his first night of restful sleep since his observation of the robbery. The next morning, Harold waited downstairs to talk to him.

"I'm going to take the day off," he said. "We'll walk around Portishead, and you can see the wharf and the warehouse. But first, have you heard of the Ancestry Book, the one by our ancestor who started the town of Tipton? Surely, Edmund has told you about it."

"I have heard of this volume," nodded Hugh.

"That's it on the table," pointed Harold to a big book with lots of pages. "But first, look at the fireplace," he suggested.

Hanging on the fireplace was an antique sword. "Is that Sir Anthony's sword everyone talks about?"

"The one and the same. Go, take a look."

Hugh went over and pulled the sword off its holder and out of its scabbard. "Wow, it's heavy," he noted, hefting it in his hand.

"Yes, our swords today are made of lighter and stronger metals."

Hugh tried moving the blade in different defensive and offensive positions.

Harold watched him and grinned. "There's also writing on the blade." Harold explained the words. "I've put the words in our English on the inside of the book for later generations."

When he was finished, Hugh put the weapon back in its former position. "I'd like to read the book, if you don't mind."

"I hoped you would. It's very old, so be careful of the pages. Let's eat our morning meal and take our walk. You can read this afternoon. The sun will be hot to the west, and this room will be shaded by the trees on the hillside behind us. The cool breezes from the estuary will come through the open windows of the house, and reading will be pleasurable."

That afternoon, Hugh read much of the book with Harold's help. The following day, he went to work with Harold in the headquarters of *Tipton Brothers, Shipping*, learning the shipping business.

Chapter 9

At the end of 15th Century

The War of Roses The Battle near Market
Bosworth

The world in the late 15th Century was opening up
with many advancements in technology and trade. On
the continent in 1430, a Dutchman named Laurens
Costner, from Haarlem, played with his children in a
forest near his home. The day was full of sunshine as
they ran through the woods, squealing, chasing, and
pointing at the red squirrels, which ran from limb to
limb in the high oak trees, as they looked for acorns to
eat.

With nothing else to do, Laurens sat down on a
large log next to the water canal which meandered
through the forest, pulled out his knife, and started
carving their names in the smooth, soft bark of a white
birch tree. Cutting through the bark, a thought came to
him. He'd make blocks with their initials for them to
play with. Soon the children were standing around,
watching him hard at work.

"Papa, what are you doing?" Lisjbet, the oldest
one asked.

"Carving your names in wooden blocks. Here
Lisjbet, I have yours done," he responded, holding

them out in a row, so she could see her name. "Aelbert and Marij, yours are next."

He carved as fast as he could, and soon the children were lining up the letters of their names in the sandy canal bank. When they dropped a block of wood, the letter made an imprint in the wet sand.

Immediately, Costner had another idea. Could you take his blocks and use them to make an alphabet and an ink impression of the letters on paper? When the children headed home, he put the blocks in the pocket of his trousers. He would try. The more he worked at his idea, the more he felt sure it was possible.

He hired a young German, Johannes Gutenberg, as an apprentice and they strung together the blocks of wood with letters on them and started printing leaflets. Before he could complete his ideas, an epidemic of the bubonic plague ravaged the area and Laurens Costner was dead.

Gutenberg loaded up the parts of the press and the work they had accomplished and headed up the River Rhine, past the old castles, river toll booths, and the vast grape vineyards running up and down the riverside hills. He finally stopped at Strasburg, where he set up shop, and started to work on the biggest problem his former employer, Costner, had with his idea. Wood did not hold up when used over and over in a press.

Being someone taught at an early age to work with metals, he started to experiment with different ones. The result was the first movable type printing press using metal letters.

When asked about his invention, he said, *"It is a press, certainly, but a press from which shall flow inexhaustible streams. Through it, God will spread His Word. A spring of truth shall flow from it: like a new star it shall scatter the darkness of ignorance, and cause a light heretofore unknown to shine amongst men."* This profound statement would have more repercussions than the printer would ever know. In 1452, Gutenberg produced the *one book* to come out of his shop—the Latin Holy Bible.

Deeply in debt to his partner, John Fust, Gutenberg lost the printing press and the printing business when Fust went to court and sued for the money owed to him. But the first step, toward the freedom of man, in the next centuries had been taken. All the people needed was God's Word printed in the English they understood and transported to England—and this was in the making.

When George Beaufert asked William in Bristol the question, "Would there be war in England," he didn't receive an answer from him.

Trouble was brewing at home.

In 1453, two factions were vying for the throne of England, and both were determined to rule the country. The War of the Roses was between the House of Lancaster (Red Rose) and the House of York (White Rose). These families were both descendants of Edward III and both could claim the throne.

The War of Roses, otherwise called the Cousins War, began in 1455. It seesawed back and forth between the two factions. Five times the crown changed heads, and fifteen times brutal battles were fought, until the final and definitive battle at Bosworth Field. This event

occurred thirty years later, in 1485. When it was over, the English hoped it would end the conflict.

~

The whole Tipton family had assembled at Gloucester to decide where they stood in this latest battle for the throne of England. Their decision could influence whether they continued in the shipping business. It could also determine if they lived or died.

"The rumours coming from King Richard's court aren't good. There are so many reports of beheadings of opponents, the mysterious deaths of imaginary enemies, and especially the heinous disappearance of the two sons of Edward IV — one being the rightful heir to the throne. After being placed in the Tower of London for their safety, nothing was heard of them again. Our King has many dark shadows hanging over his two-year reign," said William.

Harold continued with William's thoughts. "It's not that King Edward was lily-white. After assuming the throne, he went on a spree, just like Richard, disposing of those he felt might rival him."

"Of course, the news of the landing of young Henry Tudor's fleet at the mouth of the Severn Estuary, on the Welsh side, makes our decision even more difficult, since he's close by," another relative added. "Tudor is among friends since he has Welsh blood and was raised by his Welsh uncle at Pembroke Castle. Many Welshmen will side with him. But as far as we are concerned, he is an unknown at this time. Even so, I'm leaning toward him to end once and for all this conflict. Surely, enough blood has been spilt." Several of the relatives agreed.

"What about the citizens of Shrewsbury, or Pontesbury, or Worcester," asked Harold. "They're people who supply much of the goods we ship. Our choice might affect their decision to support us, or not, and then there's the tradesman's guilds. Could they ban us from trading, or will they support us?"

William stood to address the meeting. "I don't think we can base our decision only on money, our heads, or our business. We've always took into consideration where we stood on the issues, and how the results of our choices might affect our country. I'd rather send my descendants to a war that gives careful thought to the consequences for England, for the outcome is our future." William was known for his participation in the siege of Orléans and was respected for this act.

When the vote was taken, the majority supported Henry Tudor and his claim to the English crown.

The news of Henry Tudor's landing at Milford Haven's harbour in Wales had spread quickly through the Welsh countryside and across to the Marcher (border) counties on the English side of the River Severn. As the son of Margaret Beaufort, Countess of Richmond, he was the sole claimant from the Lancastrian dynasty (Red Rose) to the throne.

The Tipton's had decided to support him by gathering arms and men. These supplies had already been shipped up the River Severn, intercepted by a branch of the family at Pontesbury, and stockpiled in a storage area within Shrewsbury town. This included the armour of six Tipton men who'd been designated to support Henry Tudor in the war. The Tipton men, all experts with the longbow, had heard it on good authority that Henry was headed toward Shrewsbury.

~

It was July 1485, and William Tipton stood at the end of Bristol Bridge, looking at his twenty-three-year-old grandson. They were the last ones to say goodbye.

Young George was named after George Beaufert, William's long-time friend with whom he'd fought in France, and who'd lived as part of the family for years. The kinfolk had buried George in the family plot at All Saint's Church in Bristol.

Young George's father, Laurence, and his mother had said their tearful goodbyes and returned to the shop on Bristol Bridge. They had taken over the store as William and Martha had aged.

"Young George, just remember everything we've discussed about fighting," William admonished. Young George had been his and George Beaufert's pupil on the longbow ever since he was big enough to hold one. His grandfather had to admit that the boy was much more adept at shooting his arrows than he. He had sharper eyes and his fingers were nimbler at using the longbow, and he was far more skilled at swordsmanship than the older men had been.

"Grandfather, I shall not forget *anything* you've taught me." He smiled at his gray-haired grandfather and patted his sword, the one given to William by Edmund Tipton, which King Edward I had given to his new Knight, Sir Anthony de Tipton at Rhuddlan Castle after he'd killed Prince Llewellyn. The rest of his supplies, light armour and longbow were packed onto a horse. He'd leave the animal at Pontesbury until his return from the impending fight.

"Do you have the address of our family at Pontesbury?"

"Yes, in my pocket." Young George would stay with his cousins until he joined Henry Tudor at Shrewsbury. "Grandfather, you fret too much. I am no longer a child, but a young man, who will soon be a father. I'll miss you, and grandmother, and father and mama," came out of his mouth unexpectedly.

Saying goodbye was beginning to get too personal and emotional. Young George hadn't realized how much he loved his family until faced with leaving it, and the possibility of not coming back made it worse.

And he still hadn't said farewell to his wife, leaving her for last. His first child would probably be born while he was gone.

"Saying goodbye to Lucia will be hard, won't it?" William observed, as his grandson seemed distracted, and this was another consequence of war the old man understood.

The old man put his arms around Young George and gave him a warm hug and kiss on the cheek, noting but not commenting on the tears on his grandson's face. Holding his grandson at arm's length, he promised, "We'll take good care of her, don't worry, and say hello to our cousins for me," he concluded and turned to walk the bridge to rejoin Martha in their quarters above the store on Bristol Bridge, brushing aside his own tears when he turned the corner and was out of sight.

Old memories flooded back with each step, as he remembered his own leaving and safe return from his time in the services of England, against the unending foe of France, which started for him at the siege of

Orléans. He and Martha were sweethearts before he left, and he hadn't asked her to wait. But Martha had remained his. And on his homecoming, as he held out his arms to receive her kiss—ah, what joy he'd felt at the reunion. A finger brushed another tear away as he remembered. This was followed by a smile at memories of first courtship and the long life of love they had shared.

He must remember to give her many kisses when he got home.

~

Nottingham was not the old 'wattle-and-daub' home of the tribal chieftain Snotta on the River Trent, encountered by Chieftain Tybba as he sailed up the river to find a home. The stone castle which now existed was first built as a Norman castle under the rule of King William, the Conqueror of Normandy, and later adorned by subsequent rulers with fantastically sculptured animals and beasts on its parapets. This was where King Richard had of late established his royal home and headquarters.

Two men walked in opposite directions on the southern parapet of the long-established military stronghold of Nottingham. Every time the lookouts passed each other, they paused to have a short conversation.

"Do you have any idea what that animal is?" asked the one clad in a blue tunic, tugging at his coat of mail, and pointing with his longbow, at a stone beast attached to the parapet. It had a mane, long fangs, and protruding eyes.

The one in a brown tunic, armed with a longbow, responded, "No, but I'd hate to meet it within the royal hunting grounds on a dark night." The nearby hunting grounds were stocked with all kinds of animals native to England.

Both men laughed and continued their sentry rounds.

On the next pass, brown tunic asked, "What was the messenger's news? I'm talking about the one who arrived hurriedly on horseback from up the River Trent. There's a rumour afloat in the guardroom that Henry Tudor is on the march here with an army."

"I heard the same thing in the tavern." Blue tunic nodded in agreement.

"What were you doing at the tavern?" asked brown tunic, who was the nosy one of the two and the bigger blabber mouth.

Blue tunic just laughed and started moving. If he told brown tunic, his escapades would be all over the army barracks, and soon his wife would hear.

With the next stop, brown tunic lowered his voice and asked, "Is it true that King Richard took captive the youngest children of the nobles in his army, as assurance against any who would not obey his commands?"

"They *are* here," blue tunic affirmed quietly, looking around the area. "There is much dissent amongst the highest in his command — some are saying the word treason is being talked about amongst some of the Lords."

"Whoever is talking had better be careful."

From below, the harsh voice of the castle Marshal demanded, "Are you two up there to gossip like fishwives or walk the parapet as sentries?" The two men jumped apart and immediately resumed their rounds—silent for the rest of their shift.

~

King Richard, hearing that Henry had landed five days ago in Wales, left the comfort of Nottingham Castle and headed south toward Leicester with his nobles. Picking up his army of around ten thousand, he marched the men four abreast with the cavalry on each side. He encamped on Ambion Hill near Market Bosworth in Leicestershire to await his rival for the crown.

Arriving early, gave him a little time to look over the area of Bosworth Field and formulate a battle plan, since this was where he would intercept the opposing army. Once Henry showed up, Richard would form a line and group his men into three distinct divisions.

Those observing his ride from afar had no trouble recognizing the King, because Richard had a strange twist in his spine. Some called him a hunchback, but his backbones bulged to his right side, making his left shoulder lower than his right one. Even if he had no crown on his head, there was no way to mistake him as King as he rode around the future battlefield at Ambion Hill.

He knew he must win this fight. Being a successful soldier and strategist, he assured himself he would, especially since his army now numbered over twelve thousand with three thousand infantry being added lately. The biggest question was loyalty within his ranks. He suspected some of his Lords were muttering against him.

After consulting with his commanders on the disposition of the army at the start of the battle, the King spent the night at the Blue Boar Inn in Leicester.

∼

Young George Tipton of Bristol and his cousin, Durwin Tipton of Pontesbury, had joined Henry Tudor as he marched his army of three thousand French mercenaries across Wales into the English Midlands. It had swelled to four or five thousand as he crossed Wales, including Rhys ap Thomas, a prominent Welsh leader, along with his men. They were willing to support Henry because of his Welsh bloodline, which came from his grandfather, Owen Tudor. More had joined the advancing men by the time Tudor arrived to the south of Nottingham. Seeing King Richard's army on top of a hill, he led his troops to an opposing one, leaving a field between the two fighting units.

Young George and Durwin, along with the other Tipton men, pitched one tent with the other groups who would fight the Hunchback's army. Standards of different groups made a lively and colorful display among the spread-out militias, and there was much comradery and nervous joking, as the troops got ready for the night.

On the evening of August 21st, within striking distance of each other, the two foes readied themselves for battle. The murmur of human voices and the sound of sharpening steel, as swords were given a final rub on whetstones, floated across the valley, audible in the darkness which was punctuated by glowing fires.

"Wonder what they're thinking and planning, concerning arraying ourselves in tomorrow's battle," asked Young George of his cousin, Durwin, nodding toward the red, fiery dragon flag of Henry of Richmond, flying above his tent where the discussion was taking place.

The Tipton men were hunkered around a blazing fire with their cousins, eating stale bread and cheese brought from Bristol, Pontesbury, or Gloucester and washing the dry food down with whatever was left in their water bottles—this was their last meal before tomorrow's battle.

Durwin glanced in the direction Young George was looking, where a light silhouetted the guarded open door. He shook his head and answered, "I don't know, but I wouldn't want to be making the decision. Do you remember hearing about the battle at Towton? So many men were killed."

"Yes, over 20,000 supposedly. I can't imagine a number that big. We don't have close to that number in our group—probably not even in both armies put together."

Another cousin chimed in, while looking at the opposite field in the diminished sunlight. "Do you think we're outnumbered?"

Young George wanted to laugh but didn't. "Yes. We are definitely outnumbered. That's what will make deciding on a battle plan so hard. The infantry will get the brunt of this battle, but tomorrow morning, we must aim our arrows well. We must do all we can to help them."

"The cannons will be the first thing we'll hear in the morning. They will be our wakeup call." Durwin said this, while looking around the group, who hunched over the warm fire, nodded in agreement.

"Who's going to sleep?" asked the youngest cousin in the group with an uneasy chuckle.

"I don't know," Durwin grinned at his cousin. "But my feeling is, it's time we stretch out on our mats and try."

Young George, standing, added, "Conduct yourselves like Tipton's tomorrow. We've got a long history of honor and steadfastness in battle. We have nothing to fear and everything to gain." He was thinking of the Ancestry Book. "Remember as we've read, Tipton men have always showed up in support of their rightful King."

"Henry's not the King," someone added.

"Maybe not, but tomorrow may change that," was another comment.

There was a murmur of understanding around the campfire, as most of them stood to their feet.

"Let's make our ancestor's proud of us tomorrow," Durwin called.

With those words, the group broke up and either went into the tent to rest or disappeared into the darkness at the edge of camp. Soon all were bedded down on their mats, with the youngest cousin snoring the loudest.

Although it was warm during the day, and chilly now, a colder night still might overtake them as they slept. Young George ran his hands up and down his forearms. After sweating through the march for most of the day, even the least dip in the air temperature left him shivering.

Keeping the fire burning was an obsession for him. He would be up some of the night with that task—not much sleep for him. Not wishing his life away, but he'd be glad when the battle tomorrow was over.

～

The cannons from both sides started shooting iron shot at first light, trying to establish the range of the enemy and draw first blood.

"Did you sleep at all, cousin?" asked Durwin, standing with his hands spread toward the leaping flames of the fire.

"Yes, some," was Young George's response, as he stretched his arms to the new dawn and shook off the last of the night's poor slumber. Shadows moved around them as others came from the tent behind where they stood. There were some coughs and muffled good mornings, but others remained silent, each thinking their own thoughts about the day's future activities.

Young George and Durwin rallied the Tiptons. They donned armour, strung longbows and procured their quivers, and headed for the other archers and crossbowmen, who were bunched up, awaiting orders from the officer in charge, Sir John de Vere, the Earl of Oxford, who had been designated as group commander.

As they gathered together, what they saw on the hill, across the mist-covered field, was not reassuring.

The vanguard of Richard's army was straight ahead, with it being in command of John Howard, Duke of Norfolk. The King was positioned beside the Duke.

Another group, under the King's banner, was bunched to the right rear and off to the side. It was under the command of the brother's, Lord Thomas, the

Earl of Derby, and Sir William Stanley. Thomas was married to Henry Tudor's mother.

The third commander was Henry Percy, the Earl of Northumberland.

William Stanley, unbeknownst to King Richard, had talked to Henry Tudor only days before on his march to Market Bosworth, telling him they hadn't decided whether they would support the King or not. With the lives of their children hanging in the balance, because the King held them at Nottingham Castle as assurance against their disloyalty, the decision they would make depended on how the battle was progressing.

"Isn't that the standard of the Earl of Northumberland to the left?" asked Young George of Durwin.

"Yes, it is. And the brother's Stanley are to the right in the rear. Who do you think they'll support, Henry or Richard?"

Young George shook his head. "I don't like the look of things."

At that moment, the Earl of Oxford, Henry's most experienced commander, gave the order of battle for his forces. The archers were to line up and shoot their arrows first. Then those with crossbows and the infantry would head across the field to confront Richard's forces while the longbowmen continued to shoot arrows above their heads. Henry would stay slightly to the right, in position with his men to enter the battle if needed.

～

The mists over the field finally cleared, leaving the opposing forces with a clear view to the battlefield.

After volleys of arrows shot by both armies, the Earl of Oxford stood Henry's infantry in a side-by-side array, maintaining a tight line of defense.

In a surprise move and before Henry's forces could march forward, Richard ordered part of the middle division of his infantry down the hill to engage his enemy's forces in hand-to-hand combat.

The strong resistance of the Earl's men pushed hard against the King's army, returning Richard's surprise move by pushing his men backward. Some of Richard's struggling forces deserted the field, running for their lives.

After several minutes and realizing the battle wasn't proceeding in the direction he'd planned, the King gave the command for the Stanley's to charge the area. To the King's shock, the Stanley's, after seeing the forces of the king, running for their lives, stood still. They did not join the fight. Neither did the Earl of Northumberland.

Did they see a possibility of the advantage going to the upstart across the battlefield?

"What is he thinking?" asked Durwin of Young George, excitedly pointing across the battlefield to the hill beyond. Henry's archers were standing to the rear of the fighting men, watching the progression of the battle, as the last line of defense in the historic clash. "Look at the King's standard. It's moving. It's moving toward the fighting men," noted Durwin.

The furious King had taken several of his personal guard, and riding his horse, he had headed down the hill towards the battle and into the fight on the end where Henry Tudor watched the battle.

Richard had decided he'd take matters into his own hands. He would kill Henry himself.

"Looks like the King wants to get this battle over with or get killed," Young George correctly deduced. "What's he up to? Where's Henry?"

"Young George," exclaimed Durwin, who stood a little taller than his cousin, "He's heading straight for Henry. Come on!"

The Tipton archers followed at Durwin's call, picking up swords or other weapons off the dead or pulling out knives from their belts. They cut and slashed their way toward Henry and his guard.

～

Realizing that Northumberland and the Stanley's were deserting his cause, Richard gambled everything and headed straight for Henry Tudor. He would end this fight once-and-for-all. He! He, the King of England!

Enraged, he thought as he rode down the hill, *I will kill this usurper of my throne, with my bare hands, if necessary, and the men who'd deserted me will be executed, along with their children, and those against me on this battlefield will die – every last one of them. No one will dare defy me, the rightly ordained King. No one!*

Seeing Henry alone and apart from the battle with his guard, Richard charged straight for his antagonist. This proved to be a bad mistake. With the rush of his charge, Richard got close, but some of the men in his personal retinue, who rode by his side, understanding at this moment they could overpower their hated King, joined in the fight against him. Richard, unhorsed, disappeared into the melee.

Realizing what was happening and risking all, the Stanley brothers and the Earl of Northumberland sent their troops into the fray, on the side of Henry. Their hatred knew no bounds. There was little resistance.

With his helmet and crown knocked from his head to the ground, Richard was hacked to death within a matter of a few minutes. In the fury of the battle, the age of chivalry was over as the victors disposed of the losers. The battle was finished and the crown acquired.

The Tiptons watched as Sir William Stanley placed the crown on the head of Henry Tudor, who was now King Henry VII. Another official coronation would take place later.

~

Young George rode up to his home at Bristol, leading the pack horse with his armour, sword, longbow, and supplies. The house was located close to the arrow and bolt works that he now operated.

All was quiet. Where was Lucia?

He quickly dismounted and went through the house. Food was on the table, and the back door was open. What had happened, or maybe he thought, *what was happening*?

He remounted his horse, leaving the pack horse standing outside his home under a tree, and rode quickly toward the shop on Bristol Bridge. Tying his horse's reins to the post at the door, he took the stairs two-at-a-time, arriving on the top step as a baby's cries rent the air.

Hurrying toward the sound, he was greeted by his father Laurence, coming from an open door. "Young George, you are the father of a healthy, very angry, little boy," he said, smiling.

"How's Lucia?" he asked.

"The first time isn't easy, but she's smiling. Why don't you go in and see for yourself?"

That's all Young George needed. He rushed through the door to greet his wife.

❧ **Chapter 10** ❧

Finish up of 15th Century
The Discovery of the New World Beginning of the 16th Century A.D.

The 1490's brought many significant and world changes around the earth, and these would soon affect the Tiptons, as England under the Tudors slipped from medievalism and feudalism into the renaissance and the reformation.

In 1492, King Ferdinand and Queen Isabella of Spain defeated the Moorish kingdom of Granada, bringing all of Spain under Christian rule. In the aura of this victory, they agreed to support the possibility of pioneering a western sea route to Cathay (China) which was proposed by a sailor from Genoa—Christopher Columbus. On October 12, of the same year, Columbus sailed to the Bahamas or somewhere close to there and claimed it for the Spanish Crown. After returning to Spain and basking in the glory of the find, he returned to the newly discovered islands several more times, and each time he added more territory for the Spanish.

In 1495, the future biblical scholar, William Tyndale, was born in Gloucester on the River Severn.

Also, in 1495, the Italian Giovanni Caboto or John Cabot arrived in Bristol and anchored on the River Avon.

Born in 1450, in Genoa (a year before Columbus), he worked for a Venetian merchant in the spice trade, sailing ships around the Mediterranean.

A year later, 1496, John Colet, an Oxford professor and the son of the Mayor of London, started reading the New Testament in Greek and translating it into English. He gave readings in English of the scriptures for countless multitudes of the public at the great St. Paul's Cathedral in London.

Translating from the Latin to English was totally banned by the Roman Catholic Church with beheading as the punishment. But Colet had friends in high places, probably more than one, so he managed to keep his head attached to his body. Colet was the friend of Thomas Linacre, physician to King Henry VII and his sons. Linacre was another Greek scholar from Oxford, who read the Bible in Greek.

~

"What is that?" asked Young George of his father Laurence. They stood looking at an unknown ship which resided at a wharf downriver from the Bristol Bridge. It was the new caravel model with several sails, one of the fastest ships on the water.

"All I know is that the captain is an Italian who's convinced King Henry, our liege Lord, to let him try to find a northern route to the Indies."

"Why would we want to do that?" asked Young George. "Columbus didn't find hordes of gold from what I've heard—nor spices, or silk cloth or ..."

Laurence held up his hand. "That's true, but I'm sure King Henry's thinking is that we're losing the race to find new lands to conquer or trade with, and

Spain's not exactly the country he's happy to stand aside and let win the contest."

"Is Spain our rival?"

"Everyone is our rival, it seems," his father said with a sigh and slight shake of the head. "Look, there's Cabot now, walking across the bridge. He's back from London."

Young George turned and saw an older man with a huge, white beard which bushed in front of his ears. It separated in the middle, running down to two points on his chest. A flat cap sat on top of his head and barely kept the sun out of his eyes. His dress was a tunic, swinging with each confident step, almost reaching the ground, and tied with a wide belt around the waist. A gold chain held a pendant with an image on the front. An imposing figure of a man, Cabot was too far away, for even the keen eyes of the former longbow archer at Bosworth, to tell what it represented.

"Do you think he got funding for his voyage in London?" he asked of his father, as he continued to watch the captain cross the stone walkway, obviously heading for his docked ship.

"Henry is not one to dole out money. He keeps a tight rein on his purse."

"Some people call him a miser."

Young George laughed. "Maybe he is, but we Tipton's aren't known for throwing our money around either, are we?"

"No. But, we will weigh a situation or outlay and support a firm investment, thinking our involvement is warranted for our shipping or business growth."

"That's very true. As far as Cabot, we'll soon find out. I know several merchants here in Bristol who have decided to support him. He's loaded his ship with goods for the voyage, even some from our store, and hired men to sail the *Matthew*. When he sails out of port, we'll be the first to know. They might find something this time, maybe HyBrazil itself."

Laurence was referring to voyages from Bristol to find the fabled island in the Atlantic where the wood of the brazil tree grew. This tree supposedly contained material from which an expensive red dye, Bristol Red, could be removed. After several attempts, the earlier sailors had never found the isle and abandoned the search.

Two mornings later, in the summer of 1497, the *Matthew* was gone. When Cabot returned, he'd discovered Labrador, Newfoundland, and South Carolina—but no passage to the Indies. The following year, he embarked on a second journey, and was never heard from again.

~

Ten-year-old Isaac Tipton, the youngest son of Young George Tipton, bounded down the stairs into the shop of his grandfather and father.

"Papa, will you take me fishing?" he asked, as George handed stocks of spices to Laurence, who stood on a ladder to reach the highest shelves in their very successful store.

Grandfather Laurence looked down at Young George and thought for a moment. He responded. "George, let's leave Lucia and my wife in charge of the store and go to Portishead fishing with Isaac. What do you think? Should we leave the women in charge?" He winked at Isaac.

"My sentiments exactly, father."

Laurence was always ready to go fishing and missed going since his father William had died. Their store was so successful, this left little time for former activities of enjoyment. "Do you want to tell the ladies, or do you intend for me to accomplish this feat?"

"I'll do it," piped up Isaac, already heading for the stairs, realizing the answer to his question was a yes.

"You'd better go," Laurence said, looking at his grandson's disappearing back. "You can keep up with him, I can't. I'll call for the buggy to be ready. Why don't we stay overnight? We can visit with Harold and Hugh. It's been some time since we've seen them both."

"Good idea. I'll inform the ladies and ask them to pack for us accordingly." With that, Young George followed his son up the steps.

In 1500, the trip to Portishead was accomplished in record time, with roads much improved over the years. Looking at the Severn Estuary, from above on the edge of the Downs, was always an awe-inspiring sight. On a curve, before the last descent, Young George stopped the buggy just so the three could take in the vista. "Look at that view."

"Isaac, don't ever forget to come back here when troubles overcome you. Somehow, they fade in the vastness of the space you see there in the distance, where the world stretches on and on in quietude and peacefulness. Will you remember that?" William asked his grandson.

"Sure, grandpapa." Isaac, sitting between the other two men, was solemn as he nodded his head.

The three sat for a minute in quiet aloneness until Isaac asked, "Will we get to board one of the big ships and look around?"

Young George laughed, "I'm sure Harold will be glad to make that wish come true—right Father?"

"Yes. But, let's leave the buggy with them and catch some fish for our supper. Late afternoon or early morning is a good time to get a string full, and we can clean them and get Harold's wife to fry them for our evening meal."

"Good idea, father. We can talk after we eat."

～

On arrival, the men, including Harold and his son's Paul and Andrew, got into a large row boat and headed for a secluded spot, a place north of the sluggish mouth of the Avon.

"There's a small stream running into the estuary. Paul, Andrew, and I often come here when the work for the day is over."

Isaac sat in front, facing backward, waving his arms as if flying like the squawking sea gulls, they disturbed in the shallows on the bank of the estuary.

They entered the brook and rowed east against the current, until they rounded a bend in the clearer water. Paul climbed out of the boat, pulled it up to the bank, and tied it to a tree.

Paul looked at Isaac as he helped him onto the shore, "Maybe we'll catch so many fish the boat will be overloaded as we go back."

"Will we sink?" asked Isaac, a frightened look on his normally sunshiny face.

Grandpapa Laurence assured Isaac, "We'll stop before we haul in that many. Come on. I'll carry your pole."

The six spread out down the bank, putting worms on their hooks and throwing them into the water. Then they settled down to the slow pace of fishing—some sitting and some standing at the stream's edge. The place was under the shadow of trees from a distant limestone cliff where peregrine falcons, soaring on the uplifting warmer air, cried their happiness at the earth below, checking out their next meal of a pigeon, gull, or mouse.

As they relaxed in the serenity of the outdoors, doing what man had done for centuries, Young George managed to get close to Harold. There was a question he wanted to ask his cousin.

"How do you think our King is doing?" He knew Harold had contacts in London and other shipping ports in England and overseas. He often heard things no one else had ears to hear.

Young George was interested, because fifteen years had passed since he was there when Henry Tudor was crowned on the field at Bosworth after King Richard III was killed. The Tiptons had backed King Henry, and he wanted to know if this had been a mistake.

"He's continued the policy of dynastic execution, especially against those who fought him at Bosworth, although he tends to show mercy at times, for the price of gold, of course. His first act after becoming King was to marry into his antagonist's family. Elizabeth of York was the perfect choice and virtually guarantees no more civil war between the Lancaster and the York dynasties, at least for now." Harold pulled in his line.

"My father says his claim to the throne was flimsy at best and based on his mother's descent from John of Gaunt, brother of King Edward III."

"That's another story, best not spoken of to those you do not know well," said Harold, putting an additional worm on his line and casting it back into the water.

"Papa, look. I've caught a fish."

Young George and Harold turned to look, as Isaac held up his fishing pole. On his line, a wriggling captive was trying to get off his hook. Grandpapa Laurence was trying desperately to grab the line and wound up chasing the fish up the bank, as his grandson sent it flying through the air.

"Very good, son. Now, catch another one." George turned back to Harold and continued their conversation.

"So, cousin, what's the real story behind the rebellion of Henry Stafford, the Duke of Buckingham? I've always wondered. Was he on Henry's side or as others have said fighting for his own interests?"

"This is what I heard. When the opportunity came for Richard to seize the throne, Stafford backed him and even helped him take possession of the former King's two small sons. Two months later, Stafford changed his mind."

"What happened?"

"We never heard exactly what happened, but there was a big row over something the two men disagreed about. After that, Stafford and Richard were distant enemies. There was always the thought in the back of Stafford's mind, that insecure King Richard, who was trying to remove or get rid of anyone with a claim to the throne, might include him on the list to be eliminated. Stafford had as much right to the throne as Richard—certainly more than our present King. Henry became our monarch through military victory, not necessarily by ancestry some claim."

"Wasn't King Henry included in the rebellion in some way?"

"Yes. When Stafford was sure of the particulars of his attempt to overthrow Richard, he sent a letter to Henry in France, giving him the date the rebellion would start, and asking him to bring his French mercenaries. Henry set out for Wales, but the weather in the English Channel was bad. He had to turn back to Brittany, where he was residing.

"That storm caused the River Severn to flood. Much of Stafford's army deserted him on the march to fight the King, and he was betrayed by one of his followers, convicted of treason, and beheaded at Salisbury in November. I think the year was 1483."

"Papa, I've another fish." The fish was flying through the air like the last one.

Laughing, Laurence called to Harold and George, while holding up their string of several wiggling captives. "You're going to need to get fishing and stop talking," he suggested.

Young George and Harold waved at his comments and finished their conversation.

"As far as our King," Harold continued. "We could do worse. Even though we pay more in taxes, he's got a better collection system, and I understand his coffers are filling up with the revenue from being a better steward of English money."

"Harold, I didn't see Hugh at Portishead."

"No, we sent him and his young children to London to facilitate our offices there. He has friends in high places who could be of benefit to us. It's a good move for our continental business. Did you know his wife died?"

"No. The Pestilence?"

"Yes. After that, he felt the change of scenery would be good for both himself and the children."

"Oops, I think I've got a fish." Laurence pulled in a big one and held it up for Isaac to see.

∾

By the 16th century, the English people had begun to recover from the first scourge of the Pestilence, although the plague did continue to ravage the country and the known world at times, but not with quite as much fury. In England, the population had enlarged, and there were more mouths to feed, which meant a demand for more of everything—food, clothes, housing, and work.

The shipping industry increased in export and import of goods, and the Tipton's wealth expanded along with this explosion of commerce, industry, and manufacturing.

Some of the Tipton family were sent to famous schools throughout the country to study law, some business practices, and some were experts on international trade. They were soon to be classed as "gentlemen, because of their intellectual ability and wealth."

As one writer of the 1600's put it, those who could *"live without manual labor, and thereto is able and will bear the port, charge and countenance of a gentleman,"* could *"for money have a coat and arms bestowed upon him by heralds…and [be] reputed for a gentleman ever after."* The Tipton family could buy and sport their own coat-of-arms.

For centuries, the Bristol Bridge, earlier known as the Anglo-Saxon, Brycgstow (bridge-place) was the only crossing of the River Avon for many miles, causing a major amount of traffic on its wooden surface. Realizing the need for a crossing which could stand heavier loads, a stone bridge was built with stores and houses atop. These merchant structures were along each side of the span. The successful Tipton store on the bridge was viewed and visited by an endless stream of onlookers and purchasers.

The industry of the region changed also.

Hides were tanned along the Severn and Avon and then used in the manufacturing of leather goods in the river towns. Instead of sending metal ore abroad, it was smelted and cast at home, and no longer was wool sent to the continent to be processed, dyed, and finished. Equipment was purchased, and it was treated and handled in the Midlands and elsewhere.

Through the guilds, the Merchant Adventurers controlled shipping from the ports of England, including Bristol. The finished goods were sold by the piece or made into clothes and purchased at the market place. The Tipton family, as long-time members of the Guild, maintained a small office in Ireland. They expanded their operations in Waterford, London, and the continent.

ЭС Chapter 11 ЭС

The 16th Century
The Reformers, Henry VIII, Hugh Tipton

The Reformation, one could say, started a little before 1415 with the Lollards, and the dissident priest and professor at Oxford, John Wycliffe, who translated the Bible into English from Latin. This was strictly forbidden by the Catholic Church—who controlled most of Western Europe in ecclesiastical matters. Wycliffe denounced the Churches growing wealth through indulgences. His translation, which was handwritten with limited copies, would soon mean a decree of death for anyone caught possessing or reading one.

The Reformation continued with John Hus or Husinec (translated Goosetown, and abbreviated to Goose), who studied Wycliffe's writings. The writings were causing a stir on the European continent, especially in Bohemian Prague, where Hus preached at Bethlehem Chapel, to three thousand people in their native language, not Latin.

Like Wycliffe, he preached against indulgences. He said, *"When the Lord gave me knowledge of Scriptures, I discharged that kind of stupidity from my foolish mind."* Asked to recant, he refused. In 1415, he was burned at the stake for his stance, and while the flames leaped around him, he was heard to be praying and repeating the Psalms.

In 1453, the fall of Constantinople, with its three defensive walls, to the Ottoman blockade and Sultan Mehmed, virtually ensured the continuing advance into the western countries of the languages familiar to the Greeks and Hebrews. As the scholars fled the collapsing city, they spread into the western city-states and other developing countries, taking with them the original classics in Greek and the Hebrew Bible.

From Germany came a man named Reuchlin, a renowned classic Greek and Hebrew scholar, and teacher who published a Hebrew grammar in 1506. Reuchlin was not shy. This caused him to be much battered by the learned of the day. His stance on Jewish teachings and other subjects of the Catholic Church did not help.

His grammar came into the hands of Martin Luther, who used it as a help to translate the Latin Bible into German. Although, some of Reuchlin's teachings, Luther he did not agree with.

When Reuchlin heard of the Lutheran papers and held a copy in his hands, he was heard to exclaim, "Thanks be to God, at last they have found a man who will give them so much to do, that they will be compelled to let my old age end in peace."

The stage was being set for the greatest return to Biblical Christian teaching since the Catholic Church commandeered the Bible.

～

The Reformation continued in England under Henry VII with English Renaissance scholars learning to become proficient in Greek and Latin—reading Greek classical literature and other ancient works. This soon transitioned to the Scriptures.

Upon comparing the Greek Scriptures, to the Catholic Church's translation in Latin, the learned men Thomas Linacre and John Colet realized the difference in the wording.

Linacre, a physician to Henry VII and VIII, once said, *"Either this is not the gospel* (the original Greek), *or we are not Christians."* Once these men and others started the fires of learning the truth, nothing would stop others from doing the same.

Enter this scene Martin Luther. Living in a monastery in Whittenburg, Germany, he was haunted by his insecurities concerning his salvation. Throwing himself into the monastic life did not solve his problem. It took a mentor, who told him to focus on Christ alone to find his answer.

After he obtained his doctorate at Whittenburg University, he began to teach the Psalms and Paul's epistle to the Romans. The Word enlightened Luther's mind. He understood for the first time that righteousness is a gift of God's grace. It couldn't be bought or sold or worked out within the Church. For himself, he had discovered the gift of salvation in the doctrine of justification by grace alone.

This doctrine was not new. This Word became flesh with the birth and death of a perfect man, Christ on the cross. The discovery set him afire, as he reflected on the cross and Jesus' sufferings. He accepted that salvation was through grace and faith in Jesus' promise of eternal life.

Martin Luther affectionately referred to Hus as the *"goose who had been cooked for defying the Pope,"* It's possible he was thinking about being cooked in the same manner, when he tacked his 95 theses to the wooden door of the Wittenberg Church in Germany. Luther's stance wasn't popular with the papal hierarchy either, but as Hus did, he refused to recant. Luther strenuously objected to the corrupt Roman Catholic practice of selling indulgences and believed in only two sacraments—The Lord's Supper and Baptism. Although he was excommunicated from the Catholic Church, he continued to speak and write in Wittenberg. He was never cooked for defying the Pope.

With the start of the Reformation and the Renaissance as a backdrop, Henry VII died in 1509. He left his second son, Henry VIII, a secure throne and full coffers. At eighteen, the young Henry was handsome, athletic, and a spendthrift. Lacking the miserly ways of his father, the young man quickly drained the treasury of the crown, which his father had painstakingly amassed.

In 1517, eight years after Henry VIII became King, Martin Luther tacked his 95 theses to the door of the Wittenberg Church. At first, this only enraged Henry VIII, who railed against this heretic of his church. Sometime later, he started a defense of the Catholic Church's sacraments. Who, better than the King, to refute this common priest's claims?

Discussing his thoughts with Cardinal Wolsey, who was appointed by the Pope and who became the King's confidant and right-hand man, he wrote for months his objection to Luther's ideas, making sure every detail was correct according to the Catholic Church's teaching.

A light rain, driven by the wind, pinged against the windows of the Palace of Placentia at Greenwich in

London. King Henry had padded around the room for several minutes, his hand stroking the beard on his chin. He was thinking. He went to a window and threw it open, disregarding the mist falling on the stone floor. The rush of cool, moist air felt good on his flushed face. The fire, burning in the fireplace, flickered briefly at the movement of the air within the room.

Through the late afternoon's foggy haze, he looked across the expanse of clipped grass and over the gardens he'd walked among in the morning. This was the palace where he was born and where he felt most at home. It had everything he needed — a place to hunt, entertain, and play tennis with his nobles and family. He held court in the Great Hall on the raised dais of his father's making, and went to chapel in a small building across the courtyard, where he heard Mass and took Communion. The guest rooms were always filled to capacity with the most influential and wealthy persons in England — many of them his relatives.

For most of today, he'd sat at peace in this room, writing in his bedchamber. His clothing consisted of a loose shirt with looser sleeves and knee breeches. He shut the window and, turning toward the open door to his royal rooms, he called, "Lord Chamberlain."

Isaac Tipton got up from his chair in the hall and came immediately into the King's bedchamber.

Henry looked at him. "Who are you?" he demanded.

"Isaac, Sire. The Lord Chamberlain went to his rooms, as he was sick." Isaac thought it was amazing. The King didn't know his name after the time he'd been at the palace and even in this very room today, keeping the fire going, and straightening up after his majesty.

"Where's his assistant?" demanded Henry.

"Sick also, Sire."

"Is there something going around that they're both sick?" Henry quickly held up his hand, meaning he didn't need an answer. "Today, you are the Chamberlain," he commanded.

"Yes, Sire," responded Isaac with a bow.

"Go and find Cardinal Wolsey. Bring him to me immediately."

"Yes, Sire, immediately."

Isaac turned and grinned at the word Chamberlain. He'd just been promoted, and the current Lord Chamberlain would not be happy at that. He hurried out of the King's bedchamber and almost bowled over the Master of the Wardrobe, whose arms and hands were filled with the King's clothing to be replaced in his closet.

"Isaac, what on earth is wrong with you? Watch where you're going," the irritated man exclaimed, rearranging some of the clothes which had almost fallen from his arm.

"Sorry, sir. I'm on the King's business. He wants Cardinal Wolsey immediately."

"Shouldn't you inform the Lord Chamberlain and let him take care of the Cardinal?"

"I would if he were available, but he's sick in bed, and I don't think I want to disturb him."

"And the Valet de Chambres, where is he? Are they both sick?"

"Yes, sir."

"Don't let me detain you then. You'd better hurry. His Majesty has not been in a good mood today." The man turned and watched Isaac as the young man hurried down the long corridor, calling after him. "Better check the chapel here first, and if he isn't there, you'll need to take a carriage to Fulham Palace."

No one was in the chapel or the attached vestry. Both were completely deserted. Isaac knew Fulham Palace was where the Cardinal lived and had his official offices. He hurried to the stables. Normally, there were several men working, cleaning the stalls, and grooming the horses. He only saw one man. Walking quickly to the groomer, he ordered a carriage and horses from the Marshal's assistant.

"Who are you to order a carriage and horses?" demanded the groomer, who carried two buckets, which were full of feed for the royal steeds. He stood looking Isaac up-and-down.

"I'm the King's Chamberlain," stated Isaac— tongue-in-cheek, not using the word Lord and realizing he wasn't dressed like his superior, although he was trying to put on the man's self-important air.

"Aren't you a little young?" complained the man, but he'd put down the buckets and was heading for harness and horses.

Isaac decided not to answer. He stood his ground and waited on his conveyance just as he'd seen the real Lord Chamberlain do. "Is there no one to drive me?" he asked, when the man returned after what seemed like an hour, leading the team and hooked-up carriage. In the back of his mind, the image of Henry pacing up and down appeared.

"Not today, at least not now. You'll need to do the driving yourself. I have orders to stay here."

Isaac drew in his breath and let it out in a rush. Nodding at the man, he mounted the carriage steps and flicked the reins. He could handle the trip. He and his father often took trips around Bristol with Isaac driving the team of horses.

The trip from southeast London would take several minutes—more time than he had, after the delay in hitching up the horses. He would go to the London Bridge, cross to the north, and then west to Fulham Castle. The route was through the heart of busy London.

Isaac could have gone by boat on the Thames River and avoided the London traffic, noise, and smells. The King, his family and nobles often took boat rides to visit places within the city. Returning to the castle steps, they disembarked at the gate nearest the water, and walked into the building's interior.

Cardinal Wolsey did not appreciate being called from his afternoon nap. He had dined on duck, carrots, and rice. Meticulously picking the meat from the fowl's bones, he'd eaten every morsel, and now his digestion was disturbed. With a lace handkerchief to his nose, he didn't appreciate the furious journey through the foul-smelling London streets and the jerking carriage which dodged horses and pedestrians, which by his looks was being driven by a lout.

At the palace, he walked stiffly on small feet, with his Cardinal's robes swishing just above the stone walkway to the King's rooms. Overweight, he was panting by the time he came to the open doorway, where the King was growing more impatient.

Isaac rushed into the room to announce his presence. Standing just inside the door, he said, "Sire, the Cardinal is here to see you."

Henry looked up at his self-appointed Chamberlain and said sternly, "Send him in."

Isaac went to the corridor. "The King is ready to see you. Please go in."

After the Cardinal disappeared inside the room, Isaac breathed a sigh of relief and resumed his seat by the door. He could hear the conversation inside the room.

Indicating a notebook of papers which lay on his desk, Henry said, "Lord Chancellor, the defense of the seven sacraments is finished. See that it gets published, sent to every Catholic Church in England, and that Pope Leo, the Tenth, gets a copy." Henry picked up the stack and handed it to Wolsey.

Some said the Cardinal was Henry's *alter rex*, with as much political power as the King. He *was* a master manipulator in getting his way, and Henry's commands he always executed in a prompt manner. He was the most powerful churchman in England and the major power behind the King's throne. No one challenged the Cardinal, for he was also Lord Chancellor. The Cardinal did not disobey Henry. He did give advice when asked for his consul.

Now he gave a slight duck of the head. "Sire, I'll see that it's done. The Pope should be especially satisfied with your defense of the sacraments. And I've more news. Reports of another burning of hundreds of

Luther's books and writings came today in letters from our Cardinals in Flanders and Antwerp."

"Glad to hear of that. Is the investigation of the present Duke of Buckingham continuing? We haven't talked of him lately."

"Yes, Sire. Our spies are everywhere. I should have information on my return from York."

Henry was nodding in response to Wolsey's words, as he started to pace around the room. "I will expect a full report when you return. Do you leave in the morning?"

"After the noonday meal, unless you need me to do something."

"No, I think I'll be playing tennis and enjoying some hunting until you return. England's return to warm weather has me wanting to get outside the castle and enjoy the spring sunshine. Go in peace." Henry dismissed the man with a wave of his hand. "Wolsey," he called before the Cardinal could go out the door.

The pudgy man turned to receive the King's words. "Yes, Sire?"

"I dedicated the paper to the Pope."

Cardinal Wolsey nodded his head and said, "I see. I'll make sure that His Holiness takes note of your words." With that, Wolsey disappeared through the door, passed Isaac, and walked stiffly down the hall.

In the carriage, which with a proper driver would take him back to Fulham Castle, he leafed through the papers defending the sacraments. It was signed in bold handwriting,

Henry the VIII, by the Grace of God, King of England and France and Lord of Ireland.

Nowhere was the Cardinal's name mentioned, although he'd done much of the research and made suggestions. The man leaned his head back to the carriage's side, lost in his own thoughts, and took a brief nap on the drive home. He didn't put the lacy handkerchief to his nose.

～

Twenty-two-year-old Isaac Tipton stood courtside, holding a towel, as King Henry VIII played tennis with three of his nobles. The constant movement and whacks at the ball were interspersed with loud comments coming from the players.

"Tenez," yelled Henry, showing his muscles and dexterity, as he returned a ball across the net to the other two opponents. *Tenez* meant here it comes or watch your head, because the ball was hard and would hurt if it hit your body.

"Henry's in rare form this morning," Isaac whispered to the Duke of Buckingham's assistant, William Tipton, who stood with Sir Edward Stafford's towel.

"Yes," said William, with the towel held up to cover his mouth, trying to keep his talking from being known. "I've noticed the court's ladies-in-waiting, who are observing the match, twittering behind the nets alongside the court, and pointing out his physical qualities. He does cut a figure in his flowing, white silk shirt and shiny knee britches."

"Ouch," yelled one of the King's opponents, as his royal highness scored a direct hit and the ball hit his opponent's hip. The man limped a few steps before continuing.

"Sir John, you're going to have to move faster than that," observed Henry, laughing as the man continued to hobble while moving to return the ball.

"I've been thinking," said the King as he continued to go after balls coming his way. "I should invite Francois, the King of France, to a royal match. We could sell tickets and bet on who'll win."

"That's not a bad idea," said Edward Stafford, who was Henry's partner, grunting as he jumped to return a serve from Sir John, who was showing his temper, which Henry took pleasure in stirring up.

When the game was over, Henry walked off the court in long strides without comment, heading for the entrance of the enclosed playing area. He was followed by Isaac, practically running with the towel, and an assembly of other court officials and tennis observers. Henry nodded as he grasped the cotton square which was offered to him, and kept walking across the green, sculpted lawn, toward his rooms at the Palace of Placentia. He wiped his arms and face as he walked, and then he threw the towel to Isaac.

Edward Stafford caught up with him. "My Lord, will the Cardinal play tennis with us tomorrow?" he asked. Edward had felt a change in Henry's attitude towards him. He didn't know why.

"Yes. Wolsey will be returning from York today with news of the area. I'm sure he'll be ready to play." Although Henry had begun to suspect the Duke's allegiance to the crown, he was a good tennis player, and the King of England enjoyed a hard game and liked to win. When Wolsey came home, he'd be Henry's partner, and Stafford would be an opposing player. The King liked to play with, and also play against the best.

～

The hierarchy at the Palace of Placentia made many bedfellows of the attendants. Even though the tension concerning the Duke of Buckingham was escalating, the two Tiptons had become close friends, supporting each other when difficulties arose. King Henry's vast palace was filled with intrigue and reports of women in the King's bed chamber.

With his father's approval, Henry had married the widow of his deceased sixteen-year-old brother, Arthur. By her, he'd sired several children. The match with his older sister-in-law was made to produce an heir, with no love lost in the process. Although Catherine of Aragon gave him several children, none of the males survived from infancy. The only female to survive was his daughter, Mary.

Not wishing for a woman to inherit the throne, he soon started thinking about getting rid of his Catholic wife. She had become barren, and he needed a son and heir to the kingdom, for he had decided no woman would sit on the throne.

The Pope had given permission for him to marry Catherine, since marrying a brother's wife was strongly opposed by the Catholic Church. Now, he needed an annulment or another special dissolution by the Pope in Rome. How hard would that be? After all, he was the King of England, and he had supported the Church against its enemies.

He was thirty-one. Time was becoming important, and although he hoped not, disposing of her might prove to be harder than he imagined.

~

As Isaac Tipton had explained to his distant cousin, William, "Henry needs a male heir. His daughter, Princess Mary, will not do as the future queen, and his present wife is too old to have other children. So, he actively seeks a young, fruitful woman to fulfill his need of a son."

"He certainly found one in Mary Boleyn, but she's married."

"There were rumours about her before she came to England. I pity her poor husband." The two were rushing behind the two men talking in front of them. "I hear Mistress Mary's sister, Anne, will be coming from France to join her soon, as Maid-in-Waiting to the King's wife."

William had an answer to his friend's comment. "This morning, I heard Sir Edward say she was already here. I'm going to go, Isaac. I see Lord Stafford's servant motioning for me."

"Will you be around for a few days?"

"For tomorrow anyway, so they can play more tennis."

"I'll see you then." Isaac hurried to the kitchen. There was just enough time to eat and rest, before helping the Chamberlain put Henry to bed. Another reason to rush might be his hope of an accidental meeting with Eleanor, a maid in the chambers of Mary Boleyn. When he got to the kitchen, she was nowhere to be seen. He sat down at one of the tables, ate his food, and went to King Henry's rooms. The Lord Chamberlain nor the King had arrived, so he put his aching feet up on a stool in Henry's closet and went promptly to sleep.

~

Isaac had been recommended for the position by Hugh Tipton, who ran the Tipton shipping business in London on the River Thames.

Hugh had fled Tipton on the Tame, when he and his family were threatened by Three Fingers and Sir Weldon Haywood. He ended up in Portishead, helping his cousin Harold, who eventually sent him and his children to London after his wife died.

When the Marshall of the Palace of Placentia, who was Hugh's good friend, had asked if he knew someone, who was both trustworthy and discrete, Hugh had said, "Let me send a letter. There may be a Tipton for the position." Whereupon, Hugh had sent a letter to Young George, in Bristol, asking if Isaac might want the job.

Of course, Isaac, who was around twenty at that time, thought this was just the lark he needed. He soon found out that all that glitters is not gold, and living as a servant in the King's employ was not easy. Especially since you were on call day and night.

He'd toughed it out, and as he wrote his mother, *"You'll be surprised, because I actually get up by myself in the morning. No one has to pull me out of bed."* There had been a few exceptions to this, like when he became sick with a fever.

His thoughts turned to William. Unlike his master, Sir Edward Stafford, who was from Wales, William was born in Gloucester, on the Severn River and knew Isaac's Tipton cousins who lived there. William was his best friend at court, where they shared their thoughts and dreams.

After the tennis match, Henry stomped around his rooms at the Palace of Placentia. Even playing and winning at tennis couldn't keep his mind off the problems at hand. And there was more than one. Catherine had lost their last child, a son, and now he wanted another wife, one who could bear him a son. He was tired of trying with her. That was his conundrum in 1519, and he was intent on solving it.

Then, there was the matter of loyalty. There were nasty rumours floating around about the Earl of Stafford, Edward, the 3rd Duke of Buckingham and Sir Ralph of Staffordshire's descendent. Was he interested in the throne? His father, the 2nd Duke of Buckingham was executed for treason after the failed Buckingham Rebellion against the hated King Richard III. Would Edward turn out the same way? Wolsey had cautioned the King more than once not to trust the man. He awaited the Cardinal's report to determine the man's fate and expected the account tomorrow on the churchman's delayed return from York. As usual, justice would be swift in Henry's court.

The tennis match, Isaac and William had expected the next day never happened. Sir Edward was arrested and accused of listening to prophecies of the King's death and intending to kill the King. He was tried by his peers and taken to Tower Hill. In May, Sir Edward Stafford was executed on trumped up charges of treason. The Cardinal gloated. He had managed to rid himself of one man he despised. There were others on his list.

Henry said calmly, after hearing the deed was done, "Like father, like son."

❧ Chapter 12 ❧

The 16th Century
Tyndale, The Holy Bible in English, A Visit Home

No one knows the exact birthdate of William Tyndale. His ancestral family came from Northumberland just south of the Scottish border. They moved to East Anglia and then to Gloucestershire on the Severn, where he grew up. He studied at Oxford. In 1515, he received his Bachelor of Arts and Master's degrees. His Master's degree allowed him to go to Cambridge, where he studied theology. He wanted to study the Holy Scriptures, which he could have done immediately in Greek and Hebrew. His comment concerning this part of his education was thus:

"They have ordained that no man shall look on the Scripture, until he be noselled (nursed or trained) *in heathen learning eight or nine years and armed with false principles, with which he is clean shut out of the understanding of the Scripture."*

After leaving Cambridge in 1521, Tyndale became the chaplain and live-in tutor for Sir John Walsh's children at the manor called the House on Little Sodbury in Gloucestershire. He went as an ordained priest.

Since the children were small, his teaching position gave him ample time to proceed with independent

studies in the Scriptures. He'd read all the writings he could get his hands on of Wycliffe, Desiderius Erasmus— who made the Greek New Testament available on the continent in 1453 and at Cambridge—and studied Martin Luther's papers. When he delved into Hebrew texts, he began to realize the appalling untruths of the Catholic Church's teaching. To stand against this religious hierarchy meant death, which others like Hus had found out.

The Walshes, being of the nobility in Gloucestershire, hosted many Catholic Abbots and Priors from the area. They were often invited to dine at the manor. Many times, Tyndale was seated at the afternoon meal with Sir John Walsh, taking meat with these churchmen and interacting with them. He noticed that a lot of them, even though they could read Latin, the language of the Catholic Church, did not know very much about the Bible.

Because William was asking questions, it was obviously making them uncomfortable. Not only were they ill at ease, but he was upset that they were able to read the Bible, which they did not take seriously, while the common people, who wanted to read the Bible, couldn't because of the language.

When the discussion became more heated, the Prior to his side whispered, "Better to forget God's laws and follow the Pope's laws."

Tyndale raised his eyebrows and turned to look at the speaker with a shocked face. He replied, *"I defy the Pope, and all his laws; and if God spares my life, ere many years, I will cause the boy that driveth the plow to know more of the Scriptures than thou dost!"*

Tyndale got up and strode quickly out of the room. Later, looking out of the upstairs window at the moon and the stars in the night sky, and watching the ornate carriages of the churchmen as they left, he murmured, "For if God be on my side, what matter it, who be against me, be they bishops, cardinals, popes, or whatsoever names they will?"

He stood for a few more minutes, until the sound of the departing religious men diminished in the distance, and then he closed the window, striding into the room with determination in his steps. He talked to the room again, "Lord, give me the strength to do what thou hath commanded me."

The statement he'd made to his dinner partner got him into trouble with the chancellor of the Diocese of Worcester, John Bell. But the charges against him were dropped. This particular area of the western midlands was more open to Tyndale's arguments on the Catholic Church, because of similar statements made by John Wycliffe's followers, the Lollards. They had brought his Bible to Worcester, reading and teaching from it in secret for several years.

The Bible was originally written in Hebrew, Aramaic, and Greek. Tyndale now had two of the languages he could use to translate God's Word into English—both he knew very well. By lamplight, he started his task.

Isaac managed to go home one summer to Bristol. His grandfather and grandmother were gone and buried at All Saint's Church. He and his aging father Young George walked around the graveyard, looking at their family headstones. The latest one was his mother, the grass not fully grown back over the disturbed ground.

"I wish I'd been here," Isaac nodded at his father.

"You're here now."

Suddenly the church bells rang. Young George jumped at the sound, clutching his son's arm.

"Wonder what's going on?" asked Isaac.

Out popped a bride and groom, with people streaming from the church behind them. They left in a horse drawn carriage to the cheers and laughter of those standing by the roadside.

"Life goes on." Young George gave a heavy sigh and a perceptible nod of his head with a slight knowing grin.

Isaac and his father headed back to Bristol Bridge.

The Tiptons on Bristol Bridge had saved their money, and Young George no longer had to work seven days a week, or all day for that matter. When he wanted to, he closed the store and went fishing or walking on the pathways beside the River Avon. Now, he walked alone. His family was spread up and down the River's Avon and Severn.

"Isaac," he said.

"Yes, father?"

"What do you think about me selling our house here on the bridge and moving to London? We could room together. Or, Hugh Tipton is getting old, and he might need some company. Like me, all of his children are grown and living in different areas of England."

"Are you lonely, Father?"

"It is awfully quiet after Mam died." George admitted, using the name for his wife that the children had used. "There might be enough money for you to quit at the Palace of Placentia, and we could travel and see the area where Tybba lived and ride a boat on the

River Tame and River Trent. I've always wanted to do this after reading the Ancestry Book."

"We could go to Oswestry and see Offa's Wall and Tettenhall where Meta received Aethelflaed's sword." Taking some time away from Court and its intrigues sounded good to Isaac. He was tired of the uneasy atmosphere and frenetic pace at the Palace.

"What do you think?"

"I think we've got a plan," said Isaac, realizing this meant leaving Eleanor, who was starting to be important to him. "I'll look into it when I return to Hampton Court."

The two were standing in front of the Tipton business, reluctant to go inside. Although the store was stocked with all the items as before, the place just wasn't the same. Two chairs sat in front of the store's windows on the stone bridge.

"Let's sit awhile," Isaac suggested.

When they were comfortably seated, Young George continued, "I heard about Sir Edward Stafford. The word I hear is there was no evidence that he was planning anything against Henry."

"I thought so, also, and William and I said as much to each other. But I didn't dare open my mouth to anyone else."

"I talked to William Tipton."

"Yes?" Isaac looked quickly at his father. This was the first he'd heard of his friend since the Duke had been executed. Everyone associated with Stafford had immediately left London and scattered in all directions. "How is he?"

"Since he was directly under the Steward of Thornbury Castle in Gloucestershire, and a confidant of both the Duke and the Steward, he knew the happenings at the castle."

"Yes, I know. We were great friends at The Palace of Placentia and Hampton Court, when the King stayed there as a guest of the Cardinal."

"Did you know William came to me and asked for help?"

"No, I haven't seen him since the Duke was executed. He disappeared."

"After the Duke was arrested, William feared for his life, as I'm sure most of Buckingham's acquaintances and staff did. He hurried here, because you were his friend, and he knew I would befriend him. I never asked our relative about the Duke's intentions. Was securing the throne for himself the Duke's aim, only in the back of his mind, or not even thought of? But we'll never know, will we?"

Isaac didn't answer his father's question. Instead he asked another, "What happened to William?"

"He stayed with me for several days. When things settled down, he returned to work with Edward Stafford's son, Henry. I never heard from him after that. I hope he's all right."

"The Staffords won't be back in court. Not while Henry is King."

〜

"Isaac, are you ready to leave?"

"Oh, Poppa. I've come home to rest and relax," called Isaac. "Why? Why?" But Isaac appeared in the doorway ready to go to church, a big smile on his face.

George led the way off Bristol Bridge toward All Saints Church. Then he made a detour, heading straight west.

"Where are we going, Poppa?" asked Isaac, knowing this wasn't the route they should be taking.

"I wanted to check something out. There's a rumour of a new priest who gives a message outside of Bristol Cathedral after the regular services. The talk is he follows Wycliffe's and Luther's teachings in his presentation. I wanted to hear what he says. Then we'll walk to The Hatchet on the quay and eat our noon meal before going home."

Isaac looked puzzled. "Why doesn't he lead the service inside the cathedral?"

George shook his head. "The Catholic Church wouldn't approve."

"I've heard of rumblings in the Court, but don't know the particulars. I know that Cardinal Wolsey has had Luther's writings burnt, and the King has published a book denouncing Luther's writing. In fact, before I left, the Pope declared Henry a 'Defender of the Faith', and with pride, he's added it to his official title."

"What does his title look like now?" George asked.

Isaac gave a chuckle and responded, *"Henry VIII, by the Grace of God, King of England and France, Defender of the Faith, and Lord of Ireland."*

"That's a mouthful," exclaimed George, narrowly avoiding a loose cobblestone in the path. "Since you mention Ireland, is something different going on there? I've heard rumours, and the Tipton branch located at Waterford says there's military buildup around Dublin. Is that true?"

"No, not from England. The Pale, those four counties around Dublin, are ruled by Irish nobles. Maybe they have a reason for an army. The rest of

Ireland, including Waterford, is under the Lordship of Henry. I think the King's only concern is that the Spanish will get a foothold somewhere on the isle and use it to invade England. I heard him say this is not likely, because he's increasing the naval boats in the area."

"That's good to know. I'll let the Tiptons at Portishead in on your information."

"If you leave here, who will run the Bristol end of the Tipton boating empire?"

"I have no doubt someone will step up. Maybe Paul or Andrew. You did know their father, Harold, is dead." Young George nodded and continued. "We're here. Let's go in to the services. We'll stand close to the back and listen for Tyndale to come."

Listening to Tyndale, standing outside the Bristol Cathedral, was the first time Isaac had heard the true message of Jesus and his cross, but it wouldn't be the last time. And the next one would come from the most unlikely source.

~

Tyndale stayed with the Walsh family for two years. His dedication to translating the Holy Scriptures into English from the original Greek and Hebrew did not lessen, but he realized he needed to be wholly devoted to the process to make significant progress. Working at night by candlelight or lamplight tired him out and wasn't fair to his young charges.

Hearing through the church hierarchy, about the new Bishop of London's former assistance to Desiderius Erasmus in translating the Bible into Greek, he decided to visit this patriarch of the church. He needed the blessing of this man to continue, especially if he remained in England. Tyndale quit his tutoring job with the Walshes and headed for London.

～

"Please be seated," said the priest in his long robes, returning through a heavy, wooden door at the back of the vaulted room in Fulham Palace, where resided the offices of the Catholic Church in London. "The Bishop of London will see you shortly." The man stopped at an ornate, gilded table outside the inner rooms and ruffled papers on his desk.

The couch, which the priest indicated, was of a beautiful scarlet and gold satin stripe and obviously very expensive. In fact, the whole room was one of opulence—pictures in gold-gilded frames and side chairs with gilt colored arms. Fresh flowers in vases and a thick rug of scarlet outlined in gold lay on the floor. Marks from a recent brushing still remained on the carpet's surface.

Tyndale looked at the delicate settee and wondered if it would hold up should he ease his body onto it.

The priest was staring at him.

"Thank you," he said and sat down, pulling the satchel holding his papers onto his lap.

The settee held.

Outside of an open window, a dove flew onto the casement and cooed at the inhabitants inside. It pecked at seeds, obviously strewn there for it to feed on.

"I place food on the windowsill each morning," said the priest, looking at the bird. "We are friends, the bird and I." At last, he was smiling.

Beyond the window, the manicured lawn and fountain rested between the huge building and the road which was lined with trees. He could see a passing carriage on its cobblestone surface, although no sound came through the window. The River Thames would soon stop its progress, unless it turned onto the road heading west toward Hampton Court.

Tyndale tried not to fidget while waiting on the Bishop, but the response he received from this man meant his staying in England or heading abroad. He intended to finish what he'd started in the satchel, a translation from German, Greek, and Hebrew to English of the New Testament. He'd brought only enough for the Bishop to perceive what he was doing. He had a copy in his quarters in London.

Finally, another priest appeared, and he was escorted down a long hall into the Bishop's anterior room. Here he waited again, until the man at long last showed up.

"Master Tyndale, I presume." Bishop Tunstall didn't bother to tell Tyndale he'd heard his name. Now was a good time to find out if the rumours were true.

"Yes, Sir."

"How may I help you? Oh, and please sit down." The Bishop indicated two chairs, where they could comfortably sit side-by-side in intimate conversation.

William pulled out several sheets of paper tied into a roll. He untied them and put them in the hands of the Bishop. Then he explained what he was doing.

The Cleric sat still as Tyndale described his intention to translate the Bible into English.

Bishop Cuthbert Tunstall had not been in the office long, but long enough to understand his words and position had influence with the King and the

Church. He was a conservative and defender of the Roman Catholic doctrine, as Tyndall was about to find out. Tunstall wasn't afraid to express opposite views, but once a precedent was set, he enforced the new standard.

After Tyndale finished his whole speech to Tunstall, the Bishop stood and walked around the room, reading some of the pages Tyndale had put in his hands. "Is this from *Martin Luther's* translation in German?" he asked.

From the way the man said Martin Luther, Tyndale decided to hold his admiration to a minimum. So, he only said, "I've read him, but my translation is from the original Greek and Hebrew."

There was more silence as the Bishop continued his walk.

When he came back to where Tyndale was sitting, he towered over the man and said, "I forbid you to finish this. It is heresy, and if you persist, I will see that you are tried for putting false doctrine in front of the Church and the people of England. May I repeat again. This is heresy. Do you understand?"

"Yes, sir. I do."

"I don't want to see any more of *this* out there." He jabbed the papers into the air, strode to a can under his desk, and calmly and deliberately tore each piece into bits. "Your audience with me is ended." He rang a bell on his desk, and Tyndale was escorted from the room and the building. Although Tunstall did not agree with Tyndale's project, he did nothing to prevent the young man's continuing work.

Tyndale decided to remain in London and go underground in his labour. Consulting three different translations of the Scriptures, Latin, Greek, and Hebrew, took time. William was thorough in his mission, and this required a quiet place to work—uninterrupted. He was soon out of the money he'd saved for his trip to London, but by this time, he had a suspicion where he could go for help.

～

The door to the largest cloth supplier and drapery manufacturer in England swung inward at Tyndale's touch. He was dwarfed by the collection of colored and print bolts, which went clear to the ceiling with ladders to facilitate getting a preferred one from the top rack. The place reminded him of many along the River Severn, but this spacious building would swallow those little establishments whole. The room smelled of dye, wool, and other types of cloth, and included a table of expensive gold Lamé silk.

A young woman in a gray dress came from the back of the store to greet him.

She smiled and said in a business voice, "May I help you, Sir."

Tyndale smiled back. "Yes, I'm looking for your proprietor, Mr. Munmouth, I believe. I'd like to have a word with him, if possible."

"I'm sorry, sir. But Mr. Munmouth doesn't take many visitors." The young woman turned to go.

Tyndale decided to risk all. "It's about the Brethren," he said quietly, but loud enough for her to hear, since there were other customers in the store.

The woman stopped, turned, and came back to talk.

"What do you know of the Brethren?" she asked in a low voice, staring at him.

"I know enough to appreciate what they're trying to accomplish." He wasn't sure of her involvement or knowledge of or with this group.

"I see," the woman said, looking him up and down. She noticed his hands were covered with stains—ink stains? "Do you write?" she asked.

"Yes."

"What is your name?"

"Tyndale. William Tyndale," he answered.

"I'll give Mr. Munmouth your name. Wait here." When William said Tyndale, the lady put two-and-two together. He was the man who was translating the Scriptures. His name was whispered among the Catholic Church dissidents who supported the Reformation. There was no question her father would want to speak to him.

～

Humphrie Munmouth became the mentor Tyndale needed. While William was in England, Munmouth and the Christian Brethren supported the Scripture translator, and when it became necessary for him to leave his native country, they paid for his passage to Germany and filled his pockets with money.

Standing on the deck of one of Munmouth's ships, the owner said, "When it becomes necessary to ship your New Testament back to England, let us know," he told William.

"Yes, there are many ways to ship product where it will go past the watchful eyes of the Catholic Church, Cardinal Wolsey, and Henry's spies," another of the Christian Brethren stated.

ॐ **Chapter 13** ॐ

The 16th Century
Henry VIII and Anne Boleyn

Lady Anne Boleyn became a member of several courts on the continent, starting in 1513 as a young twelve-year-old at the palace of Margaret of Austria, who was Regent of the Low Countries (today's Belgium, Holland, and Luxembourg), where Anne became a Maid-of-Honor. This position was treasured by the elite of royal society and secured for her by her father, Ambassador to France, Thomas Boleyn, as a diplomat and confidant of Henry VIII.

While in the Low Countries, Lady Anne became fluent in speaking and writing French, and participated in the events of a Renaissance court. Her activities included dancing, hunting, and tournaments. She conversed with and observed the greatest philosophers, artists, poets and musicians who came to the palace festivities, while developing her taste in art, music, and books.

There was a brief period as a Maid-in-Waiting to Henry's sister, Mary Tudor, who had married Louis XII, King of France. He died only months after they wed. Louis had no sons, so Francis I, his son-in-law, succeeded him to the French throne.

Lady Anne entered the household of Francis I's wife, the 15–year-old Queen Claude. At the royal residence in Amboise, perched on an outcrop overlooking the Loire River, she met the artist Leonardo da Vinci, who lived just outside of Amboise. At the same time, the exposure to French reformist writers—like Jacques Lefevre d'Étaples and Clément Marot—would inspire Anne's interest in religious reform.

This fashionable and gifted young lady, who came back to England in 1522, knew the behaviors and traditions of a royal court. Lady Anne Boleyn's arrival at King Henry's court did not cause much excitement. She was betrothed to marry her Irish cousin, James Butler, but for some reason the engagement was ended.

Because of her father's influence at court, she became a Maid-of-Honor to Henry's wife, Catherine of Aragon. While in the Queen's court, she fell in love with and became secretly betrothed to Henry Percy. When found out, this man's father, the 4th Earl of Northumberland, refused to support the union.

And in 1524, Cardinal Wolsey refused the match, so Lady Anne was sent back to Hever Castle to rest and contemplate her loss.

∾

George Boleyn looked out the window of Hever Castle at the carriage carrying his sister, Lady Anne, home from the Palace of Placentia. Hurrying down the steps of their home, he helped her from the carriage and greeted her with a kiss.

"Dear Sister, I'm so glad you are here. There's no one to talk to but the birds in the garden." He led her up the steps to her rooms and sat down in a chair, waiting for her to refresh herself from her long ride.

"How are you?" he called as she went to her closet to remove her hat, gloves, and cloak, giving them to a waiting servant.

She returned to her drawing room, sat down, and removed her shoes. She sat rubbing her feet through her hose. "Tired, I suppose—in every way … body, mind, and spirit. I'm beginning to see why Cardinal Wolsey doesn't have many friends. Did you hear what happened?"

"Yes, we heard. Father came back with the news. I'm sorry."

"I'm much better now. King Henry was very attentive during the debacle."

"That could be good and bad, depending on the mood he's in," George gave a short chuckle. "Everyone's saying he's shorter tempered these days."

"He seemed to be in a decent mood when I left. At least, he came to bid me goodbye."

"Next week, our sister, Mary, and her husband, William Carey, are coming from the palace to visit." George stated matter-of-factly, his eyes darting toward Anne to see her reaction. Even though married, Mary's actions toward King Henry had been more than friendship. "She's bringing young Catherine with her for Father and Mother to see."

"I hope they have a safe trip," was all Anne replied, not wishing to get into palace intrigue.

George decided to change the subject. "I have more writings from the last jaunt I took with Father to France. I'll go get them for you so we can discuss the particulars. Did you hear about Tyndale?" asked George, standing up. He and his sister often discussed the problems of the Church and the new movement caused by the translation of the scriptures into English. They read everything George could get his hands on during his travels abroad with their father, Sir Thomas Boleyn.

"I knew that Wolsey and King Henry were pursuing him relentlessly in Germany, putting pressure on their many allies to arrest and send him back to England. Is there something else?"

"Father said the Church has expelled him. What do you think of that?"

"I would have expected it, given his stance on many of the Church's doctrines. I assume it won't make any difference to Tyndale at all."

"I think you're right." George lowered his voice. "There's also whispers going around that he's almost finished with his translation of the New Testament. I want to get a copy of that to read. Do you want a copy?"

Anne stood for a minute, thinking. "Yes, get me one too. I can't imagine reading the Scriptures in English." She turned as her servant entered the room.

"Lady Anne, a note just came for you." The woman came forward, curtsied, and handed the note to Anne. She left the room.

Even George could tell the impression in the wax seal was the royal signet. Anne pulled the note apart and blushed. She looked at George and rolled her eyes, then handed him the sheet of vellum.

It was a note from the King.

Dear Lady Anne,

It is with some trepidation that I take my pen in hand to send you greetings. From the moment you left, I've been wishing for your return. Please let me say that I thoroughly enjoyed our lively discussion on the merits of my future government with Cardinal Wolsey in charge. You may be right, Wolsey's attempt to levy heavy taxes has inflicted a greater burden on the poor. Your advice to be careful of Wolsey's meddling in the political affairs of the continent, since it might hamper the flow of goods from England to the Low Countries and beyond, was well thought out. I will carefully ponder your advice. In anticipation, I look forward to your return.

Your servant, Henry, rex.

～

In 1525, Cardinal Thomas Wolsey, Lord Chancellor of England and a Henry VIII confidant, established Christ Church College at Oxford. Wolsey's idea was to refute the ideology being spread by the reformation, because despite executions and imprisonment, the movement wasn't abating.

Wolsey received the exact opposite of what he intended. The Reformation awareness had struck Oxford some years before. Several students admitted to this new college, including John Frith and John Clarke. Smuggling of books was rampant from the continent where Luther's ideas were slowly taking hold, and these banned and heretical writings came especially to Oxford and Cambridge, where John Clarke, inspired by the German reformers, started a series of Bible studies. Many of the new students at Oxford favored the Reformation.

When Wolsey found out what had happened, he had ten students, the leaders of the group, imprisoned. These included John Frith and Clark. They were held in a foul, unsanitary fish locker for six months. Four students died in this dirty, contaminated place. Finally released, Frith left England for Antwerp and became Tyndale's most valuable helper in translating and printing the New Testament.

∾

William Tyndale leaned back in his wooden chair and pushed his legs out in front of him. On his desk was the last stack of papers written in English, ready for print.

"John, I think we're through," he said to his helper, John Frith. "If you're ready, I want to walk the rest of our copy over to our printers."

John looked at William, "Could you read me the last verses you transcribed?"

The Scripture translator drew from the bottom of the stack one page and read these words from Revelation 22:18-21.

"I testifye vnto every man that heareth the words of prophesy of thys boke. Yf eny man shall adde vnto these thynges, God shall adde vnto him the plages that are wrytten in this boke. And yf eny man shall mynyshe (take away or change) *of the words of the boke of this prophesy, God shall take awaye his parte out of the boke of lyfe, and oute of the holy citie, and from thoo thynges which are wrytten in this boke. He which testifyeth these thinges sayth: be it. I come quickly, Amen. Even soo: come lord Iesu. The grace of oure lorde Iesu Christ be with you all. Amen."*

"Amen," said John, nodding. "I'm ready to go."

The two men got their hats, walked from their quarters and down one of the cobblestone streets of Worms to the printers. Entering the door, they found the owner was not present, but one of the typesetters of the movable-type printing press was hard at work on an advertising pamphlet.

"Do you know when your employer will be back?" asked William of the man.

"He's eating the noon meal with his family. I can get him," the young man said, motioning to the stairs leading to upstairs rooms.

"Are you his son?"

"Yes, I'm Wilhelm," he replied with a toothy grin.

"Let him know William Tyndale bids him hello and give him the rest of the manuscript we've been working on so diligently. Tell him it is finished, and to complete the typesetting, and tell me when the first copies will be ready to ship back to England. I will write a letter and have a ship in the harbour to take them home."

"I'll make sure he gets your papers as soon as he appears. I heard him tell Mother, he's going to print thousands of copies."

William and John left the printer's building. "John, I feel like a meal of splendid baked fish," stated William, walking briskly back toward their writing quarters.

"If so, let us stop by Hermann's Fishery on the wharf. His boats will have brought in the fresh catch of the day, and he and his wife know how to cook tasty fish."

"Good idea. We could use a few minutes to rest. Can't tarry long. The Pentateuch is next, and Adam, Abraham, Joseph, and Moses are waiting to speak to us words of truth."

Tyndale was happy. Part of the task he'd set for himself was done. He might rest easy for a day, but tomorrow he would be back at his ink-stained desk, working in a book he loved with all his heart—a book which did speak words of truth to his mind.

As they walked along, the two men discussed their next step in translating the Old Testament. Reaching their destination, they went inside to sup.

Upon receiving William Tyndale's letter, advising him of the finished translation and its delivery to the printers, Humphrie Munmouth ordered his carriage and set off with his driver for the businesses located on the wharfs of the River Thames. He was headed for one in particular. One which stocked watertight boxes and barrels for shipment of wine and other goods on the high seas. This company had the reputation for dependable service and high quality, and Humphrie wanted the best for the product he had in mind.

Telling his driver, that the business was just ahead, they pulled up where the sign said, *Tipton Brother's, Export and Import — London.*

A ship sat at the wharf in front, and men scurried in all directions off-loading cargo which was being transferred into a large warehouse, awaiting delivery to other parts of the city or the interior of England.

Munmouth had never purchased from this company, but he'd shipped barrels and boxes made by them for his other customers.

"I hope I won't be long," Munmouth stated as he stepped from the carriage. "Find some place to stay warm." He flipped a coin to his driver and turned to walk across the wharf.

The chilly winds of October whipped his long cloak around his legs, causing him to walk briskly toward the front door of the Tipton establishment. He opened it and went quickly inside. As he shut the door, he pushed the hood of his cloak back and noticed an older gentleman behind the counter. Going up to him, he said, "Does it seem colder this year in October, or is it just my imagination?"

The man laughed, "Or the other option is our ages. Thinner skinned might we be. May I help you?"

"I'd like to talk to someone about watertight barrels and boxes."

Hugh Tipton looked down his spectacles at the man standing before him. Bearded, like most Englishmen those days, he had clear blue eyes and reddish-brown hair cut to the bottom of his ears. "May I introduce myself. I'm Hugh Tipton, and as the proprietor here, I can help you."

"Humphrie Munmouth, at your service." And he pushed his hand toward Hugh.

The two men shook hands.

"Is there somewhere we can sit and talk?" Humphrie asked.

"Of course. Please follow me."

The two men went into the office area behind the counter.

"May I take your cloak and gloves?" said Hugh, holding out his hand and indicating a stand where his were hanging. He realized this man intended to stay awhile, and he might as well be comfortable.

Munmouth removed his covering and gloves.

Hugh placed the clothing on the rack and replenished the fire with wood. Then he joined his new client at two chairs in front of a desk. "May I get you something to drink? My wife makes the best hot spiced cider. We grow apples at our home outside the city and she manages to keep some into and through the winter. I have some on the hearth, warming. It may be a little strong, since it was made early this morning and brought into London."

Humphrie nodded a yes, thinking a hot cup would at least warm his hands, and Hugh poured two steaming cups of golden brew into china cups and returned to the chairs.

After being comfortably seated and taking a sip, Hugh asked, "How may I help you, Master Munmouth?"

"Please, call me Humphrie, because I hope our relationship will be long and cordial."

"Of course, and my name will be Hugh."

"I have need of several sizes of special watertight boxes and barrels." Humphrie took out a paper from his shirt pocket and handed it to Hugh. He watched as the Tipton man looked over the list.

"What's this trunk with a secret compartment in the bottom?"

"Possibly where a woman would protect her most precious jewels on a trip or at home," said Humphrie, matter-of-factly. "The inside bottom needs to be removeable, but not so you can tell, should it be inspected."

"Must be the queen's jewels," said Hugh, his eyebrows going up and looking dubiously at the other man. "Are you a thief?" he asked directly.

"No," laughed Humphrie. "Just a man in need of several watertight containers."

Then Hugh asked the obvious question. "Why so many sizes?"

"I have my reasons. I just need them made. Can the Tiptons supply them?"

"I'll send a post to Bristol and ask the question. It's just a matter of time. I'm sure they can build them. When do you want these *special* parts?"

"As soon as possible. I want to take them to Germany to be loaded with supplies for England. I need this same order for the next six months. These will go inside watertight barrels for shipping wine, olive oil, or other liquids.?" Humphrie stood to leave. "Would you like an advance of money on the first shipment?"

"No. I realize these are different sizes than we normally build, but I believe you are a man of honor."

When Hugh went to get Mr. Munmouth's cloak and gloves, another thought occurred to him. "What on earth are you shipping inside the barrels that you need them to be watertight? Are you smuggling something?"

"Mr. Tipton, the less you know, the better. When can you let me know they will be made and what time they will arrive here on the River Thames, so I can have my ships ready to receive them?"

"I should have an answer the middle of next week."

"Then I bid you good day, Sir, and wait for your answer. My address is on the sheet I gave you."

Hugh walked the man to the door and shook hands.

"Oh," Humphrie said, "I almost forgot. No outside markings of any kind on the barrels and other containers."

A perplexed Hugh stood there until Humphrie mounted up into his carriage and watched until he was out of sight. What was the man into, and did he really want to get involved? Still, as long as he didn't know, he could always refute any allegations. When he turned, going back to the office to write the letter so he could get it a local messenger, he realized there'd been no talk of price. The man hadn't asked, and Hugh had been so engrossed in his guessing game, he hadn't thought to inquire.

◞◟

In January, 1526, six thousand copies of the New Testament were printed at Worms. Munmouth's ships, resting on the Rhine River in Germany, were loaded with Bibles in every kind of watertight box, chest, and barrel—even wrapped in bales of cloth. These floated within wine or olive oil barrels. Upon reaching England, they would be opened, the inside containers taken out, and the Bibles distributed among The Brethren and other reformers, for spreading to the far corners of England. Without realizing it, the Tipton's had become an integral part of the dispersal of the Gospel to the man who plowed the field, just as Tyndale had predicted.

◞◟

The same year, 1526, Lady Anne Boleyn returned to the Palace of Placentia. Her return started a chain of events which would eventually culminate in her untimely death. Anne was anything but timid. She had thoughts of her own and didn't hesitate to express them, much to Henry's delight. Of a good, noble family of the court, beautiful but not stunning, she was elegant in the square-necked fashions of the age with her pearl neck choker and long pendant dangling from her slim neck.

Henry laughed, thinking of young Lady Anne Boleyn. Her eyes mesmerized him with her heart's thoughts showing in their depths. He was definitely interested in her. More than anyone else, he knew. Soon Henry was pursuing her, sending her daily letters which became love notes, declaring his devotion. But Anne proved to be a hard catch. Henry pursued, and Lady Anne remained elusive, resisting and holding the King at arm's length.

Those in the palace were amused. Henry could normally snap his fingers and have no difficulty of getting his way.

~

Isaac sat eating the noon meal with Eleanor in the palace kitchen.

She gave a low chuckle, "Do you think Anne Boleyn will be the one? Her sister, Mary, has left the Court. I haven't seen her for days. Has she been spurned?"

Isaac shook his head. "At this time, I don't think Henry's made up his mind. Anne is lively and that's what Henry needs, someone to make him laugh."

"Does she realize what she's getting into?"

"Probably not, but that's not our concern."

"Her brother, George, was here last week. He gave her a copy of Tyndale's New Testament and told her to hide it, since having one is punishable by death. I saw her sitting in her closet with a lamp and the new book. I wonder what she's planning on doing with it?"

Isaac shook his head. "I don't know, but I heard Cardinal Wolsey tell the King, they've readied a pile of the new Bibles to be burned here in London, and the Cardinal and Henry are in a desperate search to find Tyndale. They've written letters all over Germany and anywhere else he might possibly be. Did I tell you I've heard Tyndale speak?"

Eleanor looked at him in surprise. "When was that?"

"Remember when I came back and told you Poppa wanted to join me here in London? During that trip, we went to the Bristol Cathedral and heard him deliver a sermon."

"What did you think?"

"He's definitely got some ideas which are different from the Church, especially when it comes to indulgences and sacraments—the basis for money into the coffers of the Church. I've only heard him this once, so I don't understand his statements on justification by faith in Jesus Christ—extremely foreign to the Church's teaching."

"What does he say?" asked Eleanor in a lower voice, since two others had come into the room. "Why is he different?"

"He says indulgences or works can't buy anyone's way into heaven and that there's only two sacraments mentioned in the Bible, and they are Baptism and The Lord's Supper."

"How would we know, if we can't read the Bible?" asked Eleanor.

"Exactly. Maybe we should try to find one and read it."

After some minutes of silence and to hide her uncertainty on the prospect of committing what she thought of as heresy, Eleanor asked, "Isaac, how is your father?"

"Poppa has adapted well to his move. He often takes off walking for miles to visit Hugh on the River Thames, and they go to eat the noon meal. Then he walks back, and we go for the evening meal. That is on the nights I'm home. He wants me to consider leaving the King's service and for the both of us go traveling. I haven't made up my mind."

Eleanor reached across the table and touched his hand. "If you leave, who will be my friend?"

"You might go with us?" said Isaac, counting her fingers and nodding at her.

"Are you asking or suggesting? If you are, I'll think about it. Please ask me my answer before you decide to leave. Promise me?"

"I'll definitely ask." Isaac grinned at her.

Eleanor stood. "Back to work," she said, and taking her plate to the washing station, she waved as she left the room.

~

In England, Cardinal Wolsey, Henry VIII's friend and confidante, condemned Tyndale as a heretic. He and the King sent spies to the continent to find the scholar. Tyndale went into hiding, in Hamburg, Germany, still translating the Scriptures. How long would Tyndale escape capture?

Chapter 14

The 16th Century

The Reformation, Henry VIII, Anne Boleyn Consort-in-Waiting

In 1527 and within the Catholic Church, Henry started serious annulment proceedings from Queen Catherine of Aragon. They had been married for eighteen years.

During this time, Henry had been a constant defender of the Catholic faith, but now he had a problem. Cardinal Wolsey was his go-between with the Pope in Rome, and the Pope was refusing his request. The result was a stalemate. But not for long, Henry decided.

Although he openly supported the Catholic Church, privately he thought more and more, the burgeoning Church needed its authority challenged. And since he needed money, the church had plenty he could make use of.

Even as Lady Anne became unofficially Henry's consort-in-waiting, she continued to read and study the materials of the Reformation brought to her by her brother, George. She didn't conceal the pleasure she found in such reading. By now, the New Testament was

prominently displayed on a lectern in her bed chamber for all to see and read.

~

Eleanor hurried toward Isaac. She was to sup with him and Young George Tipton and stay the night in their quarters. She would cook the meal they would eat. The two men loved her cooking and the pleasure of having a female presence in the house. She was doing this more and more as the two men prepared to travel around England.

Then, adding a wall into their little house, for a small bed chamber, they had invited her to come and share the friendship found within.

"Isaac, I have some news to tell you," she stated when she was close enough for him to hear without disturbing other people walking on the path nearby.

"I have some to tell you, also." Isaac was now twenty-seven years old and his father was approaching fifty.

"The King is in possession of a copy of Tyndale's *'The Obedience of a Christen Man, and How Christen Rulers Ought to Govern.'* Guess where he got it from?"

"From his consort, Lady Anne."

"How did you know?"

"You tell your side first," suggested Isaac.

"Lady Anne gave the book to Nan Gaynsford, my fellow worker last week, after she wondered out loud within the Lady's hearing what she was reading. My Lady handed her the book and said, 'Here, you can read it for yourself.'" Eleanor paused as they crossed the street. "I was there when she gave Nan the book."

"Then what happened?" asked Isaac as they continued on.

"Nan told me, she was fascinated by its words and sat reading the book when her suitor, George, you know him, the equerry or helper in the royal household, came to see her the next day. He snatched the book from her hand and wouldn't give it back."

Isaac continued, "Yes, George, like a complete imbecile, took the volume to the Chapel Royal and sat reading it during the service on Sunday. What was going through his mind?"

"That's a good question, because Dr. Sampson, the Dean, saw him during the service and asked for the book afterward. Realizing what he'd just confiscated, he took it to Cardinal Wolsey, who, thinking he would get back into the good graces of Henry, because he'd been falling out of favor lately, decided to take the book to the King. But the Cardinal had more pressing things to do and delayed this meeting. Whew." Eleanor stopped to get her breath. "Lady Anne, upon hearing the details of the book's seizure, went to the King to ask him to get it back."

"Let me continue," said Isaac, "because I was there at this juncture. So, when the Cardinal approached the King with the book, Henry took it and abruptly excused the man. His only intention was to return it to Lady Anne."

"Yes. Henry came directly to Lady Anne's rooms and gave it to her. I was nearby when he came. She seemed preoccupied for some time after he left, and finally, she told us she was going to see the King. She took the book and went to the Great Hall where Henry was seated."

"That book is listed as one of the heretical writings, as it contains every doctrine which Luther,

Tyndale and others of the Reformation have put forth. It's hard to believe the King would read it," said Isaac, shaking his head.

"He said he did read it, and my Lady had marked pages she thought he'd be very interested in taking particular notice of as he read. After his perusal, his very words to Lady Anne were, 'This is a book for me and all Kings to read.' At least, that's what she told us."

"Knowing our King, I'm sure he picked out and chose the words to his liking," Isaac stated.

And Isaac's statement was right.

The words inside put forth the impression that the headship of the Church should be the King of the country and not the Pope. That was all Henry needed. This was going to be his reason for breaking with the Catholic Church and creating the Church of England. But this did not happen immediately. He would exhaust every means with the Pope first, and that's were Cardinal Wolsey fit into the picture.

Because the Cardinal's attention was consumed elsewhere in the affairs of State on Henry's behalf, he could not devote uninterrupted energy toward dissolving the marriage. After a series of delays and mistakes by Cardinal Wolsey, the annulment proceedings were suspended or postponed in 1529.

At least, this was Henry's position on the matter, and he began to wonder whose side Wolsey was on. The Cardinal fell out of favor with Henry, whose patience ran out at the postponement. He needed to be free to marry Lady Anne, his consort-in-waiting, and he had a plan which he now set it in motion. He no longer needed the Cardinal.

Feeling the brunt of Henry's anger, Wolsey retreated north to fulfill his duties as Archbishop of York, but this was not far enough away from an irate King Henry. In 1530, he was summoned back to London to stand trial for treason, a favorite way for Henry to dispose of people who were no longer in his inner circle and rejected by the King. Dead men or women do not cause problems, but to Henry's dismay, the Cardinal died on the way.

Henry called a Parliament filled with reformists, the chief of whom was Thomas Cromwell. He, along with Lady Anne, pushed Henry to ignore the Pope. In 1531, Henry VIII made claim to the church title, Supreme Head of the Church of England, based on Tyndale's writings, although he still hotly pursued the man.

In May 1532, the Church of England surrendered to the authority of the monarch and the following year, the Statute in Restraint of Appeals abolished the right of the English clergy and laity to appeal to Rome on matters of matrimony, tithes and oblations and left this to the Archbishops of Canterbury and York, whom Henry now controlled.

Finally, Henry had accomplished what he set out to do many years before. He had established his *legal right* to marry Anne of Boleyn when the new Archbishop of Canterbury, Thomas Cranmer, secretly issued the annulment of his first marriage to Catherine of Aragon. This was easy considering he was a friend of Lady Anne.

Henry, feeling a bit guilty after cutting himself and England off from the Catholic Church, wanted support for his future marriage, so in 1532, he took Lady Anne and went to France to see his friend, Francis I. The King of France greeted Anne and gave Henry his hearty approval on the Field of the Cloth of Gold, where Henry used some of the wealth that had been hoarded by the late Cardinal, to put on a sumptuous display.

Upon returning to England, Henry quickly married Anne in a secret private ceremony in November. Anne immediately became pregnant so there followed a more public ceremony in January 1533.

Also, publicly at last, the Archbishop of Canterbury declared the marriage of Henry to Catherine of Aragon null and void, and a few days later his marriage to Anne was declared valid. Just as quickly, Pope Clement VII excommunicated Henry.

Lady Anne was now the expecting Queen of England, and Henry was satisfied. But Queen Anne needed to produce a boy.

∼

For several months, the Kingdom of England was in a whirl.

In July, John Firth came back to England from Germany. He was promptly arrested and burned at the stake. He was thirty years old. How close were they to arresting Tyndale?

In November, Princess Elizabeth was born. She was a disappointment to Henry, but adored by her mother.

Also, in this month, November 1534, Henry was declared the Supreme Head of the Church of England by Act of Supremacy. Although he stayed with the Catholic doctrine, he had eliminated the Papal Authority from the country.

All the monasteries were dissolved, and according to the Act of Treason, the priests and those who supported the different divisions of the Catholic Church had to swear allegiance to the Church of England and sever financial ties to Rome. The religious hierarchy of England had been turned upside down. When would it return to normal?

In 1535, Henry, who was of the Welsh Tudors, attempted to fully incorporate Wales into the Kingdom of England, by the Laws in Wales Acts. Part of the first Act said, *That this said Country or Dominion of Wales shall be, stand and continue forever from henceforth incorporated, united, and annexed to and with this his Realm of England.* This was a start, but not the end.

Also, during the same year, Tyndale, hearing of the turmoil in the religious establishment in England and Queen Anne's stalwart support of certain members of the Reformation, decided to make her a gift. Secretly getting the help of his friends in Germany, he made a specially bound version of the New Testament in blue morocco with beautiful illustrations printed on vellum.

Somehow this book was put into the hands of her brother, George. When he took it out of his diplomatic pouch and presented it to her at Hampton Court, she saw in gilt gold these words, *ANNA REGINA ANGLIAE,* OR ANNE QUEEN OF ENGLAND.

Her reign as Queen would be short lived. In January 1536, Anne miscarried for the last time, a son. Not known for his patience, Henry gave up on Anne, as he had on Catherine of Aragon, and in his philandering way, he was already involved with Jane Seymour.

Queen Anne was tried on trumped-up charges and convicted. Taken to the Tower of London, she was later escorted to Tower Green, where an expert swordsman, hired for the occasion and brought from Calais on the French coast, waited to be her executioner.

Standing, she addressed the crowd, but did not admit guilt. What she actually said is according to which side of the political or religious spectrum one related to. When her words were finished, she knelt and was blindfolded. The executioner drew back his sword, her neck was small, and with one swipe accomplished the task. She was buried within the Tower grounds in an unmarked grave.

Henry was married the next day to Jane Seymour. She did give him a male heir, but she died days later of sepsis.

With Queen Anne's death, Eleanor was released from the Queen's chambers and Isaac, who was now thirty-six, took a leave of absence from the King's staff. Isaac, Eleanor and Young George journeyed to Bristol, where the couple was joined in matrimony. It was a marriage of friends, with cordiality and respect built in. A year later, these two, along with Young George, went north into the lands of the Ancestry Book.

Turning south and upon arriving at Tipton, Young George became ill. He died and was buried with his ancestral fathers at Summerhill. Eleanor and Isaac continued on to Bristol to take over the Tipton investments there. Isaac never went back to London.

∼

For eleven years, Tyndale had managed to evade the capture of the English monarchy. But a fierce campaign was launched, and he was arrested in Antwerp, Belgium. For four hundred and fifty days he stayed jailed and shivering in the cold castle of Vilvoorde outside Brussels. In 1536, he was convicted of heresy, taken to the scaffold, and chained to the stake. His last words were, *'Lord! open the King of England's eyes.'* Then he was strangled, and his dead body burned at the stake.

This was more merciful than many reformer's deaths. He did not have to feel the hot flames upon his body as John Frith or experience suffocation by smoke as Jeanne d'Arc. He died in October, five months after Queen Anne Boleyn.

The following year, Humphrie Munmouth, Tyndale's supporter and financier, died.

In many ways, Tyndale and Queen Anne had their words fulfilled. When Henry became head of the Church in England, she suggested he needed his own Bible, and this got the King to thinking.

Before long, he authorized the Great Bible, which contained Tyndale's translation of the New Testament and some of the Old Testament. Tyndale's translation was not finished, but the rest was completed by Miles Coverdale.

Thousands of copies of this Bible were printed. It was known as the Chained Bible, because worshipers wanted to take it from the church to read. When the people removed it, they treasured its words so much, they didn't return it, but kept it for reference.

This translation was placed in every parish church in the country, where any person, be he peasant or noble, could go and read the Scriptures in English. The Great Bible of 1541 contained the authorizing signature of Cuthbert Tunstall, the man who had rejected Tyndale's first translations at Fulham Palace.

King Henry remained of the Catholic persuasion until his death. And, although Queen Anne had read Reformation literature and aided those of the changing times, there is no indication she became a Protestant or adopted Tyndale's stance on his biblical translation of justification by faith due to God's grace.

God used a philandering King and a young English woman to focus the world's attention back to his Word, Jesus Christ.

~

Henry VIII died in January 1547 at the age of fifty-five. He was buried by Jane Seymour, who gave him his only living son and heir.

❧ Chapter 15 ❧

The Last of the 16th Century
One King, Two Queens, and Hugh Tipton

Directed at Ireland, one of Henry VIII's policies was known as Plantations.

The political system of the Irish Catholics was starting to become more centralized around Dublin, extending out into the countryside with a ragged government of Parliament, Commons, Lords and nobles. In other words, this small nation might rise up and defy their English governors. Henry decided to nip any idea of a rebellion in the bud. This proved to be harder than the King realized. While this happened, the English continued to govern the land through the Lord Deputy of Ireland—a cohort of the ruler of England.

With the support of Thomas Cromwell, the King's policy or Plantations was implemented. It simply stated that all Irish noblemen would *surrender* to the King their lands and the King would return them by *regrant* under a Royal Charter. This would create the Kingdom of Ireland and the elite of Ireland would be given English titles. In Henry's thinking, this would establish a new Irish loyalty to the crown of England. The Irish Lordships accepted Henry as just one of their overlords and carried on as they had before.

Adding to the unrest above, the English Reformation caused disquiet, since most of Ireland was Roman Catholic. Some of this was assuaged by giving the dissolved monasteries to the Irish nobles, something which few of them rejected.

The English, on the mainland, had come a long way from the local tribal warfare which existed in Tybba's time, over five hundred years back. But the separate Irish clans were just that—separate and tribal. Between clans, on the small island, there were wars of succession, land disputes, and private wars within the country. Some clans continued the tradition of raiding other clans—just because their ancestors had done it.

When the English ruler started forcibly replacing the Catholic Irish with Reformed Scottish and English people from the mainland, successive rebellions broke out. Former combatant relationships between clans started breaking down, and the separate Irish clans started to unite. This bond would spell trouble in the future.

The unrest in the Irish country continued under Henry's son, Edward VI, when at nine years of age, he was crowned King of England. His reign was short—only six years, but he took his father's changes more seriously. Or rather, his advisors did. So, on his behalf, they continued to impose the Protestant religion and caused harsh penalties to be inflicted on those who acknowledged or continued in the Catholic Doctrine.

As the young King grew weaker, his Lord Protector, John Dudley, one of the descendants of Dudley Castle of Staffordshire, convinced the King to name his cousin, Lady Jane Grey, as his successor, totally bypassing his illegitimate stepsisters, Mary and Elizabeth.

After Edward's death from tuberculosis, Dudley's design soon failed, when support for Lady Jane dwindled and Mary I, the daughter of Catherine of Aragon, took the throne.

Dudley was quickly beheaded.

Lady Jane was kept imprisoned in the Tower of London. She was convicted of treason, but not immediately beheaded until her father was involved in a rebellion against Mary's wish to marry King Philip II of Spain.

The people rejoiced at Mary's coronation. But their happiness was short lived. As a Catholic, she made a vigorous attempt to reestablish the Roman Catholic Church in England, and many people died, earning her the nickname 'Bloody Mary.'

She married Philip II of Spain, but they had no children. Always a sickly child, she remained so during her whole life, and during the five years she was on the throne. She died in 1558. Again, the people of London celebrated in the streets—this time at her death.

After so much turmoil pertaining to the monarchy, the people were ready for relief. They found it in Queen Elizabeth, who was a mature, intelligent, level-headed, twenty-five years old when she sat on the throne of England. One of her first actions was to establish the English Protestant church, of which she became the Supreme Governor.

Brought up with her brother on the Protestant teachings of the Reformers, her ideas varied from her father's, Henry VIII, who maintained his Catholic concepts from the start of the Church of England. Elizabeth I was more moderate than Henry and his advisors and somewhat more tolerate of other religions.

She was a red-headed, wise ruler, who established a group of trusted councilors to advise her on problems connected to her reign. She was often heard to say, "I *see* but say nothing." She had a great sense of humour, and must have found pleasure when she wore a dress, she had had commissioned, made with jewels stitched on it *in the shape of eyes.*

Her ministers set up a secret service. These were spies who reported on happenings within the territory and abroad. In this way, she was on top of problems before they escalated.

Elizabeth never married, preferring to flirt and tease her suitors, keeping them dangling and in suspense as to her feelings.

～

In 1558, the first year of Queen Elizabeth's reign, the grandson of Hugh Tipton (the old man who was of Tipton, Portishead, and London) returned to Seville, Spain as the consul of The Andalusia Company, after first holding this position for a very short time under Henry VIII. The grandson's name was also Hugh (Hew Typton was the way he signed his name), and he was sailing with his wife, Joan, and two sons, John and Harold.

All morning their ship had been passing other vessels, heading toward the open Atlantic Ocean. These ships flew the flags of nations who traded with Spain and the other cities along the Guadalquivir River. They were coming from Seville or Sanlúcar de Barrameda, the largest and busiest seaports on the river just west of the seaport of Cadiz. These ports facilitated the meeting and transfer of goods from the cities of the eastern Mediterranean Sea known as the Levant, and the western countries and isles of Europe.

The family stood at the rail of the Tipton's ship, *The Avon*, sent especially from Bristol, to transport the family to Seville. Looking north past the last merchant ship to pass, they strained to catch the first exciting glimpse of their home. The captain's instructions were specifically to check out the possibility of trading with local wine merchants in Andalusia, and especially Seville.

"Poppa look. I see the top of a tree," exclaimed John, who was the oldest boy at twelve. He had been standing on his tiptoes near the port rail, looking intently toward the bow, at the route his father had pointed out, as the probable site where they would leave the expansive ocean waters they'd been sailing through. If he had seen the biblical dove with the olive branch coming back to Noah's Ark, he could not have been more excited.

In the bright sunshine, Hugh sat reading a book about famous men of Spain under the shade of the forecastle. He looked up, put his book on the bench where he was sitting, and stood to join his son at the rail. Straining his eyes, he tried to see what his son had sighted. When the ship crested a wave, just momentarily there was something, but he wouldn't go so far as to say it was a tree.

The rest of the family came running and crowded around. "Where, John?" asked Harold, looking in the direction his older brother John was pointing.

Hugh looked at his wife and grinned. "He's got better eyes than I."

"Look, Poppa. There!" Now he was jabbing his finger again in the same direction.

"I see it, Father," said Harold. "But I don't think it's a tree."

At this point, Hugh decided to share some history with his sons. "Do you know what famous man called this part of the ocean home for many years? He wasn't born here, but spent much of his life sailing in and out of the river we are going to live on."

The two boys looked at each other.

Hugh headed back to his bench to get out of the sun. The boys followed, and he added, "He was buried here, but a few years back, his body was taken to the West Indies."

They needed help, so turning to look at her they asked, "Mother, do you know?"

Joan was still standing at the rail. "I'm not getting into this. Your Poppa will tell you." Joan grinned at her husband.

"Do you give up?" asked Poppa Hugh, as they turned back to look at him.

John looked at Harold who nodded. "Yes, we do. We don't think we know."

"He was born in Genoa, Italy in a little house on a hill overlooking the port. He could see ships in the harbour and ships heading out to sea. He longed to sail on one of them, so at the young age of ten or so, he went to sea."

"That means," said their mother, laughing, "we could put both of you on a ship and send you sailing."

"But Mother, you would miss us," said Harold, who was a mama's boy. He came to share the bench with his father, who scooted over to let him sit down.

"Whether your mother would miss you or not, is not the story here. Once Columbus—oops." Hugh had let the cat out of the bag.

"Oh, Poppa. You gave him away," laughed John. And everyone started laughing with him, including Hugh.

"So, who is it?" asked Hugh, looking at the son who was standing in front of him.

"Christopher Columbus," said John.

"John, that's the way we pronounce his name in English. What is it in Genoese or Spanish? Do you know?"

John shook his head.

"In Genoese it's Cristoforo Colombo and in Spanish Cristóbal Colón."

"Poppa, I think I like the English version better," said Harold.

Hugh ruffled his hair. "I do too, my son. Now let's get back to the story. Once the young Christopher Columbus got on a boat, his feet were always home on the deck of a rolling ship. No place was too far for this young sailor, and soon he, as an older man and ship captain, was dreaming of going far from the coast of Spain."

Joan interrupted here. "What body of water did Columbus want to cross?" she asked, joining in the questions as she stood by the rail.

"I know the answer to that question," responded John. "Grandfather always called it the Green Sea of Darkness. I'd be scared to venture into someplace where no one's been before."

"Yes," Poppa Hugh laughed and continued. "Was Columbus a very smart man or crazy? He had people on both sides of this question. But Columbus wasn't rich. He needed money, men, and supplies. Who gave him the money and boats to sail toward his dreams?"

"King Ferdinand and Queen Isabella," said John.

"Very good. And where did he sail to on the Green Sea of Darkness?"

"He went to the New World, or what he thought was China and India,"

"Why go west, John?"

"Because he wanted to find a more direct route to the places where spices and other exotic goods could be bought and brought back to Spain."

"That's true, but he didn't find those, did he?"

"No, Poppa. He found islands which he claimed in the King and Queen's name."

"What were they called? Or better, where were they located?"

Harold responded, beating his older brother to the answer.

"The West Indies and Jamaica. Am I right, Poppa?"

"Yes, you are."

Joan motioned to Hugh and pointed toward the coast of Spain.

The boys, seeing Hugh's hesitation, turned and rushed to where their mother was standing. She said, "And this is what Columbus saw as he left the mouth of the Guadalquivir River after leaving the port of Seville." She threw her hand out in a sweeping motion and let it fall to her side.

Before them were the vast sandy beaches of Sanlúcar de Barrameda. The tide was out, and the afternoon sun glistened on the beige crystals of sand, the brilliance causing them to shade their eyes.

Hugh made one last observation. "Columbus stayed here at Sanlúcar de Barrameda for a few days before the sailed."

The Avon was flying before the wind, and the Captain ordered the mainsail raised to slow her speed as the boat entered the narrowing mouth of the river. He called to the family, "We'll be in Seville tonight, and you'll sleep in your new beds at the consul house." The home would be different from their last one, and they were anxious to see it.

After slowly passing a hundred small fishing boats, anchored all over the shallow sea harbour at Sanlúcar de Barrameda, *The Avon* pressed on with the tide into the main channel and through the salty marshlands.

"John and Harold, come here," called their mother.

The two boys hurried to the right side of the boat to see flocks of stalking, pink-orange flamingos and white egrets, dipping their beaks and feasting on the crustaceans and minnows living in the tidal basins of ocean water.

"Hugh, the flamingos seem much more beautiful than I remember," said Joan, standing by her husband. "The color against the dark-green marsh grass and reflected in the water is awe-inspiring. Makes me want to get out my easel, canvas, oils, and paint. Maybe we'll have time during our extended stay this trip."

"My dear, you will have plenty of time to travel Andalusia and paint to your heart's content," returned Hugh. "We can take trips to Cordoba and up and down the river. You can go with me on diplomatic missions — you paint, and I'll make sure our people are well represented."

The Avon had gone to a crawl as a pilot boat approached to lead them gently to a berth at Seville. The English flag designated the area for them to anchor.

"Look, Joan. I believe that's William Ostriche," Hugh said, squinting in the bright sun and looking at a man standing on the wharf. As they drew closer, they saw that the gentleman was dressed merely in loose white shirt, white hat to shade his eyes, and knee breeches — the weather being hot and muggy.

Hugh was appointed to permanently replace Ostriche as the Consul.

Ostriche was selected by Henry VIII in 1530 as a representative of the newly established Andalusia Company, serving in this capacity for several years.

This Company made up entirely of English merchants, including those of Bristol, oversaw the transactions of their fellow Englishmen in dealings with the Spanish companies in Andalusia.

The consul's responsibility as a government official was to live in a foreign country, protect, or help the English citizens who were traveling, living, or doing business there. Tipton's authority extended beyond Spain to the islands off the coast of Africa. Ostriche had written letters to Hugh while he was gone, telling him he would have ample opportunity to earn his pay when he returned.

"Hello," said the man standing on the wharf, waving his arms wildly. The dockhands tied the ship up to the pylons. "How are you, Hugh?"

"Better, now that I'm here," said Hugh, waiting until the gangplank was pushed from the ship to the shore, and then guiding his wife, who shepherded the children, he strode forward to shake the man's hand.

"The new consulate is only a short walk. We'll go on, and I've given instructions to my men," he pointed to several standing together on the wharf, "to bring your baggage round."

The group headed down the street, which was bustling with activity. After escorting Hugh's family to their new upstairs living quarters in the consulate, Ostriche led Hugh to his new office on the ground floor.

"You will soon find out that Seville has become the melting pot for business and politics from the east and the west and from the north to the south," he told Hugh. "We're still the sorting ground for manufactured goods coming from the West Indies, the Levant, England, France, the Mediterranean, and all countries in-between. Only this week, I heard multiple different languages being spoken, and you'll find the large contingent of fellow Englishmen living here in the city, has grown. Plus, there are many more in Sanlúcar de Barrameda."

"That's good to know. My sons will have English playmates."

"Yes, and we also established an English School, which you will conveniently find next door." Ostriche pointed through another window which overlooked a smaller building.

Hugh nodded and asked, "Refresh my memory, what do the English ships bring into the area, and what do they return to the homeland?"

"Good question. The English bring cloth, good cloth to the Spanish shores. We have had some problems with quality of these goods, so inspection of them is necessary. Other than cloth, we receive the metals, lead and tin, calf hides and skins for making leather products, copper and pewter vessels, wood for shipbuilding, and lately, staves for building casks for oil and wine."

Henry's ears perked up when Ostriche mentioned casks.

"Is there a market for hogsheads (large barrels) for wine and oil shipment?" he asked.

"Yes, since this is the biggest grape and fruit tree growing area in Spain. There is much opportunity."

"What about shipments to England?"

"The English love the citrus we ship them— oranges, lemons, figs, and raisins. We also send almonds, salt from the marshes along the river to the south, and soap from the factories across the river in Triana. Seville pottery and floor tiles end up in English homes. Of course, Spanish wine and olive oil are the major products on board a returning ship."

Hugh went to an open window overlooking the bustling harbour. "The view is amazing." Hugh saw a river clogged with boats—boats of different sizes.

"Yes, it is." Ostriche stood in thought. "I knew I'd forgotten something. Let me mention, the Spanish love smoked and salted fish of all kinds, including the pilchards from Ireland, cod and herring. They've only recently been introduced to this delicacy."

Hugh immediately put another note in his mind— remember this statement.

Ostriche kept up a running account of his dealings with the merchants. He told Hugh of his new efforts in dealing with authorities when the English got rowdy or broke the laws of Spain.

"We have some who are languishing in the dungeons and prisons of a local town, awaiting ransom or release. Your responsibility now, since I'm leaving. The authorities are strict, sometimes I think too strict when it comes to the English," he stated.

"When are you leaving, William?" asked Hugh.

"I will be sailing at the end of the week. Plenty enough time to acquaint you to the new people, and problems you will face. We will have an evening of festivities and invite many of the people you will interact with before I leave. There will be many different faces. It's good to have a social life with the authorities."

~

Hugh Tipton and his family stayed twelve years in Seville. They visited many places where Joan could sit and paint for hours, while Hugh pursued the diplomacy of her majesty the Queen of England.

Joan's favorite painting was of the *Flamingos in the Marshes*, as she titled the canvas. She and Hugh had spent the day rowing into and out of the lowlands. He'd sat reading another book under a large umbrella while she worked.

When she had painted to the point where she could finish the canvas at home. Hugh had remarked, "If flamingoes could commission portraits of themselves, like the English do of Hans Holbein, you would become famous, my dear." Then he raised his eyebrows and grinned at his wife.

She in return, threw her hat at him. He ducked, and it flew into the water. Hugh fished it out and brushed it off, receiving a kiss in return.

Another place where the whole family visited was the cartography building where Ferdinand Magellan, who organized the first circumnavigation of the globe, and Amerigo Vespucci, two great explorers and map makers, had worked. Both men were dead at this time.

Hugh explained. "This was at the start of "The Age of Exploration," when sciences like astronomy and cartography were surging in the Renaissance."

"Look, Harold," said John, pointing as usual. He went forward to a giant map hanging on the wall. "This map is by the German cartographer, Martin—." He read and then stood, while trying to wrap his mouth around the word *Waldseemüller*, which was the last name of the mapmaker.

"Wall-see-mule-r," Hugh tried out the name and shook his head.

Another mapmaker in the room came to their rescue. *"Waldseemüller,"* he said correctly, and coming over explained its significance. "This map was published with information from Vespucci's travels to the South Atlantic. He made copious notes and named many of the areas he visited." Then he pointed to a name on the map—America—written on the large landmass to the south of the Caribbean Sea. "It's named after Amerigo Vespucci."

Hugh bent over and observed, "This map was first printed in 1507."

While Hugh Tipton was in Spain, he sent many letters home to the merchant company's headquarters and this one to his family's headquarters in Portishead, Bristol, and London:

Dear Family, I hope this letter finds you well. I am recently come to the region of Andalusia, Spain and more importantly to the port of Seville. As you know I'm now the consul, and as such I wanted to alert you to the possibility of placing Tipton barrels here for shipment of wine, olive oil, and other goods to the world markets. Can you envision the Tipton Crest on barrels all over the known world? I can give you the name of a contact, but I will need you to send a letter asking about this possibility to my office here in Seville. Then I'll see that it gets to the right person.

Also, there is an opportunity to participate in the trade of smoked and salted fish, especially pilchards, cod, and herring. I know there was talk of trading with Ireland, so, if you haven't done so, as yet, this might be just the chance to get started. I look forward to hearing from you.

Your servant and cousin, Hew Typton.

To Hugh Tipton's credit and in response to his good work, in 1561, King Philip II of Spain described him in a decree as a *"persona honrizada y rica"* or an honorable and noble person.

The Tipton family went home in 1570, during the Spanish trade embargo against English goods. Hugh's youngest son, Harold, continued the tradition of his grandfathers, working in the shipping business in London.

Many Englishmen continued to trade with the Spaniards through smuggling supplies — sending them by partners of other countries or clandestinely landing on the forbidden shore to off load to other smugglers. Wine and oil continued to flow from Spain to England into the port of Bristol and others.

The English and Spanish maintained a tit-for-tat relationship, mainly because of privateering and pirating of boats in the West Indies and along the coasts of both countries. The fact that both imperial countries wanted the same land contributed to their discontent with each other. Depending on the decade or the year, their allies switched sides — first siding with the English and next with Spain.

As the English and Spanish continued to abrade one another, the situation soon came to a boiling point. War was on the horizon. King Philip II of Spain ordered the invasion of England.

The seacoast port of Cadiz, only a few miles east from Sanlúcar de Barrameda toward Gibraltar, became alive with shipbuilding, and the great Spanish Armada was conceived and being built in its extensive shipyards.

Elizabeth's spies soon informed the Queen.

She was not disposed to sit idly by and let the Spaniards build up a fleet of warring ships. She sent Sir Francis Drake and a flotilla of English ships to handle the matter.

"Singeing the King of Spain's Beard" was the term used by Sir Francis Drake as he informed the Queen of his escapades in Cadiz. Writing a letter, he told of staying in the port of Cadiz for three days, destroying ships, raiding, and burning the city. He told her Majesty that he'd only slowed the Spanish down. She could expect them to build again.

❧ Chapter 16 ❧

The End of the 16th Century
John Tipton, Elizabeth I, and Spain's Armada
Shakespeare and Dudley Tipton

Official relations of friendship and co-operation between Algeria and England began ten years after Hugh Tipton left Andalusia. It seemed that Tiptons were great representatives of the English government, because John Tipton became the first unofficial English consul posted to Algiers in 1580. After William Harbourne became the English ambassador to the Ottomans in Constantinople in 1582, Tipton's title soon became official. He was working for the English government.

He was appointed at the behest of London merchants who were interested in the North African market. He worked for the Turkey Company or the Levant Company, which was established under the reign of Elizabeth I. During the latter's reign, political relations between Muslim Algeria and Protestant England were founded on their shared hostility towards Catholic Spain. This alliance safeguarded English ships from assault by the notorious sitar-wielding, Barbary pirates, causing trade to flourish between the two countries.

Tipton's first view of the white-washed city was from the forecastle of a ship flying the Cross of St. George. Algiers was built on a hill with houses in layer after layer hugging the hillside.

He wondered at his reception as the ship anchored in the harbour. But he shouldn't have been concerned, because an official reception waited to greet him at the wharf. He was taken to the walled residence of the ruler and made especially welcome, by a light-skinned man. Tipton was astounded when the man spoke very good, even excellent English.

Because Elizabeth refused to renew privateering licenses, many of her subjects became pirates, and as renegades went to Algiers and other places. Because they spoke English, they rose through the ranks to command positions in the state. One of these became the treasurer of the ruler. His name, Assan Agha. The name sounded Turkish, but he proved to be an Englishman, one Rowlie, who was the son of a Bristol family, taken in the ship, *Sea Bird*.

John Tipton soon found there was plenty for him to do. English subjects, imprisoned in Algiers, were eager to send messages home asking money for their ransom. He worked as intermediary in obtaining their freedom and assured them of safe passage back to England. Then he often met English vessels coming into port to do lawful trade. There was no assurance their cargo would not be stolen while the ship was at anchor, so he offered advice on how best to secure their cargo and interceded if there was a problem.

This friendly association with England would deteriorate in the future, when the English started negotiations with Spain, and John Tipton would return to his native country.

～

When Sir Francis Drake informed Queen Elizabeth to get ready for a Spanish invasion, he told the truth. The Spanish couldn't have known that Elizabeth's coffers were empty, her ships starved of gun powder and ammunition, and her soldiers untrained and useless against an experienced and determined enemy.

Although they didn't know it, for the Spanish, this was the right time and the right place. But—something happened.

In July 1588, a Spanish fleet, of one hundred thirty ships, set sail under command of the Duke of Medina Sidonia. His orders were to wait off the coast of France, for a seasoned army of 27,000 men, being commanded by the Duke of Parma and sent overland from Flanders and the Netherlands, which at this time were part of the Spanish territory. If they could be landed on the English Kent coast, where coastal fortifications were practically nonexistent, they could go straight and quickly into London.

Tired of England's interference in the countries under their control and the privateering in the Americas, the Spanish King was ready to fight. Intending to land Parma's army by large, seagoing barge, the fleet would protect this transfer on its way to overthrow Queen Elizabeth and her establishment of Protestantism in England.

The Spanish King made one mistake. The Duke of Medina Sidonia was not a battle-hardened warrior and was subject to seasickness. He knew nothing about fighting at sea, and the weather in the English Channel was fickle.

~

As a warning and in preparation for a future coming invasion, beacons were established on the highest hills in England, warning the populace of the Spanish approach. These were positioned at fifteen miles apart and manned from March to October. Along the southern coast, forty-three were in place, with another twenty-four on toward Dover. These extended northward to Sedgley in Staffordshire and from there, east towards Great Barr and northwest toward the Wrekin Hill in Shropshire. The view from one to the other was unobstructed, making the lights clearly seen.

When the purchase of arquebuses (guns) from Holland fell through, some militiamen were armed with bow and arrows. Surely Sir Ralph Stafford and Roger Tipton were turning over in their graves at the sight of these untrained archers.

Sir Francis Drake's fleet of lighter and faster ships, coming from Plymouth harbour in Devonshire was joined by the Queen's commanders, Lord Charles Howard of Effingham and Sir John Hawkins.

When the Spanish were sighted as they entered the English Channel, the warning beacons were lit. Soon those in London and most of England would know the enemy was on the way. The Spanish, sailing in the crescent formation they were known for, were chased and easily attacked as they moved east up the English Channel toward Dover. They anchored in a crescent off the coast of France, awaiting Parma's army.

After a day of fighting, Sir Francis had a plan, and he explained it to the captains of his ships. The weather conditions were perfect. "All of us know our ammunition and gun powder is low, so I'm proposing we sacrifice eight of our small ships to stop the fighting," he said, standing on the aft deck and looking down at the commanders of his ships. Then he listed the ships he'd chosen and what he expected them to do.

Before nightfall, the ship's crews set his plan in motion, which became more spectacular since it was carried out in darkness. Loaded onto the selected ships were pitch, brimstone, gunpowder, and tar—selected for their ability to burn and explode and arranged in an order to cause as much havoc as possible. Eight ships, known as fire-ships with large amounts of explosives stowed on board, were towed upwind and in darkness set afire. With sails pushing them toward the Spanish fleet, and flames leaping amidships, the crews abandoned ship. The English watched their progress. There would be no sleep tonight.

The Spanish were in pandemonium as the ships approached. Not waiting for orders, the captains of the ships sent men to cut their anchors and the boats scattered in all directions—the closely-knit, crescent formation broken.

And as if sent by God, a quickly moving storm came from the Atlantic Ocean up the English Channel, pushing the Spanish past the white cliffs of Dover, into the North Sea and toward the coastline shoals. By now, the Armada was too far north to recover its position to pick up Parma's army. There was nothing they could do but sail before the wind—northward.

In daylight, Drake pursued them until he ran out of ammunition and then he pulled back, leaving the rest of the pursuit to his commander Lord Howard of Effingham, who mainly made sure none of the ships touched England's shore. The Great Armada limped along the coast of England on winds from the south. It rounded Scotland and faced the open Atlantic on the west coast of Ireland. The winds continued to play havoc with the Spanish ships. Storms from the open sea pushed those having no anchor against the rocky coast of Ireland, where they were battered by wind and waves and lost.

∼

In early August, the aging Robert Dudley, Earl of Leicester and a descendant of the Dudley's of Dudley Castle in Staffordshire, had assembled a force of 4,000 militia at Tilbury Fort, which was east of London toward the mouth of the River Thames. He had long been rumoured as a suitor for Elizabeth's hand. Not knowing of the Spanish fleet's plight, she rode to Tilbury and gave a speech to her loyal army. In part of it, she said…

> *Under God I have placed my chiefest strength and safeguard in the loyal hearts and goodwill of my subjects; and, therefore, I am come amongst you as you see at this time, not for my recreation and disport, but being resolved, in the midst and heat of battle, to live or die amongst you all – to lay down for my God, and for my kingdoms, and for my people, and my blood even in the dust. I know I have the body of a weak and feeble*

woman; but I have the heart and stomach of a king – and of a King of England too.

She was a vision dressed in a vest of white armour over her white robes, with a plumed helmet, holding a white and gold baton, while sitting on her white horse. Determination written on her face, she rode amongst her army, with Lord Dudley leading her horse. Although Elizabeth didn't know it, the sea battle against the Spanish Armada was already over — a great victory of her country — England.

~

After the speech and reviewing her army, the Queen returned to her palace at Greenwich, once known as the Palace of Placentia, where she had been born. Here was safety and rest. Unlike her father, Henry, she was only extravagant in her dress, and did not desire to have the largest palace or gardens in the country. Ten years would quickly pass as she continued to rule England.

~

The winter of 1598 was over, and spring was in the air. With her servants trailing behind, supposedly out of sight, Elizabeth would often walk the brick lined and pebbled paths of the gardens at Greenwich. If she stopped to smell a rose, someone was close by with a pair of scissors to cut her a bouquet. She loved violets and pansies, and the sweet smell of the honeysuckle, blooming near a marble seat in a bower where she sat, closed her eyes, and rested for a too brief moment from the world's problems.

The flowers at Greenwich reminded her of Hatfield, where she was a young girl, and the problems of state were nonexistent—of studies, of dancing, and of hunting—all the things she loved and enjoyed. She was sixty-five years old, hard to amuse and getting harder to please. When she walked, she hurt all over from the effort and sometimes, on bad days, used a cane to aid her balance.

Once, she remarked to Sir Francis Walsingham, her Secretary and the official coordinator of an intense intelligence network in England and abroad, *"To be a king and wear a crown, is a thing more glorious to them that see it, than it is pleasant to them that bear it."*

"Yes, Your Majesty," was his return, since he was old like her, he could agree wholeheartedly. "You seem cold today." He would suggest, and "Would Your Majesty like some hot tea? Some say it has a healing effect on aging bones."

He did not wait for her to answer, but went to order the repast, and then to build up the fire in her bed chamber, not waiting for others to perform the task.

When tea and small almond cakes arrived, he did not protest when she invited him to join her. This was the least he could do for his lonely Queen. He often wondered if she regretted not marrying one of the men who had become her suitor. She and the Steward would take a seat on the couches before the fire and enjoy the heat of the brew as it slid warmly down their throats, barely saying a word, sipping gently out of a fine china cup.

There were afternoons when she would sit and watch a jester or listen to a comic, who was on the retainer of and supplied by one of her nobles.

Actors and playwrights were sponsored by or under the patronage of powerful men of the court. The playwright, Christopher Marlowe had Lord Charles Howard, the Admiral who chased the Spanish Armada through the North Sea as his patron. William Shakespeare had Lord Hunsdon, the Lord Chamberlain to Queen Elizabeth.

Shakespeare and his troupe, The Lord Chamberlain's Men, were just down the lane at the newly constructed Globe Theater on the south bank of the River Thames in a seedy part of London called Southwark, a short drive by carriage from Greenwich.

Theaters were built out of the city limits so they could put on plays every day of the week, including Sunday. Inside the city, the Puritanical elements of the residents were stricter, thinking most of the productions were sacrilege or irreverent, with prohibitions for Sunday performances.

It was rumoured, Shakespeare had a new play he was ready to put on stage.

Elizabeth did not leave the palace very often, and if she had, she certainly wouldn't have gone into the area where the Globe was located. This area, west of the palace where she resided at Greenwich, was reported to be full of rogues and thieves and others of ill repute. She preferred having plays and other entertainment in the Great Hall of the palace, where she could sit or recline in the security and peace of her well-known surroundings.

Asking Sir Francis to check out the rumour of a new play of William Shakespeare, she awaited his reply.

For Sir Francis, walking in to talk to the Queen was almost like speaking to his wife—almost. He often grinned as this thought came to mind. "Majesty, your information was correct. He does have a new play called *As You Like It*, and he is ready to stage it at The Globe Theatre. He prays your Majesty to let him know your pleasure, as he will be glad to bring props, actors, and preform the presentation for you first."

"Then Francis, give him my thanks and the first open date for Saturday afternoon and let me know." Elizabeth waved him out.

"Yes, Majesty." Sir Francis backed out of the room. *"Almost,"* he thought and grinned again. Finding the palace Marshall, he asked his help in finding out the information for the Queen.

∾

William Shakespeare was in a hurry, calling out orders to the other actors in this afternoon's command performance before Her Majesty, the Queen.

"Be sure and don't damage the table and chairs! And get the new costumes, the Duke brought for us to use this afternoon, and the racks they hang on. Don't take the ratty ones we normally use." The actors usually got some fancier clothes passed on from the nobles when they bought new wardrobes or died.

"Thank goodness someone takes pity on us," said Nathan to Robert and Nicholas, as the three carried a wooden tree to the cart which would take the props to the palace.

"This thing is heavy and unwieldly," complained Nicholas, trying to keep the limbs with its green leaves tacked on balanced as they loaded it.

William continued to run down the existing props, taking some and leaving many. "We want just enough to make the performance look authentic," he said. "Remember the way they must be placed behind the curtain, so they can be moved easily."

With the final cart load, he joined the crew, sitting on the driver's seat. "I'm sure glad it's rather cold today. In the summer heat, I'd be sweating profusely."

Upon arriving at the palace, he checked out the stage area. It was raised slightly from the floor of the Great Hall. On each side was a door for actors to leave and enter the stage. Between these doors was a curtain, which split in the middle and pulled to each side. It hid the props, which were strategically placed so they could be moved easily into position during the play. At the very back of the props was a rock wall, part of a hallway, leading to a door into the outside gardens.

The one handling the props backstage was the driver of the cart. He and the other actors were pushing and pulling the last set of props in place. All was ready, the actors dressed. They awaited the Queen.

"Grandfather Harold, are we going to see the lions today?"

Harold Tipton, son of Hugh Tipton, looked down at his ten-year-old grandson, Dudley Tipton. He had promised to take him to The Tower Menagerie to see the animals lodged there—lions, monkeys, and elephants.

A zoo had been at the Tower for hundreds of years. It wasn't unusual to hear a lion's roar or elephant's trumpet when traveling by the place.

"Dudley, we won't be able to go today. Grandfather has to make a trip to the herbalist to get your grandmother some medicine—a far walk, I must say. We'll go another day."

"But grandfather, you promised we'd go," complained Dudley.

Harold walked around the counter at Tipton Brother's Import and Export and sat on a chair in front of a picture called *Flamingoes in the Marshes*, which his mother had painted while the family was in Seville, Spain. "This is what I'll do," he said, drawing the young boy between his knees, and pushing back the hair from his eyes. "Remember the park you've wanted to visit on our trips to our pie maker, close to Greenwich Palace?"

The pie maker was a friend, who made excellent concoctions in crusty dough. Dudley's mouth started to water. Like any young boy, he was always hungry. "Yes, sir."

"We'll go and have a pie and you can play in the garden. Jeffery will watch you while I continue on to the herbalist, and I'll pick you up on my way back. You like Jeffery. He's your friend. Will that work for you? You'll have plenty of time to play and make new friends."

Dudley acquiesced, and the two soon set off. The day was bright with sunshine for a change, since many days from the adjustment of winter into spring were gloomy with mists in the morning hours. The two walked briskly, hand-in-hand, along the street from his father's office near the River Thames, where boats nosily plied the river, going upstream or down.

Before too long the pieman's cart came into view. It stood close to one of the entrances to the Palace of Greenwich. His clients were among the nobles entering the home of the Queen. "Good morning, Jeffery."

"Good morning, Master Tipton and young Master Dudley." He bowed slightly, a usual habit with him. "Where are you two off to today?"

"That's a good question, and I need a favor, if you please. But first, we need two of your mutton pies."

Jeffery went to his brazier, which was filled with glowing charcoal, and took two crusted pies off the lid. On top of the iron pot's lid they stayed warm, toasty, and ready to eat. A water bucket, dipper, and tin cup provided liquid to wash the delicious pastry down.

Between bites, Harold explained his quandary, and asked a question, "Would you watch my grandson, while I visit my herbalist? He's a long walk into London, and I need to pick up some medicine for my wife, and — "

Jeffery stopped Harold in mid-sentence. "Of course, I'll take care of him. We're great friends, aren't we, Dudley?"

Dudley nodded, absorbed in the carts moving in and out at one of the side entrances of the palace. What were they doing? He didn't see his grandfather leave.

"Would you like a fruit pie to finish off your meal?" asked Jeffery, holding out the dessert in his hand toward the boy, and noticing his interest in the movements on the side of the palace.

Dudley took the pie and the container of honey to pour on the pastry. "This is de-e-licious," he exclaimed, smiling at Jeffery. "What are they doing at the palace?"

"Ah, a famous playwright named William Shakespeare will perform his latest production for Queen Elizabeth this afternoon. It shouldn't be long until they start. The last cart has unloaded, and the props are in the door." Jeffery craned his head to see if he spoke the truth. He knew everything which happened in the palace. The nobles who stopped to eat his pies were a wealth of information, and he was a master of drawing from them the details of palace happenings. It was amazing what a delicious meat pie could accomplish.

A thought occurred to him. "Dudley, would you like to see the play? I have friends who can get you backstage, and you can listen and peek through the cracks in the doors or curtains." Jeffery was often present when musicians came to play. He loved the different sounds and rhythms the instruments made when played, and with singing and dancing, so much the better.

"Wow, yes. That would be great." Better than playing outside with the children in the park, he thought. Going into the palace—wow.

The door keeper at the palace was happy to let Dudley into the side entrance. Jeffery often gave him a meat pie and sometimes sent extras home to his family.

Dudley noticed a stack of firewood cut and placed next to the stone wall outside the building. The guard cautioned, "Don't go anywhere but to the back of the stage, and you can walk the long hall until it ends, but no farther than that. Do you understand?"

"Yes, sir." The young boy slipped through the door.

Inside the palace was the back of the stage and props.

The cartman waited in the semi-gloom of the enclosed area for the play to start. Observing an intruder, he said, "How did you get in here? Don't touch anything," he admonished Dudley, but he didn't shoo the young lad away.

Before Dudley could answer, the play started. He was mesmerized as he watched beside the curtain's edge but in the shadows. He had a clear view of the stage as the actors came and went. When the curtain was opened between acts, he backed up and was careful to stay out of the way of its movement.

He was astounded, because all the actors were men, and he snickered as the men played women.

Once the cartman asked him to help push a table onto the scene and move chairs before the curtain was pulled. He jumped to help.

The play opened with the hero, Orlando, and his brother at odds with each other. The play continued as Orlando wrestled and won a contest with the champion of the Duke's court. This didn't enhance the hero's stance with the Duke, who hated him.

Celia, the evil Duke's daughter, and Rosalind, her beloved cousin, were watching the match from the manor's steps. Rosalind is attracted to the young Orlando and he, seeing her, loves her immediately.

Warned that the evil Duke would see him killed, he left with his older friend Corin for the Forest of

Arden and safety, thinking he would never see his beautiful lady again.

When Rosalind is banished by Celia's evil father, the two women left together, dressed as men, heading for the Forest of Arden where another banished, but good Duke, the friend of Orlando's father lives.

As the play progressed, Dudley helped the cartman move more props. Telling the young lad, before the next scene starts, two large trees must be moved into position, the cartman pointed to the area and each tree and left.

"I'll be back in time to help," he whispered, and then he disappeared down the long hall.

Dudley thought … to help? Was he now in charge of props?

Finally, the curtain closed. But the actors, still speaking, remained on stage to complete the scene, providing time for the scenery to be moved.

Dudley managed to push one tree in place, but the other was larger and unwieldy. When he pushed it, the top-heavy tree fell over with a loud crash.

The actors on stage raised their eyebrows and looked dubiously at each other, but continued as if nothing had happened, knowing that's what was expected of them.

Dudley looked in horror at the downed tree. What would he do? The cartman wasn't back. He couldn't raise the tree by himself. Suddenly, he remembered the wood stacked outside the palace. He hurried to the door, opened it, and grabbed something from beside the stack. When the curtains were pulled, there stood Dudley, beside the fallen tree. He had his foot on the trunk with an axe over his shoulder. No one observing the play would know any difference. He stood there until the next scene was over.

The curtain closed, again, and the cartman returned. He smelled loudly of ale.

The play continued with Dudley pondering one of the lines. *"All the world's a stage and all men and women merely players."* What did that mean? Maybe Jeffery or his grandfather would know.

Slowly the acts went by and Dudley forgot his grandfather, Jeffery, and time.

The cartman started discretely moving props through the door to a staging area outside.

The play ended. In the last scene, the couples got married. Rosalind to Orlando. Celia with Orlando's brother. All ends well.

There was energetic clapping among the audience in front of the stage as the final curtain was drawn. Soon, the audience was milling around, talking or getting ready to leave.

As Dudley turned to go, he was tapped on the shoulder by a man with piercing dark eyes, black hair, and pointed black beard. "How does it feel to act in a Shakespeare play?" the man asked.

"B-but I was standing very still," was all Dudley could say, thinking he would soon be chastised for the falling tree.

"Young man, you are a quick thinker," the bearded man stated. "And your actions fit right into the play."

"Thank you, sir."

"Where was my cartman?" The man asked, looking around the area for the deserter, who had carried a prop outside and hadn't come back into the building.

"He went on an errand, sir."

"And didn't come back, huh. The errand was probably to an inn. I'll be talking to him. Hold out your hand, young lad."

Dudley did as he was told.

"Here's two pence for a job well done, and should you need work in the future, come see me." The darkheaded man said this with a slight smile on his face, as he turned to accept congratulations from those in the audience.

Dudley looked down at the shiny coins in his hand. Then he headed for the door to the outside. "Who is that man?" he pointed and asked of the cartman, who had just come inside the palace to the rear of the stage.

"That was William Shakespeare, hisself."

"Oh," said Dudley, turning to leave. Trying to put his coins in his pocket, he dropped one.

The penny rolled. He followed it across the stone floor and stooped to pick it up. When he stood upright, before him was an older woman dressed in a beautifully jeweled gown with pearls and precious jewels embedded in the fabric. Startled, he noticed some of the pearls were in the shape of an oval. As he looked at them, they were looking back at him.

Her hands, held at her waist, revealed long fingers full of expensive rings. Dudley looked up into her face. Her hair was almost red with streaks of gray.

"Who might you be, young lad," the woman asked rather sternly, her brown eyes turning mischievous, as she peered intently at this young man who'd suddenly appeared before her.

Being startled, he replied, "Dudley, madame."

"Yes?" she said, a question mixed into her answer, and then she quickly quipped. "Then I'm the Queen of England."

Those standing around close caught the joke and laughed, but Dudley wasn't old enough for royalty gossip and didn't understand. Not knowing what else to say and not understanding the lady's nuance, Dudley made his escape through the back door, and hurried toward his friend, Jeffery.

"How was the show, Dudley? Did you like the play?" the pie man asked.

Dudley told him all that had happened. "Where's your pennies?" asked Jeffery.

Dudley pulled them from his pocket, dropping one into the grass.

Jeffery stooped to rescue it, saying, "Better keep them safe in your pocket." He looked up. "There comes your grandfather."

Before he put his pennies back in his pocket, the young boy ran to his grandfather to tell him the story.

Harold waved at Jeffery and continued down the street with Dudley jabbering away.

After the two left, Jeffery loaded up his pie cart and started down the path toward home. Something shiny caught his attention. He stooped and picked up a penny. "Findings keepings," he murmured. But he kept it safe, and returned it to Dudley the next time he saw him.

∾

Elizabeth ruled for four more years and died in 1603. She was known as the Virgin Queen or Good Queen Bess. Having no heirs, she was the last of the Tudors to reign.

Taking them on the road, Shakespeare continued to produce plays. In 1597, he was in Bristol, playing in the Guildhall before the mayor, and in 1603, the year of James I's ascension to the throne, he performed in Shrewsbury as the plague ran rampant in London. While on the River Severn, he performed *Hamlet* and *Othello* on Castle Street.

When James I came to the throne, he was granted royal patronage by the King, and the troupe became known as The King's Men. In 1611, the same year that the King James Version of the Bible was printed, Shakespeare retired to Stratford-on-Avon, as a rich man, and he died there in 1616.

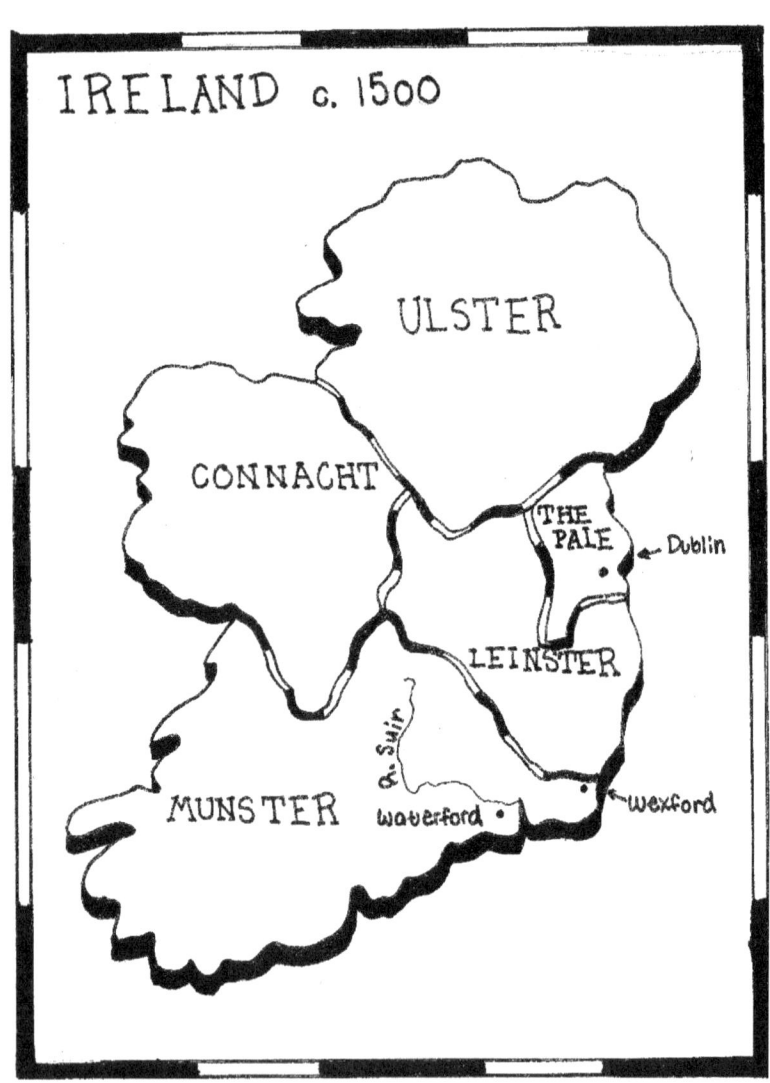

❧ **Chapter 17** ❧

The Early 17th Century
James I, Charles I, and Oliver Cromwell

The forced removal of the Irish Catholics from their ancestral land started with Henry VIII's policy called Plantations. This same policy of re-conquest and removal continued with Mary I and Elizabeth I.

When the Irish rebelled against the surrender and regrant program, land was confiscated, and English plantations established. Some of these plantations were settled as examples for the Irish to follow. Others were intended to punish the Irish nobles who rebelled—taking their land and giving it to English settlers with no intention of returning it to the former owners.

The feelings of revolt among the Irish were building with smaller battles in different parts of Ireland. While the clash between England and Spain continued, these Irish rebels were supported by the Spanish.

Elizabeth did call a halt, after hearing of several bloody massacres which took place against the Irish, wiping out whole families—men, women, and children. When she died in March 1603, the issue was unreconciled.

When the Stuart, James VI of Scotland became James I, King of England, he escalated the repopulation program with mass confiscations of land, pushing the Irish west toward the Connaught. This part of Ireland was the most desolate and poorest land in Ireland—many starved to death.

James I was not a favorite of the English people. He did unite Scotland and England, calling the country Great Brittania for the first time. Neither was his son, Charles, a favorite, as his arrogance put the whole country into confusion.

～

It was during this time a ship part-owned by Christopher Jones, called *The Mayflower*, set sail from Plymouth, England for the New World. There was an estimated one hundred and two passengers and a crew of thirty. These people, known for their separatist views against the Church of England, wanted religious liberty, and they were willing to risk death on the high seas to gain such. Their story was one of strife, adventure, starvation, and disease, but the Puritans, as they were called, survived and started the colony of Plymouth in Massachusetts. The English continued to establish colonies up and down the New World, in Massachusetts, New Hampshire, Maryland, Connecticut, Rhode Island, and into the West Indies.

～

In 1625, James died, and his son, Charles I of the house of Stuart, became King. He was much like his father, stubborn and very much his own King, preferring his so-called Personal Rule, where he ruled by decree, rather than a Parliament elected by the people.

From the Magna Carta in 1215, the English people had started to voice their opinion on matters concerning their country's position on affairs, those which affected their lives and fortunes. Although many died for speaking their convictions, the Parliament arose slowly through the years, nibbling away at the rigid monarchy until the people had enough power to express their sentiments and make a difference in English law.

This is where Charles I found himself—with Parliament having a mind of its own and the voice of the people.

Something had to give, and it started with a series of revolts all over the English Isles. Charles lacked money to carry on any lengthy conflict.

The nobles had plenty of money and the people behind them. The conflict started in Scotland, went to Ireland, and extended into England. The house of Stuart was in shambles and losing on all fronts.

This series of battles was as much a religious war as a political one as the Protestants and Catholics, holding their noses, aligned with the Royalists and Charles, while the Puritans went with the Parliamentarians.

Nottingham was again at the start of a war, if we remember Richard III, whose base was there, too. As Richard lost his life to Henry V, so would Charles surrender and eventually be beheaded by Oliver Cromwell and his followers.

In Ireland, the escalated Plantation Policy under Charles I failed when the Irish took to the hills and bogs. They started a hit-and-run attack against the English, raiding and killing the new English transplants who were settled in the Irish homes taken by the forces of James I.

Finding the English dead in their homes, or where they worked in the confiscated fields, was not unusual as the policy of resettlement continued. At this point in time, there was no organized resistance to the English invasion of the land. But, fed up with the Plantation Policy, the beleaguered Irish rebelled in 1641, and struck with a vengeance, killing several thousand of the settler population. This only exacerbated the problem, and soon a man would come into power in England which would make Irish lives a living nightmare.

In 1642, the English Civil War started in earnest. This War of the Three Kingdoms, which included England, Scotland, and Ireland ended up tearing the countries to pieces. Both sides maintained that they stood for the rule of law, yet civil war was by classification a matter of force.

~

Oliver Cromwell was the great grandson of Thomas Cromwell, who served Henry VIII. He had risen through the ranks as a staunch and outspoken Puritan. Elected to the Parliament, he never hesitated to voice his opinion, and when activities necessitated the establishment of militias to support the group he joined, he proved himself capable of organization and leadership. As Captain, his first appearance was at the Battle of Edgehill, October 1642, which was the first major battle of the Civil War.

Cromwell was part of the Roundheads who fought against the royal family or Royalist sympathizers. From this internal conflict, he emerged as the Lord Protector of England, when in 1646, King Charles surrendered and in the end was executed. Thus, begins the short-lived Republic of the Commonwealth of England.

~

If the Irish thought the Kings and Queen were terrible, Oliver Cromwell, a Welshman, turned out to be the devilin-disguise. His hatred of the Irish Catholics stemmed from his Puritan roots. Most Puritans were tolerant of other religions, but this did not extend to the Roman Catholics. He sent the English fleet and military to Ireland to kill the Irish Confederates, their Royalist and Scottish allies and confiscate their land. He continued the Plantation policy started by Henry VIII, and led the invasion himself.

In 1649, Cromwell started in Dublin, which was situated in The Pale, in the center of the east coast. It was the only port city the English retained. He sailed in fifty ships, landed troops, and equipment, and the fighting continued northward and southward.

Going north, his army under Robert Venables subdued Ulster.

The full extent of Cromwell's invasion and the atrocities or lack thereof will never be known. With the northern part and western ports of the island secured, he turned his attention southward, towards the ports of Wexford and Waterford on the Irish Sea.

When Wexford fell and the garrison there was massacred, Waterford was next on the list of ports. A siege started and lasted until December, but the cold, winter weather moved in, and the citizens of the area were given a reprieve.

In his winter quarters, half of Cromwell's army of 6000 became unfit because of disease. In May 1650, Cromwell left the country to continue his fight with the Scottish on the English mainland, and the renewed siege of Waterford began again in earnest in June 1650.

～

After Harold Tipton had sent Hugh Tipton to London in the 1500's to run the operation there, Hugh had written an aging Harold that the products found in Ireland were in demand in London and could possibly be introduced into France via the underground trade.

At first, the Tipton's sailed their ships to Waterford and waited until they could fill their holds with fish, hides, and other goods for sale on the wharf. As the situation on the isle became more tenuous and supplies were iffy, and their business expanded in the continent, they decided to rent a small building and warehouse. They could buy and stock supplies and start a larger shipping operation, which the grandson of Paul, the young Samuel Tipton, eager to be an integral part of the company, was to head. They would stay until the situation in Ireland became too unbearable to continue.

~

As an Englishman, Samuel and his shipping operation were exempt from the raids being conducted by Cromwell's New Model Army, or so he thought.

Receiving guarantees from General Thomas Preston, a Catholic in charge of the Irish Confederates, he'd managed to get the other side's assurances for his own safety within the city of Waterford. A few coins in the right place always helped.

With all sides covered, he maintained this belief until the following spring, when the New Model Army started to nibble into the area around the city of Waterford's walls, and siege artillery was moved in to batter them. Tensions within the city rose, and he immediately became an outsider with ties to the enemy.

How long would he be able to keep this part of the company open? Those in Bristol understood his plight and sent word not to risk his life or the ship. Samuel understood their reasons, but he had another reason to stay.

~

Samuel Tipton walked out onto the quay and looked over at the company ship, *The Bristol*, a rented Dutch fluyt, anchored at the port of Waterford on the River Suir. This three-masted ship was built to haul cargo with a limited crew. The financially independent Dutch were still masters of building seagoing vessels, and to all things pertaining to the sea.

Samuel had been busy all morning directing the loading of barrels filled with pilchards, small fish like sardines smoked locally or at a distant fishery, a delicacy sold and eaten in Bristol, London, and their newest customer, Spain. The fish, smoked in burnt alder and oakwood, left a faint but unmistakable odor which came from the watertight Tipton barrels made in Gloucester or Bristol, England and shipped from Portishead.

The Tipton Brother's had maintained a small shipping operation for many years in Ireland, and specifically this small town. His wasn't the only ship at harbour, but it was the only English one at present. Several of the ships were Irish privateer's and friends of his, who preyed on shipping in the Irish Sea. He'd heard rumours they were soon to sail to more friendly harbours, because running the English blockade outside the port continued to be hard.

As Samuel turned to head into the office of the company, he was hailed by a lass with long blonde hair coming down the wharf.

"Samuel, wait up," she called as she walked faster to catch him before he entered the door.

Pausing, he noticed she was dressed in his favorite red dress, long to her shoes, and sleeves with lace around the wrist. A white collar surrounded her neck and waved in the air as she hurried to greet him. She put a hand up to hold it down and one to hold her straw hat, which had a red ribbon. In the ocean breeze, it streamed out behind her.

This outfit was the one he'd noticed the first day he'd seen her. The day his heart said she was the one. It fit her slim frame perfectly.

Samuel smiled and called, "Keera, you are early." She was to come later, and he was to follow her home for the evening meal at her father's manor. This same scenario had been going on for several months, long enough for Samuel to think he might talk to her father and ask to take her for his wife. He was almost certain the father would not object, because he'd been subtly hinting for several weeks.

Samuel gave her a hug and led her into the office.

Keera lived in a manor about two miles outside the stone walls of Waterford. Despite Samuel's encouragement, her stubborn father continued to live there, knowing he was putting his family in danger. So far, the Roundheads or Cromwell's army hadn't bothered the area, preferring more strategic and lucrative targets elsewhere.

"It was such a beautiful day and my work was done, so I decided to take advantage of the warm sun and walk here to see you."

"I'm glad you came. The May sun does feel good," he said, striding behind the counter and picking up the paperwork for his ship's captain, going over it, and making sure it was correct.

"Did you have trouble getting your complete shipment of pilchard fish?" she asked. Keera was always interested in his activities and kept abreast of his progress in the shipping business. Would she make a good helper in his office? He thought so. Tipton couples tended to work together.

"The *Naomh Bréanainn or St. Brendan* was a little late, but not enough to cause difficulty in shipping today's barrels this afternoon. The captain did say getting through the blockade was hard, but with his smaller boat, he accomplished the run last night after midnight, when the moon was covered with clouds."

"He woke you up, didn't he?"

"Yes, banging on the door, but I was glad to see him. We'll make it to Bristol in plenty of time to offload the cargo and transfer it to other ships waiting at the wharf."

"Do you know the story of St. Brendan?" she asked, smiling up at him with beautiful green eyes.

Samuel returned her smile and replied, "I didn't know there was a story. I'm assuming you'll tell me."

Keera walked to the front of the counter opposite him and sat on a stool nearby. Crossing her legs, she placed her elbows on the worktop and related the story. "St. Brendan was one of the Twelve Apostles of my country, and it is said he first discovered the New World." She raised her eyebrows, pursed her lips, and waited for his response.

"If that's true, why haven't we heard of this feat?" asked Samuel, wishing he could give her a kiss, and thinking he must tell her father soon of his wish to take her to wife.

"I don't know, but he made a curragh or leather-clad boat, of wickerwork and covered it with tar, much like the ones today, took some monks with him, and went in search of the Garden of Eden."

"Did he find it?" Samuel found the tale interesting, but he didn't believe it.

"What do you think?" she asked.

"I think I need to get this paperwork to my captain." He grinned and waved the pages in the air. "Once his crew comes back to the ship, he'll be ready to sail. Come on. You can go with me and see the boat."

Outside, they walked toward the gangplank of the ship.

Suddenly, the loud sounds of yelling pierced the air. "Keera, Keera," yelled her younger brother, Aron, running down the wharf. "They've killed Father and Mother," he shrieked.

Keera turned toward the sounds just in time to be knocked backwards by her brother who grabbed her around the waist. "What are you saying, Aron? Who's been killed? And how?"

Aron caught his breath, looked up at Keera, and explained between gulps of air, "The soldiers came to the house shortly after you left and broke down the door. Father stood up to them in the Great Hall and they ran him through with a sword." Tears coursed in streams down his face.

"How do you know this?" asked Samuel.

"I saw them through the kitchen window. When they attempted to take our sisters, Mother stood between the men and Roisin and Ciara. I moved to the back steps, trying to decide to go into the room. I heard her blood curdling scream and fled down the steps, through the arbor and over the stone fence. They didn't see me. I watched as they left after ransacking the house, taking with them Roisin and Ciara, hands tied together with a rope. What will happen to them? I shouldn't have run. I should have stayed to help." He rubbed his running nose on his sleeve, and remembering, he started crying even harder.

Keera looked at Samuel, tears welling in her eyes at her brother's grief and shock, and the possibilities he'd uttered.

"Keera, first let's go and check out the house and see if we can determine what has happened." Stuffing his captain's sailing papers in his pocket, he headed up the wharf with the two following close behind. "Aron, did you see the soldiers as you came to the wharf?"

"No, it looked like they were headed for the manor to the west."

"Then, we will not run into them. Let's hurry." Samuel picked up his speed. They didn't have a minute to lose.

He'd been afraid this would happen. Oliver Cromwell had vowed to get rid of the Irish barbarians, and that was the nicest word he'd used about them. He intended to take over their lands and give the best Irish plantations to his English friends. He was doing just that. At times, he even commanded his generals to kill the people wholesale and without quarter. They were to take those who did not resist, or could be taken without much resistance, in irons to staging areas.

Rumours floated around on the River Suir that ships waited in nearby harbours which were full of Irish men, women, and children, waiting to be taken as slaves to Barbados in the West Indies.

At present, none of these ships were in the River Suir, so any from the area of Keera's family's location would be marched some distance to be boarded.

The sugar plantations in the West Indies were booming, and although African slaves were becoming numerous there, Cromwell's friends needed more hands for the fields and to maintain the houses of the owners. Slaves from Africa cost money. The Irish prisoners did not.

∼

Upon reaching Keera's home, everything was quiet, as silent as death, with no noise around the grounds or on the house's porch. The manor's ornate door was standing wide open.

"Stay here," Samuel advised as he walked up several steps to enter the house. "There's no reason for you to see this." Carefully, he went in through the door and immediately found Keera's father stretched out in the hall. His last move was a hand over the wound in his chest. Blood still oozed between his fingers and ran onto the floor.

Samuel continued on into the back rooms and kitchen. Here, he discovered the mother. She was wounded, but she was not dead. "Keera and Aron, come around the house to the back and into the kitchen," he called loud enough for them to hear, and then he knelt beside her to examine a wound to her side.

Keera appeared through the back door and ran to her, "Mother."

The woman's eyes fluttered open at hearing her daughter's voice. "What happened," she asked in a whisper, as Keera knelt beside her, avoiding another pool of blood.

"The soldiers came. Roisin and Ciara are gone. The men took them."

Hearing this news about her daughters, she closed her eyes and didn't move.

Keera looked at Samuel. "Can we get her out of here? She's going to need a body physician."

"Sure. Is there a cart or maybe a sheet? We could make a hollow out of the cloth to carry her. Wonder if any of the servants are left? We'll have a hard time moving her with just the three of us. Aron, see if you can find anyone outside, and look for a cart."

⁓

Two of the male servants had returned to the small homes provided for the plantation workers. The rest had fled at the first sight of soldiers. The two men were collecting what few possessions they had, ready to return to the hills and hide.

A cart without horses provided transportation back to Waterford, being pulled by all of them at times. As the group clattered down the wharf, Captain Peter Walton came down the ship's gangplank.

"What on earth happened?" he exclaimed when he reached the ragtag group, observing the bloody woman in the cart.

Not waiting to hear the explanation, Keera ran for the body physician to tend her mother.

While she was gone, Samuel explained the situation to his captain.

"Peter, we'll all be sailing with you, today. This will be the last time our ship will dock here, at least until this fighting is over."

"I see," Captain Walton nodded, agreeing with his employer. "I don't have a problem with that. I've been increasingly uneasy about sailing here, even with St. George's Flag flying from the main mast. I figured I'd end up in the West Indies, chopping sugar cane."

Samuel continued, "We'll have to stow the women in your captain's quarters below deck until we clear the blockade."

"Yes, Master Samuel, and a few coins in the right palms will help our passage through the blockade. We may not have any trouble at all."

"Send some of your men to round up more supplies from my warehouse. We'll need food, blankets, and cots."

The captain gave orders to his crew, those who were standing around, listening to the account of the onslaught of the manor.

Keera had managed to pack a small group of possessions for her and Aron, while he looked for help and before they fled the manor—with the idea, they would go to relatives in the fishing village of Duncannon.

Samuel went to look at the meager supply. "Please take all the extra supplies which are on the cart and stow them in a dry place." There was no way Keera was going to stay in Ireland. He would see to that.

After this was done, Keera's mother was carefully lifted aboard and placed under the forecastle out of the sun. She groaned at the pain caused by her movement onto the ship.

While waiting on Keera to return with the body physician, Samuel went into his office to pack wooden boxes with his belongings and others with company papers.

He hefted one of the boxes and walked outside to a commotion. Keera, along with the physician and his whole family, stood on the wharf.

"Samuel, he wants to go with you, and Mother will probably need him on the trip." Keera looked at him, her eyes saying, "I'm sorry," but also, pleading for a positive response.

Did everyone want to leave Ireland at the same time, he thought and nodded yes.

Persuading Keera to leave Ireland with Aron might have been hard, but the captain had loaded her mother on the ship, so she didn't have much choice, especially if she intended to take care of the wounded woman.

"My dear, the English are raiding Irish plantations, and staying is not safe." Samuel realized she was in shock. How hard it must be to believe in him—a hated Englishman? But, after a long conversation, he convinced her it was for the best. Her safety lay in sailing with the ship into the harbour at Bristol—to his family, and he hoped into his life. He wanted to take care of her. He decided now was not the time to tell her of his plans.

He promised they would head for the Caribbean Sea Islands to find her family.

While the physician tended to the mother, he gave the plantation workers the option of going or staying.

Both ran home to get their families and what few goods they possessed. The prospect of leaving their home was hard, but Samuel promised work in England on his family's dock at Portishead or in Bristol.

With their families on board ship and extra supplies for the voyage, the odd-looking group was ready to set sail.

The captain managed to get all the women and children into his cramped quarters below deck. Everyone else was outfitted to look like crew members. After running the blockade, they would be welcome to come back up the ladder into the open air. "Draw anchor," he called, and the ship was headed down the River Suir to the sea.

After the initial shock of the escape from Ireland was over, Captain Walton sailed on his regular run to the West Indies, and with Keera's mother on the mend, Samuel Tipton decided to take Keera on a buggy ride to Portishead. The day was bright with sunshine as they stopped in a secluded and shaded spot just above the rough quay.

He descended from the buggy and stood, breathing deeply of the warm, salty air. The tide was out and in the mud flats, sea birds ran nimbly from one puddle to another pecking at animal life—crustaceans and minnows caught in the sea water.

He thought back to the Tiptons' love of the sea, which he'd read about in the Ancestry Book, starting with Tybba, who before he was joined to his beautiful Gemma, sailed with his Roman friend, Cassius Aurelius, around the big rock at the mouth of the

Mediterranean Sea. It continued with Eggen, who became tied to the sea with his small export and import business. Sometime after that, the Tiptons had changed their blood to saltwater, and became a part of the sea, becoming captains of their own ships.

From the first Tipton, who'd come to settle here, several more houses dotted the hillside on the north and south side of the Avon. More than one ship was anchored offshore, waiting for the tide to rise, so they could either sail safely up the River Severn or the River Avon.

Samuel stood briefly, shading his eyes in the bright light and peering at the ships. He pointed, "Keera, see the one with the flag of St. George, the red cross on white flying in the wind? The Tipton crest is below it."

"Yes," she said, looking intently in the direction he indicated. "Is that the ship Captain Peter commands?"

"No. He's not expected back from the New World for two more months. My brother, William, is the captain of the ship. You haven't met him."

"Will he be in Bristol tomorrow?"

"Yes, you'll meet him then."

Samuel had decided this was the day. His palms were sweaty, and he was nervous. "Keera, please hand me the coverlet and the basket of food." He had thought eating outside, with the picturesque scene of the Severn Estuary before them, was the perfect place to ask for her hand in marriage.

Putting his hands around her waist, he helped her down from the buggy. For a brief moment their eyes locked. He thought he read her answer in their depths. They walked from the road down a trail to the edge of the rocks, which sat near the water. A short span of sand soon touched the sea, where the water had a slight chop from the breeze

He spread the coverlet on the grass above the rocks and set the basket atop. He couldn't wait any longer. Kneeling on one knee in front of her, he asked, "Keera, I love you. Have since I first saw you in your lovely red dress as you walked along the wharf at Waterford. Will you become my wife?"

He didn't expect her to start crying. But, she did. Through her tears, she nodded a yes.

Samuel got to his feet and pulling her to her feet, took her into his arms as she sobbed her heart out.

∾

Later, when asked what they ate for their noon meal, he said, "Hugs and kisses." He couldn't remember a thing, except promising her they would soon be going to look for her sisters.

The service took place in the new Anglican Church, where his family had become members when Henry abolished the Catholic churches in England. The people were the same as always and most of the services little altered. Only the church's money went to a different place.

Keera's mother was present.

∾

In 1653, after two years and the birth of their first daughter, Samuel kept his promise. *The Bristol* sailed for the Caribbean with the exact crew which took them from Ireland to Bristol.

Samuel had decided to wait until the best sailing time, which was around November, to set out for the

West Indies. The worst storms of the Atlantic would be abating, and the winter weather would turn to freezing in England.

They would escape the cold and head to the warmth of the Caribbean.

Since the Tiptons were experts in making barrels and casks, these wooden containers could be made on site, and they were the perfect reason to go, and if there was other business to be had, so much the better. The company already made regular spring and summer trips to the New World, taking passengers, barrels, and cargo — filling their holds in summer with tobacco from the New World for the return trip.

Barrels of sugar from the islands could fill their holds in the winter when tobacco could not be grown in the New World. In this way, they'd set up a longer route and included the Caribbean Islands in the trip, and communication from home, for Samuel and his family, would not be cut off.

"It's the perfect circle," said Samuel to Aron, as they stood on the wharf at Bristol. The young man stood as tall as Samuel, and had gained muscle strength since being in the employ of the Tipton's.

Aron had taken to life on a ship like an old hand and made several trips to London and one to the New World with one of the Tipton captains.

"At least, we won't be carrying slaves," Aron spit the word slaves out of his mouth like it was dirt.

"Are you thinking about your sisters?" asked Samuel, putting his arm around his brother-in-law.

Since most of the kidnapped Irish were sent to Barbados and sold as slaves, the Tipton's decided to set up a shipping and building operation on this island. Finding the two sisters would be accomplished in this way.

"I suppose so, but also about the captains of boats here on the quay who brag about the money they make in the illegal trade."

"No, Aron. You have my promise, the Tiptons *won't* be involved in the slave trade." At present, this traffic in slaves was light at Bristol, but some were beginning to be enmeshed in the triangle trade of taking goods to Africa, loading up with dark-skinned natives, and taking them to the Indies. There they sold humans and took on cargo for the New World and home. "The Portuguese are known for starting such disgusting actions, taking their captives to the sugar plantations of South America."

The two stood, watching a small boat being rowed upstream.

Aron leaned over and looked until it disappeared under the stone bridge. "I'm ready to go right now," Aron exclaimed eagerly as they continued to stand looking down the busy Avon.

"I don't know what we'll find over there. Certainly, the land and its people will be more primitive, but we'll have to make the best of it. With the backing of the Tipton Brothers' company, there's no possibility of not being successful." Samuel paused, and added, "Is that Captain Walton, coming across the bridge?"

"Yes, he's been back a couple of days," Aron said, peering at a tall man dressed in long, white shirt and black trousers, who appeared to be swaying a little. He was still having trouble with his sea legs.

A few steps later, the captain hailed the two and joined them. "It's a good thing we put off going to the West Indies until November," he said. He'd just returned from a special mission to Barbados, sailing along the future trading route the group would take to the West Indies. His task was to establish partners in different ports for trade, and look for a great location for their company's operation on the island. If found, he had permission to rent or buy and some equipment to offload.

"Welcome back, captain. Why do you say that?" asked Samuel.

"Barbados had a great hurricane in July. I found much destruction while I was on the island. And after talking to the local people, I discovered there was one the year before. They barely recovered from it before this one hit."

"Don't tell my wife this."

"Samuel, I don't think it would make a difference. Keera's determined to go." Aron added, "Besides you and the baby, all she thinks about is finding our sisters."

The company had decided that Aron and Keera would help with the operation in Barbados, along with the Irish plantation workers he'd brought to England and some adventurous men from Gloucester. They would make the core of the startup operation. As the business grew, native men from the island would be added to the work force.

"Did I hear my name mentioned?" asked Samuel's wife, coming up to them and smiling at her husband.

"Yes, my sweetheart, you did. Captain Peter, Aron and I were just discussing the prospects we'd find in our new home."

Keera held their first child, Anne, a girl with a head full of dark hair, which was about all you could see, since she was wrapped tightly in a wool blanket. She had passed her first birthday. "So, what have you three decided? When will we sail?"

Samuel went over to peek at his daughter who was clothed in a cotton gown and fast asleep. He gave his wife a quick peck on the cheek. "What do you think, Captain Peter? In one week, can we be loaded, on the sea, and headed for Barbados?"

The captain answered, "Make it two."

And, they were.

∾

One item, the captain loaded very carefully in an airtight box. It contained the Ancestry Book and Sir Anthony's antique sword. These were given to Samuel by his grandfather, Paul.

"Maybe, I'll come and see you someday. Until then, keep these safe."

"I promise grandfather, and I'll see you soon."

"Add your memories to the pages, and make sure your son reads the words of your forefathers and writes his own story on its sheets."

The old man embraced his grandson, and for a second, gray hair mingled with brown hair. There was a brief kiss on the young man's cheek.

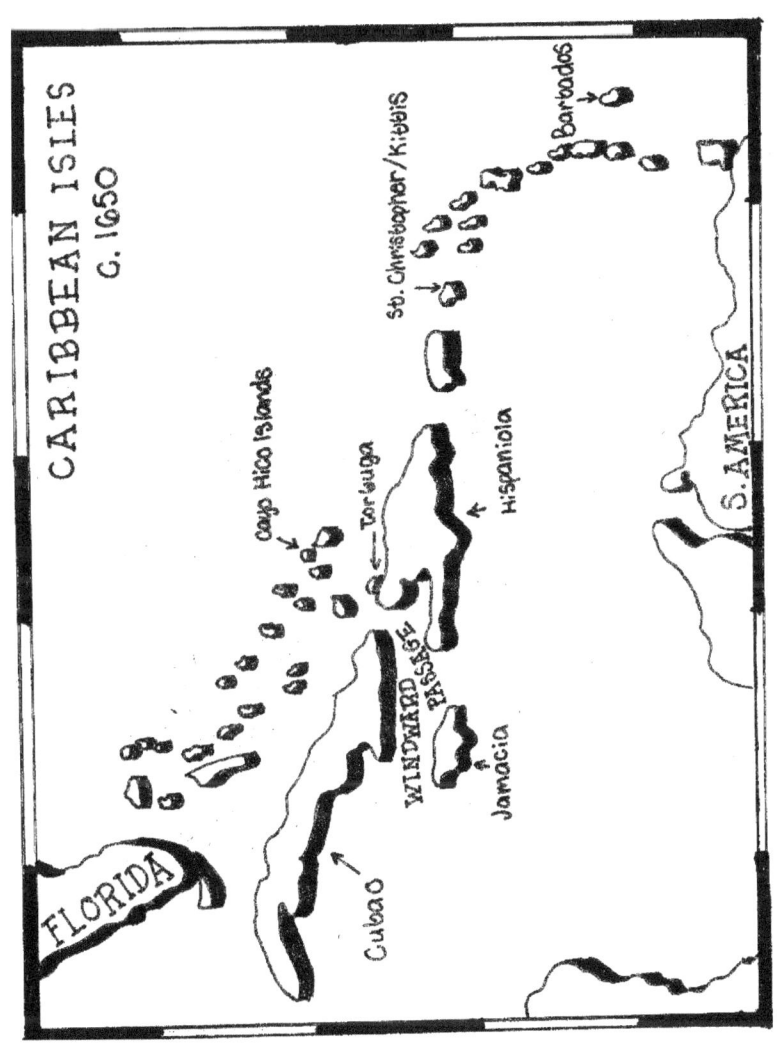

❦ Chapter 18 ❦

17th Century, West Indies

St. Christopher (St. Kitts), Master Jeaffreson

After sailing for two months, Samuel and Keera stood at the ship's rail, watching the aqua-blue of the sea and the white foam of the wake roll by. Periodically, islands appeared out of the ocean, their volcanic peaks standing starkly against the blue sky as *The Bristol* with her tall sails passed them by.

"What are those darker splotches on the sea's surface?" Keera asked, pointing in the direction of a large, dark spot on top of the peaceful water, which appeared to be stationary.

"My dear, look at the sky. What do you see?"

"I see a few clouds—oh! The dark spots are the shadows of clouds on the water. I can't believe I didn't know," she laughed, a soft sound, not harsh, at her inexperience.

They stood for a few minutes in comfortable silence, watching and feeling the phenomenon of the gently undulating sea. Samuel put his arm around her.

"What do you think Barbados will be like?" she asked, her breath against his cheek as she gave him a kiss.

Before he could answer, they were hailed by the captain. "We are going to put in at St. Christopher for some repairs to one of the cross bars on the center mast. Nothing major, but needed for the sail to work properly," he explained, "and they have good craftsmen there, I'm told, at the Jeaffreson plantation which is north of the port. I met the current owner, Samuel Jeaffreson, Jr., when I visited earlier this fall. The family were seafarers in England, before coming to St. Christopher. We'll rent a cart and pony and see if they will help."

"How long do you think we'll be in port?" called Samuel.

"Two days. No more than that."

Samuel turned back to Keera. "There may be shops near the wharf. We'll have to row into the town, but if you'd like to visit them, we shall."

With the ship at anchor not far off shore and, rowed by two of the crew, Samuel, Keera, and Captain Peter went ashore. The baby stayed with Keera's mother.

"I'll keep the boat at the wharf, should you want to return at any time of day," the captain noted. "Later in the afternoon, I don't know exactly where I'll be or when I'll return." He instructed his crew to wait with or close to the boat and headed off the wharf to rent a conveyance. Only minutes lapsed until he returned with a horse, carriage, and driver.

Keera, who'd been looking around, was amazed at the condition of the houses near the wharf. As Samuel helped her into the cart, she asked, "What happened to the houses?"

Captain Peter explained. "The hurricane last year in September and the one in July destroyed many of the homes, and they haven't been rebuilt."

～

The trip to Jeaffreson's The Red House did not take very long. They traveled beside the picturesque beaches along the western or Caribbean side of the island. Since it was early in the morning, several small boats rested in the calm waters just off shore. The captain stopped the carriage.

Men cast nets into the water and struggled to pull in large catches of fish. Their silver sides flashed in the sun. "Jacks, I'm told they are called—large schools of them, swimming just off shore," said the captain. "And, you won't see them in Barbados. They tend to stay north of there. Do you see the boat which was just pulled ashore?" He motioned to open wooden buckets full of fish which were being carried up the beach to waiting carts near the road. "They'll be taken to the local market to sell to customers for their noon or evening meal."

The cart moved on, rising at times as hills needed to be crossed.

"Is that a windmill?" asked Samuel upon observing a tall, round, block building with four large panes, which were covered in cloth and attached to it. The panes were moving in the wind.

"Yes," answered the driver. "The wheels inside turn to grind the sugarcane to separate the pulp from the stalk."

Keera, noticing the middle-aged driver appeared to be English, asked, "Are you from England?"

"Yes, Mistress. From London."

"How long have you been here?" she continued.

"I came as a young, inexperienced seaman with Sir Thomas Warner and the Jeaffresons—a cabin boy. Samuel Jeaffreson, the patriarch, has died recently, but his son is running the plantation. I decided I didn't like the seafaring life and given the chance to remain and work for the Jeaffresons, I did. There's not been an idle moment since."

"How long has Samuel Jeaffreson, the son, been in St. Christopher," asked Keera.

"Young Master Samuel sailed here with Sir Thomas, who was their neighbor in Suffolk, England. All the Jeaffreson men were mariners. And so was Warner, who became the English Governor of the Leeward Islands. His office was based on this island."

The driver pulled through an ornate gate and headed down a tree-lined drive toward a large white house. It sat shaded in a grove of trees far away from the sugar cane fields. There were barns for storage, and through some of the shed's open doorways they saw stacked barrels for the future making of rum and for storing molasses and sugar.

Keera nudged her husband when the barrels came in sight. They consisted of many different sizes.

After crossing a small stream of running water, the group gasped at the biggest tree any of them had ever seen.

Hearing their astonishment, the driver explained. "It's a saman tree, the biggest one on the island."

"What's that unusual noise, which sounds like a bird?" Samuel asked the driver.

"It is a bird—either a thrasher or a mockingbird. Only seeing it can you differentiate between them. Some of their calls are the same."

The cart continued through tightly arranged gardens, where shrubs and flowers with yellow, red, and purple blooms grew in profusion. Then they were at the door of the house. "The house is nothing extraordinary," Samuel whispered to Keera.

The driver heard him and laughed, "Yes, we've learned over the years not to build expensive homes. Hurricanes play havoc with the whole landscape when they come through, and houses are the worst hit." He hopped off the cart and held the horse's halter. "I will wait for you outside the house. Take your time. The meals here are very filling." He patted his round stomach. "I've had a few," he added.

Captain Peter got down, while Samuel helped his wife off the cart. A pebbled walkway led to the door. Here a window stood open with a wooden bench underneath. The captain knocked.

Keera was taken aback when a white woman opened the door who spoke English. She was dressed as a servant, in a beige linen petticoat which went halfway to her ankles. A white apron covered her front, and a coif held her hair in place. The only decoration was a ruffle around the bottom of the petticoat. "Welcome," she said, standing aside. "Please be seated in the Great Room," she waved her hand, indicating a room with couches and chairs. After asking their names, she curtsied and said, "I'll get the Master."

She left, picking up a large bouquet of freshly cut flowers in a vase from the gardens outside, leaving a whiff of their perfume floating in the air.

While deciding on places to sit, the three avoided a large armchair, obviously where the owner of this place rested.

The chair was positioned by a large, open window which looked out over the extensive gardens and fields, and in the distance, if you looked carefully, fragments of the blue waters of the sea appeared through the branches of the trees.

Through the window, the Caribbean wind moved the leaves on the limbs and several fronds of the coconut palms twirled with its motion. A perfect place where the Master could sit and watch the world go by.

As they waited, Samuel got up to glance at Jeaffreson's collection of books within a large glassed bookcase running along one wall.

"Young man, pick out one to take with you. I've read them all and will not miss one." The gentleman speaking was tall, gray-headed, and dressed in a white linen shirt, waistcoat, and trousers. His shoes were black leather with buckles. Although it was hot and humid outside, a blue coat covered his shoulders and arms. A slight smile rested on his face.

"Thank you, Sir, but I wouldn't think of taking your books." Samuel went to introduce himself. "Master Jeaffreson, I'm Samuel Tipton from Bristol-on-Avon. This is my wife, Keera, and I believe you've met the captain of *The Bristol*, Peter Walton.

Mr. Jeaffreson grasped his outstretched hand, acknowledging Samuel. Then, he walked to the captain and shook his. "Good to see you again, Peter.

Perhaps, we'll continue our discussion on the merits of the many kinds of ships on the seas." Finally, approaching Keera, he took her hand, bowed low, and kissed it, saying, "Madam, I hope you enjoy your stay here on St. Christopher."

When he was settled in his chair near the window, he looked at Samuel with a puzzle on his face and said, "My father knew a John Tipton who was a representative of The Levant Company in Algiers and Tripoli. I've heard him speak highly of the man. A consul, I believe."

"Yes, he was an ancestor of mine, as was Hugh Tipton, John's father—both consuls. John was appointed by William Harbourne, the first English ambassador to Turkey under Queen Elizabeth."

"Quite an accomplishment by Harbourne, becoming ambassador to the country, I think, since the English Christians were considered dogs by the Muslims."

"Yes, it was, but Harbourne was an expert in diplomatic and commercial relations," replied Samuel. "Even though the empire of Turkey was dabbling with one of our enemies—Spain."

"I'm not familiar with Hugh Tipton," Jeaffreson responded, putting his fingertips together and becoming amazed at this young man's expertise while enjoying a conversation about their mutual interests in the shipping world.

"Hugh's mother and father lived in London, taking care of our interests there. He went to Spain as a representative of The Andalusia Company in Seville. Our shipping family is based in Bristol and Portishead with smaller branches elsewhere. We have many contacts with merchants around the Mediterranean and in the New World."

"Are you here on business?"

"Not here in St. Christopher, although if you need airtight barrels or boxes for shipping, we would be an excellent supplier. At present, Barbados is our destination."

"Ah, now I know where I've seen the name—on containers for shipping. Yes, we may do some business. What brings you to The Red House?" asked Master Jeaffreson, leaning forward in his chair.

"I'll let the captain tell you."

While Captain Peter explained his mission for repairs and received assurances he'd be helped, Keera looked around the room, observing the beautiful pottery and hand-stitched table covers. The house was spotless.

Jeaffreson noticed her perusal. "Mistress Tipton, do you have children?"

"Yes, sir. A daughter, Anne, who's just past one."

"I noticed you looking around the room. Would you like a tour of the house? My wife isn't here at present. She's on the island of Antigua, with our children and her sister, but Roisin can show you around."

A jolt, like hitting your elbow on a hard object, ran through Keera's body. Roisin? Could it be her sister worked for this man? "Yes, I'd love to see the house."

The owner rose. "Gentlemen, I'll be right back." He indicated a door and left the room with Keera proceeding him. "Roisin," he called as they stood in the dining hall.

Keera trembled, waiting to see. Another white woman came to his call, but this one was not her sister. Her knees feeling weak, she grasped Master Jeaffreson's arm.

"Mistress Tipton, are you alright?"

"Yes, sir. I fear it's the heat." Keera did not want to tell him the truth.

"Roisin, get the Lady a glass of cold water." He pulled out a table chair and helped Keera to it, making sure she was seated comfortably.

The serving woman returned with the water, and Keera drank deeply. "I should be just fine now, Sir. I'll sit here a moment and then tour the house. Please return to my husband and the captain. I'm sure Roisin will be a fine guide of the house." She smiled a bit weakly at him and nodded at an obviously Irish woman. What questions would she ask her, during the tour?

"I'll leave you in Roisin's capable hands." Jeaffreson turned and left, heading back to the Great Room.

∽

When Captain Walton and the Tipton's left The Red House, after being treated to a sumptuous meal, another cart accompanied them—the workers, who would fix the mast's crossbar.

And, during the conversation around the table, Jeaffreson ventured a suggestion. He needed a bigger barrel to transport his bourgeoning sugarcane crop. If the Tipton's could supply the size he named, he would buy it, and he was sure, dependent upon quality and price, several more of the plantation owners would be interested.

With the measurements for the barrel in hand, Samuel was delighted with the turn of events and promised to make the barrel and price happen as soon as possible.

Heading back to the ship, Keera's questions for the driver started as soon as they pulled onto the road. The one she wanted answered was the first one she asked. "Are there a lot of Irish on St. Christopher?"

The driver obliged. "Yes, Mistress, there are many, but there's more on Nevis, the island you can see in the distance and others on Monserrat." He waved his hand at a greenish-gray image, across a short span of water. "That's Nevis."

"How long have the Irish been here?"

"Only a few years. They came from Ulster and Drogheda in the first slave ships to arrive on the island. Oliver Cromwell sent captured Royalist troops along with the Irish. Most work in the houses and the gardens. The Irish don't survive in the hot fields."

"Are there any here on this island from southern Ireland?"

"Not to my knowledge."

Keera looked at Samuel and asked one more question. "Do you know of other Irish people in the islands around here?"

"Only rumours of ships carrying people from *many* of the English lands here to these islands — some as indentured servants and some as slaves. They're needed to be masters over the natives of the islands. Mistress, do you know that story — the story of the Caribs?"

"No." And, Keera didn't know if she wanted to hear it. Instead, she said, "What is the story?"

The driver continued to relate the history of the island. "The Caribs, fierce warriors, lived on the island, when the English under Sir Thomas Warner first came in 1623 to establish a colony. Leaving his family here, he went back to England and brought the Jeaffresons and others back to found homes and plantations.

"They obtained permission from the Carib chief, Tegremante, to build houses and cultivate the land. As the English began to encroach on territory that the chief hadn't agreed to give them, tensions arose, and the chief sent messengers and sought help from his friends on other islands to fend off his aggressors.

"Their planned assault on the English was found out, and during a great party with Tegremante and some of his followers attending, the English laced the Carib's drinks with rum. In 1626, during the night while they were drunk, the Caribs were slain in their sleep. This included the chief, Tegremante.

"The following day, the rest of the warriors from the other islands were encamped next to a river, intending to raid and kill the English settlers the next day. The English surprised them, killing about 2,000 men. Their bodies were dumped into the river. The encampment was named Bloody Point and the river, which ran red with blood for several days, was named Bloody River."

Samuel put his arm around Keera. The stories she'd heard today were heart-wrenching.

The driver continued, "Then the French came. To avoid major conflict, the two countries split the island up, with the English taking the middle lands and the French both ends. The French built large estates and one Frenchman, Montagne, built a large castle. I can take you to Bloody Point and to the castle, if you wish, Mistress."

Keera shook her head. "No, I believe you."

"When was sugarcane introduced to St. Christopher?" Captain Peter asked, changing the subject, because this Englishman was full of information about the area.

"Maybe ten years ago. Tobacco was the first crop, along with ginger and indigo dye, but the New World colonies could produce tobacco cheaper and of better quality than we could. That's the way it is on all the islands—sugar cane is the money crop." The driver pulled up next to the docked boat, and his passengers alighted.

"Keera, do you want to go back to the boat or browse through this section of town?"

"I believe I'll go back to the ship. I need to nurse Anne, and I'm a little tired after today's excitement, even a nap would be welcome."

"I was hoping you'd say that. I could use some rest myself," said Samuel.

"I'll stay here and wait until you are comfortably on board. Then, send the boat back for us," advised the captain, as he helped the couple into the boat. "I need to show the men the mast so they can get started with repairs this afternoon. By late tomorrow morning, I hope we'll be back sailing on the sea."

"Yes, consider it done, Captain. Tomorrow Keera and I may come ashore, while you and your men finish up, and tour the stands here on the wharf."

∽

277

In later years, when some of the Jeaffresons came to the New World, the name was spelled Jefferson, and those had a son named Thomas.

❦ **Chapter 19** ❦

Early 17th Century
Barbados At Last

After the repairs were finished, *The Bristol* headed for Barbados. Occasionally, the afternoon sky was full of drifting, mottled clouds with snow-white tops and gray-to-charcoal underbellies, from which areas of rain dropped in hard showers on the ship, water, and land, if it existed. These colors were against a graduated sky of pale blue at sea-level to darker blue overhead.

Days passed as they sailed to the isle most east in the Atlantic Ocean, passing in the distance volcano topped islands, their points protruding into the blue sky and ringed with clouds.

"The ocean's so beautiful," commented Keera, as she and Samuel stood at their favorite place near the ship's rail. "I could stand here all day."

"And, you never know what you'll see next," added her husband. "Just think, it's been over one hundred and fifty years since Christopher Columbus was the first to see these islands."

"I would imagine not much has changed since then."

"No, settlement didn't really start until the 1600's, and this proved to be dangerous due to the fierce tribes, bad weather, and diseases, which the early adventurers much to their sorrow found out quickly."

"That seems to work both ways, doesn't it? The native tribes suffered also." She said this remembering the conversation at the Jeaffreson plantation.

"Yes, they did, but it's hard to stop progress and colonization. People are always looking for other opportunities and other lands. England has a history associated with this. People coming into their country, and people leaving for other places. But they're not the only ones. It's called survival of the strongest or fittest. It requires an inventive, exploring, and a need-to-know mind and with those attributes, it doesn't hurt to be lazy. Lazy people search for ways to keep from sweating and invent things. It's been the same since the first man and woman were created, and civilizations started."

"Do you believe the Bible, Samuel?"

"Yes, I do. More than ever, since I now have a copy in English. We can thank Anne Boleyn, our late King Henry's second wife, for that."

"Then I believe too." Keera said. "Will you teach me the Scriptures?"

"Yes, my dear, and we'll find a church in Barbados, I'm sure."

Silence reigned for several minutes as each watched the ocean's gentle waves, while engrossed in their own thoughts. "Look, I see birds," Keera exclaimed and pointed at a distant flock, which they were rapidly sailing toward.

"Yes, we must be getting close to Barbados. But I don't see any land. Captain," Samuel called, turning to address the ship's commander, "are we close to Barbados? We see birds but no land."

"We are very close. Keep looking," the captain suggested. "And, observe the flying fish," he pointed to the water, just as several topped a wave and sailed through the air.

"Sure enough, they do look like they're flying," laughed Keera. She pointed at a wave's peak as a fish leaped into the air, and sailed several feet before touching the water.

"They're good to eat, also," called the captain.

"I hear you," said Samuel, waving his response and turning back to the rail. "Woah, what was that?" he exclaimed, as a bird from the flock they'd just seen swooped down and caught one of the fish in its beak. "Did you see that?"

"Yes, I did, and the flying fish seemed to be chased by a bigger fish in the water. Look," Keera pointed as a large fish jumped several feet above the water, catching a flying fish in midair.

Captain Peter called, "Look to the east."

Slowly, the gray mists of the ocean released the flat island of Barbados to their gaze. She rose as a thin strip of gray-green from the sea, becoming larger, taller, and longer as *The Bristol* approached on the rippling Caribbean. The afternoon sun was behind cloud masses in the sky, reducing the light's reflection and making observation easier.

As the ship got closer, and the sails came down, slowing the ship's progress, individual trees lined the tops of the hills in almost unbroken display, meaning roads from the western side of the island to the east were few. Palm and coconut trees along with other dense vegetation grew in profusion upon the closer hillsides, where Keera could see the occasional house top in what appeared to be a chopped-out area of the vegetation. Large plantations, with cultivated fields, both north and south, stretched to the hillsides.

"The island isn't very large, Keera," Samuel said, knowing what must be on his wife's mind as they neared shore.

"Just what I was thinking, dearest. What if we find Roisin and Ciara and can't buy them? What next?" she said, looking him in the eye while hers filled with tears.

"We'll decide when that happens. There's always a way."

"Yes, I know. I can only hope …"

Samuel nodded, "First, we must busy ourselves with establishing our barrel and box making operation, and while we do this, you need to be familiarizing yourself with the people who own plantations and their families. We'll be invited to visit, and we'll ask to tour their operations, where we can look for your sisters. If they are on this island, we'll find them."

"I'll pray every day to locate my sisters," she paused. Then she continued, "Samuel, do you realize if you hadn't been in Waterford, I'd probably be right here with them, and there'd be no way of escape?" Now there were tears. "Do you know how much I love you?"

"Yes, dear. You prove it every day." Samuel put his arms around Keera and kissed her. This was a special moment. He cleared his throat and continued, "And, we must be thankful for the Tipton Brothers'

Import and Export business, because through its financial success we are here with money to set up our operation and enough to purchase your sisters when we find them."

"I'll work hard, you know that."

"I've never doubted you."

From the captain there was, "Drop anchor."

And, *The Bristol* was in Barbados.

~

Captain Peter stood on the Indian Bridge wharf, directing traffic as he'd done in St. Christopher. "We have a contact here. He's the merchant I rented our buildings from. We'll head for them and pass his rooms on the way."

"What is his name?" asked Samuel, looking over the anchorage where several boats rested at anchor, each flying the colors of the country they'd originated from. There were Dutch, The English Flag, one with the French fleur-de-leis, and one he did not recognize. Forget the Spanish, because Brittania wasn't happy with them at the moment, and they wouldn't venture here.

"The sign over his door says, Barnabas Shrewsbury. Everyone calls him Ab, and I don't know why. He laughingly told me his name rhymes with dab. He said he uses that word because he tends to dabble in other people's business."

"Is our walk a long way?" asked Keera, feeling a bit light-headed in the burning sun. She wondered how anyone from Ireland or Brittania could work in these heat conditions.

"No, look up beyond the house with the English flag on top. That's the Governor's house and office.

His rooms are just behind that house, and our rented buildings are to the left of there."

"That means if we have any trouble, the Governor's house is only a street away," observed Keera to Samuel.

After walking uphill for several feet, Samuel commented, "When we build our barrels, we can just roll them down this hill. They'll hit the sea with a splash and the momentum will head them straight for ships bound for the other islands, the New World, or England." He laughed, took Keera's arm and trudged on.

Government House was the nicest building on the island. Made of limestone coral, it was a light gray color, with multiple square glass windows slightly arched at the top.

Ab's house had a bleached-out red door with blocks of stone and windows much like the Government House. He appeared to be a man of some wealth, if one counted his dwelling. The captain knocked loudly on the door.

"I'm coming. I'm coming." The three heard as they stood waiting outside on the stone steps.

The door opened to a balding man with a ring of hair around his head, broad smile on his face. "Hello, Captain," he bellowed in a loud voice, obviously hard of hearing. "Welcome, come in, everyone," he waved his hand into a room with upholstered couches and chairs. A table was scattered with papers and a burning cigar rested in a pottery dish. The place smelled heavily of smoke.

"Ab, how are you?" Captain Walton spoke loudly to the man.

"Tolerable after all the weather we've been having. Hurricane after you left, Captain. Just got everything back in place, besides having to replace some of the windows in the building you rented. Cabbage palm tree broke into pieces and went right into the front. This must be Samuel Tipton and his wife." There was no problem with Ab's memory.

Samuel stepped forward, talked loudly, and offered his hand. "Yes, I am, and this is my wife, Keera."

"Mistress Tipton, charmed, I'm sure." He bowed and, turning, walked to a wall and pulled a metal object into his hand. "Here's the key to your building, so you can see inside." He handed it to Samuel and continued talking, as he placed a straw hat on his head.

"Mistress Tipton, you'll need one of these should you go outside for very long." He patted a straw hat down tight on his head.

"Where may I get one?" she asked him.

"Eh?" the old man countered.

"Where may I get one?" Keera asked again, more loudly.

"Look around on the wharf. Several of the women have little carts full of woven products. These include very useful baskets."

"Thank you, I'll do that as we go back to the boat. I could use it to fan in this heat."

Ab walked to Samuel and continued, "I took the liberty of unpacking what your captain off-loaded from the ship when last he was here and setting up your supplies as best I could."

With that, the four went out the door, turned right, and approached a sizable building of stone and wood. "Your house is in the back, off the side street, and attached by a passageway to the rear of the building. Notice the windows." The replaced windows stood out in their new frames. "And, if you need more storage, I have other buildings available."

Samuel unlocked the door to a large area, where light streamed in through windows on every side. "This will be a great place to work," he noted, walking from one end to the other. He stopped to check the supplies brought on the first ship. They were unpacked, but not necessarily in the right place. He'd work on that starting next week, after *The Bristol* was unloaded. Setting up his operation wouldn't be hard, since his family had done it more than once. He intended to familiarize himself with the island, as he began the process of starting work. This would give Keera a chance to learn about the plantations and its inhabitants.

"What does the house look like?" Keera wanted to know where she was going to live in Barbados.

"Eh?"

Keera repeated her question.

"This way," and Ab led them to the back of the building, and through a door with a short, covered passageway to another stone building. This one had wood floors and several rooms with beams running overhead. Again, multiple windows let in the Caribbean sun. "It's two stories," commented Ab. "Having rooms over your head will make those areas downstairs cooler. Dust off the furniture and use what's in here. I don't need it."

"Whose house was this?" asked Samuel, loudly.

"My mother and father's house—rest their souls." This was all Ab said about the subject, although Keera wanted to ask what happened.

"Captain, we'll stay on the boat until all the supplies, including the household goods, are unloaded and set up."

"You can depend on the crew to get that done soon," said the captain, as the three went out the front door of the house and onto the street.

Samuel turned to Ab and said, "Thank you for your support. I'm sure there'll be many questions to ask."

"Eh?" returned Ab.

Samuel spoke louder. "Thank you for your support. I'm sure there'll be many questions to ask."

Ab nodded, "Of course, and if there's anything I can do to facilitate the process, let me know. I should be able to help, and if I can't, I'll know someone who can. I'll be around."

And, he was—around and around. Needless to say, there was a lot of shouting going on when Ab was around.

∼

If Keera thought she'd be at once looking for her sisters, she found out it was not to be. Setting up the house and store was the first priority.

From the ship, a large stack of seasoned wood called staves were stacked in the rented building along the wall. Coming from England, these were curved, planed for smoothness on the outside, slightly cupped and planed on the inside, and beveled on each long side. They were ready to stand in metal rings and start the process of making a barrel. Aged for three years, the staves, when put together into a barrel and burned on the inside, were ready to be used by the plantation owners to make rum, although rum was rapidly giving way to sugar.

So, with plain oakwood not burned, they could be filled with molasses or sugar for shipment to England. Cut the barrels in two pieces and they could be used as a bath for humans or water tubs for cattle.

Other stacks of wood would be left to age, and the process of cutting to size started when they were ready. Since oak was the preferred material for barrel making, planks of oak must be brought by Tipton ships from either England or New England. The English colonies in the New World were rapidly getting involved in shipping and ship building.

Most of the tools were used by hand, such as the different types of planers, broadax, drawknifes, and adze. Low benches—which could be used handily, by a worker who straddled one end, used a drawknife and shaved the optimum angles on the boards—were offloaded from *The Bristol*. A few tables, where all the hand tools were kept to be used in the assembling process appeared in the work area. Metal hoops, plus flat iron to make them were stacked off the floor on boards. The iron nails to be cut and used to fasten them into future hoops rested in a Tipton box nearby. Each hoop was driven onto the barrel by a hoop driver and a hammer.

It didn't take many tools to make a barrel, but it did take an experienced craftsman, which the men Samuel had brought with him were, so producing barrels started immediately. A good worker could produce two barrels a day. Samuel had four, plus Aron. But, in the heat of the West Indies, Samuel doubted they'd be able to work that hard. Barrels would be in demand only when the sugar cane was harvested, so, the finished product would be stacked to the ceiling on one side of the building. Harvesting the cane would not begin until next year.

～

"Samuel," called the captain, "why don't we take a drive this afternoon? We'll look at the different trees and see if any of them will suffice for barrel making. The natives say there's a mahogany tree which has hard wood. It may be a candidate."

"Sure, let me tell Keera. She may want to go with us."

The captain sat in the carriage rented from Ab, with his hands on the horse's reins. It had seating for six passengers. The old man had stashed in his many buildings, just about anything they needed. He even had a cow nicknamed Brownie, which came in handy for the baby's milk.

When Samuel came back, he was accompanied by Keera and Ab. Keera had a straw hat and one of the baskets she had purchased at the market on the quay.

"Ab says he can point out several trees we may want to use for barrels," explained Samuel, helping Keera onto the seat.

"Eh?" said Ab.

"I said we're ready to go. Any suggestions where to find mahogany trees?" Samuel asked, hopping up beside Captain Peter, and turning around to speak to Ab.

Ab pointed in a direction which took them toward the crest of the island.

As they drove, it was obvious more houses existed than Keera had seen from her first observation from the ship. The trees towered over them, obscuring their presence.

Halfway up the hill, Ab shouted, "Stop here."

Captain Peter pulled up and put the brake on, so the carriage wouldn't roll back downhill.

Ab pointed to a tree beside the road.

This tree wasn't very tall. Its trunk wasn't big, and the top spread with many branches. Samuel and Captain Peter weren't impressed. "They use *this tree* in construction of houses and furniture here on the island?" said an incredulous Samuel.

"What's its name?" Captain Peter turned around to ask, wondering if the hard-of-hearing old man had misheard their comment.

"This is a mahogany tree."

"It's not big enough for the barrel making industry," observed Samuel, talking loudly.

"Oh, this is a baby. There are bigger ones," Ab assured those in the carriage.

As they continued on, Ab pointed out the banana, coconut, plantain and mango trees. Finally, the group was introduced to the golden apple tree.

"Doesn't look like an apple tree to me," Samuel said, observing the oval shaped fruit, growing in large, compact bunches on the limbs.

"No. They're not English apples, but the fruit makes good juice—maybe a little bit sour to the taste."

"What's the tree with the vines hanging from it?" Keera asked, nodding her head in its direction.

Ab laughed, "I asked the same question. The vines are actually aerial roots, and the tree is the ficus, a type of fig. Do you remember eating figs in England? See the yellow fruit? It will turn purple when ripe."

"But the figs in England were dried when imported," observed Keera. "I see several ripe ones. Could we pick some and eat them?"

"Surely," said Samuel, grabbing her basket, jumping down, and heading for some low hanging branches which had been ravaged by the last bad weather.

"Be careful, Samuel. The wasps will sting you," called Ab, noticing what looked like a whole colony swarming the tree. "They love the sweet pollen in the flowers," he said to Keera, who gave him a hug. "And, watch the ants, they like the fruit too," he grinned.

When everyone was back in the carriage munching on the ripe figs and flicking ants aside, Keera asked, "I've been wondering how the sugarcane is made into sugar." She had more than one reason to find out, and since the group had been in Barbados, they hadn't been far from the barrel making facility.

"Sure," said Ab. "Let's cross the ridge to the other side. Most of the larger plantations are over there. I know someone who'll let us witness his whole operation."

The curvy road led to the hill's crest, where the view of the Atlantic Ocean was marvelous. The breakers, because of a brisk wind from the east, were white-capping, crashing on the sandy shoreline.

"Ab, is that a large dog or sheep I see in the field next to the stone fence in the distance?" Keera asked, squinting to see better. "It's brown, not white like English sheep."

"It's called a Blackbelly sheep, brought over on some of the slave ships from Africa. It got mixed with our English sheep and turned out with the black belly and facial stripes. It has very short hair and no wool."

The carriage continued on and down the hill toward the seashore.

"Who is this man we are going to see?" Keera said into Ab's ear.

"His name is George Calles, and while in England, he fought on the Royalist side during the Civil War. He escaped just before Cromwell would have incarcerated him and came to Barbados, as did many of the wealthy Englishmen who stood by King Charles' side."

Samuel turned around to ask, "Is there great animosity between the two sides here on the island?"

Ab laughed. "No, not great. When you start to deal with the gentry, you'll find some friction under the surface, because of all the shenanigans involved here and in the other islands."

"What shenanigans?" asked Captain Peter.

"I don't remember all of those, and please don't get George started. Keep on the subject of sugar. He'll run on long enough about that."

"Ab which side are you on?" Keera asked, wondering in the future, if she needed his help —.

"I've tried to remain neutral, but my grandfather sailed with Sir Francis Drake when he destroyed the first Spanish fleet at Cadiz. Of course, that victory didn't last long, because the next year he was there when Sir Francis, Lord Howard, and Sir John Hawkins had to defeat the great Spanish Armada. I suppose I'm partial to the Royalist side because of this, but I don't advertise my position."

⤸

George Calles was a short, fat man, whose sweaty-stained hat almost never sat on his head, but remained in his hand, fanning his steaming brow and face. He stood outside the sugar grinding operation on his plantation, gesturing toward the nearest fields of sugarcane, which after over a year of growing were getting close to harvest. No one was in the fields.

"Where are your workers?" Samuel asked, not wanting to say slaves.

"They have other duties when the cane isn't being harvested. We raise our own livestock and grow gardens of vegetables for the inhabitants of the plantation to eat. They are busy with care-giving, repair of buildings, especially after storms, and spreading the soil with our livestock's manure.

"Did you know we grew tobacco as the first crop on the island and shipped it to England? The response the growers received back was the product was ill-cured, foul, with slivers of imbedded stalks, and a strange color." George laughed, his stomach jumping up and down. "They were right about their assessment. Even the growers here on Barbados didn't smoke it."

"It's obvious you're not growing tobacco now," Captain Peter stated.

"No, the growers tried cotton following the awful results of their venture into tobacco." Ab added. "Barbados cotton was of excellent quality, the price impressive in the English market, but other islands and growers soon caught on and the London market was over-supplied, causing profit levels to drop. What was next, George?"

"It was indigo, and when everyone found out they could make money growing this dye-making crop, the same thing happened, and Barbados growers started looking again. Sugarcane became the rescuer of the island economy. The world's need for sugar is unquenchable, as we've found out."

"One of the men I met in Barbados said Brazil had a lot to do with sugarcane's introduction to this island," Captain Walton rejoined. "Is that true?"

"Yes, the Dutch tried to force Portugal from the lucrative spice and sugar trade in Brazil. This led to war between the two," said Ab.

George cut in, "The Dutch lost the fight, and needing a place to go, decided to help the English here on Barbados to plant sugarcane. They supplied money, machinery, and labour. And yes," he nodded, "they brought savages from Africa to work on our plantations."

Keera winched and paled upon hearing this. "I hear there are Irish here who are slaves or indentured workers. Is that true?" she asked.

"Yes, Cromwell is shipping them in here by the boat loads. But the Irish don't last long in this hot weather, working under this hot sun. The Africans are already acclimated to it." George said this as if he were assessing his horses and oxen, which pulled the rollers as they ground the cane.

"What happens to the Irish?" asked Samuel, noticing his wife's face.

"They die, and we replace them. Their turnover is high. I can buy two Irish to one African. That tells you the difference in value between them."

Keera was getting sick to her stomach.

"Keera, do you need to sit down?" Samuel asked, still concerned about her.

She held up her hand. "One more question. Do you have any Irish women working for you?"

"No," George said. "I'd rather buy the Africans. I do have six indentured men and women from England for house work."

Keera let Samuel lead her to a large rock in the shade. She sat there while the owner walked the others around the work area.

~

In the summer of 1654, Keera's baby was born — a boy, Peader, named for her father and the Captain Peter Walton. Peader was the Irish spelling of Peter.

❧ Chapter 20 ❧

Middle of the 17th Century
Admiral Penn, Jamaica

In January 1655, a large fleet of English ships sailed into Barbados harbour. These were not trading ships, but war ships with many cannons installed on their decks.

Ab was out of breath as he hurriedly opened the door of the Tipton facility. He rushed through the large barrel and box making operation to the table where Samuel and Keera sat doing paperwork.

"What on earth is wrong?" Keera asked, noting his breathless and agitated state. She jumped up from her wooden chair and brought another to the table where she had been sitting.

The old man sat hard on the chair, took out his pocket handkerchief, and mopped his brow. "Ships," he said. "Part of a fleet...sent by the Protector Oliver Cromwell...to wrest lands here in the islands...from the Spanish." He spoke in broken words and paused for a minute to catch his breath, then continued, "The men from the ships are rowing ashore, and I talked to one, a Captain Filkins. He said Admiral William Penn and General Robert Venables are in command. He pointed them out, standing on the wharf talking to each other."

At the name of Robert Venables, Keera sent a startled look at Samuel. "Wasn't he…"

"Yes, my dear. He was part of the invasion of Ireland."

"Part of the massacre," murmured Keera, who stood and walked through the open door into the street, looking down toward the harbour.

The ships were everywhere, taking up all the area, where typically only five or six ships sat at anchor.

Normally, the fleet floating on the sea would be an awesome and beautiful sight, but not in her eyes. She saw only evil there, with a flash of her wounded mother at her Waterford home in a pool of blood, and her father dead on the floor near the front door.

Samuel, who had followed, put his arm around her but didn't say anything.

"Dear husband, I'm reminded of the reason we came here in the first place. I've been remiss in pursuing this goal."

"Keera, you've been busy with our children. Now that Anne and Peader are getting bigger and can stay with your mother, we'll take more time in the quest to find your sisters. I have to go out to a plantation on Monday to discuss selling barrels for shipping sugar to England. Why don't you go with me and meet the wife, while I talk to the husband?"

Nodding her head, Keera agreed, and they pursued this agreement for several months with no resolution.

～

After joining with France in its war against Spain, Oliver Cromwell, his Council, and the new Commonwealth of England had declared war on the Spanish. In late 1655, Cromwell ordered troops and part of his navy to execute his "Western Design," in the West Indies—a plan to take over all the Spanish possessions in the area. What better time to sneak in on their back door, while the fight was raging in the mother country?

~

Admiral Penn looked down his nose at General Venables, sniffing a little because the climate in the West Indies did not agree with him or maybe at the presence of the man in front of him. There was no compatibility between them and little respect for each other. He had no choice but to interact with the man who would command the ground troops, while he had authority over the navy in Cromwell's fight with Spain. His seamen were well-prepared. His ships seaworthy.

Venable's men were a ragtag group, hastily assembled, ill-suited for war, and not well equipped or supplied. Penn wondered if Cromwell had sent the man, only to him get him out of Ireland and England.

Venable considered Penn to be arrogant. Penn made Venables feel small.

After several days of meeting for discussions, there were many disagreements on how to proceed. Finally, all supplies were aboard for the battle, and the ships with the admiral, general, and their fighting men headed for the Spanish-held Hispaniola, and its capital, Santo Domingo. Cromwell had ordered its capture.

～

Keera had gone to the market on the quay. On returning, she saw Ab sitting on a chair outside his home. "The Admiral's fleet has left," she stated, as she stopped to adjust her heavy basket, which was full of fruit and vegetables.

Ab jumped up and took charge of the basket. They continued on toward the Tipton quarters. "Yes, Captain Filkins said they were to attack Hispaniola's capital, Santo Domingo. Protector Cromwell sent orders for its capture. Filkins said they expected a short battle, and that he'd be back here to Indian Bridge soon to celebrate. Seeing them stream out of the harbour was exciting," he said as they walked up the hill.

"Wasn't Hispaniola the first Spanish Colony in the islands?" asked Keera.

"Yes, settled just after Columbus was there in 1492. Filkins and I talked this over during his last meal on Barbados. I learned much about Hispaniola. Unlike here, the natives during the first years could supply gold, which was what the early sailors like Columbus were after. The Spanish put the indigenous people to work, digging gold and growing food. Due to warfare and severe enslavement, their numbers were reduced."

"Did they find much gold?"

"Yes, but they also found disease, and the natives started dying of smallpox brought by the sailors. They died in great numbers, until only a few were left. Then, the Spanish bought African slaves from the Portuguese."

"So, African slaves have been in the islands for over one hundred years?"

"It seems so."

"Did all the ships leave our harbour?" Keera asked, loud enough for him to hear.

There was hammering and scraping in the background as they entered the Tipton home, where Ab deposited his load on a convenient counter.

"There's one small transport ship still left, loading more supplies on board, but it leaves as soon as the hold is full." Ab noticed she was putting on her straw hat and gloves which were resting on a kitchen chair. "Are you going somewhere?"

"Yes, Samuel has an appointment with another owner on the northern end of the island. I'm going with him. He'll be here shortly. You and Aron are in charge until we get back this afternoon."

"Keera, is there something I don't know about you? I get the feeling something's missing, some information you aren't telling me. It seems to be floating in the air—between us."

She smiled at him and nodded. "One day, I'll tell you the story."

"But—."

Samuel arrived at that moment. "Hello, Ab. Are you ready, dear?" he addressed both of them at the same time. "Ab, the boats have left."

"Yes, I was just discussing with Keera their departure."

"We'll be back soon. I have a call to make on another planter, and, we should have another load of oak from England or the New World soon. Be looking for it. It might come today. Its captain is my brother,

William. He hasn't been here before. He'll need help finding us."

"Once I hear of its arrival, I'll send my servant to the harbour to greet him. Consider it done and have a safe trip."

~

The great battle for Hispaniola turned into an embarrassing escapade for the English invasion force. Even greatly outmanned, the Spanish, mulattos, and Africans under the command of the governor, Bernardino Bracamonte successfully resisted over ten thousand troops under Venables.

Being fearful of going back to England with the awkward and humiliating loss, both Penn and Venables decided to go on to Jamaica with the remainder of their forces, many of whom were dying of dysentery. Venables was sick from this disease, leaving Penn to take over and orchestrate the whole fight. Which he did.

Taking this island was easy. Since it wasn't well-fortified or well-manned by forces of the Spanish, the battle only lasted six days. The aftermath would further jeopardize their position with Cromwell, when the Spanish residents freed their slaves, who were called Maroons. They went to the high mountains, established homes, and from this redoubt started guerrilla warfare against the English.

It seemed nothing the two men did together turned out acceptable, and conquering Jamaica was no different. The English troops began starving because of lack of provisions and with the addition of disease, died by the hundreds.

In August 1655, there was nothing left for the two to do but head for home. Both Penn and Venables headed for England. Penn arrived first, and after an audience with Cromwell, was promptly thrown in the Tower. When Venables landed at Portsmouth, he was quickly arrested and sent to the Tower as well.

Because the Spanish had been on Jamaica for over one hundred years, crops brought from the Mediterranean were being grown. These were the expensive tamarind, ginger, and indigo. Citrus trees grew in groves of sweet and sour oranges, lemons, limes, and fields of sugarcane. Other crops were harvested like plantains, bananas, and avocado. Over the next years, the English took over the fields and groves, expanding the tillable ground, and sending the surplus to the other islands or England.

The perishable items could not be sent to the mother country, but the New World was expanding north of the islands in the colonies of Virginia, Massachusetts, Connecticut, Rhode Island, and New Hampshire. This was a new market for the West Indies crops.

The northern lands were a hodge-podge of peoples, including English, Dutch, French, Spanish, and even some Russian settlements. At first, the religious thinking ran to Catholics, Puritans, and Jews. In later years, Anglicans, Protestants, and Lutherans mixed into the group.

The late 16th century was one of merchants, ships, and competition between the European nations with the intent to acquire as many colonies as possible. The English business ventures in the New World were predicated on this intent. Although they were an outlet for England's unemployed population, the primary aim was to enrich the sponsors.

In England, because wool became the way to wealth, the land was given to pasture for the sheep, which meant fewer people occupied the fields and those not working, lived in poor circumstances.

The New World, in the unemployed man's eyes, became a way of new life, of new hope for themselves and their families.

England itself was changing. Cromwell was dead in 1658. His son Richard succeeded him but lasted not a year. In 1660, Charles II returned and became the King of England.

Something else was changing and growing, Samuel and Keera's family. In 1657, Rachael was born, and in 1659, another girl, Joanna.

～

Soon, Jamaican sugarcane was produced in abundance, in direct competition with the other English colonies. Hardly without knowing it, Tipton barrels and boxes were in great demand on this island. Tipton ships were spending more time on the seas, trying to keep up with demand. The distance to England and the isles became an issue.

Because of the enlarging and changing economic scene, there was a discussion of a new facility, with Captain's William Tipton and Peter Walton, an aging Paul Tipton who'd sailed to Barbados from Bristol, and Samuel Tipton in on the conversation. This one, they decided, would be in Jamaica. They left the decision of overseer to Samuel and Keera.

～

The Tiptons had been on the island of Barbados for six years. Was it time to move? Maybe, but Keera had two more plantations to check out. She was still hopeful of finding her sisters alive.

Looking for her sisters was put on hold, while Samuel, Paul who was Samuel's grandfather, and Aron sailed to Jamaica to investigate another Tipton venture. If Samuel and Keera went to Jamaica, Aron was the choice of overseeing the Barbados operation.

"Keera, I've enjoyed my time spent with you and the grandchildren," said Paul, as he waited to walk down to the quay to board the Tipton ship. Samuel had had to run a last-minute errand to the Government House to pick up some shipping papers.

"The children have enjoyed having someone else to spend time with. They get tired of the games we play."

"The islands here in the West Indies are much different from those around England. I think I'll miss the palm and coconut trees. I'll start looking at ours for fruit which can drop on your head," he laughed, remembering a close call he'd had on a picnic they'd taken on the other side of the island. "We don't have missiles dropping from the trees at home, if I don't count apples or pears or peaches. They don't slice your head open."

Keera laughed. "Yes, things are different here, but I've gotten used to the hot weather, the hurricanes, and the excitement of a different ship in the harbour."

"Yes, my love, you have," said Samuel, returning and flourishing some papers which he gave to Keera. "Take care of these for me. We'll fill them out should we decide to open up our facility in Jamaica." He turned to Paul Tipton. "Poppa, are you ready to go? Captain William is on the boat and I'm sure he's wondering what's delaying us. The row boat is waiting to take us to the ship."

"Yes, I'll head on down. You can catch up with me. Keera, take good care of my grandchildren." Paul realized Samuel needed to say goodbye to his wife. He came close and gave her a hug and goodbye kiss. He wouldn't get off the boat when it came back to Barbados. He would head on to England to load supplies for the return trip to set up the operation in Jamaica, if needed. He started down the street, turned, and waved goodbye. Then, he headed to join Aron and his son, William, on the boat.

"We won't be gone long," stated Samuel with his arms around his wife.

"How long?" asked Keera, tilting her head back, looking into his eyes and insisting on a definite time.

"Probably one month or less. Don't worry, Ab will take care of you, won't you Ab?"

"Eh?" the old man said.

Everyone laughed.

Samuel kissed Keera goodbye and whispered in her ear. "That will have to last until I get back." Then, he walked down the hill to the small row boat, climbed in with his father, and they were rowed to Captain William Tipton's tall ship. The three of them would make the final decision on the new outlet as they sailed back to Barbados.

Keera walked outside. The last she saw of the ship, the sails were being unfurled and opened to the wind. As they billowed, the ship picked up speed and disappeared from view into the ocean mists, heading west from the island.

Samuel was no more out of sight, when Keera got an inquiry from the largest plantation on the eastern side of the island. The note said the owner, Richard Marshells, extended an invitation to visit the sugarcane operation and discuss the purchase of barrels for shipment. Realizing the distance involved, the company's representatives were welcome to stay the night. The note bearer would wait for a response.

After consulting with Ab and realizing they could close a purchase as well as Samuel, Keera sent a note back, saying to expect two representatives on the following Monday. Then she and Ab made plans to go.

❧ Chapter 21 ❧

Middle of the 17th Century
Juntu, Marshells, Roisin

The Portuguese started the slave trade in the Atlantic.

Some of their islands were just off the coast of Africa, where sugarcane was grown by slave labor from the Gambia River.

The Portuguese moved across the Atlantic, going south and seeking other merchandise to include in exports to their customers. In Brazil, they found brazilwood which produced an expensive dye This dye, depending on acidity, could be yellow or red. It was used in the dying of luxury fabrics in the capitals of Europe. The Portuguese used the natives in the harvesting of brazilwood.

When the demand for sugarcane and other agricultural products increased which necessitated increased labor, they imported African slaves to grow and harvest tobacco and cotton. The Africans grew crops, whereas the natives of Brazil did not adapt to plowing and harvesting.

The Portuguese were followed by the Spanish, in slave trafficking. They brought Africans to the Caribbean to tend sugar cane and other crops on Jamaica and Hispaniola. The Spanish didn't arise to the level of the

Portuguese's trafficking in slaves, who dominated the slave trade for one hundred and fifty years. Soon the Dutch joined the slave trade, followed by the English and French, who dealt with the slave merchants. The slave merchants raided the banks of the Gambia River and the vast, forested flat lands of Senegal or Mali, taking their captives to the island of Goree, a little north of the mouth of the Gambia River. This was the point of no return for a black native.

At first, the transport of humans was light, but as sugarcane was grown in increasing quantities in the West Indies, the demand for black bodies mounted. They were habituated to the heat and became the best workers in the fields.

∾

A young, muscular black man, named Juntu, lived far up the Gambia River in Senegal, West Africa. He was the head of his tribe, a position passed down by his father, and respected by all. His village wasn't right on the river, but was only a short, tree-lined walk up a low hillside, on the red-colored soil found in most of Africa.

His village was laid out in families, whose patriarch ruled its activities and reported to Juntu. These tribal men often met the chief at his home, taking the traditional friendship tea in the afternoon. The village was clean and neat, and the houses made out of mud bricks with roofs of river rushes or wide leaves on a wooden rod grid put together with lianas from the forests, and held up by a central pole.

When necessary, Juntu called a meeting under a large baobab tree in the midst of the village. This 'meeting tree,' in the presence of the whole village, was where disputes, the union of men and women, baby naming ceremonies, and celebrations were held.

News from other tribes was shared, under the tree's wide arms with thick leafy canopy. This included the appearance of men the color of flax in the area. He hadn't seen one, but his visitors said these white-colored men stole people. Juntu had laughed at this preposterous news, but the visitors insisted.

∾

His woman, along with her friends, had taken the children and gone to the river to wash clothes and cool off. He sat on the hillside above them, listening to the slap, slap, slap of them beating the rough cloth on the rocks in the flowing water.

Everyone was happy, laughing and enjoying the cool, running stream. The children ran naked in its shallows, splashing water droplets, which looked like orbs of crystal, flashing in the sun. Juntu laughed at their antics.

His dugout canoe rested on the bank, pulled up to keep it from floating away — water from leaks pooling in the bottom. Two other men joined him as he sat, relaxing in the morning sun. They hunkered down beside him.

"Are you ready to go hunting, Juntu," the one with a red spear asked. They had planned on being gone two days.

"Ah, the sun feels good," he replied. But he got up, picked up his spear and pack, and the three of them headed down the wet, slippery bank, got into the canoe, knelt in the puddled water, and paddled down river. They wouldn't go too far, because the largest species of the hippopotamus and crocodile always inhabited parts of the western, flowing stream, not far from the village, and they were dangerous.

When the sun rested overhead, they heard and saw a family of baboons, swinging through the trees — black bodies stark against the green foliage. Females held babies, and the males watched, their black beady eyes following the men, as they sat in the middle of the river.

A brief discussion ensued. Should they take one or two as their prey and return home? Juntu overruled the suggestion. His mind was set on a larger animal found in the scrub brush along the river and inland savannah which they were approaching. The waterbuck had large horns, and if they could find one, the animal would feed his tribe for days. He would regret this decision later.

The three moved on, and all was quiet on the Gambia River.

A few miles later they stopped, hearing strange sounds coming from down river. As he had been taught by his father, he and the others pulled the dugout to the bank. The three got out and went quietly on foot toward the sounds, intending to discover the meaning of the noise.

They proceeded a few paces when suddenly, from the brush around them, men emerged. Their skin was white, and they were accompanied by men of Juntu's color. The three from the village instinctively formed a triangle with spears pointed toward their aggressors.

One of the black men spoke his language. "Put down your spears, and go peacefully," he commanded.

Red Spear understood what he said, and pushed his spear at the man.

A loud report rang out, and Red Spear fell to the ground. Juntu and his companion had never heard such a sound. Their ears rang with the noise. They were both afraid.

"Put down your spears," the man said again.

Juntu considered his options. Then he put his spear on the ground. His fellow villager did the same. The two didn't have time to examine their friend to see if he was dead or alive.

Prodded downriver by the thing which made the loud bang, they were pushed into a boat. Days later they were rowed to an island off of a large city on the coast. Juntu didn't know for sure, but the word Goree seemed to be the name of the place.

Richard Marshells stood rigid and aloof at the entrance of his sugarcane liquid reduction operation, flicking his hand toward seven large round pans called coppers or clarifiers. In reality, his were made out of iron. They rested in a descending row, over places where wood or charcoal fires were burning. The intense heat could be felt even at the distance where the three stood.

Marshells had expected the owner, Samuel Tipton, not this woman and old man.

Keera had pulled off her straw hat and started fanning her face. She continued to listen to the drone of his voice as he explained the process used at his plantation. She didn't have to listen to him, she could plainly see for herself. She'd seen this same operation tens of times, although this one was, she had to admit, larger.

Several African slaves tended the fires, stirred the pans, and skimmed the liquid of impurities from the top of the hot liquid. Some went quickly in and out of the penetrating, scorching hotness of the flames. They skillfully tended the fires and the pans, checking the thickness of the evaporating fluids.

Testing was done by ladling a bit of sugar to cool and using either an elbow or fingers in the hot liquid to determine the stage of reducing.

Keera noticed the designated African boiler had large elbow scars and mis-shaped fingers, where the liquid must have been too hot.

When she pointed this out, Marshells laughed and said, "You have two elbows and ten fingers. Doesn't keep him from working. You just use another one while the burned one heals." He continued, "The boiler is a skillful worker, and a good one is hard to replace. Joseph is a good one."

Hearing his name, Joseph, the muscular African, turned and looked at the three white people who stood at the door. He did not smile.

The plantation owner studied Keera's features closely. He would have preferred a man, so he could be himself—the course, vulgar man which he'd always been. He was definitely uncomfortable dealing with a woman on business, especially one as pretty as she. He had his own ideas on the role of women and their place in the world.

And then there was the old man, who was hard of hearing.

He shot a look at Ab and continued, "As soon as the first pan is emptied, it's filled with freshly ground liquid and the process keeps going—night and day. It doesn't stop until the cane runs out. And since we stagger the growing plants, we quit only when the maturing season is over—about six months from now."

How many times have I heard the same story? thought Keera.

"Once reduced to the stage where sugar crystals float in the pan, it's ready to pour into large wooden barrels called hogsheads or to conical clay molds and taken to the curing house. That's where your company comes in." Marshells was sure when he mentioned the quantity he'd be talking about, these two would bend over backward to help him. He needed barrels immediately. His old supplier, whom he'd despised, had sold his operation and gone back to England. The present owner had told him, in no uncertain terms, he didn't need his business.

"The curing house is there." Marshells pointed to a building which was open on each end, to facilitate the finished result, moving large carts with heavy barrels of molasses and crystalized sugar. "Would you like to visit?" Marshells took a step in this direction, turned, and paused.

"No. I can imagine your operation is comparable or superior to the others I've seen." Keera had no need to see the building. She didn't understand her feelings, but she was beginning to have a bad taste for this pompous man. Was it the way he carried himself, the way he spoke like she didn't know the sugar making process, or didn't he like women? She couldn't say.

Marshells continued, "It is there the hot sugar mixture has water added to it and for at least a month, the containers are placed over sugar pots where the syrupy molasses drains into the under vessel, leaving behind a golden, brown sugar in the upper pot. Both are put into barrels for shipment to England, where the crystals are refined even further." He turned, shaded his eyes, and looked down the rutted path toward the cane fields.

"Ah, here comes another loaded cart. Let's follow it to the grinding shed." The owner led the way up a slight hill.

Inside the cart, pulled by a horse and stacked upright, were sugarcane stalks tied in bundles ready to be put through the grinders of the mill.

～

The impressive windmill was positioned on top of the hill, where the wind constantly blew, moving the lumbering and heavy vanes. Once started, they were hard to stop.

In case of the wind shifting, two oxen waited to be harnessed to the tree tail, a long slender tree trunk going to the ground, which moved the whole windmill top into a position of facing the wind. Another, lower protrusion was an open gutter, which transported the liquid squeezed from the cane to the boiling house in a constant stream. Insects buzzed around the raw liquid as it ran down the open trough.

The rumble of the turning, huge rollers was almost deafening, as she and Ab watched the cane being fed in bundles into the biting jaws of the grinders. The bundles were immediately returned by pushcart to be refed as the wheels continued to turn.

An African man and several women fed the cane into the grinding wheels. As Keera watched, a bundle got caught on a sharp metal edge, which held it from going through. The woman pushed and pulled to free it. Overbalanced, when the bundle suddenly released and continued into the wheels, the man caught her and pulled her back. What might have turned into a terrible accident was averted.

"How long has she been working today?" Keera asked, thinking the woman might need to rest. She'd heard horror stories about working conditions at other plantations.

"Since sunup," replied Marshells. "My slaves are expected and used to working long hours. Rest will come at sundown, when the night workers start. Why don't we make our way to the house for afternoon tea and cakes? My servants will be expecting us about now."

They had barely gone through the door, when a piercing scream rent the air. Keera turned and ran back into the building, as a machete slashed the air and through the lower part of the arm of the woman who'd been feeding the rollers. The arm moved on through the machine as the woman collapsed on the ground, grabbing at the end of her severed limb. Tears streamed down her face, as she rocked in obvious agony.

Keera moved in her direction, only to be stopped by the owner's hand on her arm.

"They'll handle it," he said, tugging her away. She untangled from his grasp and stood still while looking at the scene before her.

The man hurried to a nearby shelf, pulled a rag from a stack, and came back to the woman. Quickly, he tied the exposed bone and muscle in an expertly affixed bandage. He'd done this before, probably more than once, she realized.

"Come, Keera." Ab, noticing she'd turned pale at the sight, was at her elbow. She let him steer her toward the carriage, where the owner waited to help her up. They headed toward the manor house.

Even the ride wasn't without scenes which became fixed in her mind—worse than those she encountered elsewhere. The slave houses were no more than the wattle and daub structures no doubt similar to those she'd read about in the Tipton Ancestry Book. The only difference was these had plantain leaves for a roof instead of thatch. These small, rectangular huts sat alongside gardens of maize, yams, and other food items. The occupants grew a few chickens, to provide eggs for their small children, who ran as wild as the hens.

～

Tea was the last thing Keera wanted. After making small talk for an hour, she asked to be taken to her room for the night. "I would like to lie down for a while before the evening meal," she told Marshells.

Marshells rang the servants bell. "Of course, I'll see you at dinner. There's a wonderful view of the gardens from your room, as you will see. It was my daughter's room when she was here." He pointed to a circular staircase leading to an upstairs landing.

"Where is your daughter now?"

"She's in Liverpool with her mother," he said as a servant came to show Keera to her upstairs room.

Keera looked at the flight of stairs and wondered if she could make it. Her knees were like jelly.

Someone crossing at the top of the stairs caught her attention, and she mustered the strength to gain the landing above. After being led to her room, and comfortably attended too, she dismissed the woman who'd hovered over her, by asking, "Was that an Irish servant in the upstairs hallway?"

"Yes, Mistress," answered the white woman in English. "She comes from Waterford."

Keera, surprised, thought of several questions she'd like to ask this servant, but she decided to wait. At present, her mission was to find her sister. "What is her name?"

Keera already knew the name, but she wanted it confirmed. "Roisin, Mistress. Is there anything else you need?"

"No, thank you."

Keera had stumbled upon one of her sisters!

At first, she wanted to run and find her. Then she thought better of it. Even if it was her, at the moment, there was no way she could take her off this plantation, and that's exactly what she wanted to do. In fact, taking her to Indian Bridge wasn't such a good idea. She needed to get her off the island.

Suddenly, moving to Jamaica seemed a great idea, and selling barrels to Richard Marshells was the least of her worries. She decided not to say anything to Roisin, but to keep the fact that she was her sister to herself. No one would know except Samuel, not even Ab or Aron.

She stretched out on the bed to take an afternoon nap, knowing her search for one sister was over.

Where was the other one? Maybe Roisin would know. She fell asleep with this thought.

❧ **Chapter 22** ❧

17th Century

Roisin, The Plan, Jamaica,

When Samuel and Aron returned from Jamaica, Keera had to wait until she could get her excited husband aside to tell him the news. Samuel was full of reports of Jamaica.

"Poppa, William, and I found an abandoned warehouse next to a wharf to start our new business on Port Royal. It's on the inner-harbour which looks toward the mainland, and not on the main port side, which is situated on the peninsula, as it curves out into the ocean. Our house will be up in the hills where other owners of businesses live, and you can see the ships come in and go, through the windows. No more standing in the street." Samuel kept on with a glowing report of the area.

"Sounds wonderful, Samuel. A great place to start again."

"No more rowing ashore for us, because our ships can tie up at the wharf," he said. "And, I met some of the people who've been buying from us here at Indian Bridge. They are excited at the prospect of a closer supplier. There is one drawback."

"What is the problem?" Keera asked, wondering what could be so bad after all the good words he'd said about the island.

"The port is full of pirates and privateers, which the government actively encourages, and you know what that means — all the happenings which go with them." He didn't want to name the goings-on he'd seen.

Keera started laughing. "Samuel, I've not known you to joke about such things. Pirates and buccaneers indeed!" She'd heard of the raiders on the seas. They attacked the ships of other countries. But here on Barbados, they had never been concerned about these robbers of ships. Captain Peter and Captain William avoided the area where they swarmed as they came to Indian Bridge.

"I wish I were joking, but I'm not. We'll have to be careful with the children, and you'll need someone with you when traveling into the main port for supplies."

"It's that bad?"

"Yes. There's lots of drinking and rowdiness. I've chosen the quietest spot for the business, but that doesn't mean some drunk won't wander into the area." Samuel had sat down in a chair to rest. Telling his wife, the circumstances of his trip, had been weighing on his mind.

"How will you protect the business from such? Will I be able to help you?"

"Dearest, we'll just have to wait and see." He changed the subject. "What's been happening here, while I've been gone?"

Now was the time to tell Samuel of her sister. Keera pulled up a chair and sat with him.

"I think I've found Roisin."

"What! Where?"

Keera told him of the trip to Richard Marshells' plantation. She related the scenes she'd observed while there and told of seeing her sister in the house.

"Did you talk to her?"

"No. I knew if I confronted her, I'd want to remove her right then. This wasn't possible until you came back with the news of whether we were moving to Jamaica. Since we are, I hope we can get her away from Marshells' home and take her with us. He wants to talk to you about barrels. I've heard a rumour since I came back that some of the people around here don't like him. I sure don't, and as his barrel maker won't sell to him, I think he's desperate."

"I'll go see him as soon as I can. Maybe we can cut a deal for your sister."

"I wouldn't suggest it, until you sound him out. You'll see what I mean when you talk to him. I don't think he cares much for people, whether free or slave, but to use them for his benefit. When will Captain Peter be here?" She asked this because Samuel's brother, William, and his grandfather had sailed for Bristol, England as soon as Samuel and Aron had come ashore.

"He's due in a month, bringing supplies for Barbados. If necessary, I could divide them between here and Jamaica." Samuel was thinking of how moving earlier than he'd planned would work. "We'll make that decision, when the situation with your sister resolves. But we should be prepared, either way, to sail from here to our new home when he comes, just in case your sister leaves this Marshell's plantation."

"I'll start packing," Keera said. She was determined to take her sister away from that man.

"I'll start working on a plan to get your sister away from the plantation."

∼

Samuel sent a servant with a letter to Richard Marshells telling him when he planned to arrive at his plantation to discuss his purchase of barrels for his sugarcane operation. Meanwhile, he and Keera thought they had a foolproof plan to secure the escape of her sister.

On the appointed morning, he and Keera got into their rented covered buggy and climbed the hill overlooking Indian Bridge harbour, stopping for a brief picnic at the summit in a grove of coconut and banana trees, where others had been before.

"I'm nervous," Keera said. "What if she doesn't want to come with us? She has no idea what her life would be like if she leaves him."

"That's true. The change will be drastic for her, after being a slave for so long, but we must try, sweetheart. There's always the possibility she won't come."

"I've wanted this for so long." Keera pulled in a lungful of air and let it out slowly.

"Yes, you have, my dear. You've been faithful to your ambition and never wavered."

"We don't have far to go until we put our plan into action," noted Keera.

"No, about two miles down this hill and we'll start. Are you ready?"

"Yes." She started putting the noon meal items back into their basket. There were two baskets extra for what might transpire in the next days.

Eight miles from the manor house, or halfway back home and off the main road, they obtained a room for two nights. This was part of their plan for before and after rescuing her sister. They off-loaded their extra supplies and continued on.

Just as Keera and Ab did before, they would stay overnight at Richard Marshells' manor, leave the next day, and come to this rented room. There they would stay until dusk. Then they'd head back toward the plantation and wait.

Sometime, after dark set in, Roisin should leave the house, walk down the road in the shadows, and meet them about one mile from the entrance to the plantation. When she showed up, they would ride by buggy to spend the rest of the night in their wayside room.

Anyone looking for Roisin would not associate them with her disappearance, because supposedly they'd left the day before.

Once at the manor today, Keera would ask to rest in the beautiful room she'd stayed in before, and Samuel would ask to see the operation he'd heard about from Keera. While he went with Marshells, Keera would look for Roisin and talk to her. At least, that was the plan.

～

When the two arrived at the plantation house, all was in an uproar. The African slave, Joseph, who was an expert on boiling sugarcane to perfection, was nowhere to be found.

As the Tiptons pulled up in the buggy, Marshells was shouting instructions to four white men, who appeared to be guards, and sending them on their way. Two of them carried clubs and the others had whips on their belts and held guns.

"There's too many people on this island, and not many places to hide. We'll find him," he angrily stated to Samuel, completely ignoring Keera. "He'll rue the day he left here. No one's gotten away with that. I'll make sure he suffers when my overseers bring him back." He slammed his fist into his palm to punctuate his sentence.

Keera's heart skipped a beat at his last comment. *No one*, she thought.

"I wish I could help you, sir," Samuel stated lamely, not knowing what else to say, and silently being on the side of the runaway.

"I'm sorry this happened and today of all days." Marshells stuck out his hand. "You must be Samuel Tipton — Richard Marshells," he said.

"Yes, I am, and you know my wife, Keera."

With a slight bow in her direction and a small shrug, Marshells replied, "Yes, we had a nice chat when she was here before."

"My wife's feeling the effects of the hot weather today. Since she's seen your operation and with your permission, she prefers to go and rest at the manor while we walk over your sugarcane operation. Is this okay with you? I think she knows the way to the room."

"But of course. Let me get someone to escort her. She can use my daughter's room as she did before." He walked over to pull cords hanging outside the house, selected one, and tugged it. Marshells didn't want her running around his house by herself.

The same servant who'd assisted Keera before came from the interior of the house. "Please take Mistress Tipton to her room and make sure she is comfortable," Marshells ordered.

"Yes, Master," she said with a curtsy.

As the two men headed off, the servant led the way to the stairs and the upper bed chamber and made sure she was comfortable. "Would Mistress like some coffee or tea?" she asked.

"Yes, tea would be wonderful," answered Keera. "With sugar, please."

While the servant was gone, Keera peeked out the door and decided to walk the landing on the second floor. She was hoping she'd see Roisin as she strolled along, but there didn't seem to be any activity or noise in any of the rooms. Of course, she didn't open the doors, so she couldn't be sure.

Back in her room, she looked out her bed chamber window. Down below was an extensive flower garden and a path through an arbor where taller shrubs and bushes grew. Momentarily, she saw a flash of white as someone moved among the plants. The form was familiar. It was Roisin.

Tea arrived at that moment. She seated herself at a low table and waited for the servant to pour the dark, amber brew. Given a linen napkin, she put it in her lap.

"Do you want me to put the sugar in your cup?" asked the woman before her.

"No. Everything's fine, but you could answer one question."

The servant smiled for the first time. "Yes, Mistress?"

"I see some beautiful flowers and a walk below my window. Do you think I could stroll there before I rest? How do I get there?"

"I'm sure the Master would have no objection. He is proud of the garden and the flowers are beautiful." She explained the steps needed to leave the building. "If you have trouble, just tug the green cord, and I'll take you."

Keera finished her tea in record time, and following the servant's instructions, walked out into the garden, where multiple scents greeted her. The perfumed air wasn't what she was after. She quickly followed the path in the direction where she'd last seen what she hoped was her sister. Rounding a bend, she came upon her, weeding a patch of purple flowers. The woman was singing softly to herself, a song Keera's mother had sung to them and taught all the girls to sing.

Keera stopped to listen, closing her eyes. The song was called *A Bhean Úd Thios* or O Lady Down Yonder. Keera smiled, thinking the tune was suitable, because it was about a woman captured by fairies to take care of the fairy babies and sung as a lullaby with multiple verses.

"Roisin," she said lowly and gently.

The woman jumped up and took several steps back to curtsy. "Mistress, is there something I can do for you."

"Roisin, don't you recognize me?" Keera smiled slightly and held out her hand.

Roisin looked more carefully at the woman standing before her, a look of disbelief and then one of delight slowly appearing on her face. "Keera?"

"Yes." With this one word, the two ran into each other's arms—the hug worth many years of searching and struggle. Standing back at arm's length, they looked again and this time with tears, streaming down two faces, embraced each other.

"How? How?" asked Roisin, stepping back. "I've dreamed of this for so long, but I didn't know what happened to you? I had hoped and prayed that you'd escaped the soldiers, since you went to see Samuel at the wharf."

Keera nodded. "I did, and we are married with four children. I've been looking for you all these years. It's a long story, and I'm sure we don't have time to relate the whole of it. Samuel is here with me, and we have a plan to get you out of this place."

"Oh, Keera. I wish, but it's too late." The tears started again.

"Why?"

"I too have children."

"You're married?" Keera assumed. "He can come with us and the children."

With tears running down her face, Rosin said, "No, you don't understand. It's the Master."

"Oh." This statement rocked Keera back on her heels. Now she knew why she didn't like the man. Her original appraisal of him had proved true. He was a user of both men and women, but in different ways. "We'll take the children with us when we leave. How many do you have?"

"A boy and a girl. Listen!" Roisin put her finger to her lips. "The Master. You must return to the house."

"We will speak tonight. Come to my room. There must be a way, dear sister." Keera leaned toward Roisin and gave her a quick kiss on the cheek, then she disappeared down the path, meeting Samuel and Marshells at the front door.

∼

Keera and Samuel discussed the situation while they dressed for dinner. She wondered how they'd get Roisin's children away from the other African woman, and if it were possible would her sister take the chance and come with them. Her concern was great. She didn't remember much of the evening meal and the chatter afterward. While the men enjoyed a social hour downstairs, Keera went upstairs to the bedroom.

When Roisin came, they sat inside the open window with the distant sound of the windmill grinding cane.

Roisin explained her problem. She wasn't raising her children. The Master had taken them away—his way of making sure she caused no trouble, and that she assented to his will. The African boiler's wife was tending them. Since he had disappeared, she would be under close scrutiny, and the chance of removing the children was impossible.

Keera asked, "Would the African boiler's wife want to go to?"

Roisin slowly shook her head. "Is that possible? How?"

Samuel came upstairs. Talking in low tones, he filled Roisin in on the last few years. Then he said, "Yes, it's possible. All of you would need to stay undercover until we sailed for Jamaica. We already had plans for you. We would just expand them, and everyone would be responsible for keeping out of sight."

"Roisin, what happened to Ciara?" In all the excitement, she'd forgotten to ask about her.

"She *was* with me, but she was always the stubborn one, refusing to be led. The Master sent her to the field, and like all the Irish in the fields, she couldn't make it. I can't show you her grave, because many of those who sailed with us are there in the same ground."

After a period of emotional silence, the talk resumed again.

"Will you find out about the African woman in the morning and let us know. We plan to leave mid-morning. Here's the rest of our plan." Samuel cautioned her about how she approached the woman and outlined how the escape would work.

Heavy footsteps on the circular stairs caused them to stop and listen. They went past on the upper landing.

"I must leave," Roisin whispered. "It isn't safe."

Samuel opened the door to the room and casually walked out onto the landing, looking around. He motioned to Roisin. She came out and disappeared quietly down the stairs. Neither noticed a quick movement in a downstairs hallway, as Roisin left the main house.

Keera and Samuel undressed and went to bed.

"I don't think I can sleep," Keera said as she rolled over on her side, face to face with him.

He rubbed her arm and kissed her. Then in a low voice told her of his visit to the fields of sugarcane. Before he'd got past the first acre, she was a lump in his arms, eyes closed, and fast asleep.

Samuel was the one finding it hard to sleep. He wondered what the outcome of their visit would be. So many scenarios ran through his mind. Later he awoke with a nightmare, slipped out of bed, and went to the window chair. That's were Keera found him the next morning — uncomfortable, but asleep.

~

Keera took a walk in the garden, while the men concluded their business and the carriage was readied to leave. She would meet Roisin here and find out the results of her talk with the African woman.

"Psst," came from behind the garden well. "Keera."

Keera walked over and sat on the rock edge. "I'm here," she whispered, her back to her sister.

"She will come with us."

"Great. You know what to do."

"Yes, when it's safe tonight, I'll sneak over to her house, and with her and the children, we will walk cautiously down the road until we find you. You'll be looking for us?"

"Yes. Here comes Samuel with Marshells. Be careful, dear sister. Keep your eyes and ears open and watch the path for obstacles." Walking away from the well, Keera called, "I'm here, Samuel," and then she hurried down the path and linked arms with him.

"We are ready to go, Keera." He helped her into the buggy, and turned to Marshells. "You've driven a hard bargain, Marshells. I'll see that you get your barrels. I believe we have enough in stock to fill your order." Then he shook hands with the man, climbed into their transportation, and drove out of the driveway.

Once they'd cleared the gate and *his eyes* weren't on them, Keera gave a sigh of relief. "The African woman and the children are going with us. I don't know the particulars, but we shall see them tonight, when it's safe for all of them to be on the road."

Samuel wiped his handshake hand on his trousers, as if it was dirty.

~

In the dark of night, four people and two children showed up as Keera and Samuel waited by the roadside—the African woman and to their surprise, her husband, Joseph. Roisin and the two children came, along with the servant who led the household and served Keera while she rested in the bed chamber—six in all.

Samuel might have explained the sister and children, but the rest of the group—he shook his head. If caught, everyone on this trip was in serious trouble—subject to being hanged or shot.

Samuel loaded them onto the carriage, hid then as best he could, and prayed that the strange looking group, didn't alert suspicions, as they traveled, on a lesser-known path, toward their rented room.

The group mostly stayed inside and out of sight the next day until late afternoon. Then, Samuel shepherded the group from the rented house into the carriage, concealing them with two coverlets. They made a lumpy, weird looking group as they headed toward Indian Bridge in the shadows of the setting sun, but no one stopped them, and no one interfered with their progress.

There would be the possibility of danger until the group of fugitives were loaded on the incoming ship and on the way to Jamaica.

Darkness had descended on Barbados, as the group arrived at Indian Bridge. Only a few candles and lamps cut through the night.

When the group arrived at the Tipton home, Samuel and Joseph helped all from the carriage, guiding them through an open back door into safety. They were given cots in the upstairs rooms, where each bedded down for the night. Tomorrow they would make other arrangements, but for tonight, this would suffice.

Marshells' armed men continued to search in Indian Bridge homes for his escaped slaves. When they heard that Keera was nursing old Ab, because of a mysterious illness and fever he had acquired, they gave the Tipton house a wide berth.

They didn't know this tale had been concocted by Ab himself, after Keera told Ab her story and introduced him to Roisin. He was happy to help.

Three weeks later, Captain Peter arrived with supplies to be offloaded for Barbados.

"We're taking your barrel staves and other supplies to Jamaica," Samuel explained, as the captain came into the barrel making operation.

"You're going early and not waiting on William to return?" asked Peter. He'd had a conversation with Captain William and his father in the Chesapeake Bay port where they had stopped to load tobacco on the way home to Bristol. This was a normal occurrence for the two ships—a good way to exchange news of the weather and happenings at home.

"Yes. Here's what's happened." Samuel told of finding Keera's sister and of the escaped slaves in his possession.

"You are in a dangerous position, my friend," commented Peter.

"I am," agreed Samuel. "And I need to put the fugitives aboard the ship as soon as possible. On board the ship, there's less chance of discovery, and I can breathe a sigh of relief."

Then he and Captain Peter came up with a plan. First, the people were loaded aboard the ship that night after dark, meaning concern over their being discovered declined. They were cautioned to keep low in the boat—preferably in the captain's cabin or under the fore and aftcastle of the ship. In this way, they were less likely to be seen.

The next morning, the furniture, equipment, and supplies being taken to Jamaica were rowed to the ship—those which they needed other than what the captain already had on board. When the few supplies for Barbados were offloaded, the ship pulled anchor, ready to sail.

Ab and Aron stood on the wharf waving as the ship moved in the harbour. They remained there until *The Bristol* was out of sight. Then Ab, totally cured of his mysterious illness, clapped Aron on the back. "We're in charge now, young man. Let's go run a business." They laughed together and walked back up the hill.

Keera and Samuel stood in the exact spot where they had stood seven years ago, watching the coast of Barbados and Indian Bridge slip from sight. The flying fish sailed over the waves and the frigate birds feasted on the unfortunate ones.

"How long until we get to Jamaica?" asked Keera.

"With favorable winds, probably four or five days."

Keera nodded and before Samuel knew it, she kissed him and said, "I love you."

"Somehow, I knew that," he said, grinning.

Across the deck and standing at the rail, the African Joseph stood watching the aqua-blue waters roll by, his thoughts on another voyage he'd taken some years ago. He remembered a dark-dank hole, being chained to another black man, and, if he tried to sit up, banging his head on the top of his resting place. The putrid smell did not remind him of the green forests of his homeland, where men ran free, and animals were animals—not men. There, life went on at an easy pace, not plunging up and down, on a slave ship, in the ocean. Thousands of miles away his old wife and children were on the banks of the Gambia, running free, and he hoped well.

He'd decided he would be free again while at the big plantation of the Marshells man—free or dead. He would not be chained to any man—white or black.

Turning his head, he took a quick look at the white couple on the rail. The days he'd spent with them had been different. They cared about him as a human, and as the man named Samuel had made known, he was welcome to stay with them or leave. He could make that choice when he got to this place called Jamaica.

Wasn't that freedom — making your own decisions? He turned back to the rail, took a deep breath, and squared his shoulders. Making his own decisions felt good.

❧ Chapter 23 ❧

17th Century
Port Royal, Jonathan, The Hurricane

Spain controlled the island of Jamaica for 146 years, until the English wrested it away. Even after Spain was defeated in Jamaica, the Spanish rulers kept trying to reclaim the island.

Because of this, in 1657, the English Governor of Jamaica, Edward O'Oley, invited the buccaneers, who were no more than pirates, to make their base at Port Royal.

The buccaneers or *boucaniers* (barbecuers of meat and some say their earlier human enemies) were descendants of the cattle-hunting people of the island of Spanish Hispaniola.

They turned to piracy after being robbed of their land and livelihood, and subsequently concentrated their attacks on the Spanish ships, which came through the area from Spanish Central America, and their possessions in the Caribbean Sea. These ships contained much gold, from the Incas and Aztecs, and other items of wealth.

Known as the *Brethren of the Coast*, with them there were no scruples, except among themselves. They were joined by ships of European origin, especially the English who shared the buccaneer name.

After the pirate's arrival, Port Royal became open to almost anything. As a utopia for these thieves, it was known as the "Sodom of the New World."

Most of the residents were pirates, cutthroats, or women of ill-repute. Even the parrots and monkeys had a bad name, becoming reliant on the tavern ale, walking around with an unsteady gait.

This was the atmosphere that Samuel and Keera were entering.

～

After his family moved to Jamaica, Jonathan Tipton was born in 1661.

Proceeding his birth was the death of the Protector Oliver Cromwell in 1658. This was followed by the attempted rule of his son, Richard, who soon died.

The Monarchy was restored when Charles II returned to the throne of England in 1660. King Charles continued Cromwell's practice of sending prisoners of Irish and Scottish descent to become slaves in the West Indies. Into the mix he added some common criminals.

English Americans from the North American mainland, along with people from the English mainland, arrived as immigrants seeking a different life—some as indentured servants, some with money in their pockets. These people spread over the West Indies.

Susceptibility to tropical diseases and harsh working conditions kept the white population from increasing, while the products of Jamaica, especially sugarcane, started growing and increased at a quick rate. To take care of the labour shortage, slaves were imported from

Africa, being sold in the central marketplace in Port Royal.

In 1670, when Jonathan was nine years old, the Spanish and English signed the Treaty of Madrid in July, ending the war for Jamaica. The island could now free itself of pirates, who were no longer welcome. It could grow and flourish, and Port Royal would soon become the largest town in the Caribbean.

~

The first sign of looming disaster had started the previous day. A portentous quietness filled the sky and not a leaf stirred on the trees. The birds stopped singing and disappeared.

At sunset the orange glow of the western sun shown in every Jamaican window and colored the tips of the ocean waves. The next morning, on October 7th, the eastern sun was red, the winds started to stir, and grow in intensity.

Keera was fixing the noon meal, when nine-year-old Jonathan came running into the house on the hill. He was followed by two of his sisters. "Mam, come outside and look. The sky is funny, and it looks like it will pour the rain."

"Well, I wouldn't be surprised, since we are at the end of the rainy season, and we're getting close to the afternoon—when it usually pours," Keera added, laughing at her young son.

"See, we told you it was nothing." Joanna stood with her hands on her hips, and Rachael mimicked her.

"No, mam. This is different. Please just look through the window toward the ocean."

To please him, because he seemed so intense, she went to the window and looked out. What greeted her were angry black clouds, piled to the heavens. As she looked, a gust of wind blew some of the coconuts off the trees at the front of the house. They flew through the air and barely missed her new pot of flowers at the entrance of the walk to the house.

"Hurry, Jonathan. Run outside and close the shutters, and girls, see if you can close the back ones. We don't have a minute to waste."

Jonathan left as she ran to the iron stove, pulling her pots from the fire. Food would have to wait. She wondered if Samuel knew about the approaching storm, and what about the surge? The Tipton business wasn't as susceptible as those on the lower peninsula, but a large storm — she didn't know.

She hurried after her son, praying as she went and pulling a wooden box of nails from a shelf, grabbing a hammer from a cupboard.

Not prepared for the blast of wind, when she opened the door, it slammed against the wall. Her eyes filled with dust. She struggled against the wind as she went to find him. "Jonathan, where are you?" she called over the increasing sound of the wind's whine.

"Here, mam."

Keera headed for the sound of his voice, blinking rapidly to remove the dust in her eyes. Jonathan appeared at her elbow.

"Mam, let me have the nails and the hammer. I can nail the shutters shut. I helped Dad during the last storm."

Keera was glad to let him. She stepped behind a tree for shelter, and still rubbing her eyes saw Samuel,

Peader, and Anna coming along the road in the buggy. They went straight to the carriage house, unhooked the horse, and pushed the buggy inside.

Samuel left Peader to close the door and rushed to his wife.

"Help Jonathan," Keera pointed.

Samuel hurried to Jonathan, "Here son, let me help you. Peader, get the ladder, so we can reach the top windows," he yelled at his son.

The ladder hung on the outside of the carriage house, and Peader was already standing behind him with it held in his hands.

"Good, Peader. Jonathan, do you remember where the iron bars for the windows are kept in the kitchen behind the stove."

"Yes, Dad. I'll get them." The family worked to close the house as tightly as they could to the approaching storm. The bars were placed across the top windows of the house, two-to-a-window.

When the house was secured, the ladder placed in the carriage house, and its doors secured with iron bars, Keera asked, "What about the warehouse?"

"We boarded up the windows and doors as best we could, and I sent everyone home. We left Roisin and the children at her house to collect supplies. She should be headed here now. I told them our house of stone would be safer."

"Good, let's get in the house. The wind's getting stronger, and there's danger of getting hit by flying debris." Keera rounded a corner of the house and headed toward the front door. Roisin and her children hurried to her.

"Everyone inside," ordered Samuel.

When all were in the house, they stood and looked at each other, wondering if there was something else, they could do. "I smell food," said Samuel.

"Yes, I will warm it." suggested Keera, going to the stove and testing the foods warmth by dipping a spoon in a pot and sipping carefully.

Everyone got plates from the cabinet and forks from a drawer. They gathered around the table and ate from the warm pots and pans being passed between them. Water was dipped from a bucket on the counter near the door.

"I know what we forgot to do," exclaimed Samuel. He jumped up and got the metal bucket used to clean ashes out of the stove. Quickly, he opened the door of the firebox and scooped the live coals into the bucket. "Peader, get some water and douse the fire." The coals left in the stove and bucket were soon put out. "Smoke from the stove would've made staying in the house almost impossible."

Within the hour, heavy rains driven westward by the ferocity of the windstorm hit the island. The gusts were strong, sending roofs flying off buildings, rattling windows and battering the shutters. The homes around them with wooden walls collapsed like they were made out of paper. Then all was quiet.

"Dad, may I look out the door?"

"Yes, we're probably in the eye of the storm." Samuel replied, "But be careful. You don't know what the winds have blown against it."

Jonathan took the inside bars off the door and slowly opened it. He ventured onto the walkway, followed by all the people in the house.

The sun shone overhead, and all was quiet for fifteen minutes, as they walked around the house, checking for damage.

Then, the sky darkened and the family went back inside. The raging storm hit again from the other direction. The stone house shook with its fury, but stood firmly against the howling wind. Water was sucked in between the cracks of the windows and doors and collected in puddles on the floor. This hurricane was small but intense. After five hours of battering wind and rain, the sky settled down to a steady pour, with erratic gusts of wind. Then, the sun came out as if the last few hours hadn't happened.

~

Jonathan stood on the wharf in the inner harbour, watching several men turn huge winches with ropes attached to a large sailing ship. The tide was going out and the ship slowly careened toward shore until it rested almost on its side against the bank. Several men rushed into knee-deep water, while others carried ladders to the exposed hull. They were attempting to fix a leak, and they were brushing hot tar onto the bottom of the ship. The open tar container sat over a fire built on sand next to the ship. The window for tarring the bottom was tight, if the fix was to be done before the tide came in and the ship refloated.

From where Jonathan was standing, the narrow harbour was full of ships, some trading in slaves from Africa, some bringing supplies to the island, and some loading barrels of sugarcane into holds for shipment to England by way of the New World.

There at the ports on the Chesapeake Bay, tobacco was placed in the remaining space or stashed on deck with the other supplies for the remainder of the voyage to England.

Jamaica was open for business.

A Tipton ship, with their coat-of-arms as its banner and flying the flag of the Cross of St. George, remained at the farthest part of the wharf, unable to get any closer. He wondered what news the ship had brought of England and Barbados.

At nineteen, Jonathan was heading toward the Tipton's warehouse to help his father. Like Peader and the others, he was an expert cooper, adept in the art of barrel-making, having soaked up his father's teaching, and actively participating in the art of making barrels. The African Joseph and his wife had remained with the facility, and Joseph had actually taken over the shaping of trees cut on the island to make barrel staves. He had a natural skill and talent for this work.

Joseph smiled as Jonathan entered the warehouse to the sound of hammers hitting iron rings, driving them onto another new barrel. Jonathan stopped to observe a new part of the operation.

Following the idea of the careening of ships and with the blessing of his father, he had set up a cable and gears system to help with the final finishing of the barrels. With the cables wrapped around the bottom of the barrel, a man on each end of the strong wire turned a large wheel, pulling the lower part of the staves together. This tightened the staves so the final rings could be installed. Trial and error had made the system work very well.

After this, the final firing of the barrel could be made, if necessary. The firing made them airtight for the long sea voyage to England and helped age rum, if used for that purpose. Shipments of sugarcane or other goods did not require the barrels to be fired.

"Jonathan," Samuel called from the rear of the building, where he stood, looking at a stack of papers on his work table. "Captain Peter has brought news from England and Barbados." A slim man, Samuel Tipton was now in his sixties with graying hair at his temples.

The captain grinned at Jonathan. "How's my young inventor?" he asked, sticking out his hand for a shake.

"Great, what's the news of England and Barbados?"

"We have a new helper in Barbados. He will take over Ab's place and give Aron a rest, since he's had the whole responsibility of the operation after the old man died. He's our cousin, Richard, from Gloucester."

Ab hadn't made it through the last hurricane. He, as usual, thought he could lick the high winds, and venturing down to the harbour was struck by flying debris. When Aron found him, it was too late.

"Yes," Captain Peter explained. "A recent outbreak of the plague wiped out Richard's family, except for his wife and one child. He was ready to leave and start anew somewhere else." Captain Peter continued, "I saw him in Bristol, and suggested he come to Barbados, since he knows about the barrel making process."

"Aron will be glad to have him. I went over for a few months to help out, but my heart is here in Jamaica," Jonathan told the captain.

"There's other news of Barbados. It's about Marshells, the plantation and slave owner. His wife and daughter refused to come back to the island, and after Joseph and the others managed to get off the island, he started drinking himself into a stupor. He has shot himself, because he was bankrupt."

Jonathan would normally say he was sorry to hear of this man's unfortunate circumstances, but he didn't know him like his father did.

"Will you tell Roisin and Keera, Poppa?" he asked.

"No. I don't think I will."

The men stood for a few minutes watching the staves being pulled together by Jonathan's new invention. Joseph had asked for the privilege of running the new creation. He liked the mechanics involved.

Then Samuel asked Peter, "Is it true that the wool trade in England is in decline? We've heard growing sheep isn't as profitable as it once was."

"The market is flooded with wool and the price has dropped so low, that the cost of supplemental winter food and laborers outweighs increasing their flocks. It's either feast or famine, cold or hot, rainy or dry at home. I don't know how the merchants and their suppliers stand the extreme fluctuation in the business climate and weather."

"Captain Peter has brought other news." Samuel continued to shuffle papers on his work table.

"Yes, the growth of tobacco in New England has necessitated the thinking of a warehouse for barrel making in the Chesapeake Bay area. Right now, we can ship enough from England, but in the near future, we'll probably need to make a decision on a facility."

"Yes," said his father. "And I've been asked to sail to the Chesapeake to look at the area. So, my son, how would you like to go with me? I'll probably include Peader on the trip, also."

Like all Tiptons, Jonathan was ready to sail to any destination. It was decided. He would go with his father.

～

Standing at the rail of *The Bristol*, Jonathan looked at the low coastline of the Chesapeake Bay, where a jumble of green trees grew down and it seemed into the water. This would be followed by areas where the shrub brush was gone, burned off, and easily accessible by horse, exposing the flat, arable lands on the bay.

They sailed deeper into the bay for a day, encountering smaller boats plying the deep blue waters, disturbing long-legged birds, snowy-white in colour, feasting in the bay shallows.

Occasionally, a large cleared area appeared with a house and private wharf. These were for smaller boats coming to pick up or deliver goods. Barrels stood in lines on the wooden wharves, with dark-skinned men stacking them for shipping to England. Tobacco fields stretched for many acres, until the woodlands closed in again.

Captain Peter, leaning on the rail with them, observed, "We'll soon be at the mouth of the Severn River."

"Captain, isn't there a Severn River in England? I've heard Poppa talk about it." asked Jonathan, as the water went silently by the moving ship.

"Yes, the River Severn was affected by the tidal flow much like this one. It was surrounded by lowlands, too."

"Was it as grown up with trees and shrubs? Could you get down to the riverbank?"

"With people living along it for hundreds of years, the banks were mostly accessible. The source of the river was in the Welsh mountains. Flooding, especially in the winter, was the biggest problem—for crops, cattle, and people," Samuel added.

"I wonder if I'll ever visit our homeland."

"I suppose that's up to you. I'll be glad to take you," replied Captain Peter.

A call from the ship's wheel position stopped the conversation. "We are at Providence, Captain. Shall we put in here?" Captain Peter left to take the wheel as the channel narrowed.

Samuel and Jonathan walked to the port side of the boat to observe its progress as it was steered into the mouth of the Severn River.

∽

"It's true, most of the first settlers died from malaria, but those who survived have birthed children who are more resistant to the native diseases. Our population is rising and so is our tobacco harvest." The grizzled older man talking was one they had encountered in the town of Providence, on the Severn River.

After stopping in the street to let another buggy go by, he sat with his dark-skinned driver, who held the reins of his spirited, prancing horse firmly in hand. The white man leaned toward the group as he spoke to them.

"We were exploring the possibility of setting up a barrel making operation. We're coopers from England by way of Barbados and Jamaica. This is Captain Peter Walton of *The Bristol*, he's at the helm of one of our ships. I'm Samuel Tipton." He went on to introduce Peader and Jonathan.

The old gentleman raised his hat. "I'm William Greene. My plantation is ten miles from town. Why don't you gentlemen ride home with me and take tea? I'd like to hear about the West Indies."

Samuel looked down at his clothes and replied, "We've been at sea for two weeks, and a bathhouse plus clean clothes is in order for us. Thank you for the kind invitation."

"We could talk about barrel making and the owners here who might be customers," Greene encouraged.

"Would tomorrow inconvenience you?" asked Samuel, heeding his words.

"No, tomorrow will work also." Greene dipped his head at them. "We will come for you at this time and drive you to my home."

"Thank you," Samuel replied. "We will meet you here."

The group stood in the street, watching Mr. Greene until he was out of sight.

"Talking to him was fortunate. We may find out everything we want to know in one place," Captain Peter observed.

Samuel nodded, agreeing with the captain. "Let's find a hot bath."

∿

"The Chesapeake Bay area is a one-crop economy and based solely on tobacco," ventured a man is his dress clothes, consisting of knee breeches, hose, flat-black shoes with buckle, and white wig. Obviously, the Tiptons were sitting with the elite of the community.

Another man added to the conversation. "We need more African slaves. Will you be transporting our laborers from Africa?"

"No," the captain responded. "We do transport indentured servants, if you have a need for them. We decided long ago the slave trade was not for our company."

"What is the business situation in the motherland?" asked William Greene.

Captain Peter answered, "At present the economy is stable and growing, although the wool trade is suffering."

"Then indentured servants won't come here. Our work load is increasing and our work force will become nonexistent. I tell you we need to buy slaves from Africa." The man stood, and emphasized his words with short, determined steps around the room.

The conversation turned quickly to the political, economic, and cultural aspects of Anne Arundell County. Soon the afternoon was over, and the Tipton's headed back to *The Bristol* with assurances of trade as soon as they could open up an operation in the area. This was much sooner than Samuel had planned.

As they sailed home, it was decided that the older son, Peader, would return and establish the company's startup, while Jonathan remained in Jamaica with his father. As usual, Captain Peter would return to England for supplies and equipment and come back to find property to start the operation. He would then sail to Jamaica for Peader, and those who might want to join the young man.

In the end, Jonathan's oldest sister, Anna, Peader, and Keera's sister Roisin and her children made the trip out of the Tipton family. These were joined by a base of Jamaican and Barbadian workers, including Joseph and his family. Once others in the Maryland area were trained, these last were given the option of staying or returning to the islands in the future,

Since workers for the fields were in demand, the Tiptons decided on future sailings, to bring more indentured workers from England, Wales, or Scotland to the New World. These laborers would be under contract for five years as payment for ship's passage. When the contract was finished, they would be given land by the government, and a stake or outfit, consisting of a suit of clothes, some farm tools, seed, and maybe a gun — a small price to pay for a chance at a new life.

ৠ Chapter 24 ৠ

Late 17th Century
Giovanni, Earthquake,

The next years on Jamaica passed quickly with the Tipton cooperage business expanding along the wharf from the original operation on the peninsula toward the main port. Reports from New England told of the remarkable growth of their adventure in making tobacco barrels in this different land. Even Barbados was experiencing growth with a nibble from the Portuguese coffee bean industry in Brazil.

~

The sugarcane industry in the West Indies was booming, with Jamaica becoming the undisputed capital of sugar growing production to England, much to the jealousy and dismay of the other English held islands in the Caribbean.

An older and wearier Samuel slowly withdrew from the day-to-day functions of the Port Royal hustle and bustle, confident in letting his youngest son take over the barrel making operation, while he spent his time investing the earnings in land and houses.

One afternoon in 1685, Jonathan walked down the Port Royal peninsula to discuss a shipment of iron barrel rings and wooden staves, soon to be off-loaded from an English ship from Portishead. Because of the increase in demand for barrels, these extra supplies hadn't come on a Tipton ship, and he needed to make arrangements for them to be sent to the warehouse.

Turning onto High Street, which ran the length of the largest part of the port, he heard loud noises coming from the open windows of a local rum house, The Royal Arms. An argument was ensuing. Jonathan hurried, thinking he'd get past the doorway before a serious altercation occurred.

The door opened just as he was about to walk by. A young man was ejected by two husky, bearded men into the dirty street. Jonathan made a quick step to the right to avoid stumbling over him.

"Whoa, what the…"

"Sorry," the young man said. "I was told they had rooms to let, and I was in need of one. Guess someone lied to me." He stood to his feet, brushing the port dust and dirt from his baggy knee breeches and loose-fitting shirt, as his sack of belongings was cast out of the dimly lit doorway after him. He walked to his possessions and hoisted them to his shoulder, preparing to walk away.

"What's your name?" Jonathan asked, following his steps.

"Giovanni Aurelius," was the reply. "I'm from Genoa, but I came in on the merchant ship, *Charles' Hope* out of London. She's being careened and worked on for leaks to the hull and damage to the rudder. I needed a place to stay until she's seaworthy again."

As the young man mentioned his name, Jonathan wondered if he'd heard it before. For some reason, it sounded familiar. Impressed at the man's command of

English, albeit with a strong accent, and always eager to hear of the travels of others, Jonathan extended an invitation. "Come home with me. My family has plenty of room, and you'd be welcome to spend as many nights as necessary."

"Oh, I don't want to intrude. There must be a place to stay here close by the port."

"None I would recommend." Jonathan stated, smiling and feeling a kinship with this young man and not willing to take no for an answer. "It's settled. At present, I'm headed down the wharf to talk to a ship's captain. Come with me."

"Thanks, I sure don't want to stay here." Giovanni looked at the closed door of the tavern, where raucous, drunken laughter came through the thin walls. He went with Jonathan.

After a brisk walk to the docking area, Jonathan found the ship. He climbed the gangplank and boarded, looking around to see if his new found friend was following.

"I'll stay here," said Giovanni, heading for a convenient pile of rope on the dock, where he sat down, stretched out, and closed his eyes.

Jonathan laughed and shook his head. "This won't take long."

～

Upstairs in the house on the hill above the harbour, Giovanni was given Peader's room, which was next to Jonathan's. Each day, while his ship was receiving repairs, he went to Port Royal with Jonathan, to observe the barrel making facility.

"How do you like our operation," Jonathan asked on the third day, as they walked home.

"It's very interesting. I didn't realize one man must make each barrel individually—so much handiwork and skill are involved. I don't think I'd have the patience. Do you know the whole process? Can you make a barrel by yourself?"

"Yes, I can. I believe someone should be able to make the product, the same as those working for them."

"Do you have indentured servants or slaves working on the barrels?"

"No, to slaves or indentured servants here," Jonathan replied. "But, our operation in the New World has indentured servants from England or Scotland. There aren't enough people living in that area to supply labor for the plantations. The plantation and land owners on the Chesapeake Bay have servants and African slaves. Here we have the free Maroons, who were former slaves living in the mountains. Some of them have come down to Port Royal to work."

"As soon as it's repaired, the ship on which I sail is heading for the Chesapeake Bay. The captain told me they don't often put in here at Port Royal. It's not on their regular route, but the Bay is."

"Jonathan, is that you?" called Keera, hearing the door shut as she worked in the kitchen.

"Yes, Mam. It's Giovanni and me."

"Get cleaned up. The food is ready to eat. I'm setting it on the table. And, Giovanni, the laundress, who washes the family's clothes, will be here tomorrow. If you will lay yours out, I'll see that they are washed with ours."

"Thank you, Mistress Tipton." Giovanni called back. "I will make sure you get them. I'm not good at keeping them clean. Scrubbing clothes is not a favorite job of mine."

Jonathan and Giovanni climbed the stairs to change into clean clothes for the evening meal — a requirement in the Tipton household.

When Jonathan went to get Giovanni for the night meal, he'd emptied his clothes sack on his bed. There in the midst was a book. "What is that?" he asked Giovanni in astonished surprise, as he looked at the tooled leather with a familiar ship on the cover. "Where did you get this?" he continued, thinking his new friend had been in his father's and mother's bed chamber.

"My grandfather is not in good health. He gave it to me just before I boarded the ship. He said not to lose it, that it's very old. Some of it, I can read. Some of it, I can't. Since he was ill, I don't think he thought I'd ever see him again. He raised me from a young lad, because my parents died in the plague in Genoa several years ago."

"Come, you must bring this downstairs. I want my father to see it. He won't believe you have this particular book."

"What are you talking about?" Giovanni cocked his head and looked wonderingly at his friend.

"You'll see. Come on." Jonathan grabbed Giovanni by the arm, carefully hefted the book, and steered him down the staircase. Then he hurriedly went back upstairs to a room across the hall from his. It was his parent's room. On a table was the item he was looking for — The Ancestry Book. From the wall, he gingerly took an antique sword and headed for the stairway.

Upon entering the dining room, he walked straight to the chair his father normally sat in at the table. Carefully he placed the two books side-by-side and quietly included the sword. His excitement mounted as he examined the three together.

Giovanni came to stand by his side. "Why, they have the same cover," he exclaimed. "I don't understand." He shook his head in astonishment.

"What's going on?" asked Keera, bringing food to the table. She walked around and looked over the young men's shoulders. They stood apart as she gasped, putting out a finger to touch the two books in awe. "Is this what I think it is?"

At that moment, Samuel strode into the room. "I'm hungry," he said, without realizing the drama unfolding at his eating table. "What's the group for?" he asked, approaching the table to see what the excitement was about. The three parted as he came near.

His mouth dropped open and for seconds he stood in place without moving. When he found his tongue, he picked up the new book and asked, "Where did this come from?"

"It's mine, Sir." Giovanni explained. "It's been in my family for…"

He and Samuel finished the sentence together, "for hundreds of years."

Samuel clapped Giovanni on the back. "Yes, it has. Do you know what this means?" he asked the young man.

"No Sir, I don't."

"Everyone, sit down to eat, and later I will tell Giovanni the story, which is written in this book." He touched the Tipton book with his hand. "And then, we will read your story." He nodded at Giovanni.

Giovanni stayed for six days. During which time, Samuel managed to read his whole book to the assembled family.

He read in a voice filled with emotion, at the words of a man, who lived over one thousand years before. The book recounted the story of Cassius Aurelius after leaving Tybba on the River Trent and his descendants.

'"After leaving Tybba, I traveled down the river and headed back onto the Humber Estuary, stopping for several weeks at Petuaria, being entertained by Valerius and hoping to receive word of Tybba's safe arrival at the mouth of the River Tame. Since I heard nothing, good or bad, I assumed the best, and saying a prayer to God for his safety and that of his family, I sailed for the North Sea, and resumed the visiting of those on my trading route.

"On returning to my friend's old home on the River Albis, I found Tybba's former tribe had moved to another location. I knew not where, but the wharf and some of the deserted wattle and daub houses remained. I anchored for several days, contemplated our friendship, mourned his village's disappearance, and with a sad heart, sailed away."

The book reported his marriage, the birth of five children, and twenty grandchildren, several of which became captains of ships or sailed the oceans as sailors. His descendants had written stories for the next hundreds of years of family struggles in wars, the horrors of the Pestilence, and of the city-states of the emerging country of Italy, where many of the family made permanent homes.

There were brief encounters of famous people of the Renaissance, such as Boccaccio, the writer, poet, and politician of the 1300's, from whom his contemporary, the English Geoffrey Chaucer based some of his writing.

The story continued with the Aurelius family eventually ending up in the city-state of Genoa, encountering Columbus, with one of their family participating with him in a voyage to Africa to trade for goods. He described the captain as "a very religious man" in a letter to his grandfather from Naples while on the voyage. The Aurelius family stayed in Genoa through upheavals in the many governments, which were established over the land. This is where Giovanni was born, on a hilltop, overlooking the vast shipbuilding harbour of Genoa.

Samuel closed the book and with his finger traced the ship on its cover. "Ships go all over the known world, and so do people." He looked at Giovanni. "This house with its view must remind you of yours in Genoa," he said.

"Yes, sir, it does. If I may come back to visit, I'll always feel as if I'm coming home, especially when I can see this hilltop and the house from my ship."

"From *now on*, Giovanni Aurelius, this is your home. We welcome you to it." Samuel cleared his voice, got up from his chair, and left the room. He didn't want the others in the room to see him cry.

The two young men became close friends. Before leaving, Giovanni vowed to return to his new home. Then he was off to sea again.

~

Life for the Tiptons in Jamaica returned to normal, and the years went quickly by. Giovanni did make it back. Finally, he boarded a ship where he could regularly visit his newly found adopted family.

The ship, *Julia Anne*, was a small ship, based in Barbados. It plied the waters of the Caribbean, picking up island goods and transporting them for shipment to the New World. There the goods were staged for shipping by larger ships to England or other ports. Giovanni soon worked his way up to procurer of ships supplies for the voyages, overseeing food for the ship's sailors and goods going into the holds. As he told Jonathan, "If it can be carried onto the ship and stored, my hand and loading instructions are involved."

Jonathan advised Giovanni, "If we get overloaded with orders and need more barrels in the Chesapeake Bay area, we may use your ship."

The Italian nodded. "We'll make room, somehow." Then he added, "Should you want to visit the Bay, we occasionally carry passengers there, but our ship is not outfitted for many travelers."

"I'll remember that. We could travel together."

The last time Giovanni had sailed, he'd left his ancestry book with the Tiptons saying, "This is the proper place for it to be. The books started out side-by-side, and they should end up the same way."

~

Often, Samuel would hitch the horse to the buggy and take Keera, Rachael, and Joanna to visit the wharf at Port Royal. They would watch as the rings were being hammered onto the barrel staves at the factory as well as observe the ships using the harbour.

Keera, especially, loved the sound, smell, and rumble of newly made barrels being rolled to the warehouse. She remarked to Samuel, "I miss being here and being a part of the whole operation."

"My dear, we can take care of your failure. I'm sure Jonathan would return you to the workforce." Raising his eyebrows and cocking his head, Samuel grinned at his wife. "He's always short by at least one."

Keera rolled her eyes at the love-of-her-life and suggested, "Why don't we come down and relieve him one day or afternoon of each week. Remember how tired we'd become and wish for this. A change of scenery would do us both some good."

"Scenery, huh? A bunch of barrels. Not exactly my kind of viewing pleasure. The view from our windows is enough for me. Here's my suggestion, my love. Let's pick Tuesday morning as our day."

Keera wondered at his choice, but did not argue and this became their habit.

~

Jamaica and Port Royal had become, as one of Jonathan's friends observed, the "storehouse and treasury of the West Indies", and "one of the wickedest places on Earth." It was the home port for many of the privateers and pirates operating within the Caribbean Sea. Wide open, there were as many ale houses and brothels as homes in the restricted area — maybe more. No one was counting.

The Tiptons kept a wide berth from such activities, preferring their home atmosphere and a separated area as much as possible for their warehouse, but Port Royal was rapidly surrounding them.

～

Tuesday, June 7th, 1692, started as any other day. Samuel, Keera, Rachael, and Joanna were in Port Royal to give Jonathan a day of rest. In fact, after going to the Anglican Church on Sunday, they had taken over on Monday and told Jonathan to enjoy the week off. He had plans to drive the buggy to a plantation on the western end of the island to visit a customer friend and stay several days. They'd planned on going hunting, walking in the heights of the hills, and strolling on the beach, where the waves came quietly onto the sandy shore.

Not being in a hurry and with the house quiet, Jonathan, at thirty-one, lazed around on that morning, packing a noon meal to eat. He would stop, before he rode over the hilltop and down the path on the other side, at a favorite place, under a coconut palm tree.

Leaving the house, he headed for the shed and the buggy to harness the horse. Leading the horse from its barn behind the shed, he decided not to hitch it up to the carriage, and instead put a saddle on the animal.

Frowning, he stood for a few minutes, looking around. If the house had seemed quiet, the world outside was even more muted. Why? Then he realized the birds weren't singing in the trees. There were no birds. Even his favorite woodpecker wasn't in the high limbs of the mango tree in the Tipton front yard, noisily searching for bugs or worms among the branches. He couldn't solve the mystery, if there was one. He slung his clothes and food bag across the saddle.

Shrugging his shoulders, he mounted up, and rode at a leisurely pace up a narrow path he knew well, avoiding the dirt road below. He traveled alongside groves of banana trees, so thick the light was shut out to the ground, because of the leaves' intertwining canopy. These were followed by other fruit tree groves — mangoes, oranges, and grapefruit, introduced by the Spanish. He often sent the surplus to the New World on the company boats.

Reaching the top of the hill, he dismounted, pulled his food from the horse, and sat on a rock to eat. He'd gotten though his meat and bread and peeled his banana…

The sound started slowly. Built in volume. Within seconds, it was a loud roar. Jonathan jumped up, only to be thrown back down onto the ground. The earth shook, rolled, and moved up and down. EARTHQUAKE! His horse bolted and ran with a gait so comical he would have laughed, if what was happening wasn't so deadly serious. There were shattering noises all around him as trees loosed dead limbs and anything not attached tightly, thudded to the ground. A house below him collapsed in a puff of smoke, and it wasn't the only one.

He crawled to a young sapling, pulled himself up until he stood where he could see the sea. The whole sight was surreal. Most of the peninsula of Port Royal had disappeared into the water, sinking completely until nothing was left but boats moving erratically on the disturbed sea. He stood watching in horror and shock as the rumbling and shaking continued. The whole scenario was over in a few short minutes.

Poppa, Mam, Rachel and Joanna. His workers.

He chased down his horse, calmed it, mounted and rode pell-mell for the Tiptons' stone home. When he arrived, it looked intact but strangely out of place, since those around it were flattened and on the ground. Not taking time to check out structural damage, he headed straight toward Port Royal.

Halfway down the hill, he pulled his horse up. He gazed at the sea coast, where the water had receded exposing the seabed, coral reefs, and leaving behind ponds of water, exposing the shattered port as it now sat on the seabed.

Now for the second horror, a piece of history, taking place in front of his eyes.

From the sea, a massive swell of water arose, higher and higher it came. If there was any chance his family was alive, it disappeared in a wall of water, which struck the coast. Buildings and houses disintegrated in the massive breaker. Washed inland, they became piles of rubble along the sides of the hills. Trees disappeared and joined the rubble. A boat, one that didn't sink in the massive breaker, sailed onto the hillside before him and caught on a pile of rubble which was a house. Without realizing it, tears ran down Jonathan's face. All he could do was sit on his horse, watch, and pray for survivors.

As soon as the breaker expended its energy, the water started slowly back to the ocean. The flow picked up speed, carrying anything left loose into the sea and beyond. The whole expanse was full of floating debris and something that looked like bodies from his vantage point. By squinting his eyes, barrels appeared to be floating atop the water.

He started his horse downward as people emerged from their places of safety, heading for the shore, what was left of it. The scene was indescribable with legs, arms, and wooden building parts, sticking out of the sand, which now made up Port Royal.

Jonathan passed a man, jabbering to himself as if talking to a mate. He stopped and hailed the man, who continued his babbling not realizing Jonathan was there. "We was running up the street, whilst on either side of us, we saw houses some swallowed up as holes opened in the ground and then closed over them." He threw his hands in a wide gesture, indicating the immensity of the destruction to his unseen companion. "People was running into the street, hands uplifted, asking for God's help."

Jonathan traveled on and halted his horse on the new waterfront. Dismounting, he tied the reins to a roof beam sticking out of the water and walked up and down in the sand and puddles of water, toward what had been Port Royal. He could only go so far, until the sand became a mire, sucking at his feet, while water closed around his ankles. What was he looking for? Any sign? Any evidence…

A tremor sent those on the beach scurrying for safety. Jonathan didn't run. His family was gone, and so was the Tipton barrel making business. In shock, he didn't care what happened to him. He stood facing the ocean — waiting.

When the sun started to go down, he rode for home. Worn out physically, mentally, and emotionally, he managed to pull his mattress downstairs, into the open Great Room, where the family sat to rest. The family. What family?

There'd already been two tremors, and he didn't want to fall from the second story onto the ground floor. But sleep wouldn't come. Today's unspeakable horror kept coming to mind. He relived the day over and over again. If only. If only. If only, ran through his mind.

The following morning, he was more tired than when he went to bed. Some of the shock, he'd worn out, tossing and turning during the night. Things needed to be done, and he'd best get to them.

Until the business climate steadied and started to increase in volume, shipping in and out of Port Royal became expensive as most captains avoided the area. A new town, to be called Kingston, worked feverously to restore a wharf and docking facilities. Sugarcane piled up on the plantations. No one brought the stuffed barrels to town.

Finding passage on a ship was close to impossible. Too many wanted to leave, but Jonathan remembered Giovanni's promise to take him to the Chesapeake Bay. This promise became the foundation of his labor. There was no reason for him to stay on the island. He would go to his family in the New World.

❧ Chapter 25 ❧

Late 17th Century
The Trip to Chesapeake Bay, Sarah

Jonathan was much improved when Giovanni came into port on the *Julia Anne* two months later. He had grieved over his loss and then made a plan and with his friend's help, he was ready to execute it.

Two things had happened since the massive earthquake, which struck Port Royal. He'd sold all his family's possessions in Jamaica to his friend on the western end of the island, who wanted property in eastern Jamaica. And, the friend had brought three of his massive Tipton barrels to Port Royal from his plantation for Jonathan to use—these had been made larger for storage on his manor and weren't burned inside like his normal ones.

These containers were insurance against the breakdown of his original plan.

At the sight of Port Royal or actually no wharf at all, Giovanni and several from the ship, rowed to shore. He rushed up the hill to the Tipton house, where he found Jonathan rummaging through the pantry, looking for food to eat.

"Jonathan, you're all right!" he exclaimed on seeing his friend. "After seeing the port had disappeared, I was afraid you might be gone. We heard about the catastrophe while in Barbados."

"No, Giovanni, I'm not gone, but almost everything else is. Let's sit down." After a quick hug of greeting, the two headed for undamaged chairs in the Great Hall.

Seeing Jonathan's mattress, his friend asked, "Are you sleeping downstairs?"

"Yes, we've had tremors after the big one. I didn't want to end up crashing onto the lower floor, although this house has held up well," said Jonathan, looking around the only house he'd ever known.

"It's awfully quiet. Where's Mam, Poppa, and the girls."

Jonathan told him of their deaths and related the scene he'd experienced. "I'm just now getting over the nightmares associated with that dreadful day, and I miss Poppa, Mam, and my sisters. My whole family's gone."

Giovanni had bowed his head at the devasting news of the Tiptons' deaths. No words were spoken for some minutes as the two sat in poignant thought. Giovanni cleared his throat and broke the silence, "What are you planning to do?"

Jonathan told of his plan to go to the New World and join Peader and his family. "The barrel making area was completely destroyed, and my workers are dead. I see no reason to stay here. I'm hoping to go with you when you sail."

Giovanni looked at him. "We have a full complement of crew and passengers on board—a priest of the Anglican Church and his daughter. They rowed out to the ship as soon as we dropped anchor. His church was destroyed, and his wife drowned in the tsunami. I heard him tell the captain he wants to get away for a while with his daughter. He also has family in the Chesapeake Bay area. We'll have to think of something else."

"I have an alternate plan, because I don't want to wait," said Jonathan. "Come with me." He led his friend to the shed where the buggy was kept.

"Where's the buggy?"

"Sold, along with the horse and the rest of the Tipton possessions on the island. I have the money safely hidden in the house and plan on using it to purchase property once in Providence, or is it Annapolis now?"

"Still Providence, but subject to change. You'll have a headright of fifty acres, when you arrive on shore as an immigrant. Do you need more than that?"

"Yes. I was thinking of letting Peader keep the barrel making operation and venturing into growing tobacco, a real change in the Tipton ideas of business, buying land and getting your hands dirty with soil. Later, if I need to, I can start another cooperage and sell my own barrels. I'm sure there will be other opportunities as I find them, but that's after I get there."

"All right, what's your plan for going there?" Giovanni asked, observing the barrels in the shed. On the outside, they were singed with the Tipton crest and given the numbers 1040, 1041, and 1042 on each end.

Jonathan explained what the three barrels were for. "Two of the barrels are packed with possessions — those I want to keep from my home. One of them, number 1042, includes the two Ancestry Books and Sir Anthony's sword, all placed in a flat airtight, rectangular box, which I surrounded with family trinkets. As you can see, it fits perfectly into the bigger barrel." He pointed to the wooden container.

"It doesn't look like a box the Tiptons make," observed Giovanni.

"We did make them, but long ago." Jonathan pointed to the burned crest of the Tiptons on the end. "I've also wondered at its use."

The last barrel, Jonathan explained, he'd outfitted for himself. Taking nails and crawling inside, he'd padded the interior so the rough wood was covered. He'd bored more holes in the sides of the barrel for air circulation and light, and put an inside lock on the top lid so it couldn't be opened from the outside. This was going to be his daytime home.

"Do you really think this will work?" questioned Giovanni, eyebrows raised and kicking at the barrel. He wondered if his friend was still a bit daft, from the loss of his family and the horrible scene he'd witnessed.

"Yes, I think it will, but there are always chances of complications." Jonathan explained his intentions to come out at night, when visibility was low to stretch his legs, eat, and rest.

He pointed out some dried, barbecued beef he'd packed in his barrel to chew in the daytime. Another stuffed bag for a pillow, and his money were the only other items going into the sleeping barrel.

"There are places on deck where shadows and cargo could conceal your presence, and most of the crew would be asleep below deck or under the aftcastle on the stern."

"True and the passenger's quarters on your boat are built into the aft end, along with the captain's accommodations. My end, the forecastle, contains the cook stove, eating area, and stores." Jonathan explained. "And the forecastle is less likely to be flooded by water in a strong wave, which may wash over the sides of the boat in a storm."

Giovanni was beginning to believe in his friend. "Don't forget some of the crew, including the cook, sleeps on or in the forecastle area." He was thinking. "We could stash your barrels next to or inside the galley. There they would be inconspicuous and tied to iron rings on the boat. I could say they were supplies for eating or possibly the New World—supplies for the New World would be best. That might work. My friend, I'll add your three barrels to the ship's manifest."

Jonathan's only problem would be storms, where water might enter the air holes in the barrels, or pirates might take them as supplies for their own ships should they board.

Many of the privateers had gone rogue and attacked any likely looking prey seen from their bridge.

Here on Jamaica, Jonathan remembered playing hide and seek, with his brother and sisters. This would be the adult version of his childhood game.

He grinned to himself at the pleasant memory, and then became sad—again.

That night, he and Giovanni sat in the outside courtyard of the former Tipton house on the hillside above the old harbour. Port Royal was no more—the twinkling lights on the peninsula snuffed out forever. The western sun set in a glorious glow of red-orange, as if saying goodbye to the two men. Tomorrow night, the plan would be set in motion.

～

On the day before the *Julia Anne* was sailing, the barrels were rowed to the ship and put aboard. Jonathan went out to supposedly visit Giovanni. During an isolated moment he slipped into his barrel, which rested on its side. The time had come to test his plan.

His friend came at dark. "Jonathan, all's clear," Giovanni whispered, while tapping three times on the wooden cask. "The men have gone ashore onto the mainland for one last evening of self-indulgence. Let's check for places to hide."

They tested different areas on the ship for shadow and light, stopping only as the men came rowing back to the ship, boisterously singing at the top of their voices a sea shanty known from Newfoundland to St. Kitts.

Faintly as tolls the evening chime,

Our voices keep tune and our oars keep time,

Soon as the woods on shore look dim,

We'll sing at St. Ann's our parting hymn.

Row, brothers, row, the stream runs fast,

The rapids are near and the daylight past.

Jonathan looked at Giovanni and smiled. What rapids awaited his voyage to the New World? Time to crawl into his new home. He couldn't turn back now.

The Julia Anne sailed at dawn.

~

If Jonathan planned on a calm, peaceful journey, his trip turned out to be anything but. He soon found out his barrel was very restrictive, and some days his legs cramped from his tight resting place. The tightening of his muscles became the worst problem he dealt with, and he had a terrible time not moaning at the hurt, thus alerting anyone close of his hiding place.

One evening, after the sun went down and four days out from Port Royal harbour, he left his barrel to walk the deck in the shadows. He soon realized his muscle was contracting in his left leg. The hurt became full-blown, and he sought a box to sit on in the shadows. Leaning over, he started rubbing his contracted muscle.

"Here," said a female voice from the shadows. "Let me help you. I'm an expert at muscle problems."

A woman in a flowing dress with a shawl around her shoulders came to kneel before him. In the shadows, he couldn't see much of her face or dress, but her voice was soothing and low. Below his knee breeches, she started massaging his bare leg, exploring the ball of muscle and working to gain its release.

"Who are you?" a surprised Jonathan asked, leaning back against the side of the ship, suppressing a moan. Women didn't often touch him, and this was a new, but not an embarrassing experience.

"My name's Sarah. My father was the priest at one of the Anglican Churches in Port Royal. His church was destroyed in the earthquake."

"I see," replied Jonathan, the pain so severe he couldn't utter another word.

"Did you go through the quake?" Sarah asked, working his muscle.

"Yes, my parents and sisters died in the quake or tsunami — hard to tell."

"I understand, and I'm sorry," she said, in a calm voice, her fingers digging deep into the cramped muscle. "I lost my mother."

"What are you doing out here at this time of night?" he wanted to know.

"I haven't been able to sleep, so I wait until most of the men are asleep and walk in the shadows on the deck. I find the ocean very peaceful. Why are you here?"

"For the same reason." Well, his response was partly true.

"I take it you are from Port Royal?"

The pain was starting to subside. "Yes." Jonathan said and asked, "How did you come to be an expert at muscle cramps?"

"My father has them. I remember him having one in the pulpit on one Sunday morning," she laughed. "He couldn't keep standing, until the pain went away. I worked on his muscle, and he finished his homily."

Jonathan sat mesmerized by this turn of events. There was at least two weeks to go on his trip to Maryland — maybe more, depending on the winds the ship encountered. He'd been wishing to hasten his journey. Would he now wish it to last forever?

"How is it now?"

Jonathan stood and walked around. The muscle was sore, but the cramping had stopped. "I think I'm cured. If you walk on deck after all the men are asleep, why did you trust me?"

"I've seen you on other nights and followed you. I don't feel aggression in you. Should I be worried?"

Jonathan gave a low, husky laugh. "No. Not at all."

"I think I'll go back to my room. Will I see you again?"

"We may bump into each other." Jonathan watched her shadowy figure disappear. He sat down on his box, his energy deflated, pondering this turn of events. Would she give away his presence on board the ship? What were his feelings toward her?

In the early hours of the morning, Jonathan returned to his bed chamber. He soon dozed off to sleep.

Tap. Tap. Tap. "Jonathan, I have food for you. It's safe to come out," Giovanni whispered the following evening, standing with his back to the prone barrel, which rested under the forecastle overhang out of the hot sun.

A sleepy Jonathan opened the barrel top and crawled into the darkness of a Caribbean night, the smell of roast beef stew filling his nostrils. He held out his hands for the bowl. Taking the spoon resting in the bowl, he took several bites before thanking Giovanni.

"The cook had plenty, so I brought you a big bowl." Giovanni sat down on a nearby box and watched Jonathan eat like he hadn't had a good meal in a month, which he probably hadn't.

Jonathan emptied the bowl, rubbed his stomach, and sighed, pushing air out of his mouth in a rush. "Whew. You don't know how good that tasted, and there was no bread."

"Sorry, I forgot it. How are you doing after five nights in a barrel?"

"I've slept better," stated Jonathan. "The sea has a calming effect and puts me right to sleep, at least it usually does. My biggest problem is the restrictive room, since the barrel is curved. This causes my legs to cramp and my hips to hurt."

"Ouch," Giovanni agreed. "Not much you can do but move to a new position."

Jonathan decided not to tell his friend about Sarah—at least, not now. "Are we making progress on the sea?"

"That's what I came to tell you about. The captain's knee is hurting, and he says there's a storm a coming, and he's usually right."

"How soon?" asked Jonathan.

"Probably after we pass Hispaniola and head toward the Bahamas—about two days, maybe three."

Jonathan nodded, thinking he saw movement in the shadows. "I hope it's not a bad one. Maybe it will pass fast."

"You know what they say, 'red at night, sailor's delight. Red in the morning, sailor's take warning.'"

"I'll be looking for the red warning. Does that pertain to pirates also? There are some who use red flags."

"You should know, since many of them were headquartered in Port Royal. They do love Tortuga, and we are approaching the Windward Passage, where the famous or should I say the infamous island is located."

"I'll keep my eyes peeled," joked Jonathan, knowing he couldn't see anything in a barrel. The shadow had moved again. "After we get into the Bahamas, how long to the Chesapeake Bay?"

"The currents and wind will be in our favor, but we have a thousand miles to cover, so I'm guessing two to three weeks of calm sailing."

"I've been once, but I didn't remember how long it took. It will be nice to see Peader, Anne, and Roisin again, along with Joseph and his family."

Giovanni nodded. "I'm headed back to bed. Sunrise isn't far away. Good night, Jonathan."

Jonathan watched him go, then he turned to the figure in the shadows. "Sarah, is that you?"

"Yes. I didn't want to barge into the conversation?" She stepped closer to Jonathan, but remained in the shadows. "Are we close to Tortuga? We used to have privateers in our church on Sunday. They had *letters of marque* for hunting the Spaniard ships and raiding Spanish towns."

"The letters were nothing more than a license to hunt, rob, and kill, mostly the Spanish."

"Why the Spanish?"

"Because their naval power was the greatest and they were the first to inhabit this area. The English,

French, and Dutch came later, so in most cases, they had to fight the Spanish to take or conquer land where they could find it."

"Wasn't England at war with the Spanish?"

"England's always at war with somebody. Have you heard of Sir Francis Drake?"

"I'm not sure. I think I've heard his name pertaining to the Caribbean."

"Yes, you should. He participated in the slave trade to this area for a short time. He was one of the commanders who fought the Spanish Armada about one hundred years ago in the English Channel and won. Besides that, Drake was honored as the first Englishman to circumnavigate the globe.

"Sent by Queen Elizabeth, as a privateer, on another expedition against the Spanish here in the Caribbean, he died of a fever and dysentery. They say he was given a burial at sea in a lead coffin."

"How do you know that?" Sarah was dumfounded at his knowledge.

"I've read it in a book." He didn't tell her about The Ancestry Book which mentioned Drake.

"My father taught several of the plantation owners' children to read and write. They stayed with us, and I fed them. He isn't feeling well, and I've been attending him. Just needed a respite from the stuffy cabin."

A cough from the forecastle over them stopped the conversation. "Sssh," cautioned Jonathan, putting his finger to his mouth.

They waited until steps sounded in the direction of the bow to resume their conversation.

Sarah asked, "Why do you sleep in a barrel? Don't you think that's strange?"

Jonathan shook his head. She knew everything. "There wasn't any regular passage I could buy, and I wanted to go to my family in the New World. I hatched this plan with my friend to go." Jonathan paused and added, "It's a good way to save money so I can purchase property in the Chesapeake Bay area."

"Won't you be given fifty acres when you get there?"

"Yes, if I swear allegiance to the Crown of England."

"You are a strange man, Jonathan, but I like you." Sarah changed the subject. "I hope the storm we are approaching isn't too bad. I might be seasick."

"I sure hope it isn't either."

"Have you had more cramps?"

"No. You're a good doctor," and Jonathan grinned. "For your father and me."

"I'm going back to my room to check on him. Will I see you tomorrow?"

"Maybe," said Jonathan, as he watched her go. "Good night. Stay safe, Sarah."

Sarah threw up her hand and waved.

꯲ **Chapter 26** ꯲

The Pirate, Sarah,

As a young, inexperienced colleague of the pirates, Captain Henry Morgan and William Kidd, Fredrick Borden hadn't achieved the notoriety or fame of his contemporaries. True, Morgan was dead, and Captain William Kidd had left the area, his vigor and energy for piracy waning. Not so with Fredrick. He, at forty-five, still hadn't gained the notoriety or fame and fortune which came with plundering ships and taking great riches. His ego would not let him quit until his name was known in the Caribbean for boundless and unique escapades.

He'd sailed from Nassau in the Bahamas, bound for Tortuga, stopping only one ship off the shores of Cubao, which had netted a box of bananas and a keg of water.

"Arggh."

At least, that's the way it felt, and his crew was starting to think mutiny. They wanted Spanish doubloons, gold, silver, and treasure as much as he.

Sometimes, he thought his ship was jinxed, because once it was used as a small slaver where all aboard had died of some mysterious disease, and the ghost ship was pulled ashore and sold by the merchant adventurers who owned it. He grunted, "Even they didn't want it," he hissed under his breath.

When the lookout yelled, "Ship ahoy, Captain," and pointed to the south, his spirits rose. Maybe this was just the break he needed. He walked toward the bow and mounted the steps to the forecastle. Looking south through his spyglass, he saw a small merchant ship — another box-of-bananas-and-keg-of-water ship. He spat his disgust onto the deck. "Set course for the ship to the south," he yelled to the one on the wheel in a fit of anger. Then he stomped to his quarters for a bit of liquid fortifier.

～

On day seven, the *Julia Anne* sailed by Tortuga, and everyone on board breathed a sigh of relief.

Giovanni passed Jonathan's barrel, heading into the galley and whispered, "It looks like we're safe." He no more than got the words out of his mouth when the lookout on the mast yelled, "Ship ahoy! To the port."

All eyes looked in the direction of Cubao, the group of islands north of Hispaniola and Tortuga. Sure enough, in the distance a large ship was heading straight toward them. It was so far away, only the tips of the sails were visible to those on deck. Everyone who wasn't helping sail the ship went to the gunnel to watch the approaching boat's progress. They were especially intent on the tallest mast. What flag was the ship carrying?

Jonathan almost opened the lid of his barrel to see what was going on. It was at this moment, Sarah came and stood to its side. "I'll tell you what's happening," she advised, understanding his need without him saying it. "But I need to get a little higher. I'll be back in a minute."

Jonathan heard scraping and sliding on the deck, and soon Sarah said, "I moved two boxes closer to your barrel, so I can get a better view." He heard her step upon the boxes. "If this is a pirate ship, what will they do?"

"Nothing good, Sarah. You must look for a good hiding place, if they come aboard. One where you won't be found."

"Is there room in there with you? I can't think of a better one."

"Now there's a thought," chuckled Jonathan, and upon thinking about it, it was probably her best hiding place. "Sure," he said. "I'll make room. We'll be cramped together, but we'll manage, somehow."

"The ship is still far, far away."

"Let me know when you can tell what flag she's flying."

Sarah kept talking to Jonathan as the boat got nearer.

"It's flying the crossbones and skull," called the lookout. A gasp went up from the crew. It was a pirate ship.

"All hands to the cannon or your armour," called the captain from the aftcastle.

Men scattered in all directions, some running to open boxes on deck and others manning four cannons on the gunnels. The *Julia Anne* was not set up for warfare. The battle would be short and decisive and against her.

"Did you hear that?" asked Sarah.

"A pirate ship, for sure," replied Jonathan. "Let me know when the coast is clear, and you can slide in here. We shouldn't wait until the last minute."

"Everyone's in fighting array. Even the cook's gone to defend the ship. Now's a good time to join you."

Jonathan opened the lid, while Sarah seated herself on the deck. He pushed himself farther down in the barrel, leaving the opening clear. Looking up at her, he gathered the end of her dress, to pull it into the cask. Sarah scooted her legs and then her body into the hole. The result was a jumble of legs, arms and bodies mashed against each other and the barrel. Neither could hardly move. To ease the situation, they interspersed their knees and wrapped their arms around each other. The struggle had lasted several minutes, but they soon found a measure of comfort.

Sarah said, "I'm sure if you could see my face, I'd be blushing."

To which Jonathan replied, "Better to be blushing, than be taken captive by pirates. Although, I, for one, am finding this to my liking." They were forehead to forehead, nose to nose. Jonathan was amazed at his boldness around this woman.

Sarah managed to pinch him hard on the ear.

"Ouch. Must your touch always hurt?"

Suddenly, there was excitement on the ship and running feet. What was happening? "Captain, there's a ship to the stern," called the lookout.

Now what, thought Jonathan. Were there two pirate ships bearing down on the *Julia Anne*?

Sarah put his thought into words. "Do pirate ships work together?" she whispered.

"Yes, sometimes. But this ship isn't worth the effort. It's too small. I can't imagine that happening."

They were interrupted by more sounds and yelling. "Look, mates. The pirates are turning away. They're heading for the other ship." More shouts and insults were called in the wake of the ship's leaving.

Inside the barrel, there was relief. "Guess that answers my question. Now I just have to get out of here," Sarah said.

"Are you sure you want to go?" asked Jonathan, joking of course. He was starting to sweat at their close quarters. The barrel wasn't meant for two people, and the day was hot.

Unlocking the lid, he let Sarah peek out. "We're good," she said, as the distant sounds of cannon fire could be heard. "The crew has gone aft to watch the fireworks."

Then started a scene of grunting and pushing which sent both of them into muted gales of laughter. Finally, Jonathan grasped her shoes and gave her a last push. She was gone, and he closed the lid.

The best thing to come out of the encounter with the pirate ship was the fact that he'd seen Sarah for the first time out of the shadows. She was an older, lovely woman—her hair brown with golden highlights and her eyes were gray-blue. He wondered why she'd not gotten married. In many circles, she would be called a spinster. He would ask her discreetly the next time they met. Their relationship had grown closer today, and he was happy it had.

∽

The prediction of foul weather began coming true the following day. Dark-gray clouds piled upon the horizon. The winds started rising, and the waves white capping. The boat rose and fell with the wave action.

In the bow of the boat, sheltered by the forecastle over him, Jonathan slid either forward or backward in the barrel with this movement. He began to wonder how he'd stand hours of moving in the barrel. He envisioned large blisters from chafing as a result. Something else for Sarah to doctor.

The rain came down at sunset, just in time for him to emerge into the shadows and get some fresh air. He wondered if Sarah would come to meet him. She did not show up. He thought about sneaking to her cabin to see how she was doing, but there was too much open space to cross. Too much chance of being seen. So, he did not.

He crawled into the barrel headfirst to retrieve a bar of soap which Giovanni had brought him, and in the pouring rain he washed himself and the clothes which were still on his body. Dripping wet, he walked under the overhang of the forecastle, approaching the stove, which had leftover coals from the night meal. Shivering, he stood and rotated before it until his clothes were only damp. Then he braced himself from the pitching ship by sitting at the table where the sailors ate their meals. The warmth continued to feel good in the wet, chilly, night air. He dreaded getting back into the barrel, so he risked staying close to the stove.

The storm grew worse, sending the ship's bow riding up on a wave and rolling down into the trough. Water began to crash over the bow, running the full length of the vessel, and through the rail at the back. The deck became awash with sea water.

Suddenly the door of the cook's quarters sprang wide open. It banged against the wall, and the cook came staggering through it, heading for the stove.

Jonathan was caught! He jumped up and ducked his head.

The cook, bleary-eyed from sleep and maybe drink, took one look at him, and said, "George, put out the coals for me." Then he staggered back to his room and shut the banging oak door.

Jonathan stood with his mouth wide open, holding to the table, which was nailed to the deck. Then he laughed, shook his head, and did as told. "George, will you put out the fire?" he asked himself, and George did.

Jonathan's barrel was lashed to the deck of the boat near the galley. The others stood out of sight on the starboard rail, attached to rings in the boat's walls, where they'd be easy to off-load onto the shore. He hoped the rings held. The *Julia Anne* wasn't the youngest lady on the raging sea.

The boat rocked and rolled for two days as it made the dangerous passage through the *caya hico* or string of islands bordering the Atlantic Ocean. Jonathan felt so bad, he ate hardly anything. On the third day, the winds abated, and all the *Julia Anne's* sails were unfurled. In the open Atlantic, she headed north at full speed into the Bahama Islands, following the raging storm as it ravaged the coastal areas ahead. Giovanni brought him a delicious meal of bread and stew in celebration of the calm seas.

Almost every day, he and Sarah talked long hours in the darkness on the ship. When she didn't come, he wondered where she was and what she was doing. Her father, it turned out, wasn't well, and some days and nights she nursed him.

Their talks were about their experiences in life.

Hers about losing the man she would marry in an English battle, leaving London with her parents, and coming to Jamaica to put the past behind her. Most especially she talked about her faith in God which pulled her through a trying time in her life.

He talked about his experiences in Jamaica, the hurricane, and finally the earthquake where he had lost his family. Sarah had reached for his hand as he told her of this horror. He also talked about establishing a new life in the New World.

Soon the couple knew just about everything about each other. Jonathan began to wonder what life would be like without her friendship, which was beginning to blossom into love.

The rest of the trip to Chesapeake Bay went without trouble. It was when the boat reached Annapolis, and the crew off-loaded the cargo, that Giovanni realized one of the extra barrels was gone. It was number 1042. He was sure it contained the Ancestry Book and Sir Anthony's sword.

"I'm so sorry, Jonathan. I should have taken better care of it," he exclaimed to his friend, when he came to tell him the coast was clear, and he could leave the ship.

Jonathan rested on the table with his head down, thinking after all these years, the books and sword had been consigned to a watery grave. "At least they are together," he told Giovanni. "Just as they were at the beginning, and you and I are friends. I think Cassius and Tybba would have wanted it to turn out that way."

"And here we are, sailing together, just as they did so many years ago. How did we get here at this place?" Giovanni asked.

"I'm beginning to believe there's a God, and He's the reason we're together. What do you think?"

Giovanni only nodded at Jonathan's statement. He didn't know much about gods. There were so many of them among the places he'd sailed.

"Have Sarah and her father gone ashore?"

"Yes, this morning."

"Do you know where they're going? The last time I asked her she didn't know. She said someone would meet them on the dock, and they'd be going with them to their plantation."

"I have no idea, my friend."

"Are you going to go ashore with me?" asked Jonathan.

"Yes, we are here for three days loading supplies, and then I'll head back for Barbados and Jamaica for the same trip again."

"Why don't you stay with me? We can go into business together," Jonathan suggested.

"One day I'll come back and do just that or help you. But for now, I'll keep sailing. I enjoy the sea, although at times she can be a cruel mistress."

"Life will be lonely without you," stated Jonathan, *especially if I can't find Sarah*, he thought. He'd decided he wanted her permanently in his life. The next time he saw her, he planned to ask her to be his wife. He felt like she would say yes.

"Come on. Let's get off the ship."

The two men rolled the sleeping barrel down the gang plank and put it next to the other one.

"We need a place to stay," said Jonathan. "It's too late to disturb my family, so we're going to stay at the fanciest place in town." He patted a bag with his money inside.

Jonathan put his arm around Giovanni's shoulder, and the two men walked into Annapolis. Tomorrow, they would return with a cart to collect the barrels and walk to Tipton's Cooperage to meet Peader and the others. Tonight, they'd eat a good meal, have a hot bath, and sleep in a good bed.

~

Jonathan's initial quest for Sarah came to a dead end. He didn't even know her last name, so it was hard to inquire after her, although he did in every place he visited.

For a brief time, Peader welcomed him into his business, while Jonathan put his roots down securely into the Province of Maryland's soil.

The headright system had been replaced by identifying property, taking out a patent and having a survey done to establish ownership.

He found fifty acres of land near his brother's and filed for its possession. Then he pinpointed property he could buy, adjoining this acreage. Jonathan was anything but poor. But after losing his family and business in Jamaica, and Sarah, he felt that way.

Although he needed to start cultivating his new holdings to plant tobacco, finding Sarah was more important. He could afford to take a little time to search for her, although in the vastness of the

Chesapeake Bay, finding one person was like looking for a needle-in-a-haystack. Where would he start?

～

The sky was overcast, as he rode his horse down Solomon's Island Road. His destination—London Town, which was on the way into Annapolis. He passed Larken's Tavern and noted the framed All Hallows Anglican Church, which stood beside it. He slowed his horse to a walk. He'd gone to church in Port Royal, but that was to please his parents. The sermons never phased him. The church was a social function, just like the merchant's meetings he'd attended, because he was one of the port's traders.

After his talks with Sarah on the *Julia Anne*, he'd started believing in God. Maybe a little prayer would help. After all, Giovanni showing up on the Tipton doorstep in Jamaica had to be orchestrated by Somebody. He pulled his horse to a stop and rode back to the church.

Dismounting, he walked into the dimly lit interior. Two or three people were inside. He didn't pay attention to them. He focused his thoughts on his present mission.

Somehow, before the cross at the front, he couldn't stand to say his prayer. He knelt at the altar and prayed aloud, "God, you don't really know me, but my name's Jonathan Tipton, and I have a problem. I love one of Your children, and I think she loves me. I'd like to have her as my wife. I'll take good care of her, and we'll go to church and be obedient to Your will. I just need to know where she is—please." The last words were spoken in a broken voice.

The prayer wasn't much, but the response was immediate.

"Jonathan."

The man who knelt at the altar thought he was hearing things, because he wished so much to hear her voice. Did God answer audibly and in a female voice?

"Jonathan, I'm here."

He got up on his feet and turned around. He'd heard about visions, could she be one? There was only one way to find out. Right in the middle of All Hollow's Anglican Church, he walked to Sarah, took her in his arms, and kissed her. No! She definitely wasn't a vision.

"Sarah, I thought I'd lost you."

She stood with tears running down her cheeks. "Did you mean what you said in your prayer? You want to marry me?"

"Yes. Will you? Marry me?"

"I will. My father is next door at the tavern. What about now?"

"Lead the way," responded Jonathan.

John Larken — the tavern's owner — and one of the people in the church were witnesses.

Jonathan's presence in the New World, along with his four sons, started a chain of events within the Tipton family descendants, many of whom became involved in the politics of the day, hobnobbed with presidents and governors, and continued this into the 6th and 7th generations. Others became ministers, song leaders, housewives, authors, teachers, doctors, merchants, soldiers and seamen. Some fought in wars, died in battle, and helped shape a nation. Others bought land in the mountain coves or along the famed Mississippi and farmed. They lived in every state in the union and traveled most of the world. Hundreds of thousands are numbered as his descendants.

❧ Epilogue ❧

Almost two hundred years after Jonathan Tipton landed on the Chesapeake Bay, a storm was ravaging the western coast of England.

Although the month of February had been bright with sunshine and only a little rain, the weather was about to change. In March the wind turned chilly, and by the second week wind-blown snow covered the ground. The snow piled higher and higher until the basic services of the area such as transportation halted and telegraph lines came down. Houses suffered damage to heavy, slate roofs and trees were uprooted.

By March 10th, the wind had increased to hurricane strength accompanied by a blizzard.

South of the mouth of the Severn Estuary, the tempest was especially hard on Cornwall and Devonshire, located on the eastern side of the Bristol Channel.

On the English mainland, it would be called the Great Blizzard of 1891.

Floating, at the edge of the Bristol Channel, a world traveler waited far south of the Severn Estuary, a scarred barrel with the number 1042 hesitated, bobbing up and down in the storm.

Having traveled thousands of miles, following the northern currents from the West Indies, which flowed off of the shores of the United States of America, it had passed New York and Newfoundland. Then the wooden barrel turned eastward across and through the northern Atlantic, bumping against icebergs as it floated by Greenland and Iceland.

Down the rugged, rocky, western coast of Ireland, it came and then across the wild Celtic Sea. What adventures it had experienced in these many years, no one would know. But the world had surely changed.

Stationary as it wallowed in the wakes of steamships plying the waters to exotic locations, it waited — barely moving, dipping up and down until a moisture-laden March storm, arising from the coast of northern Africa, pushed half-way across the blue Atlantic and turned north and east toward England.

The storm met northerly winds dropping cold air south from the frozen Artic. When the two met, the driving snow and hurricane force winds started, pushing the little cask, for it was small in the vast ocean, north toward the Bristol Channel. Slowly it moved while the tempest dropped fifteen feet of snow on the southwest of the English countryside, shutting down railways, roads, and burying towns in drifts of cold white — many froze to death, some drowned.

Around the little cask, a ship sank and men tried swimming in the icy water. One grabbed it and desperately tried to hang on to its round, rough surface. Frozen in the icy water, he sank beneath the stormy sea.

Gradually the barrel made its way into the mouth of the vast expanse of water, and traveled up the narrowing waterway, past Cornwall and Devonshire and into the Severn Estuary. The storm, pushing it almost to Portishead, at the mouth of the River Avon.

Here, dashed violently upon and between two rocks on the coast, it lodged. As the storm raged, sand and silt covered it up, leaving it in a sandy grave, not far from where the first Tipton barrels were made.

At last, barrel number 1042 was at peace, at rest, and home.

Waiting to be discovered, its treasure would not be gold doubloons, diamond crosses, or pearls. Its treasure was the tale of a family, started 500 years after Christ made His appearance on the earth—or thereabouts. A story worth telling...

Tipton Now 2020

Located to the northwest of Birmingham, England, Tipton is a sleepy town, except in the morning and afternoon. This is when the rush of people, heading to Birmingham or Wolverhampton, on the train and bus means standing room only, and by car the traffic moves at a snail's pace into or out of the small city. According to Keith Hodgkins, the contact person, for the Tipton Civic Society, 'Tipton is far from being a commuter town.' He continues, 'although most of the traditional, large, iron-working industries have disappeared, there is still a significant amount of smaller scale engineering, manufacturing, and service industries which employ lots of local labor.'

No one would guess that this town, along with others adjacent to it, was once the most industrialized part of England – called The Black Country. Now most large factories sit empty with broken windows, and the main street, Owen Street, has many buildings with signs saying, 'To Let.'

The best reminder, of its past for the youngest generation of Tiptonians, is the Black Country Living Museum, a high-quality example of what the town was all about – limestone, coal, iron, and steel. Some of the best known and world-changing inventions occurred here.

Let's go back to where *The Tipton's of Tybbington* ended.

Tipton in the 1700 and 1800's

The foundation of Tipton's emergence into the Industrial Revolution was the discovery of coal in Staffordshire. The inhabitants knew about this black rock and used it as heat for hundreds of years not realizing its potential.

The thirty-foot or ten-yard seam was the thickness of the coal which lay on or just below the surface of Tipton lands. As England's towns grew and timber supplies dwindled, the demand for the black fuel for heating in the cold English winters grew substantially, especially in large towns, such as London.

This necessitated a way to transport the coal inland. English roads were not good and the incessant rain made them worse.

Since England lies in most cases only hundreds of feet above sea level, and water was plentiful, a series of canals were constructed to facilitate coals easy movement in the country.

The Birmingham Canal arrived in Tipton in 1770. Over the next 50 years the town built a dense network of 13 miles of navigable waterways within its boundaries and soon became known as the 'Venice of the Midlands.' Wharfs, warehouses, industries, and canal boat building facilities soon appeared on these banks.

To transport coal and other goods, 'narrowboats,' vessels built especially for canals, plied the water, creating a new way of life. People lived on the canal, raised their children on its banks, and formed a new community of floating boat owners/operators.

In 1800, Tipton was a predominantly rural area, with a few coal mines and 4,000 residents. Then the mass building of factories associated with the coal mines took place, and resulted in Tipton becoming a heavily built-up and industrialized area with more than 30,000 residents by the end of the 19th century.

The discovery and mining of coal led to the establishment of ironworks, blast furnaces, foundries, and forges, in the direct vicinity of its mining. In 1862, while on a visit to the area, Elihu Burrit, the American Consul to Birmingham, described the region as, "Black by day and red by night."

The invention of the first successful steam engine by Thomas Newcomen which was erected at Coneygre Coalworks, and its improved model by the Scotsman James Watt can be attributed to Tipton. The area is noted for manufacturing anchors and chains, and at one time held the record for the largest anchor in the world — 20'6". The anchor chains for the ill-fated White Star Liner — Titanic were cast close by in Netherton a sister city to Tipton. The world's first steam-powered iron ship, the Aaron Manby, was built at one of the ironworks within the town.

Tipton in the 1900's

Over the years, Tipton has had many names, starting with Tibbington or Tibba (the chieftain's name) and tun (meaning farm or village). In the Domesday survey of 1086, in the reign of William the Conqueror of Normandy, the name was written as Tibintone. Between 1151 and 1723, there were 22 variations of the spelling until it eventually became known as Tipton.

Tipton expanded as did the adjoining town of Dudley, and today it's hard to tell where one ends and the other begins. All that is left of the castle at Dudley are the ruins situated on Castle Hill within the grounds of Dudley Zoo—both you can visit. In Tipton, there are still names that are reminiscent of the older history such as Lower Green, Coneygree, Summerhill, and of course the Tibbi—a large public housing estate.

With overpopulation and pollution due to the amount of manufacturing in the area, the Black Country was soon known as 'the unhealthiest place in the country.' And no wonder! This included the unsanitary living conditions, leading to the installation of clean water supplies, sewage systems, and the development of council housing to relocate occupants in poorer areas.

Tipton was not unscathed by World War I and II. An error in navigation by the German Zeppelins on January 31, 1916, dropped bombs on Union Street. Fifteen people were killed and several were injured. In November 1940, an air raid destroyed the Star Hotel, killing one person. In May, the following year, another raid destroyed Tipton Tavern and New Road Methodist Church, killing six people.

Tipton has always been interested in sports. A car, the Thunderbolt, built at Bean Cars Ltd factory, once broke the world speed record at Bonneville Salt Flats in Utah, USA. A running club, known as the Tipton Harriers, had the marathon runner, Jack Holden, as a member. In the previous century, William Perry, the famous bareknuckle fighter, bearing the unofficial title of Champion of England and known as the 'Tipton Slasher', used the Fountain Inn on Owen Street as his headquarters. A statue to him can be found in the Coronation Gardens in Tipton Green.

Not far from this statue is a church where John Wesley spoke along with a plaque to commemorate his preaching here in what was originally called the 'Wesleyan Preaching House.'

The glory days of Tipton are over, if you consider coal and the industries associated with it as the mainstay. But jobs are everywhere in the town and in the cities around it, and with new housing estates being built, it thrives. It's not unusual to walk to the library, or to eat at Mad O'Rourke's Pie Factory or the Dudley Canal Trust and meet known fellow residents on the way. And you are not too far from the outdoors. Foxes and other animals are frequent visitor's to backyards.

Tipton folk are fiercely proud of their community and remain a friendly people who welcome visitors from everywhere. These characteristics are true of their descendants who now live in America. For other material on Tipton go to www.tiptoncivicsociety.co. I wish to thank them for giving me permission to use the information from their website to write this recent history.

Books of the Tipton Chronicles

In England and the West Indies

The Tipton's of Tybbington, Before and Beyond, Part One – 500 to 1300 A.D.
The Tipton's of Tybbington, Before and Beyond, Part Two – 1300 to 1700 A.D.

In America

Butterfield Station – 1858 to 1859
Chilhowee Legacy – 1911 to 1930's
My Cherokee Rose – 1930's and Present
Tipton's Sugar Cove—Matthew – 1917 to 1921
The Six at Chestnut Hill – 2008

There will be sequels to some of my books. I can't write but so fast. Be patient. R.R.

The books are available at Amazon.com or may be ordered through your local bookstore. If you like what you're reading, go to Amazon.com/Reba Rhyne, and leave a review for any book you've read.

Ms. Rhyne may be reached at rebarhyne@gmail.com.